CUTTING WOOD

February 2005

CUTTING WOOD

For Annie ...
with unchanging respect
and affection from your
friend and sparring partner

Glenn.

GLENN HAMILTON

ISBN : Softcover 1-4134-6231-6

All characters are the invention of the Author, although based upon people known to him in the period (1952) depicted. The village of Blackfish Harbour did not, and does not, exist, although all other communities mentioned by name are real and extant with the exception of one or two specified logging camps.

This book was printed in the United States of America.

To order additional copies of this book, contact:
Xlibris Corporation
1-888-795-4274
www.Xlibris.com
Orders@Xlibris.com
25257

'For Glenda'

By the same Author:

'CHARLIE'S MOUNTAIN' (1998)
'MISSIONS' (2003)

PROLOGUE

MANITOBA

The story of Stepan Kereniuk's execution was on page four.

Two inches of cold print squeezed between an item about hailstorms over Lake Winnipegosis and a cut-price fares advertisement for Trans-Canada Airlines.

Fifteen hundred miles from the Burnaby prison farm where it was done to him to the editorial offices of the Winnipeg Free Press. *Far enough away to make it seem like nothing very much.*

'B.C. WIFESLAYER PUT TO DEATH

'Stepan Kereniuk, 56, was hanged this morning at British Columbia's Oakalla Prison for the murder of his common-law wife, Rosa Brenko.

'Kereniuk, one-time logger and salmon fisherman, was convicted for the shotgun slaying at Blackfish Harbour on northern Vancouver Island.

'Despite appeals for clemency, including a 3,000-signature petition to the Governor-General, the final conclusion was that there were insufficient grounds to warrant a reduction of sentence.'

Out there on the Coast, of course, it would be a big front-page story in the Vancouver Sun *and* Province. *Here, in mid-continent, it, and Stepan, were about as newsworthy as passing hail showers.*

*

Jack Fulton had been expecting it for the year and more since the trial and sentence, the doomed appeal which had made *this* outcome inevitable. Thinking himself ready for it, the fact of it before him now could still shock and sicken, its impact leaving a solitary rogue thought to bob in the mind like flotsam in twisting currents: that Stepan had been only *fifty six*! I never knew that . . . had figured him always for older, nearer to seventy. And, Fulton wondered bleakly, *would* that have made a difference? If Stepan had *been* old rather than middle-aged and old-looking? Might that have saved him, where nothing else could?

It was cool there in the ante-room with the air conditioning going, and silent, the mess building all-but empty. Only he was there in his grey flight suit, hot and sweaty still from the T-33's cockpit, standing, stricken, with the *Free Press* open before him . . . and that story. While, behind his bar, the corporal-barman polished glasses and remained mute, busy making ready for the after-flying rush.

Outside, there was the dry, fierce heat of mid-summer Manitoba; the hard, cloudless afternoon light shrill with the sounds of the training jets, the rushing thunder of take-offs. *Those* were reality: millions of dollars worth of sleek silver aircraft circling and dipping; gallons by the thousand of expended JP4 fuel super-heating the already hot sky . . .

For Fulton, though, in that moment, reality was this bitter pill of news: Stepan dead at the low-security prison farm. Where, unlike the grim New Westminster penitentiary, only short sentences were served—two years-less-a-day and under. Unless you were slated to hang there.

Which was the other thing about Oakalla, the awful anomaly. Where, that morning, they had done it to Stepan, bringing an end to his fifty six years . . .

And Fulton, cold and detached now in the after-shock, could make his decision to act upon Stepan's advice, given at their last meeting. Which had lain fallow for more than a year, awaiting this triggering moment. Now was the exact time to start doing something about that . . .

ONE

BRITISH COLUMBIA

"HEY, YOU . . . *HIGHPOCKETS*!" Fulton would wince and groan unavailing protest as Stepan's yell shattered the June dawn. "Best you haul your arse up lickety-split! We be go cuttin' wood!"

The morning opening fresh petals of sunrise, pastels over cool blue: the new day's first reflections high on the twinned peaks above Port Hardy; light rushing and flooding down over slopes shrouded with infinite hemlock, burning bright on the exposed scabs of the logging slash . . .

Coming awake to a loon's call across the dark, still bay of Blackfish Harbour, the water-slapping wings of a fish-gorged cormorant on its extended takeoff run, the swift, curved plummet of a leaping sockeye heard clearly through a half-mile of utter stillness. And, slowly, the senses sharpening to take in the drone of humming birds drinking from the giant fireweeds under the window . . .

"HIGH-*POCKETS* BE GOD-*DAMN* IT, EH . . . ?"

Scrambling, trembling, in numb obedience to Stepan, into wood-cutting denims and shirt, going, grumbling, to the door. Where Stepan, vastly-grinning with happy malice, would offer heart-jolting coffee stewed overnight on the wood range. The last step to total waking.

Ready then for loading the big, two-man McCullough power saw, the hammers and wedges, the peevees for manhandling the latest giant log that was, without doubt, nabbed from some boom or Davis raft southbound for the mills at Powell River or False Creek. Side-tracked, ear-marked anew, as stovewood for the two Kereniuk houses.

*

"Listen, Highpockets . . ."

"I wish you wouldn't call me that, Stepan."

"Why you not?"

"It's not my name, and I don't *like* it!"

"Pretty damn good name, I reckon."

"Not for me, it's not."

"Plenty fellas call you lots worse, I bet . . ." Stepan was laughing. "How tall you, anyhow?"

"You know very well how tall . . ." Fulton told him anyway, "six-five."

"Call that pretty high, hokay . . ." Stepan confided then, "I be five-seven. Other big fellows look you straight in eye. Me, I look you right in *pockets*."

"I'm Jack," Fulton said without hope. "And six-five is just one of those things."

"Hokay . . . fine."

"Does that mean no more Highpockets?"

"Long as I remember."

"You *always* forget!"

"Call you that because we be friends . . . account o' you Goddam good neighbour," Stepan declared in his incorrigibly-fractured English. "Be rent my liddle house, pay up on time. We be cuttin' wood together . . . never no arguments. Be *like* you."

"If you *really* liked me, you wouldn't call me that when I ask you not to!"

"Is true. Me, my Rosa, Tamara . . . all like."

"Rosa and Tamara use my proper name," Fulton reminded him, and smiled, thinking of Tamara. Feeling a pleasing warmth . . .

"Rosa fixin' supper tonight. Wantin' you be come."

"I'd like that . . . thanks." Fulton smiled some more.

"Be havin' *holopche*. You know *holopche*?"

"Don't believe I do."

"Is Uker-rain-ian grub. Green pepper full o' meat and rice and spice. Bake him all day in oven in hot to-may-to sauce. My Rosa makin' best sum'n'a'bitch *holopche* this side o' Kiev."

"I'm sure she does."

"Rosa not likin' you, for Goddam sure she not fix you *holopche* . . ." Stepan added confidingly, "Tamara be there . . . gettin' day off at hospital."

"*That's* nice." The warmth rose a degree . . .

"Damn' right . . ." An elbow dug hard into Fulton's ribs.

"*Jesus*, Stepan!"

"Make you feel pretty hokay about Tamara, eh, Highpockets?"

Fulton massaged his ribs. "You forgot again." And grinned, thinking, Stepan had got *that* right, at least.

*

The power saw and tools were in the back of Stepan's ancient pickup. "We *go*!" He ground the foot starter, and a groan emerged from beneath the hood. He muttered a Ukrainian imprecation, stabbed again with his boot, and the motor caught, filling the cab with gasoline fumes and the smoke of burned oil. "Goddam good ol' truck, eh? 'Thirty one Dodge. Never do no work on him. Never let me down."

He reversed out shudderingly into the dirt road, and Fulton gripped hard, reflecting on his misfortune in being in the hands of one of the world's most appalling drivers.

The Dodge ran down the hill in bottom gear, whining protest at the punishing revs. Fulton took what comfort he could from the knowledge that it was only a mile to where the beached log lay. With a little luck, the tormented vehicle might endure. Stepan and he might just survive.

With one hand on the wheel, Stepan bawled, "be somethin' I still don't understand."

Fulton braced his feet against the dashboard. "What?"

"Thing about you bein' in th' Service." Stepan swung the wheel hard into the corner past the barnlike community hall.

"If you mean am I in the Navy . . . yes. For now."

"And you really an *officer*?"

"Yep . . ." Fulton pondered without certainty the feelings of a man like Stepan for the officer class, and excused himself quickly. "But very junior . . . only recently commissioned."

With the speedometer needle touching forty, the Dodge remained in bottom gear. Stepan gestured, explaining mildly, "pretty Goddam steep hill. Brakes no good . . . be need the compression for stop."

They shot thus past Hawaiian Jim's gaunt brown house. Where the mean-spirited old Islander, owner of five salmon seiners, each skippered by one of his quarrelsome half-Polynesian sons, presided from his wheelchair, legs off at the knees from gangrene. Waiting to die . . .

It was established Blackfish Harbour folklore, the way that Stepan Kereniuk and Hawaiian Jim hated each other, although no one professed to know exactly why, and the two principals revealed nothing. Had Hawaiian Jim possessed legs, it was believed, they would have long since whaled the tar out of each other.

Stepan, ignoring the road, peered up hopefully at the house, and blasted the horn for long seconds. "Wake you up, old cocksucker!"

They rumbled past the high school, and down The Row of fresh white houses where the Upper Four Hundred lived, surrounded by their landscaped lawns: the high school principal, the village attorney and magistrate, the director of the B.C. Electric power plant. There, too, were to be found the Hong brothers, Chin and Chang, who owned a café and the village taxi service. And Olaf Pedersen, proprietor of Pedersen's Hardware and Haberdashery. Whose black '52 Ford sedan delivery—which served also as ambulance, morgue wagon and hearse—stood before the house, wet with dew.

Real houses, those, with electric light, bathtubs, toilets inside. If you lived on The Row, you had Arrived. You might not be as rich as Hawaiian Jim who had made his pile rum-running across the Juan de Fuca Strait to Washington State during Prohibition. But Hawaiian Jim lacked respectability, and, with his five unruly sons—the cause of the early death of their exhausted mother—would not have been welcome on The Row . . .

"Remember what I said at the start, Stepan? When I rented the house?" Fulton asked.

"Sure. But tell me again . . . so's I get him straight."

"How it was only until September? When I go back East for flying training?"

"Maybe I forget that part, eh?"

"Maybe you don't *listen.*" Fulton grinned. "Probably too drunk."

"Was not *so*, drunk." Stepan gave him a reproachful stare.

"Kindly watch the road!" Fulton demanded, "if you weren't, how come, next morning, you had that shiner?" The injured eye was still tinged with yellow and purple.

"Rosa and me have liddle fight," Stepan admitted, and shrugged. "She bust me in the eye."

"Not so little from what I heard."

"You be listen?" Stepan was frowning.

"The racket you made . . . thirty yards away? How could I not?"

"Just few liddle drinks . . . don't do no harm." Stepan looked defensive. "If I get liddle load on, don't hurt no sum'n'a'bitch. But Rosa, she get sore, go crazy sometime."

"That's women for you," Fulton offered mildly. "They tend to make their feelings known."

"I be work good and hard, eh?" Stepan sounded aggrieved. "In the woods, on my boat, bust my balls all the time. Make good money . . . see my women fed. Nice clothes . . . big house for livin'. They *welcome*!"

"Sure, Stepan. It can seem unfair . . ."

"*That* the Goddam word, hokay," Stepan agreed explosively. "Know you see it my way, Highpockets. Got good head on your shoulder."

"Why, *thank* you, Stepan."

"My Rosa take swing at me . . . hokay. I don't say nothin'. But one day, thinkin' she go too far. And I give that crazy woman . . . what you be say in English . . ." He snapped his fingers. "Yah! Piece of my Goddam *mind*!"

He slowed for the intersection with the shoreline road that ran the two miles from the Indian village on the point to the head of the bay which sheltered the seaplane base with its two resident aircraft. Between lay the white village, the fish packers' warehouses and oil company floats, the B.C. Forest Service pier, the Government dock with its yellow-walled, red-roofed freight shed, where the Vancouver steamers moored, and all the jumble and scatter of nondescript buildings which climbed the steep, logged-off sidehill to the brooding treeline.

Stepan halted at the rusting stop sign and turned to Fulton, demanding, "if I drunk . . . not listen . . . how come I remember you Navy officer? Exceptin' you not, because you *Air Force* officer?" He looked triumphant.

"None of that's easy to explain."

"So, give her a whirl . . ." Stepan added pointedly, "like *always*, I listen."

"Are we going to sit here all the time while I do?"

"Why not . . . be no traffic." Stepan peered in both directions. "No cop come nosin' around."

Indeed, Blackfish Harbour lay peaceful and quiet in the hour before full wakening. Blinds were down all along The Row. The R.C.M.P. barracks was silent, only a single outside light left on to compete wanly with the morning, the old grey Chevrolet patrol car, long pensioned off from Vancouver, standing forsaken in the road. Over the Indian village the air was silken-blue with the smoke from wood-burning ranges . . .

Stepan prompted, "so?"

"All right, like I said, at present, I'm in the Navy . . . all those things I spoke of on that first night when I had coffee with Rosa and Tamara and you . . ." Stepan nodded. "And, yes, I'm a junior officer. On what's termed extended leave-of-absence, awaiting transfer to the Air Force for flight training. But there's no course open till the Fall. So they've given me the summer off."

*

Entering the Royal Canadian Navy on a short-service commission, Jack Fulton had been the holder already of a civilian commercial pilot's licence bearing seaplane and instrument flight endorsements. He had logged more than a thousand hours.

The Navy offered carrier flying: with the breezy confidence of youth, it had seemed to Fulton that, with his existing qualifications, he was already well on his way to that much-desired goal. There would be new and complex techniques to master; the airplanes must be flown in the Navy's way. Yet, he foresaw few problems, his self-belief supported by the remembered words of a one-time flying instructor: 'they all fly the same'.

Where, Fulton reasoned, would be the problem with the Navy's thoroughbreds: Grumman Tracker airborne radar platforms, helicopters, hotshot jets like the Banshee? So what that he must become proficient in formation and aerobatic flying, in gunnery and rocketry, and learn how to handle aerial mines and depth charges. Those came under the heading of 'disposable load'; the fancy flying was, in the end, only *flying*. And they all flew the same . . .

The interview with the Training Commander at Shearwater pierced the bubble of these conceits. That was still recent enough to make him feel again the heat of his embarrassment and humiliation. When, quite affably, the Training Commander informed him that he would not become a Navy pilot.

These things he had explained to Rosa, Tamara and Stepan . . .

Stepan, characteristically blunt, had demanded, "why you want out of Navy?"

"I don't."

"So why you quit?"

"Because that's my only option if I'm ever to become a Service pilot. I wanted to fly Navy . . . the Navy said no dice."

"What for? You pilot already. You come *here* for fly."

"Seems I'm not the type the Navy wants," Fulton said, shrugging, and lived again the disappointment of that moment of rejection . . .

"Yes, Mister Fulton, you can fly," the Training Commander acknowledged. "You're not short of experience."

"In that case, sir, why have I struck out?"

"Let me make some things clear . . ." The Training Commander appeared irritated momentarily by the directness of the question. "First of all, understand that we take no pleasure from this. Regrettably, however, it's that very experience that weighs the decision against you."

"Sir . . . ?"

"A thousand hours. Time and plenty for certain undesirable habits, from the Navy's viewpoint, to have rooted themselves." The Training Commander's smile was apologetic. "Which we'd have to root *out* before we could begin to train you to our ways. Habits like rugged individualism . . . doing things your way, a one-man band answerable only to yourself. Things to make you a maverick when we're seeking integrated team members. Independent rather than *inter*-dependent."

Hating what he was hearing, Fulton was compelled—more or less—to acknowledge the points made.

"We're not unlike the airlines in this," the Training Commander explained. "Preferring our candidates with the necessary academic standards, with enthusiasm, *wanting* to fly. Now, there's no question of your not meeting those criteria. The fact that you're here now, newly-commissioned, is testimony enough."

Fulton offered a noncommittal, "yes, sir."

"Where you fall down is, paradoxically, in the fact that you *can* fly. I mentioned the airlines just now."

"Yes, you did, sir."

"Which like to recruit young people starting out. Brand-new commercial licence, couple of hundred hours logged. Starry-eyed, green as grass . . . and malleable, ready to be shaped to the airlines' needs. Lacking your kind of experience which, frankly, is seen as more liability than asset these days."

"I see, sir." Seeing, though, could not lessen the pain.

"Aviation is a small branch of a small Navy," the Training Commander pointed out. "We have just the one light fleet carrier. Unlike our next-door neighbours, every one of whom, it seems . . ." He was smiling, "keeps a carrier in his backyard. Only a few naval air stations, and nothing to match Pensacola, Corpus Christi, Great Lakes or Patuxent River. We have a limited requirement in human resources, and a waiting list coast-to-coast. Many of those on that list could be greybeards before their names land on someone's desk."

Fulton could hear the muffled aircraft sounds drifting up from the nearby flight line. A machine was taking off, lifting over the hangars, filling the room with the snap and snarl of Pratt & Whitney radial engines and Hamilton-Standard propellers: a twin-engined Expediter with its landing gear lifting into the wells. Maple leaf roundels . . . ROYAL CANADIAN NAVY in bold black letters along the fuselage . . .

It was so God-damned *unfair*!

"Nothing personal, Mister Fulton," the Training Commander was saying. "Just that, for the Navy, your skills represent a kind of negative equity. Not the best investment we can make . . ."

Tamara, who had been silent until then, wondered, "how does the Air Force come into it?"

She watched him without expression, hoping that he would accept the question as mere polite interest. Hard, though, to appear casual, making sure that, before her mother and Stepan, Jack most of all, nothing showed.

She felt an irrepressible grin working its way up, picturing their faces if they knew what was on her mind. For now, she told herself, nothing *would* show; save that for later, reflecting mirthfully, let's hope . . .

It took some doing to sit like a bump on a log, best behaviour, sweet and demure. With what I'm getting to feel brushed under the mat. With him parked before me, looking good enough to eat: late afternoon sun slanting through the kitchen window, lighting his fair hair like a halo, like some glorious, fantastic saint, or something. Talking and smiling . . . great big white-toothed grin. And now, after my dumb-arse question, here's me getting the full benefit, smile and halo all to myself! Which, Tamara decided, makes it worthwhile asking dumb-arse questions; just to corral that smile for a while.

She was smiling back; could not have done otherwise, the grin had reached the surface. Thinking, self-mocking, all teeth and gums and goo-goo eyes. Like some simp bobby-soxer. But, method in my madness: get my claim staked before someone else, less-deserving, moved in.

She felt a joyous recklessness: so *what* if I'm shamelessly on the make for this unbelievable guy who's walked into Ma's kitchen, and my life. There was heat in her face, and it felt good; she imagined, not caring much, the betraying colour that went with that.

She saw her mother watching her, the old you-don't-fool-me-for-a-minute look, and her own big, fat grin to go with it. Ma was getting the message, and there was no conning her, ever.

Tamara looked at her mother, her expression blending defiance and defensiveness, eyes demanding . . . what do you expect? You're all woman, *you* know the score: her gaze slid with deliberate meaning to Stepan, squatted there looking characteristically smug. Rules are the same for us all, Tamara's eyes said. You waited for the guy who'd turn you on, who *might* be the right one. And, when it seemed that, maybe, he'd showed up at last, you latched on, grabbed a hold, and worked every trick in the book!

Fulton watched her with covert pleasure: the young woman, darkly-beautiful, so very self-assured, yet possessing still her girlhood's long-limbed coltishness: he could picture her in that moment delightfully, running free somewhere, her hair streaming . . .

She worked as a nurse's aide at St. John's, the fifty-bed hospital which served Blackfish Harbour and the surrounding logging camps, sawmills and fishing villages. Later in the year she would go to Vancouver to begin full nursing training at the General Hospital.

He found her almost achingly lovely, attracted by her curved and supple young body, by her face with its firm, wilful chin and full, easily-smiling mouth. Her nose was straight, with nostrils sculpted as though by a delicate hand; a nose that Hollywood actresses would spend fortunes in their attempts to duplicate it.

Best, and most fascinating, he decided, were her eyes, large and dark brown, with a beguiling hint of the Orient, their veiling lashes untouched by mascara. But her stock was Russian, or Ukrainian, from lands once ravaged by Tartars and Mongols, who had left their strains behind. He found enchanting the thought of Tamara with Tartar blood . . .

He answered, watching her, "if I wanted Service flying, then the Air Force was my only choice . . . that or nothing." He joked clumsily, "they tell me the Air Force is less choosy."

"That the stupid Navy loss," Stepan declared with belligerence. Spurning the proffered coffee, he had been drinking bottled beer. "You Goddam good pilot . . ."

"Let the boy *talk*, you!" Rosa prodded him with a stubby forefinger.

Stepan gave her a sharp glance, then shrugged acceptance. "Hokay. Nobody wantin' to hear what I say."

"Nobody do," she agreed, and directed. "Be give Jack a beer . . . not be hog it all, you."

Stepan knocked the caps off two bottles.

"I say for *Jack*," Rosa told him fiercely. "Nothin' about you!"

He glowered. "Man can't drink alone."

Fulton put in quickly, "maybe I shouldn't."

"Is okay." Rosa beamed at him. "We gettin' plenty. No bugger go short around this place . . ."

"*Ma*!" Tamara was shaking her head despairingly.

"It's just that I'm flying in the morning," Fulton explained, adding lightly, "they like to have me sober for that."

"Now, I call that smart." Rosa stared hard at Stepan. "Maybe *you* begin think like so, eh?"

"Got no need . . ." He shrugged disdain. "Not go flyin' . . ."

"Best not get sassy with me . . ." Rosa began threateningly.

"*Please* . . . !" Tamara looked up, protesting, "not now . . ."

"What we do, baby?" Rosa's tone had softened.

"Ma . . . we have a guest. Do we have to fight?"

Stepan was looking sheepish as Rosa nodded agreement. "Sure . . . you right." She patted Fulton's arm. "Me and him be yakkin' all the time . . . get so's we forget sometime. Go on," she encouraged. "Be say about Air Force. We like to know these things."

*

Fulton wished to be told where he stood.

"As a naval officer?" the Training Commander enquired.

"Yes, sir."

"You can expect to serve ashore at Halifax or Esquimalt, and at sea." He looked pensive. "'Sweepers, destroyers, cruisers, maybe? The *Ontario* or the *Quebec*. Then, of course, there's the *Magnificent*, although carrier duties as a seaman officer may not hold much appeal . . ." Fulton said nothing, and was startled then as the older man suggested, "there could, though, be another chance to fly."

"Sir . . . ?"

"With the R.C.A.F."

Since the United States had relinquished responsibility to Canada for the training of pilots from NATO-member countries, the Royal Canadian Air Force had been recruiting aircrew to meet the growing demand for instructors.

The Training Commander studied Fulton's opened personnel file. "You were working towards a civilian instructor's rating."

"That's right, sir . . ." Fulton hesitated. "But, in the Air Force, wouldn't that mean tooling around in the back seat of a Harvard?"

"Have you any objection to Harvards, Mister Fulton?"

"Oh . . . no, sir." He concealed fresh doubts: it would, at least, be flying . . .

"Nice machine . . . proven and dependable," the Training Commander observed. "If you can fly a Harvard, you can fly anything."

"Yes, sir."

"But the notion doesn't thrill you."

"I'd need to think about it, sir."

"Absolutely. It's not something to rush into . . ." There was a moment's silence. The sound of a ground-testing engine came from the flight line, rising and falling to the throttle adjustments. Fulton listened enviously, waiting, until the Training Commander said, "of course, it needn't be Harvards, you know?"

"No, sir . . . ?"

"The Harvard, nowadays, is the intermediate step between *ab initio* and advanced. And advanced training, remember, is on jets. They're hiring in that department, too." He elaborated, "the T-Thirty-Three . . . five hundred knots, nice high-powered stuff. The Air Force has advanced bases in Manitoba, at Gimli, Portage la Prairie and McDonald. Now *that* might be something to ponder?"

*

"You just chop and change?" Tamara asked. "Navy to Air Force, or Army . . . whatever?"

"Maybe Foreign Legion, eh?" Stepan guffawed. He uncapped a beer bottle, fumbling, and spilled some. "Maybe Boy Scouts?"

Tamara was frowning. Rosa stared at him, tight-lipped.

"It can be done," Fulton explained quickly. "If it's what they call in the interests of the Service."

"Did they decide that for you?" Tamara watched him, and he dared to imagine something deeper, more than mere polite interest, in her steady gaze.

He told her, smiling, "I've wondered sometimes if the Training Commander was trying to tell me something? Like that old song from the First World War . . . 'We Really Hate to Lose You, but We Think You Ought to Go'."

"No," Tamara answered gravely. "I shouldn't think it was anything like *that*."

*

"Hey, lookit . . ." Stepan was pointing through the windshield, chuckling. "Here come Ichabod."

A pre-war vintage Studebaker truck was moving towards the dock, swaying and creaking. As it turned past the parked Dodge, Fulton could see on one door the crudely-daubed words: LUCKY'S TRANSFER—Freight Hauling—Phone 58Y.

Stepan explained, "comin' to meet the boat and preach."

"Who is?"

"Ichabod. He be preacher."

The Studebaker lurched on to the plank-decked Government dock at which the steamships from Vancouver and Ocean Falls made their regular stops, and picked its way out to halt by the freight shed.

"Is Lucky drivin' . . . got Ichabod with him . . ." Stepan was gazing out to the open Sound beyond the bay. "The old *Cardena* due in. Lucky meet every boat . . . got contract for shiftin' the freight." He was shaking his head. "That crazy Ichabod come too . . . never miss a boat."

With scant interest, Fulton asked, "does he work for Lucky?"

"Work for hisself. Lucky pick him up at his shack, and give him a ride down. Ichabod, he's a holy roller," Stepan said, grinning. "He collar the poor Goddam people comin' off boat, then preach 'em hellfire till they skedaddle, then he go preach at sum'n'a'bitch *boat*!" He nodded happily. "Just watch that screwball when the old *Cardena* come in."

Two men had got down from the truck, one in a plaid wool workshirt, stocky and grizzled. The other, Fulton decided, epitomised the broad definition of the 'scarecrow figure', lanky and stoop-shouldered, clad in a funereal suit, the jacket tight, the too-short sleeves exposing bony wrists.

Half-mast pants revealed grey woollen socks and vast boots. Beneath a dated Homberg hat, the middle-aged face was pale and bespectacled. It was an appearance so bizarre as to seem carefully contrived; the studied note of eccentric comedy to lend impact to the man's presence. Fulton, intrigued, wondered if the shabby, ill-fitting suit, the out-of-place briefcase in this rough-and-ready backwoods setting, the ridiculous hat, were his chosen trademark. Holding back laughter, he recalled Western movies in which wild-eyed preachers, similarly clad, rode into town on mules to the close regard of mocking, unfriendly eyes. Preachers who turned out to be full of suprises: might it be, here, that Ichabod carried a long-barrelled Colt Peacemaker under his seedy coat?

"A real doozer, eh? Man from Mars!" Stepan hooted mirthfully as Ichabod, clutching his briefcase and a clipboard, stood peering towards the point where the steamer would appear. And Fulton was moved by a sudden and unaccountable sense of pity for the lonely, questing figure. "Got his Bible, and them papers he hands out," Stepan went on. "Folks off'n the boat, he say 'em come to his meetin's. They tell him yah . . . he write down the names."

"Has he got a church?"

"Got his shack up by Indian school. Not like no Roman . . . no Orthodox . . . be make her up as he go along. Crazy as a bedbug. Hokay . . . !" He shoved open the driver's door. "We go to work, Highpockets. That old log don't cut herself."

They off-loaded the tools, the fuel for the power saw, and carried everything down to the soured, grey strip of beach where the log waited, red cedar, thirty feet long, four feet through the butt, gouged by the boom-chains, and bearing the deeply-incised marks of the forest products company, its rightful owners. It had been long in the water, its flanks darkened, festooned with weed like the drenched hair of someone drowned.

Fulton eyed the company marks apprehensively. "Nice log, Stepan."

"Is it *ever* . . ." Stepan surveyed his prize with affection. "Now we be cut him up lickety-split, eh?"

As they plied the peevees, rolling the log into position for the saw, Ichabod crossed to the pier rail to stand peering down at them with interest.

"Hey, Ichabod . . ." Stepan bawled. "How you makin' out?"

"As well as can be expected, Mister Kereniuk." The preacher raised his Homberg, and English, Fulton noted. Plummy accent. Like a stock movie butler. Rather than a gunslinger.

"Waitin' for the boat, eh?"

"Ah, yes . . . as always."

"Gettin' more souls to be save?"

"One lives in hope. There are many in need . . ." Ichabod eyed Stepan speculatively.

Stepan smirked at Fulton. "He tryin' say me somethin', Highpockets?"

"Maybe he should."

"And you, sir?" Ichabod called. "I haven't had the pleasure."

Before Fulton could respond, Stepan announced, "this Highpockets . . . Mister Fulton that come and work for Island Airways. Fly ambulance plane."

"How splendid . . ." Ichabod nodded approvingly. "And one wonders, Mister Fulton, if, between missions of mercy, there might be some need of my small services?"

Stepan muttered, "not less'n you crazy in the head!"

Fulton felt a stab of irritation: the question, friendly and harmless, was like the preacher himself. He replied pointedly for Stepan's benefit, "could be. I'm not perfect."

Ichabod brightened. "A sentiment shared. I should be delighted to welcome you."

"*Now* look what you done to yourself!" Stepan sounded wrathful.

"I'll send you a copy of my little newsletter," Ichabod promised. "Free of charge, of course."

"I'll look forward to it," Fulton assured him gravely.

A siren boomed from the Sound.

"There she blow, Ichabod!" Stepan called, grinning up. "Old *Cardena*, full o' sinners . . ." He gave Fulton a level stare. "Now, if you up to it, maybe we be cuttin' wood?"

*

The *Cardena* was ancient and shabby, from some long-past era with her unraked bow, upright masts, a single skinny smokestack and pronounced stern overhang. She swung her rusty prow towards the dock, the deck-crew waiting to pass the lines ashore. A telegraph clanged, and water boiled white under her stern.

"Hi, Ichabod . . . !" A deckhand dropped a heaving line neatly at the preacher's feet. "Do your stuff, ol' fella!"

Ichabod pulled in the line with its attached hawser, securing the eye over a bitt, handling the heavy ropes with practiced ease. More vehicles were arriving; a second Lucky's Transfer truck, two of Hong's taxis, Olaf Pedersen's black Ford. A heavy-set man emerged from the Ford, tall, with brush-cut iron-grey hair. He held the passenger door for a woman in hospital whites, a nurse's cap with two black bands. She was thin, fifty-ish, and wore a red cardigan over the white dress.

"That Olaf . . ." Stepan pointed out the man. "Biggest crook between Seattle and Alaska. They make joke about sell refrigerator to Eskimo, it Olaf they be talkin' about."

Fulton smiled. "And the lady?"

"Annie Markham . . . hospital Matron. She hokay, Tamara say. Run good, tight ship."

The Matron was waving; there were answering waves from two young women on the ship's deck.

"New nurses," Stepan observed. "Annie, she always come and meet 'em."

People were turning up on foot, among them many Indians who watched the ship with still, unrevealing eyes.

The Mounted Police patrol car arrived. Two officers in aubergine work tunics got out, a tall sergeant, a younger constable.

"Everythin' hokay now . . ." Stepan eyed the police sourly. "Goddam Horsemen come and save us all." He nodded at the sergeant. "That Porkchop."

"*Who*?"

"Stuck-up sum'n'a'bitch . . . boss o' the Detachment. He shove you in the pokey soon as look at you. Six month for spit in street."

"Porkchop?" Fulton repeated.

"Real name Prokopchuk. Uker-rainian bastard!"

"That?" Fulton stared at him. "From *you*?"

"Even Uker-rainian gettin' good an' bad." Stepan was unrepentant. "And bloody Porkchop *real* bad."

The policemen were looking down at them, and Fulton saw the war ribbons on the sergeant's tunic; one with diagonal stripes of white and purple, a tiny silver rosette; the Distinguished Flying Cross, the rosette signifying a second award. Two D.F.C.s: Prokopchuk, then, had been an airman, and a brave one . . .

He called down in a strong bass voice, "'morning, Stepan."

"Oh, yah . . . *'mornin'*, Sergeant . . ." Stepan's response blended simulated surprise with obsequiousness.

Prokopchuk nodded at Fulton. "You gentlemen are cutting wood, I see."

"Yah . . . is so." Stepan bobbed his head, the peasant before the overlord. "Liddle bit of firewood, eh?"

"Nice cedar log, that. Too good for burning." The hard, professional gaze pierced Stepan. "Nice *commercial* log. Worth a few dollars."

"One time, maybe . . ." Stepan grew evasive. "Not now so much . . . long time in the water. See all that weed?"

"I see them like that *all* the time," Prokopchuk declared. "In log booms, waiting for the tugs."

"Yah . . . maybe . . ."

"What I'm hoping is that cedar log wasn't borrowed from a boom on some dark night?"

"No chance . . ." Stepan, with a 'who, me?' expression, spread baffled arms wide. "Them marks was on him where I find him."

"And where would that have been, Stepan?"

"Out in goddam Sound . . . honest to Christ!" Stepan sounded hunted. "Off'n Sointula, when I comin' home in my boat. Gen-u-wine drift log, swear to *God*!"

"Nowhere near a boom, then?"

"No sign of one nowheres . . . no, *sir*!" Stepan grew virtuous. "There been a boom anywheres, I give him back, lickety-split." He insisted. "But, no boom. I be thinkin' hokay, they go off and leave her. So hokay for me to tow her home."

"I'd like to think that was so." Prokopchuk regarded him with enduringly sceptical eyes. "Unlawful acquisition of merchantable timber is a serious offence. Means a heavy fine . . . maybe jail."

"Is tough, yah . . ." Stepan hung his head. "But be truth what I say you."

The ship was moored; a gangway had been run on board. A small group of men, roughly-dressed came ashore to stand in bewilderment, like people made suddenly homeless. Ichabod, brandishing his clipboard, pounced upon them. The two new nurses were engaged in smiling conversation with the Matron as Olaf Pedersen stowed their bags in the Ford. Three Indian youths came from the ship to be engulfed by a welcoming party chattering in Kwakwaleth . . .

"Kids be come home from jail," Stepan explained in an aside. "Big heroes. Be make party tonight, hokay."

Prokopchuk called down, "guess it's benefit of the doubt time. Barring a complaint, we'll let it go."

"Yah, sure . . . thanks a lot." Stepan bobbed again.

"But remember about jail . . . I'm serious," Prokopchuk warned. He stalked heavily away towards the gangway, followed by the constable.

Stepan muttered at his back, "bugger off, Porkchop, and take your arse-wiper with you." He told Fulton resentfully, "Goddam truth . . . I find her off Sointula. Nowheres near bloody-bugger boom!"

The taxis and Pedersen's Ford were gone. Only a few bystanders remained. The roughly-dressed men had eluded Ichabod and were hurrying away with their duffel bags. Ichabod had vanished into the ship seeking more converts.

"Better get cutting, Stepan," Fulton suggested. "Get rid of the evidence."

"Goddam *right*!" Stepan laughed. "And screw Porkchop!"

*

By nine o'clock the log had been reduced to disc-like segments ready for splitting into manageable chunks with the hammers and wedges. After two hours, Fulton was paying the price in breathlessness and protesting muscles.

Stepan's grin was sardonic. "Is all the Navy an' Air Force in good shape like you?"

"Leave it, Stepan."

"If that so, we gettin' in a war, we all be up creek with no paddle." They reloaded the tools on to the Dodge. "Highpockets . . . I goin' to buy you breakfast."

"Just coffee. I couldn't handle food."

"Got to be eat," Stepan insisted. "Less'n you want gettin' hypoglycaemic? What happen you in plane an' get hypoglycaemic?"

Fulton gave an astonished laugh. "Where did you learn that?"

"My Tamara . . . smart gel." Stepan looked proud. "She find out at hospital. Part of her trainin' for nurse."

"So what's hypoglycaemic?"

"Is blood-sugar, right?" Stepan explained patiently, "you not be eat right, sugar go out your blood, you fall on your arse." He clambered behind the wheel.

Fulton wondered, "you're not leaving the wood?"

"What we do . . . take him for breakfast?"

"Someone could swipe it, Stepan."

"No bugger goin' to swipe all that. Not before we get back . . ." The Dodge groaned away, belching smoke. "Goddam fine truck," Stepan declared admiringly. "Now we go hotel coffee shop. Better breakfast there than Chink café."

"Up to you, Stepan."

"Forget wood . . . not going nowheres. Indian kids maybe take a liddle . . . they welcome. Know how it is with logs . . ." He glanced slyly at Fulton. "Easy come . . . easy go."

*

Fulton listened in disbelief as Stepan asked for double orders of ham, eggs, hotcakes, syrup and buttered toast for himself. "Same for you, Highpockets?"

"Stepan . . . I *couldn't*!"

"Tellin' you . . . you got to eat."

"Okay, then . . . coffee, and a couple of blueberry muffins."

"Holy Christ! Now you goin' be catchin' mal-nu-trition!"

Fulton eyed him. "Tamara again?"

"Yah . . ." He made a face. "Without her, I be knowin' *nothin*'!"

'Jambalaya', a recent hit, was bellowing from the jukebox. Fulton tried, without success, to fathom the Cajun and Creole lyrics: '. . . tum-tum-TUM . . . catfish PIE . . . chili GUMBO. For TONIGHT I'm gonna BE with my cherie-MIO . . .'

A mirthful voice demanded, "where you get the eye, Stepan?"

A man of average height, massively built, watched them, his

tanned chest bulging from a clean white shirt opened three buttons down, sleeves rolled up over powerful arms. He had a rumpled, good-humoured face, bright blue eyes, a shock of upstanding blond hair like a hogged mane . . .

"BILLY!" Stepan turned joyfully. "Old sum'n'a'bitch . . . when you get back?"

"Last night. Hitched a ride down from Sullivan Bay on a Jap troller."

Stepan pounded the huge shoulders. "Hot DAMN! Be good seein' you . . ."

The jukebox told all concerned, 'Son of a GU-U-UN, we'll have big FU-U-UN, ON th' BAY-ou . . . !'

"You, too, you old bastard. Even with that eye." The other grinned. "Who done it . . . Rosa?"

"Who else but you, maybe, and her get away with thing like that?"

"Did you have a skinful?"

"Why else she smack me . . . nice fella like me?" Stepan turned to Fulton. "Meet my best friend in the whole Goddam world. Like *bro-ther*!"

Fulton offered, "how do you do?"

"Billy Langewische." A vast freckled paw engulfed his hand. "You this old bugger's new sidekick?"

"He Highpockets . . ." Stepan grinned with malice. "He *hate* it, but still Highpockets." He commanded, "be stand up now for Billy." Obligingly, Fulton stood. "See what I mean? Thought you say you not goin' be long?" He prodded Fulton painfully, guffawing at his own joke. Fulton smiled politely. If you were tall, it was what you got . . .

He introduced himself. "Real name's Jack Fulton."

Langewische eyed him benignly. "And what brings you to town, Jack Fulton?"

Once more, it was Stepan who supplied the details. "Helpin' me cut up cedar log that prick Porkchop want be takin' away. We haul him home, split fifty-fifty."

"You in the trade, Jack?" Langewische asked.

"Pardon me?"

"Nope . . . you're no logger, not if you say 'pardon me'." Langewische laughed.

"He pilot," Stepan announced. "Island Airways . . . come here for summer work."

"That's fine . . ." Langewische nodded. "When I'm workin' up-Island, you can fly me out for th' weekend with the family. From up at Woss Lake and Nimpkish."

"Billy the best damn' scaler on the Coast," Stepan said with pride. "Even better'n me. Make hunnert bucks a day, eh, Billy?"

"On a good day."

"We friends since *forever*," Stepan insisted.

"You're makin' me blush." Langewische winked at Fulton. "I'll remember and call and ask for you."

"You might not enjoy flying with me." Fulton smiled. "I'm stuck with the ambulance Seabee. No passengers except the horizontal type."

"Well, what the hell?" Langewische shrugged. "My line of work, maybe I'll bring you some business, anyway."

"I hope not," Fulton said.

The waitress refilled their coffee mugs. Stepan looked at his friend expectantly. "How's about the party trick? With the nuts?"

"Stepan, you seen that plenty of times."

"Want Highpockets be see how . . ." He beamed at Fulton. "Hell of a trick. You do him, Billy?"

"For you, Stepan, anything . . ." He asked Fulton, "you like walnuts, Capt'n?"

"Well, yes . . ."

"Just so happens . . ." Langewische rummaged briefly. ". . . I got some here." He held out a single nut. People nearby were watching curiously.

"You get a big kick out o' this," Stepan promised.

"One peeled walnut comin' up . . ." Langewische closed his fist until the knuckles showed white. There was a crack, and he rolled his hand, producing crunching sounds, then exposed the nut kernel and broken shell. The watchers murmured, and the waitress approved, "'way to go, Billy!" Langewische offered his hand. "Your walnut, Capt'n."

Fulton chewed a piece. Stepan took what remained. "What you say, Highpockets?"

"Fantastic."

"Well . . ." Shrugging, Langewische dropped shell fragments into his coffee mug. "Show's over, folks."

Fulton said, "thanks for showing me."

"Anytime your nutcrackers let you down, give me a holler." Langewische rose, nodding affably. "Nice meetin' you."

"Likewise."

Stepan broke in, "what say we get together some night in the beer parlour?"

Langewische nodded. "Could do."

"We sink a few, eh? Tie on a doozer?"

"And what'll Rosa say to that?"

"Be hokay, we do it quick." Stepan smirked. "She feelin' bad about the shiner. Till she get over it, I can do most anythin'."

"Wouldn't bet money on that." Langewische was grinning. Silently, Fulton agreed.

"I know my Rosa," Stepan insisted. "She stay quiet maybe a week . . . passion all gone."

Fulton laughed. "Something else you learned from Tamara?"

"No, sir. I be figure *that* out for myself."

*

Bearing armsful of chopped wood, they moved back and forth, loading the truck.

The *Cardena* had gone on her way to Ocean Falls. The Government dock was deserted.

Stepan and Fulton took a breather. Fulton said, "Sergeant Porkchop'll have a hard time proving anything now."

"He got hard time prove anythin' *anytime*!"

"Thought you said he was always busting people?"

"Bullshit stuff. Few drunks . . . few fights. Some fella skip town, not be pay his fine. Porkchop go after him, get him thirty days. Is all." Stepan was laughing. "Porkchop not know real crime if she bite him in the arse!"

"Let's hope he never catches you out, Stepan."

"*That* be the foggy Friday. Sum'n'a'bitch need to get out of bed real early."

Curious, Fulton asked, "those medal ribbons he wears . . . ?"

"From war." Stepan shrugged indifference. "Big hero some say."

"One of those is the Distinguished Flying Cross . . . with a little rosette, which means he won two of them."

Stepan sniffed, "some big deal."

"The D.F.C. isn't something you get for shining your shoes!"

"I maybe hear somethin' . . . yah," Stepan allowed grumpily. "Porkchop pilot like you. Fly big bombers . . . kick shit out o' Germans. They say he pretty brave hokay." His mouth quirked. "He stupid now, but brave that time. Maybe need be stupid be brave, eh?"

"You don't give up do you?"

"Not with Porkchop, *that* for sure!"

"But . . . a Sergeant in the R.C.M.P . . . . ?"

"What so special about that?"

"To get that far in the few years since the war, you can't be completely dumb."

"Be dumb be cop in first place!"

Fulton appealed, "give him a break, Stepan. What's he ever done to you?"

"Whose side you on?" Stepan assumed an injured look. "Porkchop on my Goddam back all the time. Talk about fine . . . about jail. Treat me like second class citizen . . . like D.P.! Hokay . . . I'm a D.P., he D.P., too! Just another dumb Uker-rainian bastard like me!" He stared resentfully into the empty Sound.

"Some speech, Stepan."

"Be inside me long time all that. Sometime, I want askin' Porkchop what his problem? Maybe we go behind the woodshed, me an' him, and fix his problem *good*." He glowered at Fulton. "I say about *stupid*, eh?"

"Yes, you did."

"Now I tell you how stupid is Porkchop. He so smart, why he let woman make monkey out of him?"

"Is that what's happening?"

"You don' know about Porkchop and his woman?"

"I'm new here, remember?"

"She hospital nurse . . . run the O.R., my Tamara say. I seen her . . . blonde, good-looker, 'though she got fat legs."

Fulton offered mildly, "we can't all be perfect."

"Julie Paulen . . . Grad Nurse Paulen, R.N. Think she bloody cat's miaow. Tamara not like her one liddle bit."

"And she's Porkchop's girl?"

"Girl for any bugger she take shine to," Stepan grunted. "But stupid Porkchop plannin' on *marry* her. Big rock on her finger . . . the whole shebang." He shook his head in disbelief. "And all time Porkchop not lookin', she's got hot pants for one of the doctors. Round his house screwin' him every which way from Sunday."

"Never a dull moment in Blackfish, it seems."

"Doc-tor Denk-man," Stepan supplied with relish. "Goddam lady-killer. Whole town know . . . Indian and white. All the other Horsemen know. Only one not know be Porkchop." His stare challenged Fulton. "You say me that not *stupid*?"

An aircraft was taxying slowly out, a Beaver floatplane, the chosen mount of Mike Denholm, the Island Airways base manager. Twin white salmon seiners, the *Emma A.* and *Susan A.*, slid gently in alongside the Standard Oil dock.

"Charlie Abalone's boats." Stepan pointed. "About richest Indian on the Coast. Own seven boats, more'n that prick Hawaiian Jim ever got," he added balefully. "Contract fishin' for B.C. Packers . . . they take all his catch. Hunnert and fifty thousan' dollars a boat." He glanced quickly, slyly at Fulton. "See them names? They all name like so. Emma and Susan and Gloria. Sally-Ann, Winnie, Patsy and Edith. All Charlie's daughters . . ." He winked. "Play your cards right, you get be skipper one of them . . . get half-share."

"Say that again . . . !"

Stepan's response was drowned by the roar of the Beaver taking off. It settled gracefully on the step, cutting a pure white line across the bay that broke off as the floats lifted clear, and it began an easy climbing turn towards the mountains and Nimpkish Lake.

"Noisy sum'n'a'bitch," Stepan grumbled. "Go right through my head."

"What was that about skippers and half-shares?"

"Yah . . . is so. No shit. And three still to go, Highpockets." The elbow dug anew into Fulton's side. "Emma, Sally-Ann and Patsy. Others all spoke for. But pick from them three, you get good boat and fair-to-middlin' gel."

Fulton listened in wonder as Stepan told of Charlie Abalone, the rich Indian; of Charlie's desire to marry his daughters to white men. So great a desire that every bride's dowry included a seiner captaincy and a seventy-five thousand-dollar half-share in the boat named for her . . .

"Good deal, eh? Half the boat, all the woman? Not need share *her* with Charlie."

"You've got a weird way of looking at things."

"Make sense . . . half boat . . . nice wife waitin' . . . top price for salmon catch. And Charlie's gels good-lookers, except maybe Patsy that bandy-leg and squint a liddle."

"What's all this got to do with me?" Fulton wondered.

"Maybe you get special deal, Highpockets? Charlie gettin' white *Air Force* officer marry his gel, instead o' some rummy fisherman, maybe give you *full* share? Maybe *two* daughter?"

"You," Fulton said. "Are beyond help."

"Do that, then you be rich officer," Stepan pointed out, grinning. "Hire a skipper run your boat . . . you go be officer somewhere with pretty Indian wife. And make Charlie Abalone happy fella, eh?"

TWO

As they finished loading the wood, Fulton could ponder again, bemused, the circumstances which had brought him for the summer to Blackfish Harbour.

Facing unexpected months as a temporary civilian, it had seemed right to return home to the Pacific coast.

Drawing Service pay and allowances, he had no need for employment: he could loaf if he chose, buy a used car, drift to California or Mexico. There was his parents' home on Bowen Island, his old room waiting. Summer was beginning, with the beaches at Spanish Banks and Kitsilano and English Bay and their friendly girls; beer and wiener roasts after dark over driftwood fires. Swimming under the moon with the preferred girl . . .

But he wished for more, and it was almost reflex to drive out to the international airport on Sea Island, to visit again people and places remembered from student flying days. Where, by chance alone, he stumbled into a job. A day earlier, it would not have been there; later, and someone would have snapped it up . . .

He was in the airport coffee lounge, an old haunt, when Harry de Witt came in. Harry, who had sent him on his first solo in a Fleet 80 trainer. Who flicked bushy brows in a parody of startled disbelief.

"It lives . . . it breathes! How you doin', Admiral?"

"Everyone I possibly can, Harry. How are you?"

"Just great . . . until *this* moment."

"Park your behind," Fulton invited. "Time for coffee?"

"If you're buyin'?"

"Hospitality will run to one dime." Fulton signalled the waitress.

"What do we hear about you?" De Witt demanded. "Flying off carriers? What will our mad, impetuous Navy cook up next?" The waitress brought his coffee. "What brings you back? Leave?"

"Of a sort, I guess."

The brows shot up again. "Do I sense something sinister?"

"Some changes of plan. You'll need to revise your thinking about me."

"I did *that* the first time I flew with you!"

Fulton spoke of his disappointment, and the reason why.

"Bad habits, is it?" De Witt raised soulful eyes. "So it's *my* fault. I taught you all I know, and you still know nothing."

"I've got a maybe second chance," Fulton said. "With the Air Force."

"Dear God . . ." De Witt pretended to weep. "What did I start when I gave you the stick?"

Fulton said acidly, "Let me know when you're through." He explained the rejection, the subsequent offer, which had led to this summer of idleness. Serious then, De Witt enquired, "Jack? Would you be interested in some work?"

"Depends what's going."

"Can't promise anything, but I happen to know Island Airways is hiring. If you were to show up over there quick like a bunny, you could score."

*

The Island Airways Vancouver base was a short walk from the coffee lounge, one of a number of floatplane operations along the middle arm of the Fraser River delta.

It seemed almost too easy; within minutes he was being interviewed by Edwin Gowan, the operations manager, who asked the expected questions about flying hours and types flown: did Fulton hold a valid commercial licence and seaplane rating? The responses appeared to satisfy him.

"You could be tailor-made, Jack. We need someone until the Fall when our new permanent man joins us. A kind of stop-gap vacancy."

"Would it be in Vancouver?"

"You're not *that* lucky." Gowan smiled. "Blackfish Harbour. Know it?"

North end of Vancouver Island, Fulton recollected vaguely. Logging and fishing country, off the beaten track, accessible by sea and air.

"Not our most popular base," Gowan confessed. "A village and Indian reservation, pretty rough-and-ready, but seldom dull . . ." He ventured, "it *could* be a rewarding experience . . . ?"

Mike Denholm was the permanent pilot and base manager: there was a licensed engineer and a helper. A local woman fulfilled the functions of ticket agent and dispatcher.

If engaged, Fulton would receive three hundred and fifty dollars monthly base pay, plus five cents for every mile flown.

"Those nickels add up," Gowan promised. "Financially, it could be a good summer for you." He added then, like an afterthought, "it's ambulance flying."

There were two aircraft based at Blackfish Harbour, a flagship Beaver, flown by the base manager, and a Republic Seabee amphibian air ambulance. "Ever flown a 'Bee?" Fulton admitted that he had not, and Gowan smiled dryly. "A rare experience."

Fulton quelled a stomach flutter with the thought that . . . they all flew the same.

"From the same stable as the wartime P-Forty-Seven Thunderbolt, but a different league altogether," Gowan said. "Although, like the Thunderbolt, it's built like a brick shithouse . . ." He added, amused, "flies like one as well. Noisy, and slow as molasses in January."

From the design viewpoint, the Seabee fell into the 'interesting' category, a small, single-engined flying boat.

"It's rugged . . . can handle rough water," Gowan said. On the negative side, with its 215-horsepower engine, it was seriously underpowered. "It's the weight of that amphib gear . . . two hundred and fifty pounds. Remove the wheels and hydraulics . . . fly it as a straight 'boat, it becomes a fair performer." He grinned. "If you're in no hurry to get anywhere. Come on," he invited. "I'll show you."

*

The Island Airways dock lay along the river in the airport's shadow, a pier thrusting into swift brown water, tall pilings holding a chain of free-floating mooring pontoons, their edges lined with old tyres bolted into place to fend off delicate metal hulls and floats. Several machines lay alongside, a Norseman, a Beaver, an antique Fairchild 71. A diminutive Luscombe Silvaire bobbed lightly in the currents. On the pontoons' inner sides two Seabees were tethered side by side. All the aircraft wore the red, white and silver livery of Island Airways; on their doors a winged logo with the slightly over-optimistic claim of:

ISLAND AIRWAYS—VANCOUVER B.C.
Anything—Anywhere—Anytime.

Gowan pointed out the salient features; the wide side doors, an unusual hatch which opened outward from the blunt bow. "That's what makes it a good ambulance machine."

Fulton began to appreciate the 'interesting' design: the cockpit and passenger cabin contained within a bulbous nacelle from which extended high-set, untapered wings. The engine compartment surmounted the cabin's rear, with the propeller set behind in the unconventional 'pusher' position. There, the fuselage cut away sharply to a low hull, its top surface a mere foot above the water.

"Handy for your working engineer." Gowan indicated the hull. "He can stand there with shoulder level access to the prop and engine . . ." He gave Fulton a dry glance. "Or, in your case, knee-level." Fulton smiled back dutifully.

The tall fin and rudder flowed upward to a squared tip, and there was a small water rudder immediately behind the tailwheel assembly . . .

"And there . . ." Gowan pointed. "In an airplane only a mother could love, is the homeliest feature of all."

The main landing gear protruded from the cabin sides on spindly hydraulic legs. No wheels concealed discreetly behind metal doors; these were out-thrust blatantly, clear of the water, exposed and unapologetic, like prominent ears.

"Strictly utilitarian," Gowan murmured. "Everything you need, but no frills."

Inside, he explained the fittings, an instrument panel off-set to the left, leaving a passage from the bow-hatch to the front passenger seat. There were two rear seats.

"This is how they come from the factory . . ." Gowan ushered Fulton into the pilot's seat, and he examined the basic panel of flight and engine instruments. There was a big-knobbed throttle, controls for propeller pitch and fuel mixture, magneto switch, radio and position lights toggles, an over-head crank for the stabiliser, a hand-pump and selector that catered for flaps and landing gear.

Fulton touched the control yoke, feeling the movement of rudder pedals under his feet. He breathed in the well-known airplane smells, a subtle blending of fuel, oil, hydraulic fluid and heated metal. The Seabee felt comfortable, even familiar . . . and the excitement began to stir . . . a new aircraft, a fresh challenge.

Gowan took the front passenger seat. "This one's used for regular charter work. The Blackfish 'Bee has this seat removed so's we can load an adult-size basket stretcher through the bow, and rest the foot on the step there . . ." He indicated a small platform inside the hatch. "With the head on the rear passenger seat." Fulton nodded understanding. "Leaving your seat and one behind you for a nurse or first-aider."

Fulton wanted to know, "what if there's more than one patient?"

"You get more than one trip. At a nickel a mile, no one's complaining." Fulton smiled. "You fly out the worst hurt, then come back for the others. If it's walking wounded, you can shove two at a time in the back seats."

The most frequent passengers, Fulton learned, were the victims of logging accidents. In the main, ambulance flights were short, a matter of minutes, to the camps and sawmills in the Blackfish area.

*

A youth in an Island Airways sweatshirt stood at the bow.

"If you're ready?" Gowan asked.

"You mean . . . *fly* it?"

"That's the idea. We do need a check ride before we can commit ourselves."

"Does that mean I'm hired?"

"We'll see first how you handle the beast. Let's not jump the gun."

Fulton felt both nervous and elated. There was nothing apparent here to unnerve him: he wanted very much to fly the Seabee; it would be his first true flying boat. He had flown conventional floatplanes . . . this was entirely novel . . . Gowan promised comfortingly, "I'll talk you through . . . see you don't do anything silly."

The youth closed the hatch and released the mooring lines.

*

There were some doubtful moments during the first take-off. At full power, surging forward, a wave crunched into the bow, breaking over the windshield. Water poured through the hatch rim, soaking Gowan's legs.

"Forgot to mention that . . ." He mopped himself. "Seabees leak like sieves, only better."

The windshield cleared, but there was a considerable chop running, and the aircraft wallowed and shuddered . . .

Gowan warned, "watch your wingtip floats."

Unlike twin-float seaplanes, a flying boat on the water stood poised on a single narrow keel while small outrigger floats held the wings clear. Frail, they could snap off if allowed to dig in at speed . . .

The Seabee ploughed on sluggishly, and Fulton struggled to keep it under control. "She'll go on the step now," Gowan advised. "Forward on the stick . . . get your tail up."

Fulton obeyed, moving the control yoke forward as though lifting the tail for take-off in a landplane. The tail stayed down, the engine bellowing futilely.

"Need to break the water's suction . . . takes a little muscle . . ." Gowan advised. "Bring the stick all the way back, then a good hard shove forward . . . that ought to do it."

But *that* seemed to violate all the rules of aircraft handling: try it with most, he reflected edgily, and you'd stand on your nose . . . go over on your back. He drew the yoke fully towards him . . .

"That's it . . . let the nose come up," Gowan approved. "Be ready when I say to push forward." Fulton could feel the waves juddering through the thin hull plating. "Getting there . . ." Gowan was soothing. "Stand by."

A wave struck; one wing was dropping . . . Fulton, sweating now, fed in opposite aileron, keeping the tip-float clear. "Okay . . . *now*! Boot her *hard*!"

Fulton, wincing, booted. The control column moved through its arc, and the nose dropped obediently. More water dumped into Gowan's lap . . .

"Shit! Sorry . . ."

"I've been wet before. You just fly . . ."

The windshield was clear, water driven aside by the wind of passage, and the Seabee *felt* different now, the nose level, the view ahead unobstructed. He sensed the acceleration, and risked a glance at the airspeed indicator, seeing the needle moving up encouragingly.

"On the step." Gowan stuck up a thumb. "Couldn't have done it better myself."

Fulton's palms were clammy, and his neck and shoulders throbbed with tension. But the elation was back as, with a bound from a wave-crest, the Seabee flew.

*

He was convinced, walking back to the office, that he had blown it. "Don't call us," they would say. "We'll call you." Or, more brutally honest, "thanks . . . but *no* thanks."

He had enjoyed the Seabee in the air; it had been pleasant to handle, stable and suitably docile. Following Gowan's directions, he took them out over Georgia Strait, and Gowan made encouraging noises and talked amiably of nothing in particular. Until, deceptively mild, he suggested, "let's try a landing." Adding, "dry land . . . to help you get the feel."

The control tower gave them approach clearance to Runway 26. Gowan demonstrated the operation of the hydraulic flaps and landing gear. "Give me a touch-and-go," he said. "Please."

Fulton flew the Seabee down to the ground, holding the nose on the numbers—'26'—the point where, in theory, he should return to earth . . .

"Clear to land, touch-and-go, on Two-Six," the tower confirmed.

He eased back the power, re-trimmed, selected full flaps. The numbers, and the black rubber smudges of incalculable previous landings, drifted closer . . . he flattened the glide, closing the throttle as the numbers vanished under the nose, easing back into the three-point position . . . and enjoyed the firm gentle thump of all three wheels touching together.

The tower enquired, "will you require another approach and landing?"

"Negative," Gowan replied. "Returning to the river." As Fulton advanced the throttle to take them back into the air, he said with perceptible irony, "very nice, Jack . . . or just lucky?"

"Not sure yet."

"Let's find out."

Completing a copybook approach, Fulton flattened the glide too high, and the Seabee stalled crunchingly into the water. "Holy JE-sus!"

"Ta-a-ake it easy." Gowan sat, calm and unmoving at his side.

The aircraft bounced, and he caught it with a burst of power, easing it back into a more-or-less controlled landing.

"I think we're there," Gowan observed with mildness.

Fulton was abject. "I'm *sorry* . . ." They would never hire him. No sick, hurt logger would give a plugged nickel for his kind of experience . . .

"Like they say," Gowan suggested. "Don't be sorry . . . be careful."

"Sure . . ." There was nothing more to be said.

The Seabee rolled in the swells: Fulton pondered cutting his losses, taxying back to the dock. Get out while you're still ahead!

"You're fine on land," Gowan said. "The water landing would've been, too, but for nerves."

"Nerves . . ." Fulton repeated numbly.

"I was watching you . . . it's my neck, too," Gowan said. "This isn't the easiest small plane to come to terms with, but you've taken to it. You just tensed-up then."

"Worrying about the water conditions, I guess."

"And she felt you worrying. Airplanes are like horses . . . they respond to their riders." Gowan stared out at the choppy brown water. "You were doing fine, but you let that bug you. Now you've seen for yourself, the 'Bee *is* rugged, and forgiving if you persevere . . ." He was smiling. "The way you caught her on the hop like that was good. We all make bad landings . . . it's knowing how to get out of them, like you *did*, that counts."

"Thank you," Fulton said limply.

It had *sounded* encouraging, but walking up from the dock, he steeled himself for rejection.

*

Gowan asked, "what do you think?"

"I'm not sure *I'd* hire me."

"Should I go by your opinion, Jack?"

"You're the boss."

"That's right. But the boss thinks you did pretty well once you started believing in yourself. Those two extra landings you gave me were right up to snuff. You were working at it, figuring it out. There are some rough edges," Gowan told him. "But those can be ironed-out. So? Still feel like spending the summer with us?"

"We-e-ell . . ." Fulton released pent-up breath. "I'd really like to."

Island Airways would fly him to Blackfish Harbour in the coming week. He would spend more time before that improving his proficiency on the Seabee.

"Mike Denholm, the base manager, will check you out himself when you arrive," Gowan said. "After which, it's strictly on-the-job training."

THREE

"I be thinkin'," Stepan mused. "Goin' to lose my helper now."

"What . . . ?" Fulton came out of his reverie.

"Look to me like maybe you in business."

Jackie Seaweed was pure-bred Kwakiutl, and an excellent aircraft dockhand, monosyllabic and inscrutable. He came up to them, his face dark and enclosed, giving nothing away but a terse nod to Fulton. "Alice Royle's wantin' a talk. She's pissed-off."

Fulton was guarded. "What's eating her?"

"Reckon there's somethin' you forgot."

"Oh, shit . . ." He *had* forgotten Mrs Royle, the company agent and dispatcher. *She* took the bookings, handled the traffic, operated the radio, bullied the pilots; even Mike Denholm, who purported to be her boss. Mrs Royle was someone *not* to be forgotten . . .

"She phoned an' you never answered. Said for me to go look for you." The Indian glanced at Stepan. "Your ol' lady said where you was." And then, grinning at Fulton, "figure she's goin' to ream out your arse, Capt'n."

Fulton thought with resignation, I *know* the rules: I'm on stand-by during flying hours. With a duty to inform the dispatcher where I am. That morning, groggy with sleep, he had simply . . . forgotten. He would pay for that oversight; there was never any leeway with Alice Royle.

"See, I be right, hokay?" Stepan beamed at him. "You goin' fly for sure, and with Alice after your hide, you won't need no Goddam plane!"

*

Within a community where eccentricity was commonplace and a way of life, Alice Royle was noted as one of Blackfish Harbour's more exceptional eccentrics.

She had come from England to British Columbia as a war bride in 1919. Long-widowed, she lived in primly modest respectability, supporting herself with a small private income and the peppercorn salary paid by Island Airways.

Thirty-five years in Canada, she remained fiercely British, viewing herself as someone distinct, whose duty it was to remain aloof from her more rough-and-ready Colonial neighbours.

Reactions to her within the community varied from awe through respect and affection, to occasional dislike, and, sometimes, fear. She was a waspish, intolerant busybody, and the general consensus was that she was wacky.

The Island Airways directors loved her, and—to the sometimes despair of her working colleagues—it was made clear from Head Office that there would be employment for Mrs Royle for as long as she should desire it.

Few in Blackfish Harbour had succeeded in besting her in argument or dispute, and those few had become local legends.

In the case of blunt, rough-spoken Olaf Pedersen, it was her Englishness which proved to be her undoing.

Preparing to re-decorate her house, she had sought to purchase from Pedersen's Hardware and Haberdashery a quantity of calcimine. Which, in the English manner, she persisted in referring to as distemper.

When the nonplussed sales assistant was unable to help, she accosted Olaf Pedersen in person, demanding in her high, clear voice, "*Mister* Pedersen . . . *do* you have distemper in the shop?"

"No, Ma'am, we don't," he replied without hesitation. "Had the whole place fumigated just last week. And we all had our rabies shots, just in case!"

Chin Hong, who had come from Canton, and whose English was sparse, was the co-owner with his brother Chang of Hong's Café. Enduringly irascible, he suffered fools not at all, nor the—to him—barbarous mannerisms of those like Alice Royle.

She irritated him considerably when, at lunch one day, she demanded water biscuits with her bowl of vegetable soup.

Chin Hong thrust his ever-scowling face close to hers. "What this wat-ah bis-cuit, ha? Not know noth-thing about."

Alice Royle, shrinking back, began to explain, "*Mister* Chin . . ."

"Is Mist-ah *Hong*. Say me what want."

"*Mister* Hong, water biscuits are made to be eaten with soup."

"Not got." A determined shake of the head. "Want crack-ah? Give crack-ah."

"I have particularly ordered . . ."

"Want toast? Fix toast."

". . . water biscuits, *if* you please!"

"Not please . . . not got. Need say you two time? Give crack-ah . . . fix toast. Want wat-ah bis-cuit, give crack-ah . . . give glass wat-ah . . . you *dunk*, ha?"

For some considerable time thereafter, Alice Royle would be pursued about the village by soft, mirthful cries from points unseen: "You *dunk* . . . ha!"

*

"I had expected better from you, Mister Fulton." Alice Royle eyed him stonily.

"I'm really sorry, but I . . ."

"It's not as though you're like the others . . ." She gestured fastidiously.

"Pardon me?" He stood like a naval defaulter before the desk in her small, neat office.

She said, "I feel sure that you grasp my meaning."

"Not at all. What others are you talking about?"

"The . . . *others*." She clarified, "Mister Denholm . . . Mister Peters . . . Mister Seaweed." She was not given to the employment of first names. "None of whom possess your background. They are not 'varsity graduates, nor serving officers. One anticipates a certain laxness in such people. One had hoped . . ." She sighed, "for higher standards from you."

"I *said* I was sorry . . ."

"*Sorry* is hardly relevant, Mister Fulton."

"Yes, okay . . . fine." Resentment began to stir. There was nothing in the agreement stating that he must endure this kind of thing. "I've made a mistake. But if I've embarrassed the company, then I'm answerable to Mike Denholm, or to Vancouver. Not to you." She caught a scandalised breath. "I regret giving you problems, but it was a *small* oversight, hardly the end of the world."

"You're here," she told him icily. "To undertake emergency flights. For that you must be *available*. You are not bound by a set timetable. For you, it's here and *now*!"

"Am I to assume, then, that I'm needed now? Which, as I'm here, you should tell me more about? Instead of wasting more time bawling me out."

It was cheap sarcasm, and he braced for her indignant response, and was surprised when her expression softened.

"To which I may only respond with . . . *touché*."

He smiled at her, grateful for the capitulation, thinking, had there been witnesses to the exchange, he might have joined Olaf Pedersen and Chin Hong in the local hall of fame. He promised, "from now on, I'll stay on the ball."

"I'm sure you will." She became brisk. "Now . . . about your trip . . ."

An elderly tubercular Indian woman was to be flown to Vancouver for admission to a sanitarium.

Alice Royle made the point firmly, "you'll have ample time in which to return today."

Fulton put from his mind any small hope of a night spent in Town. Good relations were restored, but those, with Alice Royle, brought few concessions.

*

He waited, listening to the lap of water around the Seabee's hull, for the arrival of Olaf Pedersen's Ford with the patient. Jackie Seaweed, standing by the open bow-hatch, observed, "pretty nice . . . trip to Van."

"I won't be seeing much of it," Fulton said.

"Aunt Alice told you how it's goin' to be, eh?"

"Something like that."

"God-damn," the Indian said with respect. "That is *some* old woman."

The Ford drew up at the pierhead. Two orderlies picked their way down to the pontoon with the laden stretcher. In the car, Pedersen was talking to a nurse whose face was turned away.

The sick woman whimpered and muttered under her blankets and safety straps, and coughed thickly. An orderly held a sputum cup to the withered mouth. Fulton remembered some minor paperwork, and attended to it as a woman's footsteps hurried along the pontoon . . .

Tamara could see him at the airplane's controls in his lumberman's shirt, head bent, scribbling on a clipboard. She saw how the sunlight played that trick with his hair again, clean, healthy hair like spun gold: she remembered a shampoo commercial on the radio . . . 'leaves your hair light, laughing bright'. That says it all, she thought, and felt the smile again, deep inside: *that's* my man! I could probably love him for his hair alone . . .

Frowning at his paperwork, he did not look up, and she felt sudden misgiving. What if he was put-out because Matron had picked *her* to escort the old Indian woman? Or guess that she had angled deliberately for the job, and feel scorn for her manoeuvring? I hope—reflexively she crossed her fingers—it won't be like that . . . hope like crazy! Last thing I want is to have him mad with me, over *anything* . . .

She was asking, "where do I go?"

"Just step in," Jackie Seaweed told her. "Grab the seat behind the pilot."

The Seabee dipped in the water under her weight; her shadow darkened the cabin. "'Morning, Jack. How are you today?"

"Now *there* . . ." He smiled up. "Is a fine sight."

"Hope so. When they told me I was going, and who with, I made a special effort."

"It shows, Tamara."

She looked crisp and efficient in her white, figure-flattering nurse's dress, in white shoes and stockings. Her makeup was perfect, and her hair, under the cap, shone from the brush.

He told her, "pleasure to welcome you aboard."

She squeezed past into her seat, and he was very conscious of her there, close to his shoulder, and the fragrance of her cologne.

The orderlies lifted the stretcher into place, and Jackie Seaweed secured the bow-hatch.

The engine caught at the first turn of the propeller, the Seabee shuddering into wakefulness.

Fulton slid in reversed propeller pitch to back the Seabee away from the pontoon, then steered out into the open bay. Well-secured, the patient dozed, seemingly lulled by the engine's droning.

In the still air, and heavily-laden, the Seabee took a long time to get off the water, but climbed well enough through the limpid morning. Blackfish Harbour, a toy town ringing a garden pond, drifted from view behind the left wing, and the Vancouver Island mountains fell sheer into black mirroring water, their slopes furred by the land's seemingly endless wealth of conifers. Before them, Johnstone Strait led away south-eastward, crammed with rocky islands, Pearce and Cormorant, Malcolm, Harbledown and Minstrel; so many named and unnamed lining the Inside Passage between Vancouver Island and the mainland.

Kelsey Bay drifted by below, and he turned inland for the run through the pass to Campbell River and the Strait of Georgia.

Tamara leaned close and, again, his nostrils filled with scent of her cologne.

"Are you too busy to talk?"

"To you, never."

"You were doing things. I thought I'd better leave you alone."

"Thank you . . ." He glanced back, thinking how *good* she looked. "How's the patient?"

"Sleeping like a baby now."

He explained about the lulling engine sound, and mimed a yawn. "Better than knock-out drops. Gets to me every time."

"We'll have a little less of that, please . . ." Tamara hesitated. "May I tell you something?"

"Sure. It's your charter flight."

"I was watching," she said. "The take-off and all. I thought how smoothly you did everything."

"That's me. An old smoothie at heart."

She chided, "be serious. This isn't easy for me."

"What isn't?"

She ignored that. "Looking at all those dials and switches . . . so much to see to. Yet you make it seem effortless."

His cheeks were warm. "Well . . . thanks."

"I'm thinking you must have done this before."

"Once or twice, maybe."

She watched the slow-drifting mountains. "I'd no idea how beautiful it would be."

"Is this the first time you've flown off the water?"

"First time I've flown, period," she admitted, and looked at him. "Now that I have, I'm really glad it's with you."

*

Enjoying the illusion of safe distance, Fulton elected to overlook Alice Royle's admonition about a speedy return to Blackfish Harbour. Taxying in towards the Island Airways dock and the attendant ambulance, he considered the attractions of an illicit trip downtown with Tamara, telling himself that an hour or two would do no harm: he could cover their tracks for that long. They could go in on the airport bus, have lunch *a deux* at the Georgia or the Hotel Vancouver . . .

Tamara handed over her patient's documents, and briefed the sanitarium nurse. The ambulance rolled away, and they looked at each other.

"They'll gas the aircraft, and I'll have to look in at the office," Fulton explained. "Then, what about lunch?"

"That'll be nice . . ." But she looked concerned. "Don't you have to get back?"

"I'm playing hooky . . . anyhow, they only specified today." He smiled. "And summer days are long."

"Pretty sneaky . . ." Her expression had cleared.

They watched a Queen Charlotte Airlines' Stranraer flying boat—a big, twin-engined biplane of pre-war vintage—drift down to touch the water gracefully.

"Beautiful," Tamara murmured. "Reminded me of a swan."

"From a bygone age," he agreed. "Slow, dependable and pretty. I'd give my eye-teeth to fly one."

She watched him smilingly. "Maybe you will one day?"

"By time I'm qualified, any that are left will be in museums."

Tamara was unexpectedly lukewarm to his plans for lunch. "The way we're dressed, we'd hardly be popular at the Hotel Vancouver." She gestured at her white uniform, rumpled from the flight. "Would they let you in in jeans, boots and a workshirt?"

He conceded the point ruefully. ". . . although *you* look like a million dollars."

"Not so bad yourself . . . here, or at Blackfish." She coloured, laughing. "Another story, though, at the corner of Granville and West Hastings."

"But is *lunch* still okay?"

"Sure . . . if there's somewhere?"

"There's the airport coffee lounge. Fair-to-middling grub, and they don't mind what you're wearing."

"Sounds fine . . ." She reached out to take his hand. "What are we waiting for? I'm a growing girl, and starved."

*

They ordered Swiss steak and mashed potato, with lemon pie and coffee to follow, and talked easily as they ate. He thought, pleased, like old friends.

In Tamara's company, the down-at-heel eating place regained the lustre he had known there in his student flying days. As they were watching a Trans-Canada Constellation taking off, a familiar voice boomed, "Sapristi! Can it be Tailspin Fulton . . . first intrepid aviator to fly over the West Pole?" Harry de Witt beamed down at them. "Aren't you dead?"

Fulton wondered, "who writes your stuff for you, Harry?"

"Isn't it ter-RIFIC? And I'm word-perfect. They don't call me 'Da Wit' for nothin'," he punned, and held out his arms as though for applause.

Fulton made the introductions, and Tamara gave De Witt a cool smile. He stared at her, an expression of horror. "You actually *flew* with this person?"

"I did . . ." She sounded stiff. "And it was lovely."

He mourned, "why could it not have been for me?"

Tamara knew she was being unfair. Knowing did not lessen her antipathy toward the caustic-tongued intruder.

Everything had been fine until *he* showed up: her first flight through a perfect summer's morning, the landing on the busy river crowded with seaplanes: the professional handing over of her patient, which allowed her a glow of personal satisfaction.

Best, though, being *with* Jack, close in the cabin like that, with conversation light-hearted, yet subtly-revealing: the firming-up, she believed, of rapport between them.

Until this . . . *person* stuck his oar in with wisecracks that weren't funny; with an undercurrent of belittlement and mockery in every word.

An old friend of Jack's, and that, for her, aggravated the offence. She had strong feelings about friendship, not least the conviction that one friend did not use privilege to score points over the other. She would have been upset if Jack sought to make a fool of this man. So it was tit for tat wasn't it?

He can *be* Jack's friend all he wants, she decided. But I don't think he'll ever be one of mine . . .

Sensing Tamara's antipathy, Fulton explained, "Harry's the long-suffering instructor who taught me to fly."

"I have much to answer for," De Witt murmured.

Tamara was not mollified by the explanation, nor by De Witt's response to it. He had to be smart-arse, even about *that*!

He wanted to know how things were at Blackfish Harbour, and had Fulton mastered finally what he called the 'Seabeast'. And, ashamed of it, Fulton did not invite him to join them.

Until, with heavy-handed mirth, De Witt said, "don't tell me . . . three's a crowd. I'll perform the famed De Witt disappearing act . . . reserved usually for bank managers and debt collectors."

Too late, Fulton began, "Harry, there's no need . . ."

"Students await . . . hungry for my questionable gifts. I pass on my lore, and we go down in flames together . . ." He saluted Tamara. "Enjoyed meeting you, Miss Kereniuk."

"Me, too." Her answering smile was thin.

"Blackfish Harbour," he told Fulton. "Seems to offer some pleasant surprises . . ." He grinned and nodded, and was gone. Tamara gazed into her coffee cup.

"I'm sorry."

"Why?"

"Guess I was pretty mean."

"With Harry, it's love or hate . . . no half-way measures. When he was my instructor, sometimes I hated him a whole lot. Now I don't."

She chewed her lip. "Do you think he noticed?"

"Doubt it . . ." He hoped that was true. "Harry's got the proverbial rhino hide. He needs it with his job."

But the small incident picked at his mind; walking back to the aircraft, he asked, "what upset you?" He felt protective towards her, and did not want her upset.

"I'm probably being petty. But I hated the way he belittled you all the time. Acting so smart and superior."

"It's the way we are in this business . . ." He rose instinctively to the defence of a fellow-airman. But it sounded patronising, he realised; crumbs to the non-initiate. "You should hear things I've said about *him*, none of them true. It's only fun."

"It's just that, for me . . ." Tamara's gaze met his frankly. "He was spoiling a lovely experience."

*

They talked freely on the return flight.

Over Kelsey Bay once more, turning, on to the final homeward leg, Tamara said, "I'd call this . . . a *useful* kind of day."

"Getting your patient to Town, you mean?"

"That, yes . . ." She sounded reflective. "Also because of being able to know you better."

"You had no choice. Stuck with me, getting your tail bored off."

She considered him. "Why do you knock yourself?"

"I'm the nearest target."

"There's no need. So cut it out!"

"Thank you, Tamara. I'll remember that."

She said nothing for a mile or two, until, "do you mind hearing me say these things?"

"No."

"I wanted to say them. Like how glad I was when you rented our house."

"So was I . . . so *am* I . . ." He felt emboldened. "For more reasons than one . . ." But confidence waned, and he ended lamely, "it's a nice house."

"I liked it when Ma invited you for coffee . . ." And then, almost blurting, "I liked *you*."

He glanced back at her. "I think we've been sharing a wavelength."

"Now there's been today, and the feeling we've become friends." She said seriously, "and I'm always loyal to my friends. Which is why I got mad with Harry. I was feeling loyal . . . it's the way I am."

He smiled into her eyes, thinking . . . friends? Friends was a beginning, but could there be a deeper meaning? Or again, a warning . . . 'thus far, and no farther' . . . ?

She said, close to his ear, "you've gone quiet."

"Just thinking things."

"Good things?"

"The very best."

She laughed. "Going to tell me . . . or make me stew?"

"Scared I might disappoint you," he admitted. "What you said about loyalty. To me, as a friend."

"Even to the detriment of Harry?"

And Harry went out the window . . . who was *Harry*? "He can look after himself. Get to know him, you'll love him, too. Everyone does."

"Well . . . we'll see."

"Best of all," Fulton said with firmness. "I'm delighted by the thought of friendship. And I'll be loyal . . . shan't let you down."

"I'd hate it if you did," Tamara said.

The long finger of Johnstone Strait pointed ahead to its conjunction with the wider mass of Queen Charlotte Strait, the Pacific gateway: the flight's end was nearing.

Odd, then, to feel . . . *sadness*. Imminent arrival did not spell separation. Friendship was established: I live in the next house to her, Fulton thought. Why, then, this sudden feeling, beyond comprehension, of premonition and dread? The lonely awareness of . . . journey's *end*?

Tamara said, "you'll need to know my proper name."

"Don't say you're not Tamara . . ."

"That part's okay. But you introduced me to Harry as Kereniuk. I'm Brenko. Ma's name."

"Stepan's not . . . ?"

"My father? No." She shook her head. "He's more my . . . what? . . . common-law stepfather?" A frown creased her brow. "Ma and he never married. Just shacked-up, I guess. Since I was a kid."

"Was that in the Old Country?"

"No, here. Ma and I lived near Victoria. We moved to Blackfish when I was ten. With Stepan . . . for the fishing and logging." Fulton nodded. "I was born at Yalta . . . in the Crimea . . ." She grinned. "I've got this *incredible* birth certificate. A huge piece of paper covered with seals and stamps and signatures in writing no one can read. I should frame it, and say it's a degree from Moscow University."

"And . . . your father?" he asked.

"Dead," she said flatly. "Before I was born."

"I'm sorry . . ."

"Ma's told me things. He was a *kulak*. They were farmers."

"Were . . . ?"

"There are none left, thanks to Stalin. They were rich peasants . . . owned their land and property, sold on a free market. But they didn't fit in with Uncle Joe's plans, so he killed them, or put them in jail."

"Did they kill your father?"

"More or less."

"I'm sorry . . . ?" Her reply puzzled him.

"I only know what Ma said. For Pete's sake, she was still *carrying* me when it happened."

"I shouldn't stick my nose in."

"They took him to Kiev," Tamara said. "There was a trial . . . all *kulaks*. He was sentenced to a labour camp in Siberia, but never got there. Died in the Kiev jail. Ma never learned how or why . . ." She grimaced. "Sorry to be morbid."

"I asked you."

"I sound like a sob-sister."

"No . . ." He probed cautiously, "so you both came here?"

"That's about it." She shrugged. "I got born, and Ma made it on her own for a while. Until they let her leave . . . although she never mentions that. Then Stepan walked into our lives, and the rest you know."

He sensed something like resignation in the way she spoke of Stepan. An undertone that could have been . . . dislike? He did not think he had imagined it, yet what could it be about a man she had known all her life, her mother's partner, that could provoke that reaction?

Fulton liked Stepan, and found no wrong in him. True that he drank, and that Rosa and he quarrelled bitterly about that. Rosa, though, was not a woman to tolerate a man and his ways blindly. Had it been so bad, surely she would not have stayed on . . . ?

He ventured, "are there problems between you and Stepan?"

"Would that bother you?"

And . . . play it straight, Fulton thought. "Yes, it would."

"Why?"

"Because Stepan's a friend, and there was what you said about loyalty." Tamara smiled slightly, but offered no response. "I like him. We get along. I think he likes me."

"For sure," she affirmed, and mimicked Stepan's mangled English. "That one smart young sum'n'a'bitch . . ." Fulton was laughing. "Hardly qvit messin' his pants, he big-time Navy officer."

"You have a rare talent there."

"I only quote. But Stepan means it."

"Then you see what I mean when I say I like him."

"Because he says nice things about you?"

He replied, a little nettled, "because of *liking* him."

Tamara suggested without evident irony, "isn't that the man's point of view?"

"It's all I've got . . ." He was smarting still. "And the woman's? Yours?"

She corrected him, "my mother's and mine."

"It's your mother you're concerned for?"

"Who else . . . ?" She paused. "I must be fair. Stepan's always been kind to me . . . gentle. He's tried being a father . . . protecting me."

He began, "then I don't see . . ."

"*Try*, Jack . . ." There was a sudden edge in her voice. "You were there that evening . . . heard them brawling later." He nodded. She went on bitterly, "it's his damn' drinking. He starts, then won't stop. And it changes him." Her hand touched Fulton's shoulder, fingers squeezing. "I know you like him . . . wouldn't want it otherwise. Nor would Ma. She loves him. They've stayed together all my life. I know he cares for us. When he's sober, there could be no one nicer."

"Could it be that you're making too much of this?" He added quickly, "that's not a criticism. But the drinking aside . . ."

"And what it does to Ma," Tamara finished for him. "She's never touched alcohol, you know? Nothing holier-than-thou, just her preference. She's talked of the Ukraine . . . how the *kulaks* whooped it up, drinking, fighting, sometimes killing one another. She was young, and it scared her . . . made her hate all that."

*

For some time, following the Revolution and bitter civil war, the Speryatin district and its largely-kulak populace remained prosperous, seemingly unaffected. There was food on every table; no discernible shortages. Men owned land, horses, livestock, and lived in warm, solid houses. There was ample money, the returns on produce sold on a free market. For the kulaks, this was the norm: to prosper, live well, eat, drink, dance, shout, fight, make love, and savour life with few fears for the future.

Far away in Moscow and Petrograd, the politicians plotted and squabbled murderously among themselves. The cruiser *Aurora* fired from her mooring on the river Neva, and the Romanovs abdicated, were dispatched to Ekaterinberg, then into oblivion. Names came and went: Kerensky, Trotsky, Denikin with his White Army scoring successes against the Reds until fortune turned against him. While others prevailed; Lenin and, in the shadows, the Georgian, Dzugashvili, who had re-invented himself as Stalin.

The infant Soviet republics struggled to make sense of chaos unleashed beneath the banners of revolution and liberty. Certain areas, mostly central, felt the iron weight of newly-minted policies, but in the vast hinterlands there was little immediate evidence of change. Battles and upheavals, blood-letting, the settling of scores and the imposition of repressive diktats in the guise of 'civil order', were as the affairs of other worlds, as fleeting as the seasons. They came, they went, they were forgotten.

For the Speryatin kulaks, and those of Priluki, Lubny, Uman, Shpola, Brovary and Vasilkov, life, it did seem, would be as always. They went about their business in comfortable complacency: no hint yet in their lives of the alien word 'collectivisation', or the way that this would write finis to all they knew and held dear . . .

For Rosa Korchenko, crisis and politics were matters beyond interest or comprehension: of no concern by comparison with the turbulent, often violent, affairs of family and community. Kulak life and living, the material advantages notwithstanding, were always turbulent, frequently perilous, dependent upon the whims of weather, soil, drought and flood, blight and epidemic. With natural perils went those man-made; the depredations of the czars and governments, bureaucrats, soldiers and policemen. One trod a tightrope always between joy and danger, the balance forever precarious. Kulaks, like any threatened species, acquired defensive hardness as the major pre-requisite for survival; for the winning and holding of position, security and respect within the community, the ability, outside it, to outwit those who sought to bleed them dry. Kulaks, by nature, lived and played hard, and none more than Pyotr Korchenko, father to Rosa and her four brothers.

Pyotr Korchenko had learned from his own father life's hard lessons, driven home with whip and fist. From the age of eight, working at his father's side, forever under that brooding, critical eye, he came to accept in sullen acquiescence, that only maximum effort, total success, in all endeavours would ever suffice. He learned to acknowledge, almost with gratitude, the noncommittal grunts with which his occasional successes were greeted. Pyotr Korchenko learned by bitter example to the point where, aged twenty seven—when his father died in a knife fight—he had assumed unconsciously the older man's ways and methods as his own.

In young manhood, he adopted happily the traditional male kulak habits of rowdy drinking, whoring and brawling. At twenty five, there were few who did not fear his fists, or whom he could not drink under the table. He was tall, powerful, and his father now knew better than to lift a hand against him.

"I made that boy," the elder Korchenko would boast. "Shaped him into something worthwhile. Without me, he'd be nothing."

Hearing the boasts, Pyotr Korchenko would grin, not troubling himself to conceal contempt.

By the time he was twenty eight, his father was dead and, by the custom of primogeniture, the farm and property passed to him. Pyotr Korchenko was rich, and seen—his bruising nature aside—as a worthwhile catch.

He married within the community, sired children, worked ferociously hard, and continued to prosper. Sober, while a harsh, unrelenting disciplinarian, he was caring of his familial responsibilities, and a steady provider. When drunk, his rage and violence were widespread and indiscriminate, turned against his family as often as against outsiders. With the one exception of Rosa, the sole daughter. There was something about her that stirred an inner kernel of tenderness: at the height of his fury, a glimpse of her could make him abject, contrite, seeking to embrace and caress her, begging understanding and pity, seeking to explain himself. Something which he could not do, lacking comprehension of the bitter demons which drove him.

Rosa, conscious of her sheltered status, hated it, seeing only that her being spared seemed to exact higher toll from her mother and brothers. Loathing her father, sickened by his sentimentality, she longed perversely to share her mother's suffering. Her brothers, while she pitied them, *were* male, could care for themselves. But, when it was her mother he attacked, she wanted to assault him back with some heavy weapon, or shoot him with one of his hunting guns; to inflict painful, mortal injury on that raging bulk . . .

In such moments, she would look into her mother's eyes, knowing that her own violent thoughts were known, and would see the pleading there: do nothing . . . don't throw away this small blessing for something you can never change . . .

Sometimes, alone, mother and daughter would talk: Rosa protesting her outrage and hatred, only to be silenced by the mother's seemingly unalterable belief that Pyotr Korchenko was, at heart, a good man; that it was only when reliving the harsh memories of his own childhood that the dark, brutal side of his nature was revealed.

Rosa could not accept these naive explanations: she would fret over her mother's blindness: how could she imagine truth in her words when her body bore the evidence of his savagery and sadism.

What she saw as his true nature made anathema of his over-demonstrative affection: it was gross hypocrisy that cheapened her no less than it did him. In consequence, she used every ruse and opportunity to turn aside, belittling or rejecting outright his compliments and endearments. Spurning, too, the despairing appeals in her mother's eyes. She could not, *would* not . . . she would rather be horse-whipped by him, or killed. Those options would, at least, allow her to retain her self-respect.

Pyotr Korchenko could never grasp the reasons behind her antipathy: he would protest, beg explanation. What had he done . . . how given offence? She need only say and he would change things. Then, when she turned her back, he bellowed his bafflement and frustration, although bellowing, with Rosa, was as far as it went. He followed her with hangdog, resentful eyes: in Jesus's name, what *was* it with her? But Rosa would not speak of it, and, to his dying day, Pyotr Korchenko was not to know.

That day came in 1924, the year of Lenin's death. Like that of his own father, it was mean and squalid: returning drunk, from the village, he lay down by the roadside to rest, fell into a stupor, and drowned in his vomit.

The event filled Rosa with happy relief. Drawing deep, exulting breaths within the privacy of her small room, she could tell herself, "I'm free! We're *all* free!"

Alcohol flowed at the wake, unleashing a flood-tide of banal anecdote and reminiscence. Rosa, eighteen, attractive and pleasingly plump, glowing with the knowledge of her father's baleful presence forever lifted, was the object of appreciative male eyes. It occurred to one perceptive hopeful that she was not drinking, and he called for her to be given a glass, for her to join in the stream of toasts to her departed parent.

All were startled by the change in her, her face hardening, mouth drawing into a thin, bitter line; by the way, in the sudden silence, she snapped, "No!"

The abashed young man attempted jocular protest. "*Come* on . . . some respect for your Pa?" He gave an uncertain laugh. "It's a special time . . . everyone takes a snort. Or are you too high and mighty to drink with us?"

Shocking her listeners, not caring, Rosa replied in the same biting tones, "I don't drink this shit, and I'll *never* drink it! And even if I did, I wouldn't lift a glass to that pig bastard!"

*

Tamara explained, "She's not anti-drinking, not when it's Stepan having a few friendly beers. But, with him, it never stops there, and that gets her mad. Then they fight."

"Stepan doesn't attack her physically?"

"Are you *kidding*?" It was a relief to hear her laugh. "Quite the reverse." Fulton thought of Stepan's black eye, of his telling Billy Langewische of it; he had seemed perversely proud . . ."They scream at each other, and sometimes she'll bean him. Or throw him out, make him sleep in the woodshed." She shook her head. "But I don't believe he's ever raised a hand to her." She added in a low voice, "so far . . ."

"What does that mean?"

Instead of answering, Tamara mused, "okay, that evening, he was on his way, but not *too* drunk. Not the way he's been at other times." She explained, "after fishing, when he's sold his catch for cash, or a good logging contract. He's been away, no drinking. He never drinks on the job. If only . . ." She sounded wistful. "So, when he comes in, he's got this gi-*normous* thirst, and heads straight for the beer parlour, where he drinks himself paralytic. So much so, sometimes, that he's crawled home, a half-mile, on his hands and knees. Then the yelling starts, and Ma takes a swing at him, or throws him out. Sometimes both."

Shocked and fascinated, he asked, "what does he say then?"

"He makes threats sometimes."

"What threats?"

"The kind you'd expect . . ." She did not conceal her distaste. "That he'll get even . . . beat the shit out of her. *That's* a favourite."

"Pretty rough."

"Mostly hot air . . . face-saving. When he's drunk, Ma can handle him. When he's sober, she doesn't need to. He wakes up with a shiner, or a fat lip, and no idea what for. Knowing only that he's pulled another boner. He'll be quiet then, and apologetic. Ma'll give him a talking-to, then patch him up, and fix his breakfast, and they'll be lovey-dovey till next time . . ." She hesitated. "Or that's how it's *been*."

He turned once more to look at her. "Has something changed?"

She nodded uncertainly. "You'll think I'm stupid, but there's this way I've seen him look at her."

"A *look* . . ." Blackfish Harbour was distantly visible, the pale dots of buildings clustered around the bay. He pointed. "Almost home."

"Yes . . ." But she sounded distracted.

He pressed, "*how* does Stepan look?"

"You've heard the expression . . . 'if looks could kill'?"

"Hey, now . . ." He was shaken.

She retorted, "don't knock it till you've seen it."

"Okay . . . sorry."

"When he does it, it's as if he really *hates* her . . . like he can hardly hold himself back. And, I admit, it scares me, makes me think that some day he'll crack, lose it, and try and hurt Ma in some way."

*

Only Jackie Seaweed was at the dock to meet them.

Tamara looked around. "Olaf promised to collect me . . . guess he's busy. Never mind, I'm happy to walk." She glanced at Fulton. "Care to keep me company?"

"I was hoping you'd say that."

She seemed more cheerful on the walk back and, he hoped, more receptive to things that he wished to discuss with her, which had been on his mind for most of the day. "I guess you know I'd like to see you some more?"

"Of course you'll see me . . ." She considered him with amused eyes. "We're neighbours . . . friends."

"*Loyal* as well."

"You just bet . . ." She was laughing, and he thought happily, the game's begun; the old to-and-fro, give-and-take, all the posturing and manoeuvring. And she's out to make me sweat . . . "You'll be stopping by for coffee and meals. Ma loves cooking for you."

"That's kind of her," he murmured. "Although it's not quite what I had in mind."

"Oh . . . ?"

"By seeing you . . ." He ignored her widening grin: he would not be put off! "I didn't mean dropping in to free-load dinner, or waving from my house to yours."

She watched him, wide-eyed. "So what *are* you looking for?" And touched his arm then. "I'm being a bitch, aren't I?"

"You said that, remember!"

"By 'see me', you mean *see* me?"

"You're getting the drift."

"Things like . . . dates and things?"

"And things," he agreed.

"Going places? Having fun? Living it up?"

"The nickel's dropped." He beamed at her, pleased. "Couldn't've put it better. Would that be okay?"

"Absolutely," Tamara said.

Blackfish Harbour, however, posed its problems.

For two people who had chosen to go places and do things, there were few places to go, or things to do.

There was a new movie each week at the ramshackle Totem Theatre, and badminton in the community hall. The Canadian Legion held dances every two weeks or so. There was bingo, visiting neighbours, strolling the waterfront, or hanging out in a choice of three cafés and the single beer parlour . . .

Tamara wondered, "care for rugged walking?"

"Depends how rugged."

"I have a Private Place. Where I *might* just take you."

As a child, she had stumbled upon it one day.

"Tell me about it."

"Well . . . it's lonely and beautiful, and I kid myself I'm the only one that knows about it." She added dryly, "an illusion spoiled by a trail through the woods. Probably made by Indians."

"Where?"

"If I say, will you swear, first time, not to go without me?"

"Consider it sworn. If I can go with you, why go alone?"

“I’m glad you see it that way,” Tamara said.

The Private Place lay on the far side of the point which formed a protective arm around the village.

“Beach and rocks and tidal pools, and logs and trunks washed up for years by storms,” she said. “Except when there *is* a storm, it’s unbelievably peaceful there. Just water sounds and loons calling. Bald eagles sit in the trees and watch you with unfriendly eyes.”

“Probably disloyal, too.”

“Be serious when I’m waxing lyrical.”

“Grave as a judge,” he assured her. “And, yes, I’d like to go.”

“So you shall,” Tamara promised.

She told of views from the Private Place over the Sound and across Queen Charlotte Strait.

“You can see Mount Waddington. The Indians call it Mystery Mountain. Fourteen thousand feet . . . just about the highest in B.C.” She was smiling. “Eighty miles away, and looking close enough to touch . . .” She gave a little delighted shiver. “I *do* love it.”

“I’ll tell you this,” Fulton declared. “Sooner go there than a movie, *or* badminton, *or* bingo. Much more than any Legion dance.”

“We could even swim,” she suggested. “If you like glacier water?”

“Love it,” he vowed cheerfully and recklessly. “Grew up in the stuff.”

*

Stepan had got it wrong; Tamara would not, after all, be there for dinner.

“They be give her quick turn-around,” Rosa explained. “Day-shift to night-shift. Got graveyard tonight, so gettin’ some shut-eye.” Fulton hoped his disappointment did not show. “Say me to tell you she sorry . . .” Rosa confided, “she come back from Vancouver smilin’ fit to bust.” She watched him, grinning, fists planted on ample hips. “Up to her room singin’ like a Goddam lark. She one changed gel.”

"I'm glad she enjoyed it," he said with innocence. "We had a nice day."

Rosa looked thoughtful. "Maybe you good thing for her, eh?"

"She's a lovely girl, Rosa."

"You tellin' *me*! And you nice young fella. Hope my Tamara good for *you*."

There was a question in her eyes that he was not prepared, then, to answer, thinking . . . let's not rush things. He enquired mildly, "is that the *holopche* cooking?"

"Yah . . . is her . . ." Rosa peered, sniffing, into the big iron pot. "Where you hear about *holopche*?"

"Stepan said you were preparing them for dinner, and I was invited."

"Stupid bloody man!" She looked vexed. "Suppose' to be big surprise."

The table was set for three. At two places there were clean beer glasses: Rosa would not be drinking, Fulton remembered. And I'm the guest. Stepan, it appeared, was being given a little rope.

He enquired, "where *is* the great man?"

"I make him wash up. Work all day cuttin' wood . . . not have him stink up my table. Not when we got company."

He appeared, scrubbed red, shaved, wearing a clean shirt and denims. He shook hands in the Old Country manner. "Highpockets? How you doin'?" He was smiling and at ease, telling of his day. "You see wood piled up outside there?"

"That's a hell of a stack of wood, Stepan."

"Goddam good old log . . . get lots o' mileage. And half belong to you." He encircled Rosa's shoulder with a veined and knotted arm. "Hey, you . . . good old woman!"

"*What* you wantin'?" She sounded fierce, but did not free herself. "Quit horsin' around, you!" She was blushing like a girl; her smile peeled away the layered years, and Fulton saw the young mother who had attracted Stepan Kereniuk. They stood together, and it was as though they had forgotten him. And surely, he thought, Tamara could not be right? What they had discussed together failed to measure up against what he was seeing: such affection must be real, and deep-rooted . . . ?

Rosa shoved him away. "Lunkhead . . . way you act . . . what Jack be thinkin'?" He stood, grinning expectantly, and she gave him a shrewd stare. "I know you . . . you wantin' somethin'. You don't get smoochie else."

"Ah, Rosa . . . c'mon."

"You be say what you wantin' . . ." She lifted the pot lid and studied the dinner with critical eyes. "I say maybe yah . . . maybe no."

"Just be thinkin' . . ." Stepan wheedled shamelessly, "time for maybe liddle glass o' beer?" He turned to Fulton. "What say, Highpockets? Bet you likin' one?"

"Not drag Jack in . . . not pass buck." Rosa's eye glinted. "Speak for yourself, or else pipe down . . ." She softened slightly. "Okay, maybe *one*. You like a beer Jack?"

He took his cue from Stepan. "Love one."

Rosa chuckled, her good humour restored. "Be all day with my Tamara. Thirsty work, eh?"

With the swiftness of sleight-of-hand, Stepan had uncapped two bottles and filled the glasses. "Down the hatch, Highpockets!"

"Never mind no hatch, you," Rosa warned. "Take her easy."

Fulton drank some beer. When he looked again, Stepan's glass was empty.

"Hey, you!" Rosa exclaimed. "What I just say you?"

"Hokay . . ." Stepan offered placatingly, "that one for thirst. Next one be go real slow."

He winked and grinned as Rosa turned back to the dinner. He drank again, but more decorously, and Fulton relaxed, imagining the small crisis over . . . Rosa ladled food on to his plate, the green peppers bursting with slow-cooked ground steak, rice, tomatoes, onions; ingredients and spices which he could only guess at.

She watched him, pleased, as he ate. "*Holopche*? How you like?"

Mouth full, he mumbled, "can't talk now . . . having too much fun."

"Okay . . . best you eat more . . ." She dumped a fresh steaming pepper beside the others.

"Rosa . . . hold it! I won't be able to move!"

"Talkin' *stupid,*" she grunted. "You too skinny . . . need fatten up. Lookingk like blond hair wire coat hanger."

Stepan barked a laugh. "*That* no lie . . ." He refilled the beer glasses, avoiding Rosa's beady gaze.

"You two are ganging up on me," Fulton accused.

"You come again?" she invited him. "I make *holopche*?"

"I'll be beating down the door . . ." He gorged himself in the warmth of her approval.

"Next time, be make damn' sure Tamara here. Maybe not like my *holopche* then, eh? Too busy likin' Tamara?"

He could feel the blush beginning somewhere down around his knees. Rosa, looking knowing, passed the mashed potato, the string beans and pickled cabbage. Ignoring his protests, she ladled out a fourth *holopche:* Stepan—by Fulton's count—finishing his seventh, wiped his plate with bread, and belched loud contentment. "Best thing you be sleep with window open tonight, Highpockets. You be fart like bloody horse . . . an' choke to death." His chin stained with sauce, he wagged a finger at Fulton.

"Not everyone in world like *you,*" Rosa told him and thrust a paper napkin across the table. "Wipe your kisser . . . you look like pig."

He obeyed without demur, and prepared to refill Fulton's glass.

"Stepan . . . maybe I'd better not."

"What's matter?"

"If Jack say no more, then no *more*!" Rosa barked. Her face had darkened with sudden anger. "He know when to stop . . . somethin' *you* need know!"

Fulton felt trapped then, and offered soothingly, "flying, Stepan . . . you know? I should go easy."

"Sure . . ." Rosa patted his hand. "You knowin' best."

"Maybe nobody get sick tomorrow?" Stepan countered, bottle in hand. "Not have to fly?"

Rosa turned, snapping, "that none your business, you!"

"We don't know that. I have to be on stand-by *and* sober."

"Yah . . . yah . . ." Scowling, Stepan emptied the bottle into his glass. There was insufficient to fill it, and he uncapped a fresh one. "Plenty time be sober up. Get shut-eye, in mornin' you be fine."

"But hung-over. I'm not paid to fly hung-over . . ." Fulton was growing tired of the discussion.

"Hear what he sayin'?" Rosa's voice had risen. "Lunkhead . . . you wantin' lose Jack his job?"

"He company," Stepan grew rebellious. "I say have drink . . . have liddle fun . . ."

"He havin' all he want . . ." They bickered monotonously at each other.

"Enough o' what *you* call fun. Drink, drink, drink . . . never stop. Where fun in *that*, eh?" She rose abruptly. "I makin' coffee now . . . for *everybody*!"

Something ugly had been triggered in Stepan. "*No* Goddam coffee . . . not *wantin*'!"

"Please your fool self!" She turned her back on him. "Jack . . . I sorry. Feel bad you come my house, eat dinner, and see how he act, that man!"

"Please don't worry about it. I . . ."

"*Got* to be worry. Is no way be treatin' guest. I get mad, say what on my mind . . ."

It was getting worse, and he was stuck with it. He offered weakly, "Rosa, it's no problem . . ."

"I the *woman* in this house," she declared with heat. "See everythin' go right, go good. Good dinner . . . good company . . ." She spooned coffee furiously into the pot, and slammed down the lid. "It for *me* to see everyone act good. Tamara be good . . . no worry. Same as *you* good man!" She hurled her words like projectiles. Stepan was silent, and Fulton felt sudden sympathy for him. He was far from drunk. Rosa was making too much of this. Fine, a warning note *was* needed, but she could have moderated it . . .

Unseen by her, Stepan was pouring more beer, but some small sound had caught her attention, and she spun round, yelling,

"GOD *DAMN* . . . what I SAY you? What the Sam Hill you DOIN'?"

She stepped towards him, and his hands came up defensively, one still clutching the beer bottle. Fulton winced with embarrassment for them, and for himself. Thinking with despair, if it gets physical, I'll have to intervene. He could not sit there and leave them to whale the tar out of each other. I *do* something, he thought, or I get out *now*: those were the choices. Which meant *no* choice. They were friends, neighbours, his host and hostess. *And* there was Tamara. What would *she* think, knowing that he had run, leaving her mother and Stepan in a fist-fight? How would that equate with her passion for loyalty . . . ?

But Rosa and Stepan did not come to blows. "Gimme that, you!" She snatched the bottle from his unresisting hand, shaking it in his face. Beer foamed on to the scrubbed wooden floor. "Be FINISH now . . . DONE with!" she bawled at him. "Drink no more tonight in this house . . . only coffee . . . only water . . ."

He yelled back, "Goddamit . . . LISTEN . . . !"

"YOU one be *listen*!" Rosa glared, defying him, and then the fight went out of him.

"Hokay . . . what you tell me? You always got somethin' to say . . . never stuck for nothin' . . ." He had become wearily submissive.

"I say even *look* at beer one more time, you be sleep outside!"

"Oh, yah . . . ?"

"YAH!" She bent forward aggressively. "Done it to you plenty times . . . do it again!"

Rosa, like an outraged diva, swept to the kitchen sink, and emptied the beer bottle. Fulton, glancing at Stepan then, was appalled by the look of malevolence he directed at Rosa's unheeding back, a look that seemed the certain precursor to violence. This, he knew at once, was what Tamara had seen . . . and feared.

Until Stepan met his gaze, and the look was replaced by something furtive and ashamed: he gave a little shake of the head, like a denial, as Rosa, turning, banged the empty beer bottle on the table. "There! That *you* finished!"

Stepan sat with lowered gaze and, after one hard stare, she turned to the coffee, pouring out three mugs, handing one to Fulton with smiling solicitude, dumping another before Stepan. "That clear your dumb, drunk head. Now you drink him."

Without protest, he poured cream, and three heaping spoons of sugar. He looked at Rosa, and nothing showed in his face. "Now I say we talk too much." The words were quiet. "You say, and I do. You gettin' what you want. Hokay . . . leave it be, an' leave *me* be."

Fulton sensed the moment of truce between them as Rosa, sighing, turned to the wood range, peering in at the fire. "Needin' more wood . . . stupid o' me, forgettin' . . ." She moved towards the door.

Stepan rose. "I go get . . ."

"You be stay put," she ordered. "Mind our guest, and be *nice*." She turned at the door. "No more bloody drinkin', eh?"

They could hear her out there, muttering and rooting by the woodshed. Fulton, avoiding Stepan's eye, pretended an interest in the kitchen furnishings. Hoping for Rosa's swift return.

"Highpockets . . . ?" Stepan sounded diffident, almost pleading. "I needin' talk some."

"Hasn't there been enough talk, Stepan?"

"All the same . . ." He shrugged helplessly.

His wretchedness moved Fulton. "All right."

Stepan began falteringly, "I see . . . how you see me then. How I look at my Rosa . . ."

But Fulton did not want to talk of that. "Drink some coffee . . . you'll feel better." He sent a silent prayer to Rosa—get BACK here!

"Need more'n coffee for be better. Want to talk about things."

"Stepan, it's none of my business . . ."

"Mean you not wantin'!" Stepan flared. "You say me straight!"

Stung, Fulton snapped back, "okay . . . fine. I *don't*!"

A ticking clock punctuated the ensuing heavy silence. The fire lapped quietly in the range. Wood clunked outside where Rosa continued her interminable rummaging . . .

On a note of appeal, Stepan insisted, "not makin' no excuse . . . to make me look good when Rosa not here."

Already regretting his sharpness, Fulton soothed, "there's

nothing to explain to me." But he was thinking . . . explain to Rosa, to Tamara, *they* need to know.

"Just wantin' you understand . . . not be think bad o' me."

Platitudes would never work with Stepan: like it or not, his appeal must be faced. Fulton invited, "tell me if it'll help."

"It help plenty . . ." Stepan became eager, and abject. "Not much to tell. Only want you knowin' how I feel." He paused, seeking words. "About that screwball woman . . . we be together long time . . . since first come in Canada. Get together, stay together. You knowin' why?"

"Tamara's told me a few things," Fulton conceded.

"Been talkin', eh? About her Momma . . . ?" Stepan grinned uneasily. "About this fool ol' man?"

"Good things, Stepan . . ." And there *had* been those, Fulton thought.

"Yah . . . you betcha . . ." He saw Stepan's pleasure, and did not regret the deception. "Tamara like my own gel . . . never do nothin' to hurt her." Stepan met his gaze firmly. "Never goin' hurt my Rosa, neither."

"Of course you wouldn't."

"*Love* that crazy woman," Stepan asserted fiercely. "All the years since Tamara knee-high . . . never change how I feelin'. Still lovin'." He gave a sad little shake of the head. "All same . . . she got hell of a temper. You see that?"

Fulton was smiling. "I did kind of notice."

"She get mad as wet hen . . . then holler to beat the band." He stated, "now me, be like liddle drink, maybe few sometime, with frien's, else when I gettin' good week fishin' or in the woods. Like be tie one on . . . cele-brate. Y' know?"

"Sure . . ."

"Everybody like cele-brate, get liddle drunk. But Rosa not see him like that. That fine woman not touch the stuff . . . one Goddam strong-will' old broad . . ." He swallowed some coffee, and made a face. "Who put all the damn' sugar in?"

"You did. You were probably thinking of other things."

"Guess maybe . . ." Stepan eyed Fulton uncertainly. "But love that woman too much be gettin' mad when she get mad with me for comin' home stewed. Even when . . ." He gestured at his still-discoloured eye. "She hand me a shiner. Hokay . . . I be deserve, and take it . . . don't mind liddle pain." He stirred his coffee absently, the spoon grating in the sugar sludge. "That how it is till a whiles ago, when it get *different*."

"How different, Stepan?"

"She be yellin' all the Goddam time . . . never no let-up. I so much as *look* at bottle o' beer, she go apeshit. That been gettin' under my skin real bad, Highpockets." His face had tautened. "Be thinkin', first time ever, I *hate* you, bitch-woman! Don't *know* you when you act crazy that way. You not my Rosa, and I don't *want* you."

Fulton thought of Rosa and her rages. "I see how it could seem that way."

"Seem more real than *seem*. And then I get scared."

"Why scared?"

"On account, when I hatin' her, I wantin' to pop her one. Not feel so for Rosa, only for *bitch-woman*. Scare me because my head say me Rosa and bitch-woman all the same people. I bust bitch-woman in teeth, I be bustin' Rosa, too . . . and that's *terrible* . . ." He stared down at his knotted fists. "It get mixed-up in my head, and scare me bad."

*

Preparing for bed, Fulton was wondering if Rosa, ostensibly collecting firewood, might have been listening.

If that was so, he hoped that what she overheard had sunk in. Because, in his torrent of revelation, Stepan had given implicit warning. He loved the Rosa up there on the pedestal . . . 'his' Rosa. Whereas the 'bitch-woman', his own creation, threatened his peace-of-mind.

Blame could not be placed solely at Rosa's door: the shrew had evolved with cause. It remained, indisputably, that Stepan, decent man, good provider, was a drunk. And Rosa, who had suffered that for years, was reaching the end of the line. Stepan, relishing his 'little drink', his periodic beer parlour bender, could not recognise this, or that what he viewed as a harmless self-indulgence, which he could afford, could be the cause of his partner's endless distress and fear. Instead, he felt himself threatened by the spectre of the 'bitch-woman', and his deepening hatred of her . . .

Fulton stood at the window, looking across to the other house. A light burned in the kitchen; the outlines of Rosa and Stepan moved back and forth and, in a little while, were joined by Tamara. His watch showed eleven-forty; she would be leaving for her graveyard shift, and he waited, hoping for more glimpses of her.

She emerged soon in her white dress and cap, a sweater over her shoulders, bathed in the glow from the porch light. He heard her call, "see you for breakfast." She was gone then, hurrying down the hill into darkness.

From the big house then . . . nothing. No fighting, no argument: the kitchen and porch lights had gone out. Everyone and everything seemed to sleep.

FOUR

He wakened early to lie there drifting and dreaming. The telephone was silent, and sunlight flooded the bedroom: he was comfortable and at ease. A lie-in seemed like a good thing . . .

At nine, unhurried, he rose. Embers glowed still in the kitchen range; the addition of kindling produced a good flame. The morning coffee heated, and he poured a mugful and went outside to drink it in the clear light.

The *Prince George*, Canadian National's west coast flagship, was moving with grace across the Sound on its run to Prince Rupert. A big seiner steered into the bay, meeting an old one-lung gillnetter heading out. The scene, Fulton thought, would have made the perfect tourist board poster . . .

"Hi, Sleepyhead!"

Tamara was standing by the woodshed, wearing brief white shorts, a vaguely French-looking baggy T-shirt with blue and white horizontal stripes. She had loosened her hair, and her long legs were honey-gold from hours in the sun.

"You look terrific," he called.

"Thank you, kind sir."

"Talking of 'sleepyhead', shouldn't *you* be sleeping?"

"Not yet. Wanted to enjoy this incredible morning first." She stretched, arms uplifted. "I can sleep anytime."

He held up his coffee mug. "Can I tempt you?"

"Thanks . . ." She shook her head. "I've already waded through one of Ma's marathon breakfasts. Anything more, and I'd come unzipped."

"*Inter*esting proposition."

"Down, boy . . ." Tamara laughed, then pointed to the bay.

"Just watching Stepan heading off to discover the world." She indicated the dwindling gillnetter.

"Where's he heading?" Stepan had said nothing of leaving.

"He got an early call. A week's timber cruising somewhere up Kingcome Inlet."

"That should be worth a few dollars."

"And then some," Tamara agreed. "Timber cruising spells a big pay-day."

"How was he this morning?"

"He'd left before I got home." She rolled her eyes. "But I should think a little rough. Hear tell you guys tied one on last night?"

"It wasn't so bad . . ." Fulton grew defensive. "Your mother's incredible dinner, a few beers . . . you know."

"*I* know . . . yeah!"

The gillnetter was a white dot out in the Sound. Fulton, watching it, pondered the advisability of mentioning the quarrel, the change in Stepan which had seemed to bear out Tamara's fears. To tell also of the apology, and Stepan's admissions. And decided . . . not a good idea. She was just home from work; fresh anxieties could spoil her rest. The belief persisted also that, the justice of Rosa's complaint notwithstanding, Stepan *had* been provoked: there was justice on his side, too. Let it go, he decided. Some other time, maybe . . .

She walked across the yard to stand with him. "Penny for them, Jack?"

He evaded, "oh . . . this and that."

She watched him. "You okay?"

"Sure . . . fine. Why?"

"You tell *me* . . ." She grinned. "You're the one who was on a toot with Stepan."

"Tamara . . . it wasn't a *toot.*"

"If you say so. But Stepan was all set to hit it until Ma clouded up and rained all over him."

"Is that what she told you?"

"I didn't dream it," Tamara replied levelly. "You were there. Would you say she got it wrong?"

"Stepan was being silly . . ." Fulton dodged the pitfall. "Pushing his luck."

"Just an *argument*, then?" She sounded strained. "Nothing physical?"

"Not on either side." He suggested, "was that likely in front of me?"

"Who can tell?" She squeezed her eyes shut for a moment. "When . . . when I told you of Stepan's behaviour . . ." She faltered, watching him closely.

With the opportunity to speak, he evaded again, despising himself for it. "There was no hint of that. They quarrelled . . . she won."

"And Stepan?" Tamara persisted.

"Quiet as a lamb . . ." Once you begin lying, he thought, it gets easier. "He tried a stunt, and came unstuck. So he sat back and took his knocks, all verbal. Then your mother went out for firewood, and we chatted."

"About what?"

"Cabbages and kings? Chaos in the world economy . . . the starving millions in China?"

"Oh, I'm *sure*!" She gave him a look. "After a ding-dong, and Ma storming out?"

"She didn't *storm*. She went for wood."

"Semantics . . ." Tamara gestured dismissively. "Stepan really said *nothing*?"

He asked edgily, "why do you look for what's not there?" And wondered if she sensed his guilty evasions? "Okay . . . a few things. What happened wasn't just something you switch off and forget. Stepan was embarrassed that I'd seen it . . . he wanted to apologise."

"And what did *you* say?"

Too sharply, Fulton retorted, "that he had nothing to apologise to *me* for. That it was between your mother and him, and I wasn't involved."

"Nicely handled, Jack," Tamara said with irony.

"What do you expect? I'm *not* involved. Should I have played judge and jury?"

"Simmer down," Tamara said.

He was contrite. "Sorry."

"Don't be. I got your back up."

"I was hoping you hadn't noticed."

"Oh, I notice lots about you . . ." She stretched again, studiedly casual. "Well, that about does it for the fresh air session."

"Sure. You need your sleep." But he would have liked her to stay. And to have learned what it was she noticed about him . . .

"Busy night," she admitted. "Babies galore to feed . . . obstetrics was jammed to the rafters. I must've prepared gallons of formula . . ." She was turning away. "Thanks for telling me . . . what you told me."

"Nothing to tell, really. There wasn't much more than the eating and drinking."

"Especially the drinking . . ." She turned back, laughing, and stood close to him. "God . . . you're tall!"

"Tall, but not God."

"It's like looking up at the Empire State."

"Tamara, with you this close, looking like you do, you ought to know that, unlike the Empire State, I'm not made of stone . . ." His voice caught thickly in his throat.

"*That's* good news . . ." She crooked an inviting finger. "Drop down a few floors." He bent to her and her lips brushed his lightly, then she stood back, smiling, head tilted. "Now . . . why did I do that?"

"Not that I minded, but why *did* you?"

"'Cause I *wanted* to!" She threw her arms wide. "'Cause I thought it'd be nice, and it was." She wondered, "nice for you?"

"Like . . . *wow*!"

"And here's me thinking you're an old sobersides."

"You've just changed all that!"

She wanted to know, "are you flying today?"

"I'm flying now!"

"You'll blow a gasket," Tamara warned.

"A price worth paying . . ." He sobered. "No calls so far. Nothing booked. Seems everyone's staying healthy."

"I'll sleep till four-thirty," she said. "Then it's badminton night at the community hall . . . they put up the nets at five. I often play before dinner when I'm on nights. If you're free, care to meet me for a game?"

"Love to. But my badminton's pretty shaky. Haven't played for years."

Her eyes danced. "I thought pilots and officers were all athletes?"

"We are . . . as long as it's poker and pool, and liar dice. But, for the pleasure of being with you, I'll take up badminton as well."

*

Alice Royle telephoned at noon. "A quick trip to Port McNeill, A man has injured himself . . ."

Aarvo Taarkanen, an ageing Finlander from Sointula on Malcolm Island, had taken his boat across to Port McNeill to visit his daughter and grandchildren.

Like many of his kind, he enjoyed strong drink in quantity, and nothing more than his son-in-law's own potent home brew.

Aarvo Taarkanen had worked all his life in forests; in his youth in Finland, continuing after his migration to the trackless Vancouver Island woods, a 'faller and bucker', reputedly one of the best.

His greatest pride lay in his almost-virtuoso mastery of the double-bitted axe, a tool which had survived the advent of machinery in the forest industry.

Now in his seventies, he honed his skills with a little freelance logging work, and the daily splitting of wood for his own and his neighbours' fires.

Aarvo Taarkanen found endless pleasure in his unfailing ability to place the axe always in the identical cut-line, and could, he boasted cheerfully, cut with an axe as neatly as two men with a handsaw, and sometimes more quickly . . .

He had spent much of that day splitting stovewood for his daughter, hot and thirsty work which caused him to refresh himself frequently, consuming sufficient home brew to induce euphoria, an exaggerated awareness of his talents, and a certain unsteadiness of foot.

He was enjoying himself, nicely settled into the work rhythm, when, at the top of a swing, he swayed enough to bring the axe down and miss the chopping block . . .

*

He was in the stretcher, attended by a first-aider, when Fulton arrived. His injured foot, still in its caulked boot, was elevated on wadded blankets, roughly-dressed to staunch the worst bleeding.

The first-aider was grinning. "He's done hisself good this time, the old pisser. Should've give him morphine, but he's too drunk." He shrugged. "Anyhow, morphine wouldn't change nothin'."

The patient, in the hard drinker's vernacular, was 'feeling no pain', and was loud in praise of his own achievement. "By YESUS . . . I still got my know-how! Betcha ARSE!"

It was twelve miles from Fort McNeill to Blackfish Harbour, and, all the way, Aarvo Taarkanen bellowed joyfully of his prowess.

Fulton, levelling off fifty feet above the quiet water, called Alice Royle on the radio. "Foxtrot-Lima-Juliet off Port McNeill at fifty-five, estimating Blackfish . . ."

"I'm TELLIN' you, by the Lord Yesus Christ . . . !" Aarvo Taarkanen was bawling.

"Say again, please," Alice Royle begged. "We appear to have a crossed frequency."

Fulton said, "stand by, Blackfish . . ." He turned. "Could you keep it down, Mister Taarkanen, please?"

The patient squinted, befuddled. "What's up?"

"I'm trying . . ." Fulton held up the microphone.

"Needs to talk on the radio, Aarvo," the first-aider shouted. "He can't with you makin' all that racket."

"Not makin' no Christly racket . . ." Aarvo Taarkanen was indignant. "Just tellin' my story."

"If I could just finish first?" Fulton appealed.

"Sure thing, young fella . . ." Aarvo Taarkanen beamed acquiescence. "Why'n't you SAY so . . . ?"

Fulton completed his position report, and turned back to his passenger.

"Now, sir . . . ?"

"Maybe not so big story if'n you not no axeman . . ." Aarvo Taarkanen enquired, "you been an axeman, boy?"

"Sorry," Fulton confessed. "I never had any luck . . ." He advised, "we're landing soon."

"Then I tell you quick." The old man pulled his hands free of the restraining webbing, and, clasping an imaginary axe, described a long swing. "WHO-O-OOSH!"

"You'll start th' Goddam bleedin' again," the first-aider warned.

Aarvo Taarkanen waved him away. "Lose this much, li'l more won't hurt . . ."

He resumed his narrative as Fulton lowered the flaps and made the power settings for the approach. "Like I show you . . . every swipe, put the blade back in the same notch . . . EVERY time. Do her blindfold . . . in the dark . . ." Fulton held the Seabee twenty feet off the water, coasting at eighty knots towards his chosen touchdown spot. "So, there I am, startin' in the swing, an' God-*DAMN* . . . first time ever in my life . . . I miss, and plant him straight in my foot." Fulton, hand on the throttle, was judging the spot to his personal satisfaction . . . "There's all this-here blood comin' out . . . blood up the ying-yang, and I'm lookin' at this cut I made . . . wonderin' if I can plant her back in the same hole." He guffawed, and Fulton, picturing it, felt, deep in his foot, the electric surge of sympathetic pain. He clenched his teeth and, as Aarvo Taarkanen finished his story, closed the throttle, easing back on the control yoke. "So . . . I bring her down again, and by YESUS . . . in she GO! Not so much as a pussy-hair out o' place. An' I'm lookin' at that, and thinkin' . . . YEP . . . I still got the touch, all right!"

*

Tamara had brought her spare racquet. With it in his hand, Fulton spent the next forty-five minutes being run off his feet. In spite of repeatedly losing the shuttlecock in the net, hitting it maddeningly with the wooden rim, and having his few trick shots returned with almost contemptuous ease, he enjoyed himself. Badminton he could take or leave: badminton with Tamara could become a favoured sport . . .

They sat on a bench, sipping cokes. "You," he said. "Are good."

"Thank you, Jack." She was flushed with exertion and pleasure. Her hair clung damply to her forehead, and he wanted very much to brush it aside with his fingers. "But I've been playing since I could stand unaided."

"I was terrible, and a push-over. It couldn't have been any fun for you."

"Do you hear me complaining?"

He laughed lightly. "You're a well-mannered child."

"Tell me more."

"I'd sooner *ask* something."

"That's easy. Ask."

"I was wondering . . . would you have dinner with me?"

"Where? The Hotel Vancouver again, or Chinatown? The North Shore, perhaps?"

"If only we could."

Tamara nodded. "Some other time, maybe?"

He said, disappointed, "it was just an idea."

"Jack . . . I meant about *Vancouver*." She shook her head at him. "Don't go getting a trembly lower lip. Dinner sounds great, even if the means *are* limited."

He thought . . . she's right about that. Blackfish Harbour offered a niggardly choice: the snack bar at Sullivan's Inn, a greasy spoon that catered for un-choosy drunks when the beer parlour closed. Hong's Café provided passable food without frills. Or there was the hotel coffee shop, more up-market and costly, with booths to bolster the illusion of *tête-à-tête* privacy. They favoured the coffee shop.

But Tamara said, "I'll have to ask Ma."

"Do you need permission?"

"With *my* easygoing old Ma?" She laughed. "How can you *be* so stupid?"

"It's not easy."

"Only to find out if she's fixed anything," Tamara explained. "If she has, we might need a re-think. We couldn't walk out on her."

He made agreeable sounds, and prayed silently that Rosa had made no preparations. "What if she has?"

"Then I guess we'll have to dine at home." She looked amused. "Rain-check on the coffee shop."

"She might not be happy about feeding me two nights in a row."

"She'd be happy as all get-out," Tamara insisted. "And there'll be no Stepan to spoil things."

*

"Was thinkin' to fix cold cuts . . . but okay. You go, have good time . . ." Rosa beamed at Fulton. "Just be take good care my Tamara, eh?"

"Count on it, Rosa."

Tamara went to change, and Rosa gave him a beer. "Fine you be drink . . . that crazy man not here." She poured herself coffee, and sat down companionably. "Good thing, I say, you take out Tamara. Mean for me no cookin', no doin' dishes, no cleanin' up. House all mine." She gave a great, contented smile. "That old man up some mountain somewheres, and best place for him. I rest my poor feet . . . be big lady o' the castle, like in England."

Tamara re-appeared in a cotton peasant skirt, white sandals, a broderie anglaise blouse. She saw him with his beer. "God! Are you at it *again*?"

"You sound like your mother," he said.

Rosa laughed delightedly. "That tell *you*, Miss Smartie-pants!"

"Moth-*er*!" Tamara looked pained. "I'm not a kid, and *not* what you called me."

"Beat it, both o' youse . . ." Rosa dismissed them. "Gi' me some peace."

Walking down the hill, Tamara said, still aggrieved, "I hate it when she says things like that to me in front of others."

"Who's others?"

"You know perfectly well what I mean."

"It's the way parents are," he offered. "Mine frequently make me cringe."

"Count on you to defend her . . ." But she was smiling.

"She's just a sweet little old lady."

"Right. Like Mammy Yokum, or Tugboat Annie." She took his hand. "Do you mind?"

"Not as much as I might have if you hadn't done it."

She swung their joined hands high. "I've decided to forgive you for siding against me."

"Oh, thank *God*!" He mopped his brow. "I was getting in a terrible state!"

She warned then, "just remember what I said about loyalty. If you're going to take sides, they'd better be mine."

He asked with interest, "how many sides do you have?"

"Call me multi-faceted." She pressed his hand. "An enigma."

"*There's* a word to toy with."

At the coffee shop, they were shown to a booth, and ordered dinner. Waiting, Tamara wanted to hear about his day. "I heard you take off."

"Did I wake you?"

"Yep."

"I'm sorry."

"Don't be. Mike woke me as well. So did Q.C.A. It's the chance you take when you work nights." She cocked her head. "So? Tell me."

"Just the one trip." He told her of Aarvo Taarkanen. "A real wild man. In his seventies . . . old enough to know better. Had to find out if he still had the magic touch."

"Seems he did, from what you say."

Fulton shook his head. "If it hadn't been for his caulked boot, he'd have taken his foot right off. When he said about that second swipe, I nearly blew the landing."

Tamara said reflectively, "that certainly up-stages Mister Nemlander."

"Who dat?"

Mr. Nemlander had injured himself in circumstances not unlike those of Aarvo Taarkanen. Like Aarvo Taarkanen, he was contentedly drunk as he sawed lengths of plank in his yard.

Tamara said, "so much so that, quite unaware, he sawed off the tops of his thumb and two fingers. Until, happening to notice a little blood, he decided things weren't quite as they should be." She gave an incredulous laugh. "He found the bits, washed them, wrapped them in waxed paper, shoved his hand into a clean sock, and walked to the hospital to ask if someone would sew them back on."

"And did someone?"

"Oh, yes . . ." She was quite matter-of-fact. "All nice and neat, and he was home in two days."

"How was the hand?"

"Fine, he says. Stiff . . . some mobility loss. Not so nifty any more with a knife and fork, *or* a saw. But he makes out . . ."

They finished their coffee, and Tamara wondered, "care to take a walk?"

"No Broadway show? No casino or night club?"

"Who needs fripperies?" She told him firmly, "walk!"

"Next thing," he muttered. "You'll have me in a collar and lead . . ."

Outside, the dusk was deepening, stars showing against a cloudless sky. A first-quarter moon slid towards the mountains, and a breeze came in from the Sound, ruffling the bay.

"Isn't this beautiful?" She took his hand again.

"A truly lovely hand."

"I meant the evening. But if you insist."

They walked towards the head of the bay where the last village lights yielded to the darkness of impenetrable forest.

Outside the beer parlour, some drunks whistled and catcalled after them.

"Pay no attention," Tamara said.

"Such is my firm resolve," he informed her. "Unless, of course, it gets personal."

"Then what?"

"Throw you over my shoulder, and run like hell!"

"You'd do that for *me*?" She pressed against him. "My hero!"

Olaf Pedersen was locking his store. The Ford waited, motor idling. "Hi there, you two . . ." He smiled at their joined hands. "What have we *here*?"

"It's a cold night." Tamara sounded demure. "And I forgot my mittens."

"That's okay then . . . long as there's no canoodlin'." He rattled the door a final time. "Don't s'pose I can offer you a ride . . . ?" And shook his head. "No . . . didn't think so." He was gone in a gravel-spurting u-turn.

"It'll be all over town by tomorrow," Tamara said. "Olaf will tell Madeleine . . ."

"Madeleine?"

"*Missus* Olaf. And once that old blabbermouth gets on it, we'll be engaged, shacked-up, and me pregnant."

"Sounds good to me."

"Well, it would, wouldn't it?" He felt the pressure of her fingers. "Were you serious?"

"Would a yes offend?"

"Can't think why."

"Then . . . yes. I was serious . . . *am* serious."

She said softly, "thank you, Jack."

And then, it was like a stage safely reached along a chosen route. "It did worry me . . . that I might offend you."

"It might have . . . if you hadn't meant it."

A slow half-mile brought them to the last street light, where the pretence of paving subsided into the honest mud and ruts of a chewed-over logging road. Where the darkness smelled of raw earth torn by giant trucks and diesel caterpillars. Standing close and quiet, they caught, too, the heavy scents of felled timber, cedar and pine and Douglas fir, the ubiquitous hemlock . . .

Tamara murmured, "it's almost certainly been said in some mushy movie. But here, now, it's like the whole world's holding its breath."

He was conscious of her warm young length against his side, and sensed her invitation. The intricacy of broderie anglaise was under his fingertips, emphasising the firm body beneath. They stood motionless, seeming, like that world of Hollywood cliché, not to breathe. Watching daylight's last dregs seeping from the sky.

She asked, "*was* it nice when I kissed you this morning?"

"Nice, but . . ."

"Oh?" She glanced up at him.

". . . not enough."

"Ah, but that was a morning kiss . . . chaste and proper." She added, "with probably the world and his dog watching."

"Holding their breath."

"Building up to an all-new gossip-fest."

He asked, "and now?"

"See for yourself." She gestured at the enfolding darkness. "Different time of day, and nobody here but us chickens."

"An evening kiss," he wondered. "Should that be chaste?"

"Let's play it by ear."

"By ear sounds a little tricky."

"There's a time and place for your twisted sense of humour, Mister Fulton."

He saw her face, pale in dimness, indistinct, turned to him. And, this time, it was not fleeting, and she did not tease; nothing was withheld or refused, and it lasted for a long, breathless time . . .

They drew apart, and Tamara observed musingly, "no . . . I wouldn't call *that* chaste."

"Nice, though." He was smiling. "You play well by ear."

"That was to say 'thank you' for dinner."

"You're welcome. We must do it again."

"Dinner . . . ?"

"That, too."

It was for longer then, more urgent, more demanding, she no less than he: he felt her power to draw him to her, and there was no embarrassment at all in what she could do—and did—to him . . .

"That was really rather good . . ." She sounded, he thought, remarkably collected. "Fun, too."

"What *would* the chattering masses of Blackfish have to say?"

"They'd have a ball . . ." She hesitated, then reluctantly, "talking of Blackfish . . ."

"You have to get back."

"I don't want to, really. Not now."

"What would you rather do?"

"Need I spell it out?"

"I'd much rather you showed me . . ." He drew her to him, hugging her until she gasped and giggled. And then, for a little while longer, nothing was said, or needed saying.

FIVE

Stepan's timber cruising contract had been extended: it would be three weeks, perhaps more, before he could be expected back.

Meanwhile, Fulton was dealing with a rush of demands for the ambulance Seabee; logging and sawmill accidents in the main, with a sprinkling of domestics, injured fishermen and imminent childbirths.

Almost all the logging cases were ugly and traumatic, and often freakish, brought about by a moment's inattention to tasks that were always perilous and frequently fatal. The brief honeymoon spell had ended, and Fulton was witnessing first-hand the brutal side of the job he had taken on.

He flew them out daily, those who lived, those who did not. With their terrible wounds, broken heads, destroyed faces, their bodies ripped open to expose their living organs.

Among the worst was a young choker-setter, his leg severed in an instant by a rogue length of flying steel-wire strop. Gone with the leg were the genitalia.

He was loaded aboard, blood-reeking and morphine-soaked, strapped into the basket stretcher, his grey, sweating face cowled by a blanket. Two bundles went with him, one large, one small, dumped without ceremony upon the cabin floor beneath the stretcher. The larger, wrapped in bloody rags, was instantly recognisable. The first-aid man explained the other, a whitish bag, canvas, like the bags used by banks for carrying cash . . .

"That's his balls. Maybe the doc can sew 'em on if he's quick . . . they're still pretty fresh. Hope so. He can make it without no leg, but he'll never make *out* without them-there . . ."

Fulton carried several other choker-setters—they appeared to have a propensity towards serious and painful injury—and a man who had slipped off a flat-boom into the water, his pelvis crushed between two logs.

From Beaver Cove one morning, he flew a camp cook, a brawny woman, her face, hands and arms flayed by an exploding deep fryer. She lay in the stretcher, cursing her pain and misfortune in ripest loggers' language. She informed Fulton with some belligerence that her name was blanking-Sue. She did not give an unspeakable for her asterisking face; she had never been no freaking beauty. She hated, however, being strapped in this nameless basket, trussed-blank-up like a sonofagun chicken, so she couldn't see out! This was her first unmentionable ride in an expletive-airplane, and she had been looking forward to it. For all the flubbering good *this* was, she might as well have gone in a fudpucking *submarine* . . . !

There was an early morning call to bring out a catskinner from Nimpkish Lake. Crouched beside the logging road at some distance from his big D-8 Caterpillar, attending to a major and compelling call of nature, he had been charged by an irritable moose. With no hope of regaining the sanctuary of the bulldozer, he fled into the trees, clutching his pants, and tumbled into a gully where he had lain through the night with a fractured femur. The moose, losing interest, ambled away.

There could be none worse, Fulton believed at the time, than the powder-man.

The call came from Zeballos, over on the Island's Pacific shore. Where the powder-man had been dynamiting stumps on a high-level logging slash destined for re-forestation.

Moving in to investigate the misfire of a charge, he had taken the full force of the delayed blast.

There followed the nightmare journey down the mountain, the bearers stumbling on the rocky, treacherous slopes with their screaming burden who cursed them from the depths of a torment made worse by the slightest jarring movement of the stretcher.

He was still shrieking as he was passed through the bow-hatch.

"Man . . . I'm sorry as hell," the first-aider muttered at Fulton. "He's had all the morphine I can give him, but it don't make a blind bit o' difference."

"It's okay . . . don't worry about me . . ."

But it was *not* okay as the shrill, terrible sounds seemed to tear his head apart over the noise of the Seabee's engine, through the headset clamped over his ears in a vain attempt to muffle them.

"He's smashed to bits inside . . . rib-cage gone . . . both arms. Christ alone knows what they'll find when they open him up. He should be *dead*," the first-aider insisted furiously. "He's *s'posed* to be! What kind o' shitty God would . . ."

He was small, round-shouldered and middle-aged, borne down by the endless, solitary anxieties of his profession. Now, with the added ingredient of angry protest, he was close to weeping, and Fulton wondered how often he might have felt like that . . . ?

It was a bad flying day: the perfect summer weather had broken, driven out by low cloud and rain which masked the mountains. On the way in to Zeballos, he had been compelled to follow contours and valleys, his visibility reduced further by the grey rain-sheets driving in on strong, blustering winds. The passes had been filled with turbulence which shook and bounced the Seabee.

He must fly back now through that with a stretchered man who howled his indescribable agony at the slightest disturbance.

Hard to imagine, then, following a shuddering take-off through rough water, climbing in tumbling air into the Vancouver Island hinterland, the cabin filled with the powder-man's endless screams, that there might be worse in store.

It came when he discovered the passes ahead blocked-in by cloud that denied him now the short route to Blackfish Harbour. There could be no penetrating blind into unknown country where the peaks rose around them to three and four thousand feet . . .

Fulton turned back regretfully. "No chance of making it through." The first-aider nodded glum acceptance. "That leaves us the long way round the top end of the Island. I'm sorry."

"Don't know how much more he can take . . ." The other watched his patient. "Could lose him easy. Best thing'd be if the load got too much, and he short-circuited and passed out."

Over the open Pacific the cloud base was down to four hundred feet. Fulton held his course close to green, tumultuous seas that seemed to reach up for them as the Seabee heaved and groaned its slow way forward. Off to the right, half a mile distant, the land's dark wall rose into cloud. For minutes at a time, violent squalls cut visibility almost to zero. Following the shore, their heading was north-westward, which provided a fresh complication. That heading, combined with a rising westerly gale, induced a quartering headwind which slowed the Seabee's groundspeed. The wind's angle meant also a relentless sideways drift back towards the land which must be corrected by turning even more into the opposing air-stream. Through each clawed, crawling mile, the powder-man screamed and screamed.

Flight conditions were brutally rough, and, through it all, the first-aider sat without enquiry or complaint, nursing the patient, a soothing hand resting on the unresponsive head. As though, by contact alone, he might impart some measure of comfort and peace.

At what seemed little more than a walking pace, the Seabee battled its way across Checleset Bay, past the forbidding mass of Cape Cook, and on over Quatsino Sound and Winter Harbour where there was a sheltering seaplane dock. Forbidden to them now.

Until, after twenty-five slow, painful miles, Cape Scott was reached, and he could turn eastward with the wind now on the tail to send them romping homeward. Fifteen minutes more brought them into the lee of land and Queen Charlotte Strait, where the air calmed and the clouds lifted to a thousand feet. Where, without warning, shocking them, the screaming ceased as the powder-man lapsed into belated unconsciousness.

One hour and forty-five minutes from Zeballos, they touched down on the bay's flat, rain-dappled water, and spied the Ford, the two white-clad orderlies, waiting.

*

"Good *morn*-ing, Mister Fulton . . ." Alice Royle's call, and bright, crisp tones, were too early to be welcome.

He grunted back, sleepy and graceless, "what's up?"

"*You* should be, for a start. For a jolly nice Vancouver trip. Take-off at eight, please . . ." Fulton glanced outside, checking the weather, but she had anticipated him. "Lovely morning . . . all yesterday's nastiness blown away. Campbell River and Vancouver are reporting perfect conditions . . ."

Cloudless stillness out there, early sunlight gilding the peaks, painting distant Mystery Mountain with strokes of lemon and coral. Difficult even to imagine that yesterday, and Zeballos, could have been . . .

"So *changeable*," Alice Royle prattled on happily. "It *does* remind me of England . . ." She confided, "must be why I love it so much."

The trip would be another quick turn-around; there and back in a day. A patient for the General Hospital.

"It's that poor chap from Zeballos."

It was like a low blow: protest cried out in his mind . . . wasn't yesterday enough? To be burdened with *that* again . . . all the way to Vancouver! He cursed the local hospital silently, the doctors and nurses. For copping-*out*! They were there, weren't they, to *deal* with trauma and catastrophe . . . with shattered powder-men? Not to shunt it on down the line with himself as conveyor belt . . . !

He nursed his hurt as the Ford arrived, and the orderlies bore the stretcher down. Jackie Seaweed, reeling in the fuel hose, muttered with pointed dryness, "have a nice trip." He had witnessed the previous day's arrival.

A swell was running in the bay, yesterday's storm legacy, sufficient to sway the pontoon and make the orderlies' progress unsteady. Before, that would have had the powder-man screaming. Now, there was no sound, no movement. Fulton got into his seat, and one of the orderlies took the place behind him.

"Hi there . . . I'm Eric." The voice was light, slightly sibilant.

"Hi . . ." Fulton reserved judgement. Nothing said that male nursing staff had to be queer . . .

"I'm coming, too, as you've probably gathered," Eric informed him. "If that's okay?"

"Fine. We're not picky . . ." Too late, Fulton regretted the slip: it had come like a reflex; he put it down to his continuing ill-humour; anyone was in the firing line today! He wondered, though, ashamed, would I have been a sorehead with Tamara? He offered appeasement, "all are welcome . . . says so on the door."

"'Anything, Anywhere, Anytime'," Eric quoted, and giggled. "Not sure I care about being any-*thing*, but never mind." He gave Fulton a concerned glance. "Hear you had a dreadful time of it yesterday."

"All part of the job, Eric."

"Well, shouldn't be anything like that today," Eric promised. "Gorgeous weather, and . . ." He nodded at the stretcher on the pontoon. "He's in a deep coma, and a blessing for all concerned. If he'd been like yesterday, we couldn't possibly have moved him . . ."

"You guys havin' a reunion, or what?" The other orderly leaned through the hatch. His accent was heavy-Québec. "We got a body to get movin'."

"Don't get your balls in an uproar, Joseph," Eric told him tartly. "I have to brief the pilot."

"Won't need no briefin' after yesterday." Joseph winked at Fulton. "Got her easy today."

"He knows that." Eric was petulant. "I've *said*."

"Okay, Honeybunch . . ." Joseph grinned. "But better get the lead out."

The unconscious powder-man was loaded and secured. He uttered no sound. The thick, sweetish odour of sickness filled the cabin . . . Joseph called, "how you doin' back there, Blossom?"

"As well as can be expected," Eric answered stiffly. "Considering the intelligence level of some of the hired help around here."

As Fulton hit the starter button, Joseph warned mockingly, "don't let Tweetie-Pie puke all over you, Capt'n. He got a delicate cons-tit-ution!"

"Piss off," Eric told him. "You bloody pea-souper!"

*

They flew down the Inside Passage through silken air, with a visibility of fifty miles from their cool, comfortable altitude. The powder-man lay still and silent; Eric had immersed himself in a book. Fulton glanced back, curious, anticipating something lurid, but the orderly was engrossed in a heavy nursing manual. He looked up, and Fulton asked, “improving your mind?”

“Doing my best with limited resources.” Eric made a wry grimace. “Boning-up for Registered Nurse training.”

“So’s a friend of mine . . . starting at the V.G.H. In August. Colleague of yours.”

“That’ll be Tammy. We’re on the same course.”

“Tammy . . .” He considered it doubtfully: she was Tamara, and did not seem like a Tammy to him. He felt a pang of envy then: Eric would be close to her in Vancouver, sharing with her. And I’ll be far away, a continent between us . . .

“She’s a natural,” Eric was saying. “Going to make a wonderful nurse.”

“What about you?”

“Strictly run-of-the-mill. I’ll make it, but I’ll always be a bedpan-walloper at heart.” He chuckled. “With a nice diploma to hang in my boudoir.”

Denman Island lay below, and Qualicum Beach, with the long dark shape of Texada Island drifting back beyond the left wing. Over Parksville, Fulton turned east for the run across Georgia Strait to the Fraser’s mouth. The Strait was busy with shipping, a ferry leaving Nanaimo, fishboats and freighters. Two destroyers steamed in line ahead towards Esquimalt, and they brought a moment’s unexpected nostalgia, the reminder of what could have been with the Navy. As a seaman officer, prohibited from flying, he might have risen to command one of those . . .

Twenty miles out, he called Vancouver for approach clearance, and the wind and weather on the river, then switched over to report his imminent arrival on the company frequency.

“We’ll be down in ten minutes, and the reception committee’s waiting,” he informed Eric. Nodding, the orderly leaned forward, and Fulton could smell his pungent aftershave . . . and thought of Tamara’s preferred and more subtle cologne.

"May I ask you something terribly personal?"

"You can always *ask*, Eric."

"You spoke of Tammy as your *friend*?"

"Well, I like to think so."

"Then would you be . . ." Eric sounded coy. "That *special* friend?"

He felt his heart tip over. "Couldn't say. Why don't you tell me?"

"You sound edgy. Am I trespassing?"

"I'm scared of flying. It makes me that way."

Eric giggled. "I wouldn't want to talk out of turn."

"I'll let you know if you do . . ." Fulton pointed to the brownish haze over Vancouver, the North Shore mountains lofting behind. "Be quick. I'll be busy soon."

"Ooops . . . sorry . . . yes . . . well . . ." He giggled again, and that giggle was beginning to grate, Fulton decided.

Eric spoke of graveyard shifts shared, conversations over coffee and night lunch. "I help Tammy with the babies . . . she's in obstetrics a lot."

"She's mentioned that."

"With the feeding and changing . . . I simply adore babies." Fulton waited. "Well, it was during a feeding session, just us, so we could chat . . ." Eric explained, "we chat a lot. We're not *registered*, you see." He seemed piqued. "Sometimes the registered ones can be *unbelievably* bitchy."

"I'm sorry to hear that, Eric."

"So Tammy and I have chummed-up. A kind of mutual defence pact."

"Very smart . . ." Fulton tried not to think of 'all girls together'. That, too, would be bitchy.

"It was then she mentioned it. Although she wasn't entirely forthcoming, it was apparent that it must be a *fellow*. I mean, a lovely girl like Tammy, it would have to be, wouldn't it?"

"Sure hope *that's* the case!"

"There she was . . . eyes all lit-up . . . and actually *blushing*. It was quite charming."

West Point Grey slid in under the nose, and Sea Island lay two minutes beyond. Fulton picked out the seaplane traffic on the river, a Beaver taxying out, a Stranraer beginning its take-off run. Another Seabee was on final approach. He asked, "what makes you think I'm this special friend?"

"Oh . . . *you* know."

"'Fraid I don't . . . sorry about that."

"We-e-ell, no names were mentioned, but I could draw conclusions."

"Good for you," Fulton approved dryly. He began the downwind leg for the Tower-controlled approach to the river, positioned number three to land. The Stranraer was airborne, climbing out westbound. He searched out the aircraft ahead of him, the other Seabee at number one, about to touch down, next, a mile behind, an Otter floatplane in the distinctive blue and gold colour scheme of the Mounted Police Air Division. An arrowhead wake sprang out behind the Seabee; it slowed and turned shoreward. The Tower cleared the Otter to land, and Fulton to number two. He turned to Eric. "Fifteen seconds to spill the beans."

"Or what . . . ?" Eric smirked. "The third degree?"

"Just get it *said*, Eric!"

"All ri-i-ight . . . don't get owly!" Eric grew testy. "I'm *coming* to it!"

He sniffed, then, "no, no names, but enough hints. The special friend being a *close* neighbour and how much closer could you get without actually moving in? And then, during day-shift, whenever you take off, she *shoots* to the window with this gooey look on her face."

"*Gooey*, eh?"

"There!" Eric pouted, "are we *quite* satisfied now?"

The police Otter had taxied clear. The Tower said, "Foxtrot-Lima-Juliet cleared to land."

"Thank you, Eric." Fulton was smiling. "You just made it."

SIX

When he climbed out of the Seabee, Bob Peters was already up on a wing root, the cowling lifted, frowning into the engine. Mike Denholm walked across from the tethered Beaver. "Sorry, Jack . . . wasted trip." His eyes were sombre.

Fulton asked quietly, "he died, then?"

"In the ambulance, on the way to Town. Too bad."

"Yes . . ." But, was it? The powder-man had reeked of death, and continuing life, surely, had held nothing for him . . . ?

"You win some, you lose some." Denholm's regretful words closed that chapter for ever . . .

Bob Peters called down, "Mister Pilot . . . have you been over-boosting my engine?"

"To the best of my knowledge, Mister Engineer . . ." Fulton met his gaze. ". . . I have not."

"And that's *you* told, Bob," Denholm said.

"You *would* say that," Peters observed sourly. "You bloody birdmen stick together."

"Like shit to a blanket," Denholm agreed mildly. "A needed strategy in the face of our hostile friends in the 'You Bend 'Em, We Mend 'Em' department."

"'S not funny, you know." Peters sounded glum, and defeated.

"What makes you think *someone's* . . ." Fulton stressed the word with some belligerence, ". . . been over-boosting?"

"There's signs," Peters claimed mysteriously. "There's always *signs* . . ."

He stood on the wing-root, oily, lanky and lugubrious, the archetypal bush airplane engineer, worth his weight, although no one would ever tell him that. "Only need to lift the lid . . ." He rapped bony knuckles on the cowling. "Only need to *sniff*. And there it is."

"Oh, *Jesus*, Bob!" Fulton flared, exasperated. It had been a long, tiring day, with only the bitter knowledge of failure and death to round it out. "When you know for sure, write me a *report*!"

"Let's not get ugly now," Denholm suggested softly.

"Well, I'm sorry . . . but I'm being accused without grounds . . ."

"No one's accusing," Peters soothed. "But *some* pilot's done it. I just wondered if it could've been you?"

"Like the cops," Denholm murmured. "He just needs to eliminate you from his enquiries."

"Then the answer's no."

Peters nodded. "That's all I needed to hear."

"Kiss and make up now?" Denholm wondered.

But Fulton was curious. "Why did you ask?"

"Like I said . . . *signs*." Peters shrugged. "It always shows when the throttle's been overworked with the revs too low."

"Sorry to hear that . . . particularly as I have to fly the thing. But it's some other driver." He reminded them, "I'm the new boy here . . . on my best behaviour."

"Oh, *bless* you for that!" Denholm blew out relieved breath. "I'd been terrified of a change of heart!"

It cleared the air; Fulton was laughing, raising submissive hands. "Okay . . . okay . . ."

"You know me, Jack . . ." Peters was apologetic now. "I kind of mother-hen my aircraft. Overdo it sometimes, maybe." He glanced at Denholm. "Ask Mike . . . he's the boss."

"First time you've ever admitted *that*," Denholm said.

"Thing is," Peters told them. "I'll need to ground her for a day."

Denholm wondered, "must you?"

"This needs looking into . . . catch it early."

"How do you know it's early?"

"Engine's still running, isn't it?"

Denholm nodded. "Just a day, then?"

"Give me till the morning after tomorrow?"

"Okay, Bob . . . stopwatch is ticking." Denholm told Fulton, "Jack, you've got an honest-to-God day off."

"What if we get casualties?"

"Then me and Nellie will have to cope." Denholm jerked a thumb at the Beaver. "Trust me, Jack . . . I'm a big boy now. I'll try very hard not to screw up and let you down."

*

Tamara looked thoughtful. "I might be able to swing a shift-switch."

"That took talent," Fulton said admiringly.

"What . . . swing a shift-switch?"

"There you go again." He asked, "think you can?"

"Erica might . . . she's another aide," Tamara explained. "There's a boat trip and wiener roast to Nimpkish River on Thursday. Erica's goofy about Michael, the X-ray technician, and he's going. But she's off tomorrow, and I've got Thursday . . ."

"It all sounds wonderfully complicated."

"Okay. Then to reduce it to a level you can grasp, let's say I foresee a swap."

"Thank you for telling me. I might never have guessed."

They were in Rosa's kitchen. Stepan was still away, and Rosa was out, visiting neighbours. Tamara went to the phone, and he listened to the brief one-sided conversation, hoping that Erica would be amenable . . .

Tamara said, "'bye for now, Erica," and replaced the receiver, beaming. "She couldn't wait to say yes . . . and thanks a million."

"Erica . . . I *love* you!"

"From a distance, please. Platonically." She leaned down to encircle him with her arms.

He wondered, "wouldn't be jealous, would we?"

"Of *you*? Ha!"

"That's not what I asked."

Her arms tightened. "Maybe a *leedle*. You'll see why when you meet Erica." Her lips brushed his cheek. "She's gorgeous."

"So are you."

"She's gorgeous-er."

"My mind's made up," he declared. "Don't confuse me with facts."

She kissed him fully. "Thank you for that. Thank you for *you.*"

"Would 'ditto' do for an answer?"

"It would. And it earns you a reward."

"I've just had one."

"That was simply to get your attention." She enquired, "any plans for our shared day off?"

"Shall we make it up as we go along?"

"Remember the Private Place?"

"Is that my reward?"

"If you like?"

"I *like*, Tamara."

"As long as the weather plays ball."

"The weather can go fly a kite. It'll still be perfect."

"We'll take a picnic," she promised. "Ma will provide."

"Seems a little presumptuous?"

"Don't you believe it. Soon's she knows, the catering will be out of our hands. We'll be heading for the woods with grub for a week."

He sighed in ecstasy. "Food . . . and a week in the woods with you."

"I see you've got your priorities right," Tamara said dryly. "Food . . . then me!"

*

He had steeled himself for rain and wind, and wakened to a fresh, magic morning filling the house with light. The Sound lay like a pewter mirror, untouched by breeze or wave: Blackfish Harbour was breathless and still beneath its veil of blue woodsmoke . . .

"Got a little grub for you kids," Rosa announced.

Fulton eyed the bulging rucksack. "My *God*, Rosa!"

"Somethin' wrong?" She was looking anxious.

"We can't take all *that*!"

"What you sayin'?" She bared her teeth in a grin. "Too much for you to pack? Strong young fella like you?"

"Rosa . . . we're only going for the *day* . . ."

"You need be eat good . . ." She nudged him. "Got to keep your strength up, eh?"

He looked at her. "Did I really hear that?"

Tamara appeared, and spotted the rucksack. "Ma . . . you're *kidding*!"

"Kid about what, Sweetie?"

"We can't take all that!"

"That what *he* say . . ." Rosa jerked a derisive thumb at Fulton. "You not like?"

He began, "it's not that . . ."

"Act like pair o' sissies." She shook her head. "Young people all same these days."

"Ma . . . all I said was a little picnic. Some sandwiches . . . coffee."

"You goin' over the other side? Your place?"

"That *was* the idea . . ." Suddenly Tamara was blushing.

"So?" Rosa looked perplexed. "Is long haul. You get hungry. Maybe it be long day, eh? Maybe you get cut off by big tide over there . . . never know your luck. Need be prepare." And Fulton, disbelieving, saw her wink.

"We'll be darned tired, too, Ma." Tamara was resigned. "Carrying that load."

"You want take Stepan old truck? Drive to end o' road, then leave him. Then just need carry to other side. Easy."

Tamara and Fulton exchanged looks. The dreadful truck had not been part of their plan.

"I don't drive, Ma. Remember?"

"How about him?" She gave Fulton a scathing glance.

"I've got no licence," he lied.

She looked disbelieving. "You be drive *airplane* . . . not drive little *truck*? Now I hear everythin'!"

"One of those things," he offered lamely.

Rosa was shaking her head in doubt. "Walk all the way, you got a long hike. Be beat-up before you get *anywheres.*"

"I've done it before, Ma . . . it's no big deal."

Fulton put in, "it's not that we're ungrateful . . ."

"Ha! I reckon," she snorted, and shrugged. "Be please yourselfs. Don't say me I never say you . . ."

She bawled after them as they plodded down the hill, "BE EAT *ALL* . . . BE *STRONG*! NOT SO HEAVY BRINGIN' BACK THEN!"

"Do you think she's telling us something?" he murmured.

By the time they had reached the shoreline road, he was sweating, and beginning to regret spurning the truck . . .

Tamara said, "let me take it for a while."

"Never!"

"I'm pretty damn' strong you know!"

He laughed. "Sounds like the song about Stashu Pandowski."

"Oh, yes . . . ?"

"Stashu's girl-friend . . ." He quoted the line, "'She not very much good for *pretty*, but she pretty much good for *strong*'!"

"Not very much good for pretty, is it?" She giggled and grabbed his arm. "You can be quite funny sometimes." They followed the logging road deep into the forest.

"How's the load?"

"What load?" He wiped his streaming face.

"So why are your knees buckling?"

"I've never carried an entire roast ox more than a mile before."

"Almost there . . . another half-mile." Tamara grinned. "Unfortunately, half that half-mile is an almost vertical climb, the other a likewise descent."

"Are we having fun?" he murmured. "Or are we having fun?"

*

She enquired softly, "worth the effort?"

With the rucksack dumped, barefoot, pants' legs rolled up, he stood in water cold enough to burn, chilled by the run-off from

Coast Range peaks and glaciers. Savouring the peace of a place wholly undisturbed.

He smiled back at her. "Cheap at the price." He extended a hand, and she walked into the water, giving a little breathless scream. "GOD! That's *murder*!"

"Thought you were tough? Used to it?"

"Tough is okay. But you never get *used* to this."

"I'd hate to get used to anything here," he admitted.

The Private Place was a small cove where the Sound washed in, a movement like slow breathing. Miniature waves curled over grey stones and patches of coarse sand. Tidal pools from which the sea had withdrawn were fringed with kelp-ropes and pale sea anemones hanging limp without the water's support, and alive with small darting fish waiting for the next inflow to reclaim them.

The forest came to the sea's edge, encroaching in places where half-toppled hemlocks jutted out from the shore. The high Pacific tides, and the storms of decades, had raised a dam-wall of driftwood; old cut logs, long-lost, weed-tangled, riddled with the bore holes of teredos, jumping with sand fleas. Whole trees were piled there, washed in from distant places, bleached bone-white.

The silence was almost palpable, and enhanced by an unseen bird's cry, a salmon leaping, the near-distant rush of a hidden creek . . .

"Historic day, Jack." Tamara murmured. "It's now been visited by a second human being."

"The tourist rush begins." He was smiling. "Soon, it'll be popcorn, hot dogs and fries. There'll be a Ferris wheel, parking, traffic backed up to Campbell River . . ."

"No, *please* . . ." She sounded stricken. "Don't!"

He was contrite. "It'll never happen here. A bad joke in worse taste," he soothed. "Fiction . . ." He took in the full extent of the cove. "You're right about the untouched feeling. Like a brand-new planet."

She pointed. "There's Mystery Mountain."

The peak was emerging from a veil of high cloud, gleaming

under snow, its fissures shadow-filled. It possessed the air of lonely drama that enveloped all great mountains. He pressed her hand in appreciation. "I must be blind. Almost every day I fly over here, and I've never noticed it."

But, from the air, at a hundred miles per hour, the magic would not be evident. One more strip of shore where the endless forests . . . ended.

They stumbled, wincing, back to the abandoned rucksack, and Tamara lay back, surrendering to the sun. "Might've been fun to swim."

"In any water but that."

"I've swum here on colder days than this."

"No one's stopping you."

"I can't," Tamara admitted. "No bathing suit, either."

"*Still* no one's stopping you . . ."

She laughed, and confessed, "when I swim alone I never have one."

"Should you be telling me this?" His arms were around her then, and, for some time, there was no banter: kissing Tamara was an activity to concentrate the mind. The sense, he thought, of being . . . *consumed*! Eaten alive! The sweet desire to be drawn in, for each to become part of the other . . .

Tamara wanted to know, "what do you think about when you kiss me?"

"Spiders."

She jerked against him. "*What*?"

"You know . . . *spiders*. But in the nicest possible way."

"While you're still ahead," she suggested with firmness. "Maybe you should explain that."

He tried to put into words the strange thoughts and sensations; the wish to form with her a single, perfect whole.

"Sounds stupid," he finished.

"No . . ." Her eyes were grave. "A little weird, but . . . I can see it." She cocked her head. "S*piders*?"

He warned, "this may offend."

"It may indeed. But try me."

He spoke of being consumed. "That's when I remembered those spiders that mate, then, when they're through, she eats him."

"Short and to the point." Tamara accused, "that's kind of yukkie."

"Couldn't help thinking of that old male spider. Maybe Burl Ives could write a song about him? How, as he got gobbled, mindful of what had occurred, he'd be thinking 'way to go, Daddy-o!'"

Tamara wondered, "do you often get like this?"

"Only at full moon . . ." He leered. "And alone with you."

"Hate to disappoint you, but I have no wish to eat you."

"The word," he reminded her. "Was *consume*. Which is open to wider interpretations . . ." He began to laugh.

"Bad enough thinking these things," Tamara said. "Now they're funny?"

"I was thinking of your mother."

"She wouldn't be thrilled."

"Her and her ton-weight picnic. You getting home without me, telling her what you'd done, and her saying . . ." He attempted Rosa's thick accents, "I not givingk 'nough grub?"

She clung to him, laughing. "Do you want to be like the spider, and mate with me?"

He said at once, "yes, Tamara. Very much."

"Like in the movies . . ." Her gaze held his. "This is so sudden."

"Does *that* offend?"

"If we're going to get serious, we should talk it through."

He found the phrasing erotic. "I'd reached the point where I had to say it."

She wanted to know, "how long have you felt this?"

"From about the first five minutes."

"He-e-ey . . . !" Her laugh seemed nervous. "*Jack*!"

"It's true. Suddenly, out of nowhere, a girl like you? Who doesn't exactly discourage me . . ."

She drew him back down to her. "I'd like to be shown some more, I think."

He sought to be gentle, unhurried, *cool*. For everything to go right, but he trembled, and could not control the physical evidence of his *wanting*.

She wore a shirt, and hip-hugging pedal pushers: he saw her bra, the rise and fall of captive breasts, and felt doubt: should he undress her . . . wasn't that how it went? Without effort, the clothes simply . . . melted away? It was like that in novels. Novels, though, did not come with instructions manuals: how breathless, dizzy, with shaking hands, to deal with buttons, zippers, the awkward angles of limbs inside constricting cloth . . .

He retreated to the safe ground of a kiss, finding that, with their lips meeting it became, if not easier, then at least possible to discover ways. Part of the mind, detached, directing the hands on to the paths of exploration that elicited like response. Until, suddenly, she stopped. "Jack, we'd better not . . ."

She despised herself, yet was powerless to prevent it, thinking of the potential disaster that this brief indulgence could bring.

The future Tamara had worked out for herself was painstakingly wrought, each step considered, a well-known route with its milestones and landmarks, a precise map for her to follow.

Still, it held many pitfalls and hazards, few more perilous than the one before her, nor more insidious, drawing her into a situation that could write finis to all hopes.

She *was* much-tempted, *wanting* to *do* this with Jack. This once, couldn't the risk be worth taking? Fifty-fifty odds at *least* of getting away with it, probably more. The sly thought came, it was only when you made a habit of it, like Julie Paulen. Because Paulen, if the stories were true, was at it all the time with Doctor Denkman, probably with Sergeant Prokopchuk as well. Yet she seemed to come to no harm, no sudden alarms or embarrassments.

Thoughts of Paulen, she found, could put a brake on impetuosity, chilling the mind, strengthening resolve. If ever there was a passion-killer, Tamara decided, it was Paulen.

So that she could sidestep the pitfall, and place her hands on Jack's chest, pushing him away. "Look . . . I'm sorry, really."

Fulton lay, frozen there. "What is it, baby? It's okay . . . tell me."

His chest pounded; a pulse was beating in his throat. The hot tide fell back slowly, and there was no anger, nor great disappointment . . . not really.

"I . . . just *can't* . . ." Her words were muffled against him. "I was letting myself forget things."

He echoed, "things . . . ?" And when she did not reply, asked, "was it me . . . ?" A quaintly old-fashioned phrase came to mind. "Did I outrage you?"

"Out . . . ?" She half-choked on laughter. "It's hardly the moment for Jane Austen!"

He offered uneasily. "I'd never forgive myself . . ."

"You did *not* outrage me." She had recovered some poise. "You couldn't."

"Truly?"

"Do outraged women stick around? No . . . I chickened-out. That's all."

"No."

"All right? What would you call it?"

"Being wise?" he suggested. "Being smart?"

She said, "there *is* a reason. I'm not playing bitchy games. When I can find the words, I'll try and explain."

"When you're ready . . ." He kissed her softly. "Any words will do."

*

They lay, hands clasped, drowsy in the late afternoon. Tamara murmured, "there's a plane."

He heard it also, muffled and echoing, the snapping drone of a Beaver at take-off power. "Mike with a trip. Hope he's not stuck with one of mine."

The sound grew louder and the aircraft appeared, misty water streaming from its floats, touching their skins with cold needles as it passed low overhead.

Tamara declared, "he did that on purpose."

"He doesn't know we're here."

"You don't know the Blackfish telegraph. Half the population will have spotted us heading out of town."

"Reckon they put Mike up to it?" He chuckled. "Fly over and cool their ardour?"

She said, subdued, "we didn't need Mike for *that.*"

The Beaver was a dot against a vast backdrop of gold and blue. The salty spray had dried on them.

He wondered, "what should we talk about now?"

"Food," she answered at once. "And not one word about spiders!"

Despite the headway made at lunch, much of the picnic remained. Rosa, that liberal teetotaller, had included six bottles of Lucky Lager. They had drunk two; the others lay immersed in a cold tidal pool. The tide was hurrying in, and he went to retrieve them. "Like one?"

"Could we share?"

They watched the tide's advance across the sand patches, the way it outflanked the rocks and swallowed the pools. Stranded brown kelp was caught up to snake-dance in the currents, and the sand fleas fled ashore . . .

He pointed out, "we don't dare take any grub back."

"We could stay for supper?"

"God . . . there's enough for breakfast as well!"

"Are you suggesting . . ." Her amused eyes quizzed him. ". . . we make a night of it?"

"*That's* a notion."

"I agree," Tamara said.

"But . . . what you said earlier . . ."

"I haven't forgotten. I claim the woman's right to change her mind."

"Oh . . ."

She became brisk. "We can certainly stay for supper . . . lots of time. There'll be hours of daylight for getting back."

"Fine . . ." But he was perplexed by this seeming reversal, the playful game of privilege. The unanswered question—*was* it playful?—teased and needled him.

"Should we do it?" she asked.

"And what does your mother say when we don't show up till tomorrow?"

She looked rueful. "Actually . . . I meant *supper.*"

"Oo-o-oops!" He made himself smile.

"It's a great idea." She touched his hand. "I do like it. And Ma would take that in her stride."

The beer bottle went back and forth.

He had to ask, "does she approve of me?"

"Come on . . . you *know* the answer." Her laughter mocked him. "If she thought I'd let her, she'd have it up in lights."

"What . . . ?"

"Her approval of you."

He offered simply, "I'm glad. What about Stepan?"

"If it's okay with Ma and me, Stepan doesn't give a hoot. That's the side of him I *like*. He's fair and kind, and doesn't interfere. He's always insisted it's my life." She said quickly, "Jack, let's be clear, I'm not hurling myself at you."

"I'd like it if you were."

Her response to that was oblique, although not discouraging. "Stepan would be as tickled as Ma, though, if we wound up married." Her face was averted.

"And you? Would *you* be tickled?"

"If that's a proposal, then it's pretty round and about."

"It could be," he acknowledged. "But no pressure. I love you too much for that."

She told him, "it was always planned that I'd go to college. I'd thought of medicine . . . my grades were okay. That's why I took the hospital job. I thought . . . six months, a year . . . getting the feel. I'd be better-equipped." She searched his face.

"Sounds reasonable . . ." He was puzzled, though, by the line the discussion was taking.

"I wanted to go, but not in a hurry," she said. "But then, instead of working as a nurse, seems I *found* nursing. With my hand to my brow . . . very Sarah Bernhardt. Very Florence Nightingale."

"*Still* sounds reasonable."

"Dear Jack . . . always there . . ." Her hand stroked his. ". . . with the right word."

"We do our best."

The Beaver was returning, the distant engine note a faint pressure on the air; the reminder that this day was nearing its end.

Tamara spotted it first. "There . . ."

Mike Denholm was down on the water, fooling around. The distant midge grew wings, the dots of floats seemed to skim the flat sea.

"That looks like a real ball." Tamara turned her face to him. "Next time we fly together, could we try that?"

"As long as there's a next time."

"We'll find a way," she said.

And, yes, let's do that, he thought. "We'll roar off, and play games."

"Like today's games?"

"Those weren't games."

"Jack," she said. "Let's not take it too seriously yet."

"Someone should. I wasn't looking for a roll in the hay. And that certainly wasn't one."

She replied with a renewed pressure on his hand.

The Beaver passed overhead, climbing to clear the ridge, drifting from view, throttled back, descending for the landing.

They propped themselves against a bare-bones tree as the sea crept closer.

He prompted, "so, tell me about nursing."

She lowered the beer bottle. "I'm hooked, I suppose."

"Wouldn't qualifying as a doctor be a better deal?"

"Maybe . . ." She nodded. "But I can't get steamed-up about it now. It's in my head . . . I'd prefer an R.N. to an M.D."

He remembered Eric's words: '. . . she's a natural'.

"That's my first aim. What I've been winding up to tell you. Other things . . . I'm sorry, but, for now, they have to take a back seat. Once I'm on the register, I can start shaping my life around what I've achieved . . ." She glanced at him again quickly. "But not until."

"All right, Tamara."

"I *do* want to be with you, Jack." Her mouth tightened. "Stopping you and myself like that, I hated it, and had to."

"Sure. Fine . . ."

"I want it to be for *real*. Really you, really me. Nothing artificial or forced." She faced him frankly. "Does it make you unhappy, hearing this?"

"I wanted to know. I kind of guessed what was coming."

"We've talked a lot today. Things we'd never have mentioned a week ago." She hesitated. "Like . . . marriage?"

"But not just yet," he supplied.

"Please, Jack . . . ?"

"Which does seem to imply *some*time?"

"If sometime will do?"

"Fine for now. It gives me a goal."

"I don't know what the rules are about married nursing students," Tamara said. "Or even if it's allowed."

"I should think not. That could play hell with your studies."

"And be horribly unfair to you."

"Yet, if we did, I'd be taking that on as part of the deal . . ." But she was shaking her head, and he let it go.

"It'd be awful for us both . . ." She gave a little abashed laugh. "And then I'd be pregnant."

He smiled. "And there goes nursing out the window and I'd have to find employment to keep you both in gruel."

She smiled faintly. "That's something I wouldn't want to happen yet."

Sure . . ."

She said reflectively, "three years. Another year if I do midwifery. Although, then, I'd have my R.N., and could marry . . ." Her tone was dry. "I could practice my craft on *me*. If you still wanted me?"

"I'd still want you."

"And that's me," Tamara said, and asked, "what about you?"

He told her, "been thinking how we might make something of this time in between."

He talked of the Air Force, feeling his way into a new career. Like Tamara he would face a lengthy training period, the token familiarisation course on Harvards at an F.T.S. After which there would be the move to advanced jet flying, and the eventual award of wings. Which, it seemed certain, would lead back to the classroom at Trenton, the Flying Instructors' School in Ontario. "Where, I'll learn to dish it out instead of take it. All of which adds up to much work, and a social life stripped bare."

She nodded. "We'll be in the same boat."

"As long as I don't pull any spectacular boners."

"You won't," she said.

"I mentioned holding a short-service commission. Five years, normally, then a polite letter of resignation, and hit the road."

"Yes? So?" Tamara looked questioning.

"*So* . . . instead, I put in for a permanent commission. Qualified, I'd be more of an asset. It costs a bundle to train a pilot, and they like to get some mileage."

"What would be the advantages for you?"

"Job for life . . . doing something I enjoy. Nice pension at the end, and still not completely over the hill." He grinned. "We'd be in our fifties."

"Darby and Joan? Kicking up our rheumaticky heels?"

"Speak for yourself," he said.

"But, the Air Force . . . full time?" she wondered. "Would that be okay for you?"

"It beats going to jail."

She admitted, "I like the idea. It's responsible . . . caring."

"I care, Tamara. That's something you *should* know."

SEVEN

During the night, low pressure moved in from the Pacific. Fulton awakened to the lash of rain against the window. The temperature had tumbled and a gale churned the Sound to whiteness. Inland, the valleys were filled with cloud and rain.

It was pounding down still harder when Alice Royle called. "*So* sorry, but we have an accident at Nimpkish Lake."

"Where?"

"It's Camp 'C', I'm afraid."

It would have to be Camp 'C', he thought. Farthest up and most inaccessible. Lying between rock walls, where the lake, reduced to a narrowing finger, allowed only minimal turning space which, even under favourable conditions, demanded precise flying. To go in there blind, with turbulence and unknown wind-drift, could be asking for trouble . . .

"Are you still there?" Alice Royle enquired.

"Wish I wasn't. Just checking the weather."

"What do you think?"

"That it's a perfect day to be a bank teller." He heard her chuckle. "Not good, although the pass through to Nimpkish looks like it could be open. Trouble is, the terrain climbs several hundred feet to the near end of the lake. If the cloud's on the deck there, then forget it."

"Could you go and see?"

"Can do," he agreed without enthusiasm.

Alice Royle offered tentatively, "according to the camp superintendent, their weather's quite good."

"They always say that. Anything to make us fly."

"They can be naughty," she acknowledged. "Nevertheless, it places us in a quandary."

"It places *me*," he retorted. "On the assurances of some self-seeking camp super, I end up in quandary soup. Like alphabet soup, only thicker. Less easy to penetrate with all those rocks in it."

She chided, "now, now . . ."

"Don't worry. Just a little spleen-venting." He asked, "what kind of case is it?"

"One that can't be delayed. Another choker-setter . . . badly hurt."

He peered towards the pass, the visibly lowering cloud-base. "Guess I'm stuck with it."

"You'll go?"

"Don't know about *go*. But for the casualty, and our reputation, I'll give it a whirl."

*

He was airborne after a short, bumpy run. Turbulence struck at once; he held the climb through vicious down-drafts, circling Englewood and Beaver Cove to gain height before turning into the pass, with the loom of half-hidden mountains off each wingtip.

With the land still rising ahead, he ran into cloud at seven hundred feet, and decided that that was enough heroics. Letting the altimeter unwind slowly, he eased down on instruments into clear air . . .

"Foxtrot-Lima-Juliet . . ." Alice Royle sounded tinny in the headset. "Free to talk?"

"Go ahead, Blackfish . . ." The Seabee hit a bump hard enough to lift it back among the hanging vapour tendrils. He clung on, thinking of what goes up must come down. The bottom seemed to drop out of the world as the aircraft plunged in the following downdraft, and he throttled back to cushion some of the shock from the deflection of the descending air column.

"Lima-Juliet, do you read?" There was anxiety in the tinny voice.

"Roger, Blackfish . . . I was busy there."

"I'll keep this brief. Camp 'C' knows you're on your way in atrocious conditions, and that we promise nothing."

"That's telling 'em." Fulton rode out a fresh updraft-downdraft sequence. "Anything on the patient?"

"Extremely poorly. Negative details."

"I'm in the pass now . . ." The Seabee was sandwiched between cloud and the thickly-wooded ground. He saw the Nimpkish River below, ragged white where it tumbled through rapids. Mountains soared on either side, losing themselves in seeping grey vapour. He flew on through a drab tunnel filled with streaming water and tumultuous air, and could not see its end. Only the spot, a half-mile ahead, where land and cloud merged in gloom . . ."Advise them I'm doing what I can," he told Alice Royle. "I'm fifteen minutes away, but still no guarantees." And cut her off with a terse, "Lima-Juliet *out*!"

Fifteen minutes was a short flight; twenty five miles for a Seabee. Too long, though, and too far, on that day. Still short of Nimpkish Lake, he found that the tunnel had no end. Climbing ground and dropping clouds met to build an impenetrable barrier.

Fulton turned out of the pass in air so rough that it seemed to be on the point, more than once, of hurling the Seabee on to its back. Until, with relief—and some guilt—he flew out of it.

"Blackfish, I'm over Englewood, unable to clear the pass. The weather's right in the trees."

Alice Royle accepted without comment. "Roger, Lima-Juliet. Blackfish standing by."

Guilt was greater than relief: he couldn't just tamely *quit*. "Blackfish, I'll cruise the shore a few miles each way . . . look for a gap to sneak through. If I'm lucky, I'll work out a revised E.T.A., and you can inform Camp 'C'."

She replied by the book, then forgot herself enough to warn, "you take care. Don't be too venturesome."

It made him laugh, thinking gratefully . . . fine, Alice. But what are the options?

He flew without success down-coast almost to Kelsey Bay, then reversed course back into the wind's teeth, estimating his speed over the ground now at no more than sixty miles per hour. Back to Englewood and Beaver Cove, on by Alert Bay and Port McNeill, bouncing and soaring, hammered by rain. While, all along the Island's length, the overcast hung sullen and lumpish about the mountain shoulders, spilling its greyness into every valley.

He gave up then. "Blackfish, it's no-go."

Alice Royle asked him to stand by; his transmission had blocked another message. She was quickly back: it had been Camp 'C' on the radio. "It's no longer possible to reach them. Their own weather has worsened."

"That's it," he said. "Full house."

The patient would be brought down to Englewood over the logging roads. It would need two hours to cover the twenty-five miles. Could Fulton be there to meet them?

"I'll wait at Englewood," he promised. "It's the least we can do."

*

The Dodge Power Wagon bearing the casualty was late arriving.

"Sorry . . . blew a tyre half-way," the driver called. "Then the jack was fucked. Had to cut down a sapling, and lever the old son of a bitch."

Fulton asked, "how's the patient?"

"*We* made it." The driver shrugged. "He didn't . . ."

The shrouded body was carried down. "Wasn't no point you comin'," the first-aider declared. "He'd never have lived. Some dumb kid torn up to ratshit."

Fulton did not care much for the first-aider. He had a tough, thankless job, and must be objective; no room for sentiment. There could still be, though, some compassion? Caring cost little . . .

The first-aider seemed to guess his thoughts. "*He* won't give a shit now what any bastard says or thinks." He wondered if Fulton would fly the body out unattended. "No good me goin'. Only ones interested now's the coroner and the Mounties. If I go, I'll be stuck till I can get a ride back."

Only five minutes, Fulton reflected. Only another lifeless body. A short, rough trip, but the dead man was unlikely to complain about the service. And *what* was that, he wondered then, about caring . . . compassion?

EIGHT

He was with Tamara in Hong's Café when the constable found them. "*Just* who I'm looking for."

Tamara eyed Fulton. "What have you *done*, Jack?"

"I was about to ask you that." He asked the constable instead, "will I need a lawyer?"

"Not unless we bust you for the way you fly."

"That's *always* a possibility."

The constable looked at Tamara. "Sorry to break up a meeting between friends."

She assured him earnestly, "I've never seen this man before in my life."

"What they all say." He informed Fulton, "Sarge wondered if you'd stop by the office."

"Do I have a choice?"

"Not really. He wants you for a job."

"As long as it's lawful."

"With us, you can never tell . . ." The constable suggested to Tamara, "as I've put the kibosh on your coffee break, could I offer you a ride home?"

"In a *police* car?"

"It's all I've got. These are tough times."

"Thank you kindly, but perforce, no," Tamara said. "I have a reputation to live up to in this town."

Interested, Fulton asked, "What's with 'perforce'?"

"I'm a well-read young thing." She smiled with sweet malice. "By time you get back from where you seem to be going, *you* could be well-read, too!"

*

Sergeant Prokopchuk announced heavily, "I've cleared it with Alice Royle."

Fulton nodded. "So, where to?"

"Middle of nowhere . . ."

He's not in the best of moods, Fulton registered, and wondered if Prokopchuk's notorious zeal was proving burdensome. Or could it be Grad Nurse Paulen R.N.? He offered lightly, "routine trip, then."

"Take a look here." Prokopchuk indicated the large wall map of the northern end of Vancouver Island, the area of the upper Queen Charlotte Strait. "Somewhere there. We'll need to search."

"For what?"

"Two Indian gillnetters." Prokopchuk said tightly, "we may have a murder on our hands. There's a body to bring in."

One gillnetter travelling down from Bella Coola had come upon the other drifting off Cape Caution in heavy seas, its fishing gear in disarray. The Bella Coola boat had run alongside to offer assistance, but none was needed. A man lay on deck beside the net drum. Despite the sea and rain there was still a lot of blood. A gaff-hook bore signs of having been used as a weapon.

"This fellow radioed in," Prokopchuk explained. "He's trying to haul the derelict into Seymour Inlet. He'll wait until we get there." Fulton nodded. "How's about this weather?"

Conditions had improved since the abortive Camp 'C' trip two days earlier. The cloud had broken to give sunlight between showers. If the boats were found in open seas, then it was wind which would present problems. Still blowing strongly enough to raise heavy breakers in which the Seabee could not land . . .

Fulton explained all that.

"A little *wind*, and we don't go?" Prokopchuk demanded.

"That's not what I said." Fulton gave him a level stare. "We can go, we can search, and find. What I can't promise out there is a safe landing." He looked pointedly at the ribbon and rosette on Prokopchuk's tunic. "You should understand that. Would you have landed your Lancaster in those conditions?"

"Halifax." Prokopchuk smiled thinly.

"Pardon me . . . ?"

"I flew the Handley Page Halifax. Never got on to Lancs, worst luck."

"You wouldn't've landed your *Halifax* in those sea conditions, then."

"Not unless pushed. She was a landplane."

"And for all the good a Seabee could do in half a gale, it might as well be the same."

"Fair enough." Prokopchuk nodded. "Let's go take a look."

"If there's any chance of a landing, then I'll try," Fulton promised. "But you wouldn't thank me for ditching you."

Prokopchuk mused, "if this fellow's found sheltered water . . ."

"End of problem." Irritation retreated as Prokopchuk gave ground. And it's not my job to pick fights with the cash customers, Fulton reminded himself. "You mentioned Seymour Inlet. That should be a better set-up."

Prokopchuk said then, "I'll be going with you."

"Yes, of course." Fulton pondered with little enthusiasm the prospect of flying under the critical eye of a man with four-engine experience. Who had faced flak and fighters, and won medals doing it. Weighed against that, twelve hundred hours on small airplanes could seem puny indeed.

*

Prokopchuk sat in silence, studying the instrument panel and controls with professional interest as Fulton climbed the Seabee to a thousand feet. Heading for Cape Caution, sixty miles to the north-west.

He faced the same quartering headwind which had plagued the Zeballos and Camp 'C' flights, but a more kindly wind, strong and steady, with only occasional turbulence.

Its effect on the sea was disturbing. Queen Charlotte Strait looked cold and angry, with steep waves running on a surface clawed to whiteness by the nails of wind.

Prokopchuk leaned forward. "See what you mean about landing."

Fulton shook his head. "I wouldn't even look at it."

"Allow me to admit I'm glad."

The dry acknowledgement could surprise: Fulton had been prepared for a difficult passenger, one who would carp and make unreasonable demands. So far, though, Prokopchuk was quiet, seemingly at ease, riding the bumps with the familiarity of long practice.

The Seabee wallowed on, the minutes inching by on the instrument panel clock. Through showers which reduced visibility sharply: a heavy squall line ran down on them, a curling fringe of rent and matted grey cloud like dirty wool, with the opaque midnight-blue wall of the rain tramping behind; revealing with startling suddenness the full perfect circle of the airborne rainbow. They flew through the squall for what seemed a long time, shaken and buffeted, until they emerged into air scrubbed clean and sparkling, with the mountains around Smith and Seymour Inlets, the blunt promontory of Cape Caution appreciably closer. Now five miles distant, Seymour Inlet lay within its guarding arms of land, an arrowhead-shaped islet at the entrance pointing the way to sheltered water within . . .

Prokopchuk was pointing. "There he is . . . first go!"

The two small boats, lashed abeam and pitching hideously, were a mile to seaward of the arrowhead islet, a stubby wake indicating their slow progress.

"Take her down . . . give him a buzz," Prokopchuk directed. "See what the score is."

Fulton eased off power, allowing the Seabee to descend shallowly, feeling the increasing roughness of the lower air. He levelled off at fifty feet, holding the aircraft as it bucked and skittered towards the boats.

"Give me a steep turn to the left as you pass over. I want a closer look."

With resignation Fulton thought, I guess he's taking charge. No more Mister Nice Guy. He made the turn very steep, with power on, pulling back on the yoke so that Prokopchuk would feel the centrifugal force: maybe a little 'G' would remind him who was boss . . .

He glanced down as they flew over the boats. The Indian skipper, a chunky man in a yellow oilskin jacket, stood outside the pilothouse, staring up. On the accompanying craft, a still figure lay huddled over the net-drum.

Prokopchuk was making energetic hand signals, pointing shoreward. He ordered, "head off in that direction so's he gets my drift."

Biting back a sharper retort, Fulton observed, "think he'd got that before we showed up."

"Take her inside. We'll wait for him."

Fulton gave up: you'd never win with a Mountie hot on the trail. He flew obediently into the inlet where the wind *was* less severe, the water calmer. "But if I don't see something suitable . . ."

"You will. I have faith in you." Prokopchuk grinned without mirth. Maybe he sounded like that in the old days, Fulton mused. Rallying his gunners as the Messerschmitts swarmed in . . .

"There . . . *that* looks good!" Prokopchuk pointed ahead. "Try that!"

"*Jawohl, mein Führer* . . ." Fulton followed the pointing finger, and saw the cove, thinking . . . he can pick them, still. A deep indentation in the rocky shore, wide, plenty of water, well-sheltered, although a considerable swell was running at the entrance . . .

"Line up along that ridge," Prokopchuk directed. "Then left on to final approach, chop the power, and glide her in. You'll be on the water in the first fifty yards."

"You're never going to believe this," Fulton told him. "But that's exactly what I intended doing."

"Of course, sorry . . ." Prokopchuk looked vexed.

"Unless *you'd* like to shoot the landing yourself?" It was said before he could prevent it.

"Don't tempt me . . ." There was amusement, and a hint of wistfulness in the other's voice. "I'd love to, but I couldn't do it the way you do."

"I'm not sure if that's a compliment or not, but never mind . . ." In the mood now to atone, Fulton kept it light.

"I forgot myself," Prokopchuk confessed. "Bad old habits die hard."

In continuing atonement, Fulton flew the approach Prokopchuk's way, and it was an excellent approach with a soft touch-down in deep, safe water. He steered in slowly towards a strip of firm-looking sand, pumping down the landing gear so that the wheels would make first contact. They bumped gently, rolling ahead over hard tidal sand. "Looks good," Prokopchuk called. "Hardly leaving a tyre track . . ." He added, quickly apologetic, "thought you'd care to know." The Seabee surged on to the beach, water pouring off the hull.

"Now we wait, I guess," Fulton said.

With the engine shut down, the wind and wave sounds seemed very loud, and surf was beating up white at the cove's entrance.

Prokopchuk studied his watch. "He ought to be inside soon."

"He was close enough to figure out what we were doing."

"Let's hope so . . ." Prokopchuk sounded disparaging. "Never can tell what goes on in an Indian's head."

The Indian, though, did what was expected of him.

Forty minutes after landing, the sound of a powerful diesel became audible, and the two boats crept into sight, one ancient and decrepit, one sleekly modern.

Prokopchuk grunted, "he's done well for himself. That's thirty thousand dollars' worth of boat. While that other thing . . ." He was shaking his head. "The bloody wrecks they go out in. Never thinking of the weather."

"Maybe the weather killed the owner?"

Prokopchuk was expressionless. "Maybe."

The boats entered the cove, coming on slowly, and Prokopchuk waved them closer. Both rolled heavily, riding the surf at the entrance. There were tyre fenders over the sides of both to protect the hulls, and the squeal of tortured rubber came to them across the water. They were close enough now for their names, painted on the bows, to be made out: the new craft was *Caroline M.*, the other, *Weetsisiya.*

"Standard oddball Indian name," Prokopchuk said.

"What does it mean?"

"Pretty much what you want it to. Kwakiutl greeting . . . 'Hi', 'Good morning', 'How are you'. Probably dreamed up at some drunken potlatch."

"No bigotry here," Fulton murmured.

The boats, masts swaying, were almost stationary.

"If he can inch up to the sand and put an anchor over, we could wade out with the stretcher." Prokopchuk cocked an eye. "If you're game?"

"It seems I am."

"'Anything, Anywhere, Anytime', remember?"

"I don't recall any provision for swimming," Fulton said.

Suddenly, sharply, Prokopchuk demanded, "what in hell's he *doing*?"

The *Caroline M.* was backing away through a swirl of water. Prokopchuk's parade ground bellow challenged the wind, "DON'T BACK OFF . . . BRING HER *IN*!" He beckoned furiously.

The Indian, out on deck, refused with a sweeping horizontal gesture. A young woman had emerged from the pilot-house.

"Probably bloody Caroline M.," Prokopchuk said crossly.

The Indian was shouting, the wind fragmenting his words, ". . . NOT 'NOUGH *WATER* . . . ECHO SOUNDER RUNNIN' . . . PLENTY ROCKS . . . COULD WRECK MY *BOAT* . . . !"

Prokopchuk snapped, "bugger it!"

"Well, that rules out wading . . ."

"If you've nothing constructive to say, then please keep quiet!" Before Fulton could respond, he had turned away. "IT'S *OKAY* HERE . . . GOOD SMOOTH SAND!"

"I DRAW FOUR FOOT O' WATER . . . TIDE'S ON THE EBB . . ." the answer came back. "YOU GUYS . . . COME OUT TO *ME* . . . !"

"That's it, then." Prokopchuk ordered furiously, "let's go!"

"That's what I like about you," Fulton said. "No 'please' or 'thank you' or 'would you mind?' A real pleasure working with you!"

Taxying out, he thought at least I made my point.

He told Prokopchuk, "I'm not staying alongside in this water. I'll nose in, and you can step across. You'll have to work something out with the stretcher. Get those two to help you."

"And if that doesn't work?"

"Then we're out of luck!"

The *Caroline M.* lay a hundred yards distant. Boat and airplane were rising and falling on foot-high waves, their movements erratic and unsynchronised. The boats' bulk and weight were quite sufficient to crush the aircraft's frail metal skin.

"It may not matter to you," Prokopchuk said wrathfully. "But we're still dealing with a *murder* here."

"It matters, but it's your murder. My main concern is my aircraft. I'm not getting our necks in a sling for someone who's dead and doesn't care . . ." Fulton's heart was racing; he regained control, saying more quietly, "*you* know how airplanes are. We tangle up with those boats and we're in trouble."

"*Okay*!" Prokopchuk cut his hand down in frustration. "Just do what you *can*!"

The gap was fifty yards: on the *Caroline M.* the woman was at the wheel, the man busy dropping more fenders over.

"About the body." Prokopchuk was terse. "I need to examine it, then it goes to Blackfish for autopsy. Delays can destroy forensic evidence, things an autopsy might have revealed lost to conjecture, or plain don't know. Which means a lost case, someone unpunished."

He was hot on punishment, Fulton remembered. Stepan had said it: Porkchop would jail you for spitting in the street. And murder was more serious . . .

Fulton replied, "I'll do what's possible." He reached up to the reverse pitch control, flipping off the metal safety guard, ready to stop the Seabee in the water. From that point it would get tricky. "I'll need your help."

Prokopchuk nodded. "Just say."

"Open the bow-hatch, and be ready to fend us off . . . and expect to get wet."

"All right."

"We mustn't bang against his hull too much."

"Understood."

"Have the Indian grab a wingtip and hold it clear. That's vital."

Prokopchuk stood in the open hatch with the waves slapping into the bow, soaking him. "Can't say about the stretcher," Fulton called in warning. "That looks plain impossible."

"If we have to, we'll manage without it."

Fulton tried not to picture that. A stretchered corpse, decently-shrouded, was one thing. But . . . sprawled there on the cabin floor beside him, like a wino sleeping it off? He would have much preferred the wino . . . even the worst wino in the world.

"I'll lie off until you're ready to load. How long will you need?"

"Minutes? To check the body and the scene, then the actual loading. Why?"

"More than fifteen minutes, I'll have to head back to the beach. You know how it goes . . . low power settings and fouled-up plugs."

"Point taken." Prokopchuk gave a nod. "But I'd sooner you were nearby."

"Then kindly make it snappy."

The first contact with the boat surprised and pleased Fulton with its gentleness, the nose touching lightly against a fender. The Indian was in position at the wingtip, the woman stood at the wheel.

Fresh waves surged up: Fulton felt them rolling under him, saw how the nose lifted against the boat's side, metal squealing against rubber. Prokopchuk had one foot still on the step inside the Seabee's bow, the other resting precariously on the boat's rubbing strake. He bent his body awkwardly, reaching in to seize the empty basket stretcher, drawing it out past him in one convulsive movement, hurling it on to the boat's deck.

As he went to step after it, the *Caroline M.* fell into a trough, leaving the Seabee still riding the crest. Fulton saw him lurch sideways off-balance, heard him yell angrily at the pitching boat, "HOLD *STILL* YOU GOD-DAMN' SON OF A *WHORE*!" He clung to the gunwale as the Seabee followed the boat, swooping down into the trough.

Fulton shouted, "you *okay*?"

"So far! But I'm too old for this bullshit!"

A wave sprang up, soaking him to the hips: the boat lurched sideways, and he went with it across the gunwale to sprawl on the deck as boat and aircraft fell away.

The Indian released the wingtip, and Fulton reversed clear. Prokopchuk was on his feet, his cap gone, dripping water, red-faced with exertion. He turned away and, followed by the Indian, boarded the *Weetsisiya*. The wind was freshening, piling waves in the open inlet. Fulton watched them anxiously, nursing the throttle, letting the airplane weathercock naturally into wind.

In less than ten minutes, Prokopchuk was signalling him to re-approach. In which time the water had become perceptibly more choppy, the waves starting to topple. It was going to be difficult, if not impossible, to remain alongside the boat without suffering damage. He edged closer, worrying about that, about retrieving the laden stretcher, about the *time* it would take . . .

Once more the nose rubbed against a tyre fender and now the woman was at the wingtip. Air and water rushed in as Prokopchuk pulled open the bow-hatch, shouting, "no *stretcher*! We'll never make it . . . he goes as *is*!"

"Oh, Jesus . . . !" Fulton watched, stricken, as Prokopchuk dragged the limp corpse up, loosely-wrapped in sodden blankets, to hang over the gunwale, dripping. A twist of wind carried the cloying foulness of putrefaction into the cabin.

Prokopchuk was preparing to step across when boat and airplane soared over a crest. There was a crash as the bow slipped between two fenders, and into the boat's hull. Fulton did not wait, sliding the propeller into reverse. The engine rumbled, and the Seabee slid away, leaving Prokopchuk clinging to the gunwale, bellowing.

Fulton ignored him, concentrating on bringing the nose back against the tyres. For three attempts his efforts were fruitless as the wild water dipped the two craft perilously towards each other.

The fourth try brought him close enough to hear clearly Prokopchuk's shouted accusation, "you're supposed to be a God-damned *professional*! Is this the best you can do . . . ?"

"Hell with YOU!" It was monstrously unjust, and Fulton cared no longer what anyone thought or said or did, least of all bloody *Porkchop*! "I'm busting my balls, you prick! If that's how you see it, then I'm gone, and you can *stay* . . . !" They glared their shared detestation, and then, made reckless by rage, hardly caring, Fulton brought the Seabee back against the boat's side. The nose bumped and the two rode together, for the moment not dipping or sliding. Prokopchuk was gripping the body, signalling to the Indian to help, as Fulton commanded, "skip that! Leave it!"

Prokopchuk turned, staring. "What . . . ?"

"Leave it, and get in here. If you don't, I'm going . . . *now*!"

Without a word, Prokopchuk stumbled through the bow-hatch, and Fulton reversed away.

"What the *hell* do you think you're . . . ?"

"Shut the hatch," Fulton said.

Prokopchuk did it, then crouched, the water running off his sodden uniform.

"That's it, eh? We quit?"

"It'd be justified, Sergeant. The company would back me!"

"I'm telling you now . . ."

"Not telling . . . you're a *passenger*! Pilots do the telling . . ."

"We'll see about that when your precious company hears . . ."

"Complain your fill, but I'll have some things to say, too!"

Fulton taxied in a circle, clear of the boats. On deck, the Indian couple watched them, unmoving. The dead bundle swayed, forsaken, straddling the gunwale.

The turning circle was almost completed when Fulton noticed the smooth water in their wake, and remembered . . . *the training movie*.

An instructional film on seamanship and ship-handling from his midshipman days: a vessel at sea in rough water, turning at speed, the water inside the turn flattened by the circling movement. Like that now in the Seabee's diminutive wake. There had been a floatplane in the film, orbiting as the parent ship smoothed the surface for its landing . . .

He said, "there's something that may work."

"Oh? Let's hear it."

Fulton spelled it out; the ship turning, the smoothed-out water . . .

Prokopchuk looked disbelieving. "You want him to go round in *circles*?"

"Just the one. At full throttle."

"And then?"

"Complete the circle . . . stop. I'll go alongside in the flattened water, and we'll try and get your corpse." Fulton eyed him coldly. "Unless you can suggest anything better?"

Prokopchuk took the gibe without comment. "All right."

"Have him cast off the other boat while he circles. They can collect it afterwards. I want every fender he's got over the side, and anything else soft. I want to touch down on a feather bed!"

*

The Indian took the wheel, and the powerful boat jumped forward, the water lashed white under the stern. As the helm went hard over the *Caroline M.* heeled until her outer rubbing strake was almost submerged, and a widening patch of smoothed, glittering surface began to form.

Fulton turned, too, inside the circle, steering for the point where it would be completed. He was fifteen yards away when the bow hit the wake's tail, and the Indian took her astern, stopped, and the boat lay in the water, rolling uneasily. Fulton taxied in, reversed the propeller, and was rewarded by the soft squelch of the nose against cushioning rubber.

Prokopchuk bridged the unsteady gap with his long legs, seizing the body's nearer end while the Indian took the other. They heaved together, and the mass tumbled heavily and wetly on to the cabin floor . . .

Fulton gagged as the terrible stench locked in his nostrils, looking down at water, pinkish with blood, that oozed over the aluminum plating . . .

"Okay . . . get out of here!" Prokopchuk, still clinging to the boat, leaned in.

Fulton looked up with streaming eyes. "What about you?"

"I'm staying . . . I'm sure *that'll* make you happy!"

The *Weetsisiya* was evidence: the Indian couple were witnesses. Without him there, he could not count upon them to show up at Blackfish Harbour. "I'm going to see they make it. And that you get your stretcher back." He ordered brusquely, "now, *go*. I want our friend there safe in the cooler when I get in." He slammed the hatch, leaving Fulton alone with the body . . . and the smell.

*

Beginning the take-off run, with the throttle half-open, the Franklin missed, backfired noisily, and lost power. Advancing the throttle further only made things worse. Fulton pulled off power, letting the Seabee settle back in the troughs. It had to be plugs; the engine had been idling too long: they would be fouled by carbon deposits, possibly oil as well.

He was able to taxy back downwind, and re-position the Seabee for another attempt, hoping that, this time, the deposits might burn off . . .

At half-throttle, the same thing happened, the engine losing power, the aircraft subsiding into the waves.

On board the *Caroline M.*, Prokopchuk was signalling, the unmistakeable movement, back and forth, of an aircraft's throttle. And there he goes *again*, Fulton thought wrathfully. Telling me my bloody job! He yelled furiously, unavailingly, "I KNOW, GOD DAMN IT!"

Near the beach, he turned into the wind once more, advancing the throttle gingerly. The Seabee surged forward until, at twenty inches of manifold pressure, the Franklin spluttered and faltered . . .

He cursed aloud, so angry and frustrated, that, momentarily, he could ignore the presence at his side of the stinking, saturated corpse. Four further attempts to get airborne met with no success, and he began to fear for the overworked engine. Yet, an inner voice drove him on: 'keep at it, it's only carbon, and carbon burns away. And Porkchop, for sure, won't let you forget if you quit . . . !'

He turned away downwind, fast-taxying, using all the power the Franklin would provide to try and clear the plugs. He swung the Seabee hard back into wind, feeling the lurch as a wingtip float dug in, thinking . . . the hell with *that*! I can't be bothered with it now . . .

He was feeding in power, and the aircraft was answering, rising on to the step, feeling lighter, the control surfaces responsive to a hardening airflow. He inched the throttle forward and watched the manifold pressure gauge as the needle approached the critical mark . . . eighteen inches . . . nineteen . . . twenty. The engine coughed, and he shouted, "God DAMN you!" But the cough was left behind; it had smoothed out, the needle climbing to '25', nearing full power . . . the flickering response to a fresh splutter, then smoothing once more as the scrap of carbon burned away. The needle reached '30', and, holding his breath, he pushed the throttle fully open.

Waves slammed under the hull. Like a washboard road beneath a car's juddering wheels. Until, as the Seabee left the water, the drumming ceased.

Fulton remained tense; the engine could still fail. He had passed through the inlet's entrance, back out over the open and wind-lashed strait: a failure now would mean an immediate forced landing down there, almost certainly another, fresher corpse.

But the Franklin did not falter, and the Seabee climbed steadily. He throttled back at a thousand feet with the beginning, but still uncertain, hope that crisis might be overcome . . .

The slow release of tension brought its drawbacks, freeing his mind once more to the awareness of his immediate surroundings, to the hideous cargo and its inescapable reek.

He flew on, choking and nauseous, and reflected with bitter irony on the boasts of men to be created in God's image: what could there be that was remotely *godlike* in that sprawled and flopping foulness? Some irresistible compulsion made him glance down at it, and look upon a new, unanticipated horror.

The shrouding blanket had worked loose to expose the head that lolled on an old man's thin, stringy neck. The terrible face watched him, swollen and discoloured with mottlings of purple, red, black, yellow, a greenish coppery sheen, the skin tautened to bursting under pressures within that threatened to free the liquefied flesh. Pressures which pried the jaws apart in a wide, frozen grin that exposed pale gums and stained teeth, a thickened, lolling tongue: the features of some malevolent clown . . . God's dead face was stubbled and filthy, the nostrils filled with blackened blood. Thinning hair strands, matted by sea and rain, lay across the forehead.

The eyes were gone.

Choice prey for questing seabirds, only the red-rimmed cavities remaining, shredded by thrusting beaks . . .

His mind shouted at him to turn AWAY . . . why do you LOOK? There was no need: nothing now, or ever, to be done for the face, for the vanished eyes that still seemed to watch him accusingly from darkness. No comfort to offer, or secrets to share. Who but some sick voyeur would *want* to look at that, his appalled mind demanded. Yet Fulton could not turn away until he had done the one thing that he most feared and hated to do. Face crinkling with disgust, he must reach out to pull the blanket back into place. Forcing himself with the bile sour and burning in his throat, to tuck it in under the crushed head so that the head's weight might hold it in place for a little longer . . . for as long as it took.

He *could* turn away then, and see, like a well-earned reward, things that were good and right and normal, coming closer, within reach. Steep slopes dropping to the quiet bay, the houses and pierheads, the exhausted strip of road. On the dark water, Mike Denholm in the Beaver beginning his take-off run . . .

He came in high over the Private Place, his nostrils clotted with death and decay, that smell on his clothes, in his hair, now on the cringing fingers of one hand . . .

As he completed the pre-landing checks, Fulton could reflect that, in miles flown, at a nickel a mile, *this* experience had been worth just six dollars and fifty cents!

NINE

Olaf Pedersen said flatly, "no disrespect, but he's not ridin' inside!"

"So what do we do?" Fulton asked.

"Got a little trailer back at the store I can hook on." Pedersen nodded at the bundle. "He won't mind."

The Seabee was moored. Jackie Seaweed was perched on the lift strut with the fuel hose thrust into the filler pipe. He had helped with the unloading, saying nothing, showing nothing. All three cabin doors gaped wide open to let the fresh air through, and the Indian had promised to use plenty of carbolic on the wash-down . . .

"Back soon, Jackie," Pedersen promised. "Just keep an eye on buddy-boy."

The Indian did not look up. "If he comes to, I'll buy him a beer."

Inside the Ford, Pedersen wrinkled his nose. "Maybe I shouldn't let *you* in, neither."

"*That* bad, is it?"

"You're pretty ripe . . ." Pedersen grinned. "Should pick your passengers more careful."

"I agree." Fulton nodded. "Porkchop *and* that poor bastard." Away from the corpse, he could re-discover pity.

"Don't worry about it," Pedersen told him. "I get 'em in the store worse'n that, and they're *alive* . . ." He confided, laughing, "what really bothers me is them Indian dogs. They catch that scent, there'll be only picked bones time I get back. Might eat your dockhand, too . . . they're not fussy."

Longing for the shower, for odourless skin and clean clothes, Fulton crouched in his seat as Pedersen regaled him with stories of Indian village dogs.

"Everywhere I go, they chase the Goddam car, hootin' and hollerin'. Had a few under the wheels, too . . . Indian mutts are too damn' dumb to live. Don't enjoy hurtin' 'em, although there's one bugger I *really* hate. Nigh on had me off the road more'n once, till I fixed his wagon for him . . ." The dog would run beside the Ford, snapping at the doors and windows. "Got good and tired of findin' my paint scratched up by his Christly claws . . ."

On a subsequent visit to the Indian village, anticipating the now-inevitable encounter, Pedersen had been ready.

"Drove nice and slow, with the window wound down. Sure as shootin', there he was, the dumb prick, all hunkered-down like a one-mutt ambush." The dog charged, leaping at the open window. "I reach down, grab him by the neck, and don' let go," Pedersen recounted happily, "then I hit th' gas, wound the old rig here up around sixty right through the village, draggin' him with his feet on the ground. Hung on must've been a quarter-mile . . ." Fulton was laughing. "Then I leff him go, and he's sittin' back there in the road with his feet on fire, not knowin' which one to lick first. Never bothers me now . . . hightails it soon's as he sees me . . ." He glanced at Fulton. "Know what I'd do, Jack?"

"What would you do, Olaf?"

"I'd think hard on good things like that till you get your head straight again. I'd take a bath, shove your clothes in the Bendix, or maybe burn 'em. Then, all clean and fresh, I'd go callin' on that pretty nurse we both admire so much."

He left Fulton at the corner of The Row. Lying alongside at the B.C. Packers' dock was an old, battered white gillnetter. And Fulton thought, pleased, Stepan's home.

*

Seeking a favour, he took the soiled clothes across to the big house. "Give him me here." Rosa seized the shirt and denims. "Put him in the Bendix. Be fine then."

"Thanks, Rosa . . ." He explained the smell briefly. "It just seems to cling to you."

She nodded sympathetic understanding. "That poor fella. Bad as Stepan's socks when he been a week on boat."

He remembered the moored gillnetter, and was about to enquire about Stepan, but checked the impulse. Had Stepan been at home, he would have been much in evidence, loud and boisterous after his long absence. Or Rosa, certainly, would have mentioned it. A suspicion was forming in his mind, and he asked instead, "Tamara home?"

"You got no luck." Rosa looked knowing. "You stuck with me."

He smiled. "My second-favourite girl."

"Tamara your first?" She looked pleased when he nodded. "Is good thing, I say." She bundled the clothes into the washing machine. "She got to do overtime . . . not home before six. Lots o' new babbies . . . all that feedin' an' dirty diapers. And they short of staff." She set the controls, and his clothes spun into a soapy, cleansing Niagara. "You see, when my Tamara come home, she stink bad as you . . . all that babby-crap. You be two of a kind."

"That's how I'd like it," Fulton admitted. "Although not exactly like *that* . . ."

*

Early evening, and the beer parlour was still quiet.

Stepan was there as Fulton had expected. At a corner table laden with glasses, full and empty, *many* glasses. What he would not have expected was to find Stepan with Ichabod, the itinerant preacher, who leaned over the table, talking earnestly. Stepan, it was evident, was drunk.

He looked up at Fulton. "Hey . . . *High*-pockets!"

"Hi, Stepan."

Ichabod, affable and courteous, offered his hand. "*Mister* Fulton, sir . . ." He wore his shabby black suit. His old Homberg was on the table among the glasses, in a pool of beer, the clipboard and briefcase rested against a table leg. Two untouched glasses of pale beer stood before him.

Stepan invited thickly, "be drink liddle beer with ol' Stepan?"

"Sounds good to me."

Stepan waved him to a chair, telling Ichabod, "This my good friend . . . officer and Goddam gentleman. Good pilot . . . not drink too much less'n he be go flyin'."

"An admirable example to follow, surely?" Ichabod suggested mildly.

"Yah, maybe . . ." Stepan grinned in beery triumph. "Except, like I say to him before, I not be go flyin'. No need be sober for run my ol' boat. Be drunk as a skunk, *she* know which way to go." He announced, "got real *res-pec'* for Highpockets . . ." And turned his head to bawl at the bar, "DRAW TWO!"

"Comin' at you, Stepan . . ." The barman banged two brimming glasses on to a waiter's tray.

Stepan paid with a half-dollar, telling the waiter, "have one . . ." The waiter nodded thanks, and left twenty cents change.

"Thanks, Stepan . . ." Fulton raised a glass. "Health, gentlemen."

Ichabod sipped as Stepan drained a full glass in three swallows, and belched. "I be *say* somethin' . . . what I say?"

"You mentioned respect," Ichabod reminded him.

"Yah . . . is so." Stepan pursued his theme anew. "Respect man that know when to start and stop. Whole lot smarter'n one that start and keep goin'. Like me, eh?" Stepan guffawed, and bawled at the bar, "DRAW SIX!"

"On the way, Stepan . . ." The waiter hurried over with six more beers.

Stepan held up a rumpled dollar bill.

"Let me get this," Fulton said.

"Got *no* chance . . ." Stepan waved him away, telling the waiter, "his money no damn' good . . . don' touch him. I been three weeks in bush . . . got paid," he said. "Is my party . . ." He told the waiter, "have one . . ." The waiter gave him thirty cents change. Stepan added it to the pile of nickels, dimes and quarters on the soaked table. "All adds up," he remarked vaguely, and looked at Fulton with bloodshot eyes. "Somethin' else . . . big difference between you an' *him*." He jerked a derisory thumb at Ichabod. "He bad as me . . . sure know when to start in preachin', but not know when be stop . . ." Ichabod nodded amiable agreement, and sipped some beer. "Know what he try and do to me, Highpockets?"

"I've no idea," Fulton confessed.

"Change my Goddam life! Say me . . . shape up or ship out!"

Ichabod chided gently, "that's a bit much, Stepan."

"Tell me he help me change my life for good. *I* say he *wreck* the sum'n'a'bitch!"

"Oh, now *really* . . ."

"Say me I drink too much!"

Fulton began, "well . . ."

"Sayin' not be good for Rosa . . . for Tamara. For *business*."

"It *can* cause problems," Fulton ventured.

"I treat my Rosa, my Tamara, hokay. Work hard, make good money, they not be go short for nothin'. In woods, on my boat, drink only water, apple juice, coffee . . . nothin' stronger *never*." He banged the table hard in confirmation; the assembled glasses rattled, and more beer slopped. The barman glanced over quickly, then, satisfied, resumed drawing beer and loading trays. Ichabod sat in silence, his angular body bent awkwardly in the chair. Notwithstanding the force of his arguments, Stepan was in good humour. "Highpockets, I bet you somethin'."

"Go ahead. Bet me."

"For all I say is different between you an' him . . ." His sly glance moved between them. "Right now, not a bit different *nohow*. *Bet* you!"

"Say that again," Fulton said. "So that we can all understand."

"Ichabod come in here be *preach* at me," Stepan insisted. "Thinkin' now you come and do same. Feel it in my water. What you say?"

And . . . he's got me there, Fulton allowed. "I was hoping for a chat, yes."

"Heart to heart, eh?" Stepan assumed a doleful look. "Hokay, Preacher Highpockets . . . Preacher Ichabod . . . I be know when I'm licked. Too many sum'n'a'bitches up against me. So . . . know what I be doin'?" He came unsteadily to his feet, the chair legs screeching on the cement floor. "What I do is go make big pee-pee!"

He lumbered off, weaving. Nicely drunk, Fulton decided. Not *crawling* drunk, though, or falling-down drunk. And, on the strength of that, not drunk enough yet, maybe, to get Rosa into an uproar? Tough and intolerant, she remained fair-minded. On a handsome pay-day, would she be ready, for once, to look the other way . . . ?

Ichabod murmured, "I've been wondering if you're heaven-sent, or merely *Rosa*-sent?"

"I'm really sorry," Fulton told him quickly. "I said I'd visit, and I haven't. The thing is, Icha . . ." He caught his breath. "Um . . ."

"You may call me that. Others show less restraint."

"It kind of slipped," Fulton said.

"It does tend to," Ichabod agreed. "As it's a name I'm not bound to by law, I find it no encumbrance."

"*That's* good . . ."

"I am, in fact, Andrew Skilly. Which rhymes handily with silly and other less-endearing epithets to which my attention has been drawn. But there is a distiction to Ichabod which is not unpleasing. It derives from the Hebrew, you know . . . Samuel One, Chapter Four, Verse Twenty One. The meaning is of interest . . . 'the glory is departed'. I wonder if people hereabouts know of that? And desire at times, in my case, that it might be so?" Meditatively, he sipped a little beer. "You may use Andrew, Andy or Ichabod as you see fit."

Fulton agreed, smiling, "I'll go for Andy." Ichabod—Andy—reminded him of great comics, like Buster Keaton and Ben Turpin. Who never cracked a smile, yet gave the impression always that the last laugh was theirs . . . Ichabod had turned to the bar, beckoning.

"If you would kindly indulge us, Mister Foster?"

"That four or six, Ichabod?" the barman enquired. "Did Stepan take off?"

"I imagine he'll return shortly," Ichabod declared. "But, until that hoped-for moment, four should suffice . . ."

The waiter brought their beer. "Forty cents, Ichabod."

From a small leather purse, the preacher produced a quarter, a dime and a nickel. The waiter looked disappointed. Ichabod rummaged once more, and found another nickel. "Something for you, my friend."

"Jesus!" The waiter stared at the coin lying in his palm. "Last o' the big-time spenders, eh?"

As he moved away, Ichabod peered through his glasses at Fulton. "I spoke of God-sent? And Rosa?"

"Right."

"Because your appearance was so timely, coupled with your expressed wish to discuss matters with Stepan . . ." Ichabod assured him, "nothing whatever to do with your non-appearance at one of my small gatherings."

"I feel bad about that, though," Fulton said.

"Please don't. Like yourself, my immediate concern is for Stepan. I mentioned Rosa because she has spoken to me of him already. Informing me of things."

"Like Stepan and drinking?"

"The matter which arouses your own concern?"

"Rosa, Tamara, you and I know it." Fulton shrugged. "Stepan does, too." He grinned then. "Otherwise, why did he go haring off to the can?"

"Feeling outnumbered and defensive?" Ichabod suggested lightly. "Plus an over-full bladder? He could hold his own with me, but you tipped the balance against him."

"That's how you see it?"

"Frankly, I anticipate complete failure with Stepan," Ichabod confessed. "Which means that I fail Rosa, also. I promised to try and help, believing Stepan amenable to reason. Perhaps I was mistaken . . ."

"Maybe only Stepan can help Stepan."

"Doesn't that sound rather like what you refer to here as a cop-out?"

"Could be. But what else is there? Attempts to help only seem to get his back up."

"It would appear so." Ichabod nodded.

"I've seen and heard how it is when Rosa gets after him. Maybe that's why she's talked to you. Because *she* can't get through, either . . ." Fulton recounted the events at the dinner table.

"How was he then?"

"Defiant . . . truculent . . . and not half as gassed as he is now. To quote him, he works hard, and has the right to enjoy himself. For enjoyment," Fulton added dryly. "Read drinking beer."

"But after the quarrel, you spoke with him alone?"

"And behind all the tough talk, he was troubled. Worrying that, one day, Rosa will rile him once too often."

"You've become his friend . . . he has great affection for you." Ichabod asked, "what do you think of him?"

"Sentiments returned in full. He's wild and woolly, that's for sure. Same time, he's one of the most kindly, decent men you could meet. He drinks too much, and he's a little larcenous where so-called drift-logs are concerned. But I'd call those his worst sins."

The beer parlour was filling as the evening rush began. The barman had been joined by an assistant. Two more waiters appeared, tying on aprons.

"I would suggest," Ichabod said then. "That Stepan is, at best, a determined drunkard. At worst, an alcoholic."

"I thought alkies drank without cease."

"There are *those*, yes . . ."

"Stepan's never that bad. You heard what he said about when he's at work. Surely no true alcoholic would have that much self-control?"

"Alcoholism is a single hypothesis, and you argue against it," Ichabod said. "Which leaves the drunkard. Which, in turn, compounds the problem."

"Because he ignores everything and everybody, and does nothing about it?" Ichabod nodded, his expression filled with regret.

"If he can't, or won't, listen to himself, or to Rosa, how on earth will he ever heed me? Particularly when he views me as something of a joke."

Waiting, they sipped beer in silence. There was no sign of Stepan returning. And Fulton thought, with sudden resentment, why *am* I bothering with any of this, anyway? It was Stepan's life to live, or to ruin, as he wished. And Stepan would resist interference, even though it came in the guise of friendly concern.

Yet he knew—as he had known on that night in the kitchen—want to or not, I *am* involved. Because Tamara was involved, and had confided her fears and doubts. Rosa was another story: it was a pity, but she, at least, could handle Stepan. Had it been Rosa alone he could have stayed clear, certain that Stepan at his wildest would not get the better of her, even in the physical show-down feared by Tamara.

It was *she* who made the difference. His deepening feelings for her committed him, and he could not stand aside . . .

"Perhaps," he heard Ichabod saying. "We might ponder the prolonged absence of our friend, and his possible whereabouts?"

They stood to gaze about the noisy, smoke-filled room, but met with no success.

"Think he's taken off?"

"A possibility. Although I should prefer to consider the alternatives."

"Go look for him?"

"Indeed . . ." Ichabod smiled sadly. "Like faithful Saint Bernards."

"But we'll skip the kegs of cognac," Fulton said.

*

Stepan was where he had said he would be, snoring gently in a cubicle.

"Suitably docile," Ichabod observed. "We should manage to extract him."

"You make him sound like a bad tooth."

"We'll proceed with caution, then. Bearing in mind that teeth can bite."

A stranger, buttoning up, asked, "he a pal o' yours?"

"We like to imagine so, sir," Ichabod assured him with courtesy.

"I'd leave him lay," the stranger advised. "Not doin' no harm. Who's to bother him?"

And Fulton wondered . . . what if Stepan had been bothered already? "We need to get him home. His wife's pretty worried."

The stranger laughed. "She's goin' to be more'n worried when she gets a load o' the shape he's in." He wished them luck, and left.

"Andy . . . about someone bothering him," Fulton said. "He's just been paid. There could be a lot of money."

"Or again . . . not . . ." Ichabod nodded. "If someone unknown, and opportunistic, has preceded us?"

Except for themselves, the reeking latrine was empty. "We'd better take a look."

Stepan stirred, muttering fretfully in his sleep, as Fulton searched his pockets.

"Quickly," Ichabod warned. "I anticipate a loose-bladdered rush."

Fulton discovered the billfold, and stepped away quickly as three men came in. He busied himself with his zipper, and saw Ichabod at the other end of the trough urinal, eyes turned heavenward, mouth pursed in a soundless whistle.

The newcomers nodded companionably. One, spying Stepan, said, "*he's* found somewheres for th' night."

"The sleep of the just . . ." Fulton forced a smile, and, when the three had trooped out, he opened the billfold to find ninety two dollars in cash and a company cheque—Alaska Pine & Cellulose—for one thousand four hundred and seventy one dollars and sixty eight cents, payable to 'S.T. Kereniuk'. He grinned his relief at Ichabod. "Seems we got here first."

"And now, perhaps, we should remove the evidence?"

Stepan grumbled some incomprehensible complaint as they lifted him.

Another man came in, and laughed. "Takin' out the empties?"

"This one is rather full, I fear," Ichabod replied.

The early evening was bright and blustery. A heavy shower was sweeping in from the Sound.

"I shall summon a taxi," Ichabod declared.

He went to the payphone, and Fulton, supporting Stepan, tried to replace the billfold. It was almost done when the lolling head straightened, and a steely hand gripped his wrist. Stepan said, grinning tightly, "if I not know you better, Highpockets, be thinkin' you try rob an old fella."

"*Damn* it, Stepan . . . you nearly gave me a bloody heart attack!"

"Maybe you deserve, eh? Goin' around helpin' yourself?"

For a moment then, Fulton almost hated him. "You stupid old bastard! Maybe it's what *you* deserve for passing out in the john with your pockets full of money!"

"Hey! What's eatin' . . . ?"

"You're more God-damned trouble than you're worth!" Fulton said with heat. "Fifteen hundred dollars you've got there . . ."

"Been lookin', eh?" Stepan's voice hardened. "Highpockets?"

"Yes, I *have*! To find out if someone *had* cleaned you out!"

"An' no one be doin'. So what's your beef?"

"That's no thanks to *you*, is it?"

They bickered fretfully as the shower came up the bay, and the first drops hissed around them.

"You gettin' plenty smart talk for young punk still wet behin' the ears!"

"And you can forget *that* shit! If you're a prime example of age and wisdom, then Christ help us all!"

The shower hit full force, soaking them in an instant. "Pissin' like cow on a flat rock," Stepan observed mildly, and glanced sidelong at Fulton. "Highpockets, you pretty hard man to please."

Fulton stared at him, and tried not to laugh, thinking . . . we're classic examples of people too dumb to come in out of the rain. Dripping, he said sternly, "fifteen hundred *bucks*, Stepan. Why didn't you send out invitations?"

"Be no problem . . . was *you* findin' . . ."

"Sweet suffering *Jesus*!" Fulton looked up, feeling the rain, a cooling tonic on his face. "Don't you realise . . . at what Tamara makes as an aide, that's *ten months' salary*? You bonehead . . . don't you ever *think*?"

Stepan became crestfallen, but made an attempt to brazen it out. "You know me, Highpockets . . . I tell you before, eh? Easy come, easy go?"

"Would you be saying that, you birdbrain, if some bugger *had* rolled you?"

Stepan, swaying slightly, looked down at his sodden boots. "Sorry, damn it . . . *sorry*!"

And Fulton thought that, after all, his spur-of-the-moment venture might not have failed entirely. The money argument, Stepan's bluster notwithstanding, appeared to have hit the mark. Achieving, in a sudden burst of anger and outrage, what Ichabod with his enduring patience and forbearance seemingly could not.

*

A stone-faced Rosa received Stepan from their care, eyeing them, and the taxi waiting to bear Ichabod away, with deep suspicion. "Where you find him?"

"Rosa, we've been together . . ." Ichabod was subdued. "In the beer parlour . . . a glass or two . . ."

"Or *two*? Ha!"

Fulton offered, "we weren't there long."

"Not *you*, maybe. *This* one . . . different story, I bet." Rosa poked the shrinking Stepan with a finger. "Wantin' to *know* about this fool!"

Stepan began wearily, "honest to Christ . . ."

"Wantin' know how long you been *in*?"

"Liddle time, maybe . . ." He would not look at her.

"What you callin' little time? You say me, lunkhead . . . what time you get IN?"

"Two 'clock, maybe."

"Is gone seven! Where you been? No . . ." Rosa shook her head. "Let me guess. Not need three guess . . . just the *one*!"

They stood in a semi-circle before her, soaked and chilled and abject in the continuing rain. She did not invite them inside.

"No need you say . . . just be tellin' me big lie, anyhow. Save your breath. Be all day in bloody-bugger beer parlour . . . since first you get in!"

"Only *liddle* whiles . . . few beers . . ." Stepan wheedled. "Not be drunk . . . swear it . . ."

Rosa pounced. "Not drunk, what for needin' taxi, eh . . . what *for*? Why you not walk, or be crawl? You *always* walk, or be crawl!"

"Pretty wet evening, Rosa," Fulton ventured. "We got soaked, and grabbed a cab . . ."

"Need you two bring him home if he be *sober*? Bull-SHEET, I say you!" She glared at Stepan. "You! Inside! Hot bath . . . clean clothes. You stink o' that dirty boat! Stink o' beer! Just plain be *stink*!"

He edged past her in the doorway, and turned to look back. "Nice be with you fellas. Thanks a lot for everythin' . . ."

"Be get lost, you!" Rosa commanded.

Stepan got lost.

She softened then, inviting them in, offering coffee. Ichabod, hastily it seemed, declined; he had rounds to make. He hesitated for a moment. "As promised, Rosa, Stepan and I have had a long discussion." She looked expectant. "There is, however, the need for further talk."

"Talk all you like," she encouraged. "Long as it wake up that fool."

Ichabod spoke of a 'fluid situation'. Which, given the circumstances, Fulton thought mirthfully, was apt. Ichabod would, he vowed, 'get back to her'. If she could just be patient. Rosa listened, nodding, not speaking. Her face had gone cold and hard.

When Ichabod had left, she asked Fulton acidly, "you be got *rounds* to make, too?"

"Only to the house, and get out of these wet things."

She nodded. "You get wet lookin' after my bloody Stepan. Gi' me them things for dryin'."

He accepted ruefully. "This is getting to be a habit."

"Sorry, I be talk too bad . . ." Rosa smiled apology. "Be gettin' a little sore."

"Of course. Understood."

"You get goin' . . ." She sent him off then. "Time you get back, Tamara be ready."

"Ready . . . ?"

"She in the shower, washin' off babby-stink. Soon, she be bright-eye an' bushy-tail!"

*

He lay awake, reliving the evening. Rain lashed the window, and dripped steadily in the guttering. He thought fleetingly of Prokopchuk, somewhere out in the dark tumult of Queen Charlotte Strait, and felt no sympathy: Prokopchuk had wanted it that way . . .

Tamara's company aside, it had not been a noteworthy evening: Doris Day and Sylvester the Cat at the Totem Theatre, then on to the coffee shop under a shared umbrella for Pepsi shakes and hand-holding in a booth. Like high school juniors. She had wanted to know about the Seymour Inlet trip, and, although he spared her the more grisly details, it remained a disturbing story.

She shivered. "I wondered who they had in. The morgue's in the basement of the Nurses' Residence, and the lights were on for an autopsy."

"Fun for the nurses. Having that underfoot."

"Right beside the laundry lines . . ." Tamara grinned. "A big freezer room exactly like the one in the hospital kitchen."

"Long as they remember where to store the hamburgers, and vice versa."

"That's *sick* . . ." She nudged him sharply. "Although, upstairs, you'd hardly know it was there. All the same, some residents aren't too thrilled about going down at night. The orderlies like to horse around sometimes. They think it's funny."

The rain had ceased when they left the coffee shop. Ragged cloud flew overhead, and surf boomed out beyond the point. A large vessel was entering the bay, its masthead lights swaying.

"The Standard Oil tanker," Tamara said. "She's due."

He hugged her in the wind. "Not much gets past you."

"There's not much to *get.* For Blackfish, the tanker's an event."

"So are you." He kissed the top of her head. "An event." As the ship's siren sounded, she turned her face up to him. In a little while, he said softly, "Olaf got it right."

"You're thinking of him? *Now*?"

"First, you need to know what he got right." Fulton mentioned the Indian dog.

"The one with the red-hot paws?" She was laughing.

"That's him. More folklore?"

"Along with Billy Langewische's walnuts."

"Olaf knew I had the blues after that trip, and told me the shaggy dog story to cheer me up."

"And did it?"

"Oh, yes. But what he said afterwards was better."

She watched him. "*Do* tell."

"That I needed some therapeutic time with you."

"I'd call that good advice," Tamara said.

"*That's* what Olaf was right about."

The tanker was alongside, its decklights picking out the men connecting pumps and hoses. The clouds had thickened, early drops signalling a fresh squall . . .

They came up to the house, and he said regretfully, "better get you inside before you're soaked."

"Not yet. We've got the bumber-chute . . ." She shook out the umbrella. "Let's talk some more."

"Anything in particular?"

Tamara said, "earlier, you went looking for Stepan?"

He felt wary at once, and evaded, "following a hunch . . . nothing definite. Guessing . . . where he was, you know?"

"You can say beer parlour, Jack. Ma and me, we're used to it."

"I had some half-baked notion of trying to reason with him."

"Then thank you . . ." She asked, "does Ma know about it?"

"No. I didn't want her thinking I was meddling. Then, when I arrived, Ichabod was there, trying to back Stepan into a corner."

The rain was heavier, and they huddled under the skimpy umbrella.

"How did you know Stepan was back?"

"Saw his boat. Then, when he wasn't home, and your mother said nothing, it kind of fell into place . . ." He suggested tentatively, "maybe you shouldn't let it get to you so much."

"How can I *not*?" She sounded sharp. "When, with Stepan, *always*, it goes the same way!"

"Forgive me . . ."

She caught her breath. "If *you'll* forgive *me*? For getting hot and bothered?"

A small craft was moving far out in the Sound, a single wavering dot of light. Still too early, Fulton estimated, at their crawling speed, to be Prokopchuk and his two charges . . .

"Sorry to keep on," Tamara said. "But . . . how *was* Stepan when you found him?"

"Feeling no pain." He smiled.

She eyed him doubtfully. "With Stepan, that could mean anything."

"He was drinking beer with Ichabod . . ." He would not, he decided, make mention of the *several* other glasses on the table at the time.

"He was backed into a corner, you *said*."

"Well, Ichabod *was* doing the talking . . ." Fulton shifted uneasily, feeling his soaked legs, the wetness inside his shoes.

"Just looking for the facts," Tamara said.

"Like Sergeant Friday in Dragnet . . ."

"Ichabod was *lecturing* Stepan, wasn't he?"

He asked, "you know about that?"

"That Ma's spoken to Ichabod? Sure." A defiant note emerged. "Why not? She needs all the help she can get! Never mind from where . . ."

Sleep was coming down, slow and warm, fragmenting his thoughts, which lost form and substance, drifting away. He half-dreamed, smiling, of Tamara, sleeping now herself . . . picturing her on her side, the tanned, slender legs drawn up. He would touch her bared shoulder lightly, and she would turn to him . . .

"NO-GOOD, DIRTY DRUNKEN *BUM*!"

Fulton jerked upright, quivering with shock: the involuntary thought coming, there must be a window open over there. Allowing Rosa's voice, clear and loud and furious, to escape, over-riding the rain and wind.

"GOD-DAMN . . . GET *OUT*! NOT STAY NO LONGER *MINUTE* IN MY HOUSE!"

He thought, despairing, they're at it again. Tamara would not be softly-sleeping, nor anyone else within a half-mile's radius!

Stepan's answering bellow came, "*crazy Goddam* WOMAN! *What's* MATTER *with you*?"

"BE STINKIN' *DRUNK* . . . LOUSY BASTARD!"

"*A liddle beer* . . ."

"IS *BULL*-SHEET!"

"*Is* TRUTH . . . !"

"TRUTH? DON'T BE SAY ME 'BOUT *TRUTH*!" Invective flew back and forth like a ball across a net. "NOT YOUR BLOODY *DRINKIN'* I RILED 'BOUT!"

"*So* WHY *you get so stupid excited*?"

"YOU BE SWEAR YOU CALL QUITS TONIGHT! NOT TOUCH NO MORE AN' . . ."

"*Now* . . . LIS-*ten* . . ."

"*YOU* LISTEN! SHUT FACE AND LISTEN *GOOD*!"

Something crashed down over there, shattering: Fulton caught his breath, wondering if Stepan was losing it. And felt relief as Rosa's voice, unquelled, came again, jeering, "yah . . . GO on! Bust up the Goddam house . . . what you ALWAYS do . . . is all you KNOW!"

Stepan's response was more muted, as if in the realisation of having gone too far. "Don't like it you sayin' me shuddup . . . shuddup! Get in my head . . . make me *mad*!"

"Get your feelin's hurt, eh? How about MY Goddam feelin's? When you act like you think me some bloody fool-woman . . . you makin' me promises, then be makin' LIES to me?"

"Nobody LYIN' . . ."

"Drunk fool MAN! I talk you nice at supper . . . not gettin' mad. PLEASE, I say you . . . no more tonight. You say me you quit . . . I *believe*! Now I find you . . . SIX MORE BOTTLES . . . ALL *EMPTY* BOTTLES! You LIE me, and I HATE lyin' worse'n DRINKIN'!"

Stepan's reply was inaudible.

"Too LATE you be SORRY, stupid one! Sorry from you only one more big LIE!" Rosa commanded, "go be sorry in WOODSHED!"

"God DAMN!" Stepan bawled. "Is RAININ' out there to beat the band! Blowin' . . ."

"TOUGH! Little rain . . . cool you off!" Rosa was without pity. "Make you see sense! Now you GO . . . *GIT*!"

The porch light came on: Fulton, at the window, saw Rosa in the doorway grasping Stepan by the shoulders, shaking him. She shoved him, and he stumbled out into the wet night, turning unsteadily to face her. "What FOR you do this?"

"Because you dirty, drunk LIAR . . . not HAVE you in here!" She stepped back inside.

"Rosa . . . be LISTEN!"

"Don't try come in here . . . I lock doors and windows . . ." Her admonishing finger threatened him. "You try . . . I call COPS . . . you go in POKEY!" The door slammed in Stepan's face, and there was the loud and meaningful rattle of bolts. With bleak finality the porch light went out. Stepan stood bare-headed in the rain, wearing only shirt and denims, lit by the glow from the kitchen window. He raised his cupped hands to his mouth. "MEAN OL' GODDAM *WOMAN* . . . I BE GET EVEN!"

In reply, the kitchen light went out, leaving him a dim shape in the stormy dark. His point made, Stepan turned and trudged the well-worn path to the woodshed.

*

Fulton thought of Stepan in the cold; of Rosa inside, warmed by her righteous fury.

Tamara must have overheard everything, and what would *she* be thinking? Not hard to imagine her fear and anxiety as they screamed at each other . . .

He heard soft footsteps. Outside somewhere, shuffling over the saturated ground, reaching the wooden steps that led up to his plank verandah. He lay still, not breathing, as they halted outside the door.

Someone knocked lightly, but he offered no response. The knock was repeated more insistently . . .

"Highpockets . . . ?" The hoarse whisper came, "you be sleepin'?"

Relief, then anger, flooded his scared mind: bloody *Stepan*! "Not any *more*! Thanks to YOU!"

The nervous whisper pleaded, "not be yell so loud, eh? You be wake up that crazy woman!"

Fulton jerked open the door. "What do you *want*, Stepan?"

He stood there, shivering, hugging himself against the cold. "She throw me *out*, Highpockets!"

"I *know*, damn it! So must most of Blackfish!"

"Stuck in Christly woodshed. Rain comin' in . . . wind. Got no blanket . . . not enough clothes. Needin' place to go."

Fulton hardened his heart. "Go sleep on your boat."

"Sure. Only boat lock up. Key inside with that nutty woman . . ." A whining note crept in. "Give me a break? Can sleep on kitchen floor . . . you never know I there."

"I'd always know where you are, Stepan. Just look for the nearest riot." Fulton stepped aside. "Okay . . . come in."

"Highpockets, you never regret it . . ." Stepan was beaming. "Remember you in my will!"

*

Stepan's soggy clothing made a dispiriting pile on the floor. Stepan, blanket-wrapped, sipped from his mug critically. "Need show you how to make good *skookum* coffee."

"Don't knock it . . . it's free."

"Like belly-wash."

"Best I can do at this time of night."

"Sure . . . is so. I bringin' you trouble."

"It's something you do well."

"Don' mean it 'bout coffee . . ." Stepan waved the mug.

"Just me bitching. I'm seldom at my best after midnight." Fulton asked, "what went wrong?"

"How much you hear?"

"Enough."

"Hokay . . ."

"You were into the beer again," Fulton accused.

"One or two, maybe. *My* beers . . . what I pay for."

"Six," Fulton corrected him.

"What you say . . . ?"

"I heard Rosa."

"Holy shit . . ." Stepan looked despairing. "Can't do *nothin'* in this Goddam town." Fulton felt a fresh spurt of amused sympathy. With the power of Rosa's lungs, little could be secret, or sacred. "I tell you," Stepan confided. "Feel bad people sayin' I be treat Rosa lousy."

"Who says that?"

"Know-it-alls . . ." Stepan added quickly, "not *you* . . . know you for friend. Is *other* bastards sayin'. And sometime, Tamara sayin', too. This I know."

"Stepan . . . you worry her . . . scare her sometimes," Fulton said earnestly. "Rosa's her mother, and you have these brawls. She worries about it going too far . . ." He switched tack then, sensing the potential perils of that line of reasoning. "Remember at supper the other night? What you said to me?"

"About how I feelin' for Rosa?" Stepan watched him attentively. "How sometime she makin' me feel?"

"You said you could see Rosa pushing you too hard, and how that frightened you."

"Try an' put out of my head sayin' that." Stepan looked abject.

"The thought of hitting Rosa?"

"Not wantin' do that *ever*! Better off be dead . . ." Stepan's voice rose. "Stupid woman . . . *you* knowin' what I feel for her. And somethin' else I say you . . . thing which is gospel truth." Stepan's eyes challenged him. "Day come, and I hurt Rosa . . . that finish me for sure straightaway! No bullshit!"

"Stepan, listen . . ." Fulton was moved and embarrassed; the baring of souls was alien to him. "I don't believe you'd hurt her. It's not in you . . ."

He made himself suppress the memory of the night in the kitchen; the look of hatred directed at Rosa's back.

"Not scared be die," Stepan insisted stubbornly. "Dyin' happen to people, same as gettin' born. Same as . . ." He shrugged and smiled. "Gettin' drunk. I tell you, Highpockets . . . I ever do that thing, I want to die . . . goin' to be die."

He fell moodily silent then, cradling his coffee mug. Minutes ticked by, and Fulton felt his returning tiredness . . .

"Yet, same time, don't understand what *is* with her," Stepan muttered. "Why she treat me so? Gettin' plastered sometimes. Not like *all* the time."

"I know, Stepan."

"You seein' my cheque that time? Almost fifteen hunnert bucks?"

"Yes."

"You talk to me pretty strong about that. And you was *right*. That cheque for Rosa. She get it, I sign him over . . . no strings. Go ahead . . . spend . . . all yours. Only keep me change for beer money . . . for groceries in the boat. All else, she welcome. Reckon that deserve few beers . . . don't do no bugger no harm."

"You wouldn't think so."

"Still, fifteen hunnert in her purse . . . from me with love and carin', still she go throw me out in the rain . . . go sleep in sum'n'a'bitch woodshed! Like some cheapskate don't never give her *nothin'*. An' I think on that, how not right thing to do for a fella. Then I get mad, thinkin' of things I be do to *her* . . . then gettin' scared thinkin' of *doin'* them things!"

TEN

The summer moved on for Jack Fulton with work, with experiences that ran the gamut, bizarre to tragic to irritating and infuriating, then to those which were funny and outrageous.

He flew expectant mothers and sick children, the old and the ill and the frequently despairing.

He brought in a very fat man with a perforated duodenal ulcer. At three hundred pounds, he was too vast for the basket stretcher, and made the flight lying on blankets, the strength and weight of his smaller, but still immense, brother acting as a makeshift safety harness.

The spell of poor weather had passed; the sun returned, warming the air, bringing light winds from a Pacific high that lay stationary for days over the Gulf of Alaska.

But the hot, rainless days dried out the forests, and the fire hazard mounted. In anticipation of a provincial government order closing down logging and sawmill operations, the camps and mills were working flat out, bringing about a sharp rise in the rate of accidents. Accidents with power saws and axes, with chokers and boom-chains, from falls, fire, electric shock and scalding. An outbreak of salmonella at Woss Lake required nine round trips to evacuate the afflicted. For Fulton, the sum of nickels-per-mile rose steadily.

There were, in that time, two drownings, and a logger flown in from Harbledown Island, victim of a brawl, his skull crushed by a kick from a caulked boot. On that same day the Beaver flew to Harbledown with a constable to bring back the assailant. The injured man had died in the hospital, and the charge of assault was up-graded to murder . . .

*

Standing in line in the bank, Fulton heard a voice at his back. "I was hoping to run into you."

He had not seen Sergeant Prokopchuk since the Seymour Inlet trip.

The two gillnetters had reached Blackfish Harbour where the *Weetsisiya* was impounded as Crown evidence. Since then, under the pressure of work, and spending his scant free time with Tamara, those events had slipped back in his mind.

"Hello, Sergeant . . ." Mindful of the friction of their last encounter, he waited guardedly.

But Prokopchuk was smiling, and uncharacteristically affable. "Have you got time for a chat?"

"From you, that always sounds ominous."

The bank teller gave a little cough. "Your cash, Mister Fulton."

"Right with you," he promised Prokopchuk, and smiled for the teller. "Just fulfilling my parole conditions." She returned the smile dutifully, and counted out his fifty dollars. He told Prokopchuk, "I'll wait."

"I'll be a while. How about meeting in the coffee shop? I'm buying."

"*That's* too good to pass up."

Fulton was on his second cup when Prokopchuk appeared. "Been feeling bad about you, Jack."

"Can't think why."

"Come on, now . . ." Prokopchuk gave him a dry look. "Seymour Inlet?"

"Oh, *that* . . ."

"You remind me of a certain kind of suspect," Prokopchuk mused. "The one who looks blank, and says 'Oh, *that* robbery' or '*that* murder'!"

"Must be the uniform," Fulton decided. "Makes me go all coy."

"I'll jog your memory," Prokopchuk said. "Seymour Inlet, and getting picky . . . throwing my weight around? Taking out my anger and frustration on you? Losing my temper? Behaving like a prick?"

"Oh, *that*!" Fulton exclaimed.

"I was wrong on all counts," Prokopchuk declared. "Fraught that day, what with this and that. Which excuses not a damned thing. What I'd ask . . ." He looked steadily at Fulton. ". . . is that you'll accept a sincere apology?"

He had been 'fraught', and Fulton wondered anew about the allegedly wayward Nurse Paulen. Prokopchuk was not the kind of policeman to let the job get on top of him. But a cheating woman might.

One evening, in this same coffee shop, Tamara had pointed out Julie Paulen. Blonde, thirty-ish, handsome under heavy makeup. Big-busted, his male eye noted. Getting fleshy around the face. Perfect match, he had thought sourly, for Prokopchuk. They were both big and fleshy.

She had been in a booth with another young woman and two men, neither of whom was Prokopchuk.

"They're doctors," Tamara informed him. "Deane and Denkman."

"Sound more like a law firm." He asked, "I thought Paulen was engaged?"

"Oh, she *is*. She just keeps smarmy Denkman for horsing around with."

Fulton eyed her. "So it's more than a bitchy rumour?"

"A whole lot more. And neither seems to give a damn."

Looking across, he watched as Denkman's hand explored the plump thigh of Nurse Paulen, R.N. She seemed not to mind.

"See what you mean . . ."

Remembering it now, he offered his hand. "Thanks, Sergeant. Let's forget it ever happened."

Prokopchuk muttered, "I wish I could. But it won't go away."

"You'd had a rough ride . . . *and* a ducking." Fulton grinned at him. "Then the slow boat to China."

"I used to believe I was a fair-to-middling sailor." Prokopchuk confessed. "Completely lost count of the times I puked on that trip."

"Dare I ask how it's going?"

"The case?" Prokopchuk grimaced. "Dead end. Not going worth a good God damn."

"Sorry to hear that."

"Yeah?" Prokopchuk was laughing. "I'll bet . . ."

"Well, I had to say *something* nice. Now that we're pals again!"

*

During those days of nervous industry in the woods, Stepan's freelance services were in continuing demand.

The berth where his old gillnetter would lie was now empty for long periods. When he was at home, he and Fulton would spend time together cutting wood. Almost always Stepan returned with a choice length of timber in tow, and the pressing need to have it cut up before Sergeant Prokopchuk began asking difficult questions.

Fulton spied him entering the bay one morning, and went to the dock to take his lines. Stepan pointed with glee to a cedar log lashed alongside. "This bugger goin' to break Porkchop's heart!"

The log was five feet through the butt, and half again as long as the boat. "When he sees that," Fulton believed. "You'll be the one with the broken heart."

The log was clean, its cut marks still bright. It floated high, unsaturated, with no clinging weed. It bore the stamp of ownership of Canadian Forest Products Ltd.

Stepan protested, "Highpockets . . . it not *that* I be talkin' about. Anyhow, I not swipe him."

"Tell it to the judge."

"You think you so smart young sum'n'a'bitch . . ." Stepan produced a crumpled paper. "What you say *now*, eh, Bigshot?"

It was a bill of sale assigning ownership of one merchantable cedar log to S.T. Kereniuk in recognition of the payment of one dollar. "They was askin' *three* bucks," Stepan crowed happily, "but I beat 'em down!" He took back the paper. "Hey, Highpockets? I be show him to Porkchop, he not know be shit or go blind!" He wagged a finger at Fulton. "Say you be sorry."

"I be sorry."

"Say you be *very* sorry."

"I be *very* sorry, Stepan!"

"That good . . ." Stepan locked the pilot-house, and clambered ashore. "Now we go drink beer, eh?"

Fulton began, "now look, Stepan . . ."

"What you sayin'?"

"Just . . . why not take it easy?"

"I be take her easy, hokay."

"Think of Rosa."

"Every Goddam minute be think of her! Now . . . we drink beer, or what?"

They sat together in the rancid, echoing room. Fulton, sipping a beer he did not really want, told himself that he was merely keeping an eye on Stepan. And was astonished when, after four quick glasses, he wiped his mouth, announcing, "hokay . . . now I be gettin' home to my Rosa."

It *did* appear that Stepan's drinking habits were moderating, although he did not give up completely. He was as ever, in his cups, cocksure, loud and opinionated, but not now, it appeared, to excess. He managed always to walk home, erect and reasonably steady. On each return to Blackfish Harbour, however, he would still head straight to the beer parlour for his 'few beers'.

There were times, still, when his notion of a few would be in conflict with Rosa's, and a shouting match would ensue. But to Fulton, listening, they were little more now than noisy spats. As far as he could ascertain, none culminated in physical chastisement, or in Stepan's further banishment to the woodshed.

*

At the end of June, the nurses held their Summer Dance, and Fulton attended as Tamara's guest. A wing of the Residence had been made into a recreation area which, with the removal of the bridge and table tennis tables, left space for dancing, for a buffet and bar, and a corner reserved for a combo of local amateur musicians.

By nine o'clock, the room was hotly-crowded with couples swirling to a creditable rendition of 'Muskrat Ramble'. Most of the nurses and female guests wore ballgowns or cocktail dresses:

those who would go on duty at midnight were in whites, sipping decorously at ginger ale. Eric, the orderly, safely off-duty, presided at the bar.

Tamara introduced Fulton to her friends and close colleagues, and he squirmed under their speculative gaze. He met Erica, the aide with whom Tamara had exchanged days off, and Kirsty Watanabe, a smiling, half-Japanese grad nurse who ran the obstetrics wing. There was Hilde, an Austrian lab technician of whom Tamara whispered warning, "watch yourself. She's husband-hunting, and doesn't care who knows it."

From curious glances and oblique comments he gathered that he had been the subject of conjecture and debate among Tamara's cronies.

She pointed out the musicians to him. "There's Deane and Denkman, your law firm."

Deane was taking a trumpet solo, backed by Denkman on the piano.

"They're jazz-freaks. Doctor Denkman believes he was Scott Joplin in another life."

"Joplin was ragtime."

"Mister Know-it-All," she mocked. "Where's the difference?"

The trombonist doubled as manager of the local branch of the Bank of Montreal.

"So very solemn on the day job . . ." Tamara was laughing. "Strictly *Mister* de Brett, and, no, you *can't* have a loan. But once you get him on his horn, he's Smoky, and would open the safe for you if you asked him nicely."

A pleasant-faced, middle-aged woman smiled in gentle absorption over her dwarfing double bass. Fulton thought he knew her from somewhere . . .

"Annie Markham," Tamara said.

"The *Matron*?"

"Yes, indeedy . . ." She enquired bafflingly, "did that hurt?"

"Did what . . . ?"

"When your jaw hit the floor?"

He grinned. "It *was* some surprise." He watched the Matron's fingers as, with tenderness, they stroked and plucked the strings.

"She's played with symphony orchestras, and she's a whizz on jazz." Tamara pointed. "Now check out the drummer."

He looked . . . and saw Olaf Pedersen, his jacket removed, his shirt sleeves turned up to reveal a weight-lifter's arms, beaming as he beat out a riff between the trumpet and trombone solos. "Another dark horse."

"The joint's jumping with them."

Two glasses of Eric's home-made punch emboldened him sufficiently to ask Tamara to dance. 'Muskrat Ramble' had yielded to a languid blues. He drew her close. "You dance divinely, Miss Rogers."

"So do you, Mister Astaire." She winced slightly. "Sure is a pity about the feet, though."

They eased through the crush to a spot at the centre of the floor where they could stand, swaying together. He brushed her forehead with his lips, and she hugged him back, and, at his elbow, Sergeant Prokopchuk wanted to know, "and what's all *this*?"

Without looking closely, I wouldn't have known him, Fulton thought. Porkchop in tweed sports coat and flannels, a checked shirt and plain knitted tie, with a clasp shaped like an R.C.A.F. pilot's wings. Looking boyish and vulnerable with his bristling crewcut, like a college quarterback out of his depth, yearning for the locker room.

He was with Julie Paulen who shimmered in silver lamé, her plump shoulders bared.

Fulton said, "hi, Sergeant." Tamara gave one of her politely distant smiles.

"What's with 'Sergeant'?" Prokopchuk boomed. "Call me Gene . . . or anything you fancy. Long as it's not late for breakfast." Only he laughed. Tamara and Fulton held their smiles; Nurse Paulen eyed the ceiling. "Meet Julie, my fiancée." She stiffened visibly as he drew her towards him.

Fulton offered his hand. "I've heard a lot about you."

"*Have* you now?" She showed him her best white smile. "But how do I know if it's complimentary?"

And Fulton wondered if she knew what was said of her, and *if* it troubled her at all. "All professional observations," he lied lightly. "All good."

"Well, *there's* something. It looks like we're a matched pair . . ." She held Fulton's hand. "Gene tells me great things about you."

Tamara's eyes had gone cold, and he withdrew his hand with care. "That's a surprise after the ride I gave him."

"You're a good airman," Prokopchuk proclaimed in a don't-argue-with-me voice. "Knew it straightaway."

Which didn't stop you telling me how to run things, Fulton reflected dryly, and told himself to forget it; we're all the very best of friends. "Thanks. Maybe you'll give me a reference for the Air Force?"

"You're the kind they need," Prokopchuk assured him.

"When you two are through with the mutual admiration kick . . . ?" Julie Paulen gave a forced laugh.

"Seems to me, hon . . ." Prokopchuk gave her a cool look. "You started the ball rolling."

She made no answer, asking Tamara instead, "is it right what I'm hearing?"

"I give up. What are you hearing?"

The mouth smiled on, leaving the eyes chilly. "That you two are an item?"

Prokopchuk warned, "Julie, let's leave it, eh?"

"Oh, it's fine . . ." Tamara gripped Fulton's arm. "*We've* nothing to hide."

"That's a relief." Prokopchuk joked heavily, "we won't press charges, then."

Julie Paulen's expression, Fulton concluded, was what might have been called 'an interesting study', the daubed mouth smiling gamely beneath the eyes that watched Tamara with unconcealed hostility. The sight made him uneasy; Paulen was a senior grad nurse and department head, Tamara an aide. Paulen would know what lay beneath that barb, and would have many ways in which to respond to it later . . .

"Well, mustn't hold you up . . ." Prokopchuk made a fresh attempt at breeziness. "Not when you're having fun."

"You have fun, too, Sergeant." Tamara did not look at Julie Paulen. "I'd say you deserve some."

They drifted apart, Paulen a flash of figure-hugging silver, telling Fulton pointedly, "nice meeting *you*."

"Sure hope so . . ." He took Tamara into his arms to sway to Glenn Miller's 'Moonlight Serenade'.

Tamara was still watching Julie Paulen down at the far end of the room. "She looks like a foil-wrapped Hershey bar!"

"Miaaaow!" Fulton murmured.

"That bad was it?" She giggled against his chest.

"I thought you'd start swinging at each other. Then Porkchop could've busted his fiancée, and the girl I love, for riotous behaviour."

She asked with meekness, "was I wicked?"

"I was shocked and appalled," he told her with severity.

"Sorry about that . . ." She stifled laughter.

"You don't *sound* sorry."

"That's because you love me." She looked up at him. "You do, don't you?"

"In spite of everything," he said.

'Moonlight Serenade' ended, and supper was announced. At the bar, Eric invited, "name your poison, Sheriff."

"On the subject of poison," Tamara said. "I'll have some more of your punch."

"Ah . . ." Eric beamed at her fondly. "A lady with taste."

"It's the *taste* I'm trying to get rid of!"

"You can be quite un-BELIEV-ably cruel . . ." Eric ladled her punch. "Which reminds me . . . I observed you exercising that considerable talent on Nurse Appalling."

"How did it look?" Tamara was grinning.

"*She's* been looking like a dying duck in a thunderstorm ever since. Tell your Auntie Eric what you said, dear."

"Let's say . . . she gave me the chance to zap her . . ."

"And you zapped her." Eric looked pleased. The bar was getting busy, and he invited them to leave. "No loitering on the premises. Kindly adjust your garments before stepping out . . ."

They helped themselves at the buffet, and located a couple of chairs. "I suppose you're like Porkchop?" Tamara sounded defensive.

"I try not to be. What brought that on?"

"Disapproving of what I said to darling Julie?"

"Not necessarily."

"*He* disapproved no end."

"Maybe you did push your luck."

"I don't enjoy being called an item . . . especially not by *her*."

"I'm sure she didn't mean anything . . ."

"If it had been Erica, or Kirsty . . ." Tamara pursued her plaint. "Or Annie Markham, I wouldn't've cared. But not *her*!"

"Tamara, listen . . ."

"I detest her! And it's time Porkchop was given a break."

"Maybe I'm not very bright . . ." He smiled uncertainly. "But I don't get your drift."

"You must've noticed how she looked at him. Like something stuck on her shoe."

"I noticed."

"Well, then . . . it was a chance too good to pass up . . . seeing her get nailed instead."

They sat in a slightly strained silence as supper ended. The musicians were returning: couples drifted on to the dance floor. Fulton wondered, "care to give it another whirl?"

But she demurred. "In a while, maybe? *You* could dance with someone else."

"I came here to dance with you. You have an exclusive on my flat feet."

"No cheek-to-cheek with Tinfoil Julie?" She shot him a smiling glance. "She'd like that. She was clearly smitten."

"I can understand why . . . but no, thanks."

"Think what you're missing."

"That's why no thanks." He took her hand. "Would you want me panting after her?"

"I'd hate it," Tamara admitted. "But I'm being fair-minded and generous."

The band was playing 'Autumn Leaves'. Dancers drifted past,

pressed close: the too-warm air smelled of smoke and bodies and staling perfume. Eric's punch had done its work; the party had shed its earlier stiffness. Julie Paulen danced with Prokopchuk, her eyes following Denkman, crouched over his keyboard.

Tamara said suddenly, "I owe you my vote of thanks."

"If you feel that way. What did I do?"

"Gave *us* a break. Ma and me."

"I can't imagine two more deserving people." Fulton smiled. "Nor how I did it."

"Stepan," she said then. "You talked to him."

"A word here and there . . ."

"No need to be modest. It's true. Now Ma and Stepan have had a heart-to-heart, and worked out a few things." Her answering smile was very warm. "And you're to blame."

"Now the question . . ." He looked down into her face. "*What* have they worked out?"

"Seems Stepan's remembered things you told him . . . *and* quoted them. Things said in the beer parlour, and on the night Ma threw him out, and he came to you."

"*That* was supposed to be our big secret."

"Never let Stepan in on secrets . . . he blabs." She told him, "what you said to him sank in."

"Then I'm glad . . ." He was surprised: he would not have credited Stepan, for all the agreeable noises he might make, with taking heed of, or acting on, anything that was said to him . . .

"He told Ma you made sense, and helped him a lot."

"Well, good for *me* . . . I guess."

"You don't sound convinced."

"Sorry. But it does prompt the question . . . was that Stepan talking, or your mother's wishful thinking? Not trying to be a party-pooper, but maybe we shouldn't get our hopes up too much yet?"

Tamara was nodding slow agreement. "Yet, this time, I'd call it Stepan talking. And his word's good in most things."

"Other than when explaining stolen logs to Porkchop."

"Okay . . ." She laughed. "But in all else, he's strictly straight-arrow." She mused lightly, "he could be one of a vanishing breed.

Does business on a handshake, *and* lives up to it . . ." She insisted then, "you gave him some blunt talk, Jack, and scored points."

He wondered, curious, "did he mention the john? And the money?"

"Clean breast . . . the works. Including the bit about him being rolled for the equivalent of almost a year's salary for me. That got him where it hurt."

"It was meant to. I was pretty mad just then."

"Well, we heard it. The lot."

"Again, I'm glad . . ." He lifted her hand to his lips. "Maybe there *is* hope for Stepan?"

The band had progressed to the more frenetic 'Delicado', and skirts flew as the dancers jived enthusiastically. A silver lamé figure wriggled and flashed, but not now with Sergeant Prokopchuk, who was nowhere to be seen. Glasses crashed, and Eric's prim voice rose above the whoops and laughter. "Party's getting rough, boys and girls. Now I'm down to my last ten gallons of punch!"

"Let's not forget," Fulton pointed out. "Ichabod's part in this."

"But Ichabod made one mistake, doing what comes naturally . . . preaching," Tamara said. "And Stepan wont be preached at . . ." She grinned tautly. "He gets a fair whack of that from Ma."

"You could say *I* preached as well."

"But no soul-saving . . . no hellfire and brimstone. You just talked, showed him things he'd missed. Like the money, and maybe getting robbed. He took it from you, and took it *in*. And we've seen the difference." She shrugged resigned acceptance. "Long way still from a clean sheet, but better. Ma's happier, and that has to be good . . ." The band began 'A Fine Romance', and she stirred beside him. "I've always liked this old turkey."

"Prepared to take your life in your hands again?" She rose at once, offering her arms. Some of the lights had gone out; the room was dim and intimate. "Should we talk, or smooch?"

She answered, "I guess we're not done talking."

"Oh . . . ?"

"You gave me a choice, and smooch came second."

"Okay . . ." He chuckled. "Just a teensy bit more talk?"

"And the smooch?"

"Lots."

"Start talking," Tamara said.

"Still wondering about your mother's and Stepan's plans . . . if anything's been revealed?"

"She's said enough to make *me* feel better. About their long talk, and Stepan facing up to the fact that his drinking's a problem. Swearing he'll try and ease up. Nothing about actually quitting, and Ma's realist enough to accept that's beyond his reach. But he promised to try, and he's trying."

"Sounds pretty good."

"Jack . . ." Her eyes met his, and the tension was in her voice once more. "Do you think it can work?"

"Don't you?"

"I'm . . . not certain."

"I think, with Stepan promising, and knowing how he feels for your mother, there should be a chance."

"But only that?"

"Isn't it enough? For starters?"

"You know me." She looked rueful. "Wanting it all at once."

"He's putting his money where his mouth is," Fulton told her. "You're both *seeing* that difference."

"Yes," Tamara half-agreed.

"Hey, you . . ." He raised her chin, and their lips met, and clung. No one around them appeared to notice. When they drew back, he murmured, "be fair, baby. While we're handing out the breaks, we should remember no one needs one more than Stepan."

ELEVEN

July the First and cloudless blue and hot for the Dominion Day holiday, with a breeze stirring the surface of the bay. The stores were shut but, by noon, the cafés and beer parlour were doing big business.

The perfect day for Tamara and the Private Place, Fulton thought with regret. It would be peaceful there, with scant likelihood of others showing up to disturb them. But Tamara had the day shift, on duty until four . . .

Instead, the telephone rang, and Alice Royle—who observed public holidays seldom—informed him, "Camp 'A' at Nimpkish. Only a quick trip." Twenty minutes there and back, he registered automatically, plus whatever delay on the ground. "A man has been taken ill."

"What kind of ill?"

"No details, I'm afraid . . . they were not exactly forthcoming." She sounded miffed.

Fulton experienced a sudden foreboding . . .

The first-aid man, sounding harassed, greeted him at the camp dock. "He's a *bad* one."

"What's up with him?"

"Best see for yourself."

The sense of foreboding deepened. "Can't we just get him down here and get going?"

"Camp super says he'd look on it as a favour if you come up."

The first-aid man led the way to the loggers' bunkhouses. The bellowing was audible from a hundred yards away. "What the hell have you got in there?" Fulton demanded. "King Kong?"

"You should ask . . ." The first-aid man looked glum. "Goddam alkie . . . one o' the camp cooks, real ptomaine artist. Been gettin' at the lemon extract." He gave a sour grin. "Now he's seein' snakes comin' out the walls, scarin' the piss out of him. Makin' him holler like that."

In the uncompromisingly liquor-free logging camp, the cook had discovered a way to satisfy his cravings in the cookhouse supplies of lemon and vanilla extract with their high alcohol content.

"Got better uses for 'em than in lemon pie," the first-aid man said.

The patient raved without cease, fighting the stretcher straps, howling up from the depths of his inescapable nightmare.

Three men waited with him, still breathing heavily with the effort of subduing and restraining him. One, the camp superintendent, nodded tired welcome.

"You're a sight for sore eyes, Jack. Thanks for comin' so quick."

Fulton, watching the shrieking man, was thinking, I *should* feel pity . . . not this anger and disgust. But there could be little tolerance for a sentient creature that would set out, fully knowing, to turn itself into *that* . . .

"Asked Ivan to bring you up." The superintendent's eyes questioned Fulton. "We got you here. But you needn't take him. Not if you see him as a risk."

"I've had worse," Fulton said. "Although most of those were dead." There was a ripple of laughter. "My one worry is, could he get free? If he did, in flight, it would be hairy."

"Shouldn't think so . . ." The superintendent fingered his chin. "If we fixed him any tighter, he'd quit breathing."

"Now *there's* an idea," Ivan, the first-aid man muttered. There was more half-shamed laughter.

"He doesn't sound too popular," Fulton said.

"He's been a fucking pain in the arse since he come off the boat," the superintendent stated. "How such a rummy ever got hired, I'll never know. But this is the end of the line. I'm runnin' him off."

"I blame myself," Ivan admitted morosely. "Him there in the cookhouse, and I never even *thought* of them bloody extracts."

"Might've been worthwhile . . ." The superintendent was grinning sourly. ". . . if the bastard could *cook*."

The patient fought the restraints, shouting, as they debated him. Pinkish drool trailed from his mouth. Ivan bent closer. "Bit his tongue, the prick. No big deal."

The superintendent asked, "what d'you say, Jack? Yes or no? I'll respect it, whatever."

"I'm here . . . I've got to go back," Fulton said. "Might as well do it with a payload."

He heard their shared relief. For him, though, there was only the continuing foreboding.

*

As the Seabee became airborne, he was telling himself, *ten minutes*. Get through that, and it's finished. He need never see, or, more to the point, *hear*, the raving alcoholic again. For ten minutes, it was only noise. He could handle noise . . . ?

The dying powder-man had been worse, and that had gone on for much longer. With the powder-man, though, you could sympathise, feel the full depths of pity, even when the screaming drove you half-out of your mind. You wanted, with the powder-man, to help . . .

Not *this* one, he reflected coldly. A Skid Row alkie who had done this to himself, *knowing* what he did. Doing it anyway.

Since coming to Blackfish Harbour, Fulton's total of sick and injured patients had risen steadily. It *was* remarkable, he allowed then, how you could—with no awareness of a developing process—become attuned to the experiences, learning—by this mysterious means—to take them in stride. It was, he supposed uncertainly, a kind of hardening. A protective coating over such distracting emotions as sadness, anger, pity or revulsion.

Except for *this* man, this screaming and yelling piece of human flotsam, who merited no compassion. Given the choice, he thought, I wouldn't waste the effort of flying him out: he had made his decision, and could stew in it! The analogy seemed fitting . . .

His irritation, he found, was making him tense: each time the man roared out, he would grip the control yoke in anger, feeling the erosion of the smooth co-ordination between mind and body and aircraft. Betrayed in the small, jittery fluctuations of instrument needles; the altimeter and rate-of-climb, airspeed and turn-and-bank. With each fresh outburst, he would feel the responsive knotting of his shoulders, and try to will himself . . . I will *not* let it get to me. The problem was that it had *got* . . .

The Seabee was ten feet above the bay, throttled back for the landing, when the patient freed an arm from restraint.

Fulton heard the first-aid man cry out, and felt a numbing blow to the back of his head.

Stunned momentarily, he had no recollection of pulling back on the yoke, was only aware, appalled, that the aircraft had reared nose-high with little airspeed remaining, and was shuddering at the brink of a destructive stall.

He slammed the control column forward, and applied full power. The Franklin responded, the propeller biting into air, clawing for thrust and speed. Thankfully, he felt the ugly shudder in the airframe that warned of the stall recede as lifting air flowed, hardening, around the wings . . .

Pandemonium, though, within the cramped cabin, the demented patient flailing out, more wild blows landing as the first-aid man struggled to subdue him.

Attempting to avoid the blows, and keep control of the aircraft, Fulton yelled, "GOD *DAMN* YOU! GET HIM *OFF* ME!"

"TRYIN', AREN'T I . . ." The other's voice was shrill with fright and indignation. "Jesus CHRIST . . . what's UP with you? You nearly had us in the drink then . . ."

"You dim-witted son of a BITCH!" The last thread of self-control snapped. "THAT was because YOU weren't doing your JOB!"

He fought to overcome rage; this was not the time or place. He had overshot the intended touch-down point; the Seabee was heading out into the open Sound. He should, he knew, climb away, circle back, begin a fresh approach, and dismissed that: he wanted these two out of his aircraft, out of his *sight*, with no further delay . . . !

No more blows struck him; Fulton risked a furious backward glance. The first-aid man was pinning the freed arm down. He stared, hot-eyed, at Fulton. "I don't like bein' talked to like that!"

"Too bad!" Fulton ordered, "now shut up, and keep *him* off me!"

He was shaking as he gave his attention to his flying, levelling the wings, aligning the nose with the horizon, thinking only of getting down . . . *now*.

He closed the throttle once more, lifting the nose . . . but it felt all wrong: the well-established rapport with the airplane was lost . . .

Like the scared, inept student he had once been, he flattened the descent too high and too sharply: the Seabee ballooned, hanging in the air as if undecided, before dropping hard into the water. There was a rumbling crunch; under such conditions calm water could feel about as yielding as a pile of rocks . . .

The Seabee bounced high, and, still rattled, he managed only clumsily to catch it on the rebound with a burst of throttle. Almost past caring then, Fulton let it settle jarringly once more, completing what he could acknowledge wretchedly as the worst landing—definitely—of his career.

*

Six figures watched as he made his approach to the pontoon: two white-clad orderlies and Olaf Pedersen, then, a little apart, Mike Denholm and Bob Peters, both grim-faced; Jackie Seaweed, habitually expressionless, his pike-pole in hand, ready to hook on. And why was it, Fulton wondered, that there was always a crowd around when you screwed-up?

As he reached up to the reverse pitch lever to slow the aircraft, the patient convulsed, yelling, dislodging the first-aid man who, in turn, cannoned into Fulton. Cursing, he shoved the first-aid man aside, grabbing at the lever, sliding it swiftly back . . .

The interruption had lasted, perhaps, three seconds, enough time for the reversing propeller's braking effect to come too late to prevent the nose slamming into the side of the pontoon.

The impact jerked Fulton against his seat-belt: he watched, helpless, the men on the pontoon scattering. Air flooded the cabin as the heavy impact dislodged one of the plexiglas windshield panels.

He sat numbed, as Jackie Seaweed dived to retrieve the panel before it disappeared into the water, as Mike Denholm got a rope on to the nose cleat, and Peters seized a wildly-swinging wingtip.

Denholm yanked open the bow-hatch to inform Fulton in icy tones, "as dockings go, I'd call that, and your so-called landing, pretty bloody spectacular! I just hope you can explain them."

*

The patient, still yelling, had been driven away. The first-aid man rounded on Denholm. "I want to see the clown that's in charge of this shambles!"

"You're in luck." Denholm nodded, cold-eyed. "I'm that clown."

"Then get *this* in your head . . ." A quivering finger pointed at Fulton. "I swear I'll never fly with *him* again!"

Fulton looked at him. "Is that a promise?"

"Hush . . . *gentle*-men . . ." Denholm lifted soothing hands. "What seems to be the trouble here? Apart from things observed already?"

"*I'll* tell you what. He ought to be canned for a start! And I'll be tellin' your Head Office that!"

"Fine." Denholm nodded. "But let's be fair . . ."

"What's *fair* got to do with anything?"

"Two sides, sir, to every story." Denholm eyed him levelly. "We'll be hearing both. So tell us yours first . . . calmly, please."

Fulton listened glumly, watching as Peters examined the truant windshield panel. The Seabee's bow section, he saw with dismay, but no surprise, was crumpled . . .

"No bastard's ever talked to *me* like that," the first-aid man rasped. "I'll make sure your high brass fixes his wagon."

Fulton was stung to reply, "the reason I spoke that way . . ."

"Hear *that*?" the first-aid man demanded. "The bastard *admits* it!"

". . . is because you fell down on your job and nearly got us killed!"

"Easy, Jack," Denholm soothed. "Your turn's coming." He told the first-aid man, "maybe you should take it a little easy yourself?"

"I'm gettin' sick an' tired of you bastards tellin' me what to do, and what not . . ."

"Kind of free with the 'bastards', aren't you, sir?" Denholm was very quiet. "That's the third time, and pretty direct."

The first-aid man looked at him, nonplussed. "It wasn't meant like . . ."

"Used like that, in anger, by a stranger," Denholm pointed out. "It can become offensive."

No one moved, all eyes watched the now-hapless first-aid man. The flow of tidal water around the pontoon seemed unnaturally loud.

The first-aid man muttered, "guess I was pretty mad, eh?"

"You'd have to be to get that personal." Denholm gave him a thin smile.

"If it was me he said it to," Jackie Seaweed announced. "I'd clean his clock for him."

"I know, Jackie." Denholm nodded. "But that's not how we run the railroad, is it?"

"No, Boss . . ." The Indian watched the first-aid man with flat, opaque eyes. "I'd call that a shame."

"Well, maybe I was out of line . . ." The first-aid man stared at Fulton. "But I still got a beef with *him*!"

"Right. So now that point's made, shall we hear his?" Denholm invited, "Jack?"

Certain of his ground, Fulton told it fairly. "The patient was in a dangerous state. Snaky, *he* said." He glanced without expression at the first-aid man. "The camp super was willing to make other arrangements if I refused the trip."

Denholm demanded, "so why *did* you take it?"

"I had to come back. The patient seemed well-secured. So I was told by someone who's supposed to know these things."

The first-aid man snapped, "I been first-aidin' in the woods since before you was in rompers, sonny!"

"Then why such a shit job? You knew how he was, and were meant to watch him. Ten minutes . . . *that* was all."

"Would you agree, sir?" Denholm wondered.

"Guess he *was* actin' up some."

"Yet you didn't watch him?"

"Maybe not all the time. But . . ."

"No buts . . ." Denholm's voice had hardened. "A ten-minute flight, as stated, yet you managed to let the person in your care endanger life and cause the aircraft to be damaged . . ." The first-aid man made no reply, his eyes darting from face to face. "All I can say is, if Jack had handled his end of the bargain the way you've handled yours, he would no longer be flying for us. He would never have flown for us at all." Denholm was nodding thoughtfully. "You might ponder that when you call in at Head Office . . . ?"

The first-aid man had gone resentfully away.

"My turn for a roasting?" Fulton wondered.

"Need one, do you?"

Fulton's eyes followed the distant, trudging figure. "Another unhappy customer."

"He'll get over it. Have a few beers . . . fly back in the morning with me. He'll see sense by then. He's not a bad little fart . . . just gets excited."

"Maybe . . ."

"When that happens, everything's blown out of kilter. You bawled him out, made him feel stupid. For all the blah-blah, *he* knows whose fault it was. Probably more mad with himself than you."

"He could've fooled me."

"Makes you wacky living in the bush like he does," Denholm explained. "Makes a rugged individualist of you . . . that special someone you see every day in the shaving mirror. So that, when you've got a beef, you don't pussy-foot around with the hired help.

It's straight to Head Office to deal with those you see as almost, but not quite, as important as *you*!"

*

A day *off*, Fulton thought jubilantly. Instead of getting reamed-out, I wind up with twenty-four hours to call my own. Although it had not been a reward, exactly.

Bob Peters provided caustic explanation. "I can stick the windshield back in minutes, good as new. Not so easy with that nose. It's like the novelty card caption . . . 'the impossible we do at once. Miracles take a little longer'."

"That's really *funny*, Bob."

"The nose isn't, though. *That's* serious." The engineer admitted, "I don't see daylight comin' through, which is more your good luck than judgement."

"I was having some grief at the time, remember?"

Peters was unmoved. "Need to make allowance for these things. An enquiry would call it finger trouble . . . pilot error."

"And you're a one-man enquiry, right?"

"If you like . . ." Peters nodded equably. "Although that decision's between us two. Whereas, for the same stunt in the Air Force, they'd probably court-martial your arse."

"You're a hard man, Bob Peters."

"It's the secret of my incredible success . . ."

The nose repair would be temporary, sufficient to tide the Seabee over until its next major overhaul.

"She'll have a hare-lipped look," Peters admitted. "But she'll still lurch her way into the air."

*

He had showered, and was pulling on a fresh shirt when the knock came. "Just a minute . . ." He went to the door, fastening buttons.

She came in lifting her face to his. "You taste of Palmolive." She examined him quizzically. "You had me wondering today if we'd ever do this again."

"How's that?"

"After your little performance in the bay . . ."

He looked crestfallen. "You saw."

"And *how* I saw!"

He explained briefly, aware of her concern beneath the bantering tone, offering, "two sides to the coin, good and bad. What you witnessed was the bad side."

"Tell me about the good."

"The airplane, by virtue of my masterly handling, is decked. I've got a day off."

"You mean they give prizes for stunts like that?"

"You really know how to hurt a fellow."

"Oh, gee . . ." She was laughing at him. "Are you cut to the quick?"

"*And* deeply mortified."

"Quick . . . tell me how I can make it up to you!"

"Share my day off? Go to the Private Place?"

"There's a small problem."

"You're working," he said, resigned.

"Graveyard shift."

"Oh, well . . . what the hell?"

"Doesn't mean we can't go. But I'll have to be back. If that'll do?"

"*Fine* . . ." He brightened. "Anything!"

"Let's do it. Start early . . . back about five?"

"Absolutely."

"I'll initiate you," Tamara promised. "Into the joys of ice-bath swimming. You'll love it."

"Don't bet on that!"

She had come to tell him, among other things, she said, that Billy Langewische was coming to supper. "His wife's away, and he's batching. Ma wondered if you'd come too."

"Love it . . ." He asked, "will you be there?"

"With bells on," she vowed.

"Is it some kind of occasion?"

"Seems Stepan has an announcement to make, and Billy's part of it. They're springing it on us this evening," Tamara said.

*

"Be go workin' the woods together . . . partners," Stepan informed everyone happily.

Rosa beamed at Billy Langewische. "Hey . . . is *good*! Long time since last time."

"Couple of years, Rosa . . ." The big logger grinned at Stepan. "Too long, old fella."

"Damn' right! But we make him up now . . . make piss-pot full of money." Stepan toasted this belief with a commendably moderate swallow of beer.

"What you do this time . . ." Rosa's gaze upon Stepan was benign. "Scalin'? Timber cruisin'?"

"Bit of everything," Billy Langewische volunteered. "But all pay-dirt stuff." He gulped coffee as black and thick as molasses. "Four weeks . . . maybe run to six."

"Is for C.F.P.," Stepan put in. "They worryin' about fire season startin'." He waved a hand. "Big timber sale up to Vernon Lake . . . plenty wood cut already. Want him down in the water fast, before he burns up."

"Four weeks, eh?" Rosa asked.

"For *sure*. More, we be gettin' lucky."

"Hot *damn*!" She clapped joyous hands. "Four weeks you not be hang around my house, crazy man! Is to make whoopee, eh?"

"This no-good place . . ." Stepan was shaking his head dolefully. "Be quick gettin' know how people, they think of you!"

"When do you go, Pop?" It was the first time Fulton had heard Tamara call him that.

"Bright and early, liddle one." He gazed at her fondly. "Take my boat to Beaver Cove . . . ride up in truck from there. Mean old trip . . ." He looked at Rosa. "Long time no see my best gels. Be miss you pretty bad, hokay?"

"Old fool knucklehead . . ." But Rosa's acid tone was in conflict with the warmth in her eyes. "Sometime you so sloppy, come near to make me puke!"

*

Tamara wore a white bathing suit that was innocent of straps or other visible means of support, and which flattered further her lithe, tanned body. He watched her, conscious of the pleasurable stir of excitement in his groin. He could not prevent it, and did not care to . . .

He hid feelings and turmoil under flippancy. "That thing . . ." He pointed to the bathing suit. "How does it stay up in the water?"

"Womanly secrets . . ." She looked demure. "Not for sharing with crude males."

"Quite all right . . ." He affirmed piously, "I am the soul of refined sophistication."

She asked with wonder, "how could I have *missed* that?"

"So? Going to tell me?"

"Muscle-power, willpower and determination."

"No buttons and bows? Whalebone? Steel girders?"

"I have admirable muscles."

"I can but agree. He eyed the bathing suit. "But I'll bet you five bucks it comes off."

"Baby . . . you are *on*!" With swift movements she coiled up her hair, and pulled on her bathing cap, fastening the strap, then turned to the water.

"Coming?"

"It's not my bathing suit that's on trial."

"If you're hoping to see me come to grief . . ." Her hands smoothed over her body to her breasts. "You're going to have to get close and wet. In over your head."

"That's a terrible price to pay."

"Nothing's free in life . . ." Her eyes challenged him. "Well?"

He stepped, shuddering, into the sea, following Tamara who was already up to her waist.

The water rose above his knees, and he rose with it, on to his toes, trying to defer for a little longer the moment of full immersion. Not even Tamara, or her suspect bathing suit, he believed, could merit this torment. Like a vice, the water pinched his over-eager groin, and he ruminated upon the loss of potency: maybe that *was* what they meant about cold baths . . . ?

Tamara looked back at him mockingly. "Only one way, lover . . . got to be *bold*!" She plunged with a little gasping scream and went away from him in a smooth crawl before turning thirty yards out. "Come on, chicken! It's *great* . . . !" She kicked up out of the water, a malicious mermaid. "Lookit . . ." Her bathing suit was firmly in place. "Kiss your money goodbye!" She splashed ice-water towards him. "Cash only . . . no cheques!"

"Yeah? We'll see . . ." He drew a last gulp of sun-warmed air, and dived into fire and ice, stinging and astringent, thinking with grim intensity of the equation: movement equals friction equals *warmth* . . .

He came up beside her, spluttering. "Christ Al-MIGHTY!"

"Didn't I say it was nice?" She paddled gently, seemingly unaffected by the chill. "See what you'd have missed?"

"I'd . . . have done so . . . gladly . . ." His teeth chattered; there was no feeling left below his waist . . .

Tamara demanded, "Five dollars, please."

"Here? *Now*?"

"Before you try and chisel."

He said with difficulty, "n-not yet . . ."

"Why not? It stayed up . . . look." She rolled on to her back and floated.

"I'm looking, and it's . . . looking g-good. But there must be *something*? Suction cups, maybe?"

"I'm treating that crack with the contempt it deserves," Tamara declared.

"Anyhow, you're not out of the water yet . . ." He managed against the odds to grin. "There's many a s-slip between cup and . . . whatever."

"That's a lousy pun, and you couldn't even finish it."

"What counts is you haven't won yet. Calamities can still occur between here and dry land . . ." He rhapsodised yearningly. "Beautiful, *warm*, dry l-land." It's getting so that I can hardly shape the words, he thought. I'm like the guy who fell in the glacier. Ten thousand years from now, I'll come out the other end, stiff as a board and perfectly preserved . . .

Tamara jeered, "you think you're pretty smart."

"Only smart-*ing*!"

"We'll race out a hundred yards," she suggested. "That'll warm you up. And my bathing suit *will* stay put!"

"God help me. I'm in love with a masochist . . ." He had had enough: he was beaten, and knew it. "Enjoy your hundred-yard dash, Esther Williams. This-here land mammal's heading for home . . ." He turned shoreward, eager for the sun's raw heat on his body . . .

Tamara called after him, "are you a man, or a mouse?"

He raised a shrivelling arm in farewell. "Hope your mother put some cheese in the picnic!"

He stumbled ashore over sharp stones. Tamara swam on tranquilly, trailing a small wake across the blue calm. He watched her, wondering how can she *stand* it . . . ?

Flopped on his spread towel, relishing the slow drip of returning warmth, he thought of her, his eyes closed the better to savour the images that drifted in his mind.

She had looked lovely in the water, and the bathing suit had not betrayed her. Must discover how she—or it—did that, he decided drowsily. And how might it have been had I won the bet . . . he pictured her, a bare-breasted goddess rising from the sea: she shimmered in his mind's eye, smiling for him . . . that particular smile both tender and mocking.

In his deepening dream he sensed soft footfalls close to him; his skin prickled in the delicious anticipation of her touch. Her voice murmured, "hey, there . . ."

He wakened, squinting up, thinking . . . I went out like a light! The real Tamara stood over him, glistening from the sea. She had taken off her bathing cap, and was holding it over him, rounded, dripping, heavy-seeming . . .

The inner alarm was sounding too late as she said, "a present from the Pacific . . ." And emptied her brimming cap over him.

He yelled with shock, seeing her, as his vision cleared, laughing down at him, poised for flight.

"*BRENKO* . . . I'M GOING TO *KILL* YOU!" He was on his feet, stinging wet, lunging for her as she fled, squealing with fear and laughter. "No good RUNNING! There's nowhere to HIDE!"

He pursued her, heedless now of the cutting stones underfoot. She cried out, breathless, "I'll run in the water . . . you're too big a coward to follow me!"

"Not *now*! That won't save you!"

Instead, she ran on to where the cove ended at the great piled dam of driftwood, and turned, giggling, hands clasped before her, imploring, "oh mercy, pray, kind sir!"

"You'll get *mercy*!" He advanced with grim purpose. "And you'd *better* start praying!"

She wrung her hands pitifully. "How could you *use* a maiden so?"

"Easily," he retorted. "And you swiped *that* line from a song."

"Alas," Tamara wailed. "I am undone . . . !"

"You're about to be!"

She watched him, unmoving, as he reached for her, only beginning to struggle, fighting him, as he clasped her in his arms. They grappled, swaying and stumbling, half-choked with laughter and excitement. She swung her legs up, twisting her body, and almost managed to break free, but he held his grip, holding on to the top of her bathing suit, feeling the smooth fabric under his fingers: feeling it loosen suddenly as she tried once more to free herself, and the zipper rasped downward to expose her to him . . .

"Holy *cow*!" She gave a little abashed giggle. "You meant that, didn't you? Now I *am* undone!" And, looking at him, "you weren't kidding, were you?"

He stood, not moving, tensed for her fury, but, instead, wanton and deliberate, she cupped the bared breasts in her hands, emphasising their shape, a move to provoke and challenge him.

Not thinking now of the fears that had made her reject him before: those bonds were released, might never have been. There was only this, and this moment . . .

"Looks like I owe you five bucks." She felt deliciously bawdy: it was a comment that Rosie O'Grady, herself, might have approved. She gave a little shrug. "As Stepan would probably say . . . 'easy come, easy go'." She cocked her head. "How do you want it? Cash . . . or trade?"

He reached out to cover her hands with his, knowing what, now, was expected of him and what to do . . .

*

Fulton was with Alice Royle in the office when the radio call came.

"Blackfish Harbour, this is Campbell River. Over."

She thumbed the microphone button. "Go ahead, Campbell River."

"Roger, Alice . . . relaying a call for you. They couldn't raise you themselves."

She reached for her pad and pencil. "Ready to copy."

"Blackfish, the location is Vernon Lake. Upper Camp . . ."

Fulton stiffened, thinking of . . . Vernon Lake, of Upper Camp. Where Stepan and Billy Langewische were making their base . . .

"Confirm two . . . say again *two* . . . stretcher cases. Over."

Alice Royle was watching him, her expression seeming to suggest . . . it could be *anyone*. But the sick foreboding was back . . .

"Campbell River . . . can you advise on the injuries?"

"Negative, Blackfish . . ." The metallic voice punched through a squeal of static. "Contact's pretty broken up."

"No names?" she persisted, her gaze on Fulton.

"One only," the reply came, and he held his breath. "Not sure, but it sounded something like Billy *Language*. Over."

*

He spied Stepan at once, waiting on the pontoon, unhurt. Signalling frantically . . . *get* here!

There were men on the shore, and two Indian women, all gathered around the bundled shapes of the stretchered patients.

Stepan was weeping as Fulton stepped through the bow-hatch; semi-coherent and babbling. "Highpockets . . . thank Christ you come! Billy, he in bad shape. Tore up to bits . . ."

"Okay, Stepan . . . we'll get him out." Fulton gripped the shaking shoulders. "Easy, now . . . easy."

A tall young man hurried on to the pontoon. "Wes Carradice . . . first-aider. You ready to roll, man?" He had an abrasive manner.

"Get the first one loaded . . . the most serious, if there's a choice?"

"Make it *Billy*!" Stepan begged tearfully. "Be quick . . . not waste no time!"

"Look . . . let it go, old-timer," Carradice told him sharp-toned. "We know what we're doin' . . ." He shouted to the shore, "bring 'em down!"

As the stretchers were raised, Fulton said, "I can only take one."

"*Billy*!" Stepan was insisting again. "Got to be Billy . . ."

"ONE?" Carradice sounded incredulous. "*Why*, for Christ' sake?"

"Weren't you told? The Seabee takes only a single stretcher."

"Holy *Jesus*! No son of a bitch said." Carradice sounded accusing. "Why didn't you bring the bigger plane?"

"Because it's not set up for ambulance work. Plus it's at Ocean Falls on a charter."

"What a two-bit lash-up . . ." Carradice bawled at the approaching bearers, "hold everything! We got problems . . ."

A voice called back, "fella here wants to talk to the pilot."

"Yah . . . talk to him, Highpockets," Stepan said eagerly. "You see then how bad he hurt . . ."

But Billy Langewische, chalk-white and sweating, speaking in a hoarse whisper, had ideas of his own.

Fulton knelt beside the stretcher, noting the 'Morphine Given' tag attached to it. "What in hell have *you* been doing?"

"Cracked one too many walnuts . . ." Langewische was grinning. "Jack, listen . . . somethin' I need."

"Anything, Billy."

"Take the woman first . . . see she's okay. Then come back for me."

Stepan grew agitated. "Billy . . . you *crazy*? Got be go *now*! She not so bad . . . can wait . . ."

"Stepan . . . shut up, will you?" Langewische clung on to the grin. "Don't you never quit yakkin' . . . ?" He coughed chokingly, spitting blood and saliva, and told Fulton, "don't fight me on this . . . I'm the one gets to say. She goes first."

"Billy, if you're sure . . . ?"

"She's hurt bad, and havin' a kid." The grin tightened. "I'm done already with the menopause, so she gets first kick at the cat!"

*

She was a young woman, clearly in pain, but there was no morphine tag. Fulton wondered if that was to do with her pregnancy. Or that Carradice, more accustomed to the lacerating injuries of woodsmen, was out of his depth with a woman . . .

Like all the Indians he had met, she was stoical and unrevealing: a deep stillness seemed to sustain her. She showed nothing, lying quietly, bearing her pain, watching him with raisin-dark, expressionless eyes as he climbed the Seabee away from the lake.

He sat at the controls and pondered what could have brought her to this state. It was not the baby, he now knew; that was not due for several weeks. His curiosity grew: he wanted to *know* about her, and her affliction, and how, if at all, was it connected with Billy Langewische, hurt badly enough to cough up blood back there on the shore, and to need morphine . . .

Levelling off, he smiled at her. "Not long, and we'll be there . . . get you seen to." She merely nodded, and he offered, "I'm Jack. Can I ask your name?"

"It's . . . Clara."

"Hi, Clara. You okay there?"

"Yeah . . . it's fine."

He asked with care, "were you hurt with Billy? The fellow we left behind?"

She nodded yes. "Does it hurt to talk, Clara?"

The Indian eyes gave away no secrets. "Okay to talk some." She confessed almost shyly, "makes it feel easier."

"We'll get things fixed for you," he promised again. "I was wondering what happened? If you feel like telling me."

She answered at once, "an old cougar done it." As if being savaged by a mountain lion was nothing out of the ordinary. "He cut me up some . . . maybe hurt my baby . . ." For the first time, a flicker of something—fear, or anger, or both—showed in her eyes. "That big fella fought the cougar with his bare hands. Killed him, I reckon." She added sombrely, "I seen how it bust him open."

Her husband ran a trapline in the high country above Vernon Lake, and had been gone since daybreak, leaving her alone in the shack close to the big new timber sale. She had seen the two white men working a few hundred yards away with their scaling rods and notebooks, and the big one waved to her.

She was out pegging up the wash when the mountain lion attacked.

She heard nothing of its approach and, when it first landed on her, felt no pain: only a weight that bore her down, causing her to fall heavily.

At first, shocked and uncomprehending, she imagined it was Eddie, her husband, back early off the trapline, sneaking up to scare her. She was hopping mad; his dumb-fool trick might have hurt the baby.

She twisted under him, striking out, yelling at him to get *off* her . . . and saw the cat, looking with blank astonishment into the great golden eyes: there was an instant in which to appreciate its terrible beauty, the sleek head, the body's muscular, graceful length. No beauty, though, in the yawning jaws, the yellowed fangs of a carnivore with prey. No beauty in the carrion breath . . .

A woman, she thought only of the child she carried: the God-damned bloody cat could do what it liked with *her*, but if it put a scratch on her baby . . . !

She was fighting then for their two lives: she was young, strong, a half-wild creature herself, without fear, borne up by the pumping drive of adrenalin. Fighting, she screamed her rage and hate at the mountain lion.

Something fatalistic within pointed out that, with odds like these against her, the best she could fight for was *time*. Long enough, maybe, for someone to hear or see, and come and help. Although who, and from where . . . ?

As she fought and yelled, it *did* seem that she heard an answering cry. Like a man's voice, or was that vain, wishful thinking?

Until, as if it had never been, the weight was gone from her. She lay drained, fighting now for air, not knowing if she was hurt or, if so, how badly. Knowing only that the cougar was gone, and that, somewhere nearby, a terrible struggle was going on that involved her no longer.

Dimly she recognised the big man who had waved. Now, clutching the body of the cat in massive arms, shouting at the cat in a furious voice, "you Goddam no-name son of a *bitch*, you . . . !"

She tried to make sense of it; a man body-wresting a mountain lion, his hands buried in the thick, tawny hair of its throat, the cat fighting for its own survival, using all its strength, all its tricks. The powerful hind legs bunching, then spring-releasing as though triggered, the terrible claws shredding the man's clothes, ripping into his flesh, scoring murderous points against him. And *that* could be the man's death she watched, the blood flooding from his rent belly. Other things, too, that were not blood: *bits* of him in glistening colours riding the river-currents of his blood . . .

Yet, as he fought, and emptied himself into the earth, he could still shout at her, "get INSIDE, girl! Hole UP! Don' come out for NOTHIN'!"

And she obeyed, accustomed to obedience when a man commanded. Finding that she *could* obey: she had the strength still, and could stand, shaky on her feet, shocked by the sight of her *own* blood, so much soaking her shirt and denims. She knew *pain* then and saw the tears of claws in her clothing and down into her own body, and thought with terrible fear of the baby inside her . . .

Obedient, she sought the shelter of the little cedar-shake cabin that Eddie and his brothers had built, stumbling inside, thinking of Eddie's .30-30 Winchester, and how she could have shot the cougar with it, and helped the big man. But Eddie had the carbine with him up the mountain, and there was no other weapon. And all she could do was as she had been *told* to do: bar the door, hole up, *don't* come out . . .

In a while it grew quiet, no sound of conflict, not of man or lion. She should, she knew, open up, look . . . *investigate.* There was a man out there who had helped her, but the cat had done awful things to him. Yet, what if the man had died, and the cat waited for her to show herself . . . ?

The man had thought of that: '. . . hole up . . . don't come out . . . !'

She obeyed, crouching voiceless in the dim stillness, feeling the pain in her clawed belly and thighs, the warm, heavy drip of blood that formed a pool on the bare-board floor. Going out, cheap and easy, like water from a leaky faucet . . .

There was movement outside, a shuffling in the soft dirt, and it *must* be the cat, for, would the man not speak? Circling out there, seeking her: she watched the door fixedly; could it break in? Or spring over the stacked firewood and through the single window . . . ?

Deeply fearful, her mind clamouring, she did not at first register the voice until the anguished cry pierced her consciousness, "oh, by God . . . Jesus *Christ* . . . !" And then, angry, it seemed, calling to her, "YOU in there! Be HELP me . . . help my FRIEND!"

Different voice . . . not the big man. Oddball way of talking. Like some *bohunk* . . .

She stayed silent, stayed in place, watching with absorbed fascination the widening pool of blood. Realising, with each leaden, deliberate drip, that she felt funny . . . kind of light-headed and woozy. Drifting away . . . hard to keep awake, although she knew she must. Because there was another guy out there, and that would be the big man's side-kick. Calling for her help. There was something wrong with the big man, and she ought to go because he had saved their lives, her and her baby. But she was scared of the cat that had ripped her so bad that she messed her clean floor with herself . . .

"God DAMN you! Be come OUT . . . helpin' me . . . !"

Calling her again . . . sounding so *mad*.

"Why you hide in there? Billy save your bacon . . . you not help *him*?" She heard his bitterness, and lowered her head, ashamed: you didn't refuse help to people. "Sum'n'a'bitch *Indians* . . . all the same. Take everythin' goin' . . . don' never give nothin' back!"

Her pride suffered; she wanted to say how cruel and unfair that was. Bloody *whites* . . . shooting off their faces . . . never *thinking*. She wanted to shout at him, "why don't you bastards give us a break?"

But she could not be bothered with words: everything with whites was *words*, and none ever meant anything. And, anyway, she was too tired to argue with some Indian-hating bohunk that talked like a D.P. . . . couldn't even say the words right . . .

She subsided on to the table, lying there, hardly caring, guessing that she was bleeding to death. Finding that . . . it wasn't so bad. Like getting tireder and tireder. Must be worse ways to go . . .

The confused awareness of an opening door, the flood of sunlight, it seemed that she could make out the outline of a man against the light. A *man*, not a cat. And his cock-eyed bohunk voice coming from somewhere far away . . . farther even than Eddie's trapline up on the mountain . . .

"Oh . . . liddle gel . . . poor kid . . . I so *sorry* . . . not knowin' what *happen*. Billy not say me nothin' how bad you *hurt*. Be think you hidin' out . . . *sorry* liddle baby. Hokay now . . . goin' take good care o' you. Look after you and Billy . . . !"

TWELVE

"Take me with you, Highpockets!" Stepan voiced anguished appeal, "got to go with Billy, hokay?"

"Stepan, I've only got the one spare seat," Fulton reminded him gently.

"Is all I need . . ."

"I need to keep it free for the first-aider."

On the shore, Carradice was bent over Billy Langewische's stretcher. The two bearers waited stolidly.

Stepan suggested, "maybe he not wantin' to go?"

"We don't know yet. With someone in Billy's condition, chances are he will." But Fulton was moved by the misery in Stepan's eyes. "I'll talk to him. Just don't get your hopes up."

"Thanks, Highpockets. Knew you'd see it my way."

"Try not to worry."

"Can't help worry. Scared stiff for Billy."

Fulton offered, smiling stiffly, "cougar-wrestling won't stop him. And just *one* cougar?"

"You not see what I seen . . ." Stepan's tears streamed unchecked. "What that cat done to him."

No, I haven't, Fulton agreed silently. But I've heard as much as makes no difference: in stark, simple language, Clara had left little to the imagination. He asked softly, "how is it, Stepan?"

"Is terrible . . ." He choked on a sob. "His guts tore out . . . hear the first-aider say big word . . ." He searched his memory. "Dis . . . dis . . . ?"

Sickened, Fulton prompted, "disembowelled?"

"Yah . . . *that* what he say." Stepan's eyes squeezed shut. "All Billy got for hold him in one piece is bandage and cotton battin' . . ."

Gingerly, the bearers were bringing the laden stretcher down.

"Goddam fuckin' cougar be *dead*," Stepan said harshly.

"Yes?"

"Billy done it . . . crack his neck, like walnuts." Fulton thought of the party trick, the rock-hard shell crunched in one huge hand. What chance would a mere cougar have had . . . ? "Big old male, half-starved . . . see his bones stick out. No game up high, maybe, and he come down low for hunt. Figure be make meal of the Indian gel. Come close, too, except Billy choke the life out of him . . ."

The bearers lowered the stretcher. Carradice demanded tersely, "same as the squaw, then?" Fulton nodded, thinking, some day someone's going to smack you hard, and that can't be such a bad thing. Carradice ordered, "okay, guys . . . get him loaded."

"Hang on," Fulton said.

"What *now*?" Carradice eyed him. "More problems?"

"Wondering if you needed to go to Blackfish? If not, Stepan, his partner, would like to make the trip."

Carradice looked thoughtful. "No real need, I guess. The hospital people only have to remove the dressings, and there it is." He seemed heedless of the wakeful patient within earshot. "I'll stay put."

Billy Langewische smiled through it all, as though at some private joke. "You come back for me, then, Jack."

"Said I would. Part of the service."

"Told you I'd bring you some business some day." The injured man looked at Stepan. "*You* still here, you old buzzard?"

"God-damn' *right*!" Stepan smiled through tears. "Not get rid of me so easy."

"That's what worries me . . ." Langewische asked Fulton, "how's the gal doin'?"

"Clara? Just fine. Billy."

"By God . . . it's *Clara* now, is it?" Langewische choked on a laugh, and finished, gasping, "you make out with all the chicks, eh? God-damn' glamour-pants aviators!" He swivelled his gaze back to Stepan. "We're in the wrong business, partner. Soon's I'm fixed-up, I'm takin' up flyin'!"

*

Fulton had only one more trip that day to bring in a Japanese troller-man from Winter Harbour with a badly-poisoned hand. By three o'clock, he was through.

Outside the coffee shop, he spotted Stepan's old Dodge approaching, wreathed in blue smoke. It pulled up in a clatter of tappets. The power saw was in the back with the peevees and wedges and mauls.

"Cutting wood?" Fulton asked.

"Reckon a little . . ." Stepan was unsmiling. "Where you headin'?"

"For coffee. Join me?"

"Sure . . . yah." He eased the truck on to the shoulder. "Make him quick. Got the log, and chores, to see to." He stared at Fulton. "You be come along?"

"Could do . . ." Fulton considered the alternatives. Barring another call, he was at a loose end. Tamara had the four-to-midnight shift. "Why not? I'll have to let Aunt Alice know where I am."

"That's hokay. Be workin' close by the airplane dock this time. No need to come look . . . just whistle."

As they drank coffee, Fulton ventured, "the news must be pretty good about Billy? If you feel up to cutting wood?"

"Don't know nothin' about that," Stepan replied shortly. "I go out of hospital . . . quit that place. Billy in the operatin' room . . . Annie Markham say to me. No good stickin' around." He gave Fulton a sidelong, furtive glance. "Should have done, maybe. But hate Goddam hospital . . . go crazy in that place!"

*

It was a true drift-log, festooned with weed and encrusting marine life. Teredo worms had bored deeply into it.

"Got be dry out before she burn worth a damn," Stepan grunted.

It took thirty minutes to buck the log into sections for splitting. They rested briefly, wiping their streaming faces, and were reaching for the mauls and wedges when Olaf Pedersen's Ford appeared, racing along the shoreline road.

"That damn-fool Swede got ants in his pants again," Stepan observed. "Someday, he wrap hisself round a pole."

Fulton quipped, "maybe he's out to make a fast buck."

But the Ford skidded to a stop behind Stepan's truck.

Fulton muttered, "shit!"

"Come for you, I reckon."

"Alice must've sent him."

For the first time, Stepan smiled. "You pretty smart cookie, Highpockets. Every time we start *real* work, you bugger off, fly your airplane. I thinkin' you fix it so's . . ."

"STEPAN!" Pedersen stood at the roadside, staring down.

"Hey? What's eatin' him . . . ?"

Pedersen hurried down the bank towards them.

Fulton offered, grinning, "maybe he wants *you* to fly . . ."

"Oh, my CHRIST!" Stepan, dropping his maul, broke into a shambling run towards the storekeeper, crying out, "BILLY . . . ?"

And Fulton knew.

He watched them meet; Pedersen's big body looming over the slighter figure of Stepan. Which, as Pedersen spoke, gesticulating, seemed to bend as though under some terrible, insupportable load. Pedersen's hands gripped Stepan's shoulders, and Fulton, hurrying forward, heard him say, "I come straightaway . . . knew you'd want to hear. Stepan, I'm so fuckin' *sorry*!"

Words moved in Fulton's mind, words like 'why' and 'waste'. A furious question glowed like a neon sign . . . what was the *point*? What was gained . . . what improvement brought about?

*

They were at the pre-operative stage, the surgeon still scrubbing, when Billy Langewische died.

It had been quick, apparently painless, the brief onset of

Cheyne-Stokes breathing, evidence of the brain starved of oxygen. Until, there on the cart, waiting to be wheeled in, the breathing stopped for ever.

"They're callin' it shock," Pedersen explained. "He waited too long, sendin' the Indian woman back first. If he'd come sooner, he might've made it."

Stepan asked brokenly, "What about Billy's Missus?"

"She was at the hospital, Stepan."

"What they *say* to her?"

"Same's I'm tellin' you now."

"Jesus . . . *Jesus* . . . !" Stepan stared before him at nothing. "What Aggie goin' do now?" he caught a choking breath. "That her *husband* . . . my partner . . . back there dead!"

"I know that, old friend."

Stepan beat his clenched fists against his head. "It be ME! *I* make Billy die . . . !"

"Stepan, that's horseshit, and you know it!" Pedersen looked shaken. "Cut it out, eh?"

"He dead because I do nothin' for help him!"

"You were too far off," Fulton protested. "You couldn't have . . ."

"NO!" Stepan glared at him. "Billy same distance off, and *he* make it . . . *do* somethin'! I jus' *stan'* there. You don' know NOTHIN', Highpockets!" Stepan's face twisted in pain. "Billy not think twice . . . go straight and help. And I leave him go . . ." The voice dropped to an abject mutter. "Billy dead on account Stepan Kereniuk Goddam scared!"

He turned, hurrying away up the beach to the road. Leaving behind his truck and tools, the cut wood, trudging towards the village without a glance in their direction.

Fulton called after him, "Stepan . . . what about . . . ?"

"Let him go," Pedersen urged. "He knows what he needs to do."

"But, all his gear . . ." Fulton gestured at the cut log. "Someone'll help himself."

Pedersen suggested dryly, "guess that leaves *you* in charge."

"On my own?"

"You're big enough, and ugly enough." Pedersen was unsympathetic. "Take care of things . . ." He climbed the bank to peer into the truck. "He left the keys."

Fulton called, "what do you think he'll do?"

"With what he's got on his mind, could be anythin', or nothin' at all. Go to th' hospital, or else see Aggie Langewische? He'd *want* to see her." Pedersen shrugged. "Might go home. Or again, try the beer parlour."

*

For a dollar-fifty each, three Indian youths were willing to load the truck with the wood slabs, then ride up to the house for the off-loading.

The job was finished in an hour. The youths had no change for a five-dollar bill. Fulton wrote off the fifty cents to experience.

The house was empty and quiet: Tamara was at work, Rosa out . . . Fulton had no idea where.

He offered the youths a ride home, but they preferred to go to Hong's Café. One held up the five dollars. "Money to burn."

Outside the café Fulton ventured, "about the four bits you owe me . . ." They eyed him in silence. "You can buy me a cup of coffee sometime."

They nodded bland agreement. "Anytime."

"*Now*, maybe?"

They laughed and walked away . . .

Inside the hospital, he found Tamara at the nursing station. "Hi."

"You, too, hi . . ." She smiled. "To what do we owe the pleasure? You sick, or something?"

"I wouldn't come *here* if I was sick."

"Remember that next time you are, Sweetie."

He said, "you know Stepan's home."

"Yes . . ." She lowered her voice. "Billy? You've heard?"

"It's more or less why I'm here . . . looking for Stepan." He told her of Pedersen's bombshell. "He just took off. And he's not at home."

She looked anxious. "Does Ma know any of this?"

"Couldn't say. She wasn't there, either."

"She'd gone out before I left. Visiting a neighbour . . ." Tamara shook her head. "Don't think he's been here . . . there'd be no point. Billy's body went to the morgue hours ago."

"Sure . . ."

"What about the beer parlour?" she wondered.

"That's been on my mind."

She muttered, "oh, God . . ."

"This has knocked him for a loop. And he's blaming himself."

"But he had nothing . . ."

"That's *it*. He's saying he did nothing instead of trying to help. Thinks that would've made a difference."

She said in a low voice, "and now he'll go on a bender."

"He might not have . . . yet."

"Do you believe that?"

"Olaf figured he'd want to call on Billy's wife. Knowing how she must be feeling, there's a strong chance of it."

*

Stepan *had* been there, and gone away, an hour earlier. Janie Keebaugh, the married daughter of Wilhelm and Agnes Langewische, looked at Fulton through red, swollen eyes. "He come by to see Mom, and say how sorry he was . . ." She faltered.

"We're *all* so terribly sorry."

"You flew Dad home, eh?"

"Yes . . ."

She stood in the doorway, and did not invite him inside. "Don't want to sound mean, but Stepan shouldn't've come so soon. It upset Mom, and she didn't want to talk to him about it."

He offered gently, "Stepan's grieving, too. He wouldn't have wanted to make things worse for you, but he probably wasn't thinking straight."

She made no comment, but asked instead, "is it true? Dad strangled a cougar?"

"*And* saved a young woman . . . maybe her unborn baby, too."

She gave a choked laugh. "He's got these *unbelievable* hands. Cracks walnuts with 'em . . . does it all the time . . ." He noted with unease her use of the present tense.

He nodded. "He showed me."

"That cat shouldn't've tangled with Dad." She sounded defiant, and proud.

He answered awkwardly, "I don't know if they award medals for your father's kind of bravery, but, if so, he'd head the list. He did something you can remember always with pride . . ." But it sounded trite, like something from a pulpit, empty, ringing words about courage and devotion. All we need, he thought, is a brass band . . . !

"Oh, we're proud of him . . . always have been." She bobbed her head apologetically. "Could you please pardon me? Only I think I better go now."

*

Stepan was alone at a corner table with five full glasses and several empties before him. A sixth was in his hand, and he gazed into it, seemingly absorbed by the rising chains of gas bubbles.

The barman signalled to Fulton: Stepan did not look up as he edged by.

"Come to get him, Jack?"

"Maybe."

"Well maybe you know someone as will?"

"Has he caused any trouble?"

"Not yet."

"So, where's the problem?"

"Draw ten . . ." A waiter clattered his tray on the bar.

"Hang on, Jack . . ." The barman worked his spigot, and loaded the tray. When the waiter had gone, he murmured, "this looks like a real wing-ding Stepan's on. He's orderin' six at a go, which I shouldn't really serve him. That's his fourth order . . . nigh on twenty down the hatch already." He confided, "have to cut him off at this rate."

Fulton asked, "why not just do it?"

"Not easy . . . Stepan's a hell of a good customer . . ." The irony seemed unintended. "And there's Billy gettin' killed, and for sure, how Stepan's takin' *that*."

"That's true." Fulton was noncommittal.

"Thought you might sweet-talk him into goin' home." The barman watched Fulton hopefully. "It'd make life easier."

"I'll see," Fulton said. "But no guarantees."

The barman was drawing more beer. "Don't get me wrong. I'm not crackin' down."

"It's okay."

"HEY!" Stepan was peering their way. "Be draw another SIX!" All the glasses were empty now.

"See what I mean?" The barman sounded plaintive. "Twenty-four Goddam beers he's chug-a-lugged in under an hour . . ." He called across, "right with you, Stepan . . . soon's I can."

"Yah . . . hokay . . . when you got time."

Fulton suggested, "he doesn't *look* like trouble."

"Well, here's hopin' . . ." The barman was drawing Stepan's beer.

"Highpockets . . . ?" Stepan called then. "That you?"

Fulton dredged up a smile. "Hi, there."

"How come you talkin' to *him*?" A belligerent note appeared. "That get you nowheres."

"Just setting up a line of credit."

"You get credit in *this* place," Stepan declared caustically. "If you hunnert years old, an' got your Grandma be drink with you!" He gestured imperiously. "Not needin' no Goddam credit . . . be drink with *me*."

"That's something," the barman said. "You're the first he's talked nice to since he come in. Everyone else got their heads bit off . . ."

"Be help yourself . . ." Stepan pushed two freshly-brimming glasses across the table. "Get him down, then we get some more in."

Fulton began, "look, Stepan . . ."

"They want cut me off, eh? Drink too much?" Stepan's eyes flicked towards the barman. "That what he say?"

Fulton side-stepped the question. "You've had twenty-four beers . . ."

"Can handle twenny-four hokay. And twenny-four *more.*"

"That's not what I'm saying . . ."

"Sometimes be drink *fifty,*" Stepan boasted truculently. "*No* troubles."

"Except when you get home to Rosa."

"Rosa eh? That what all this about?"

"You know there'll be another bust-up. Rosa and Tamara unhappy . . ."

"*Different* now." Stepan grew sullen. "Billy's dead. Is why I here . . . Billy's *dead*, Highpockets!"

"Stepan, I know that . . ."

"Here for *Billy.*" He confessed wretchedly, "go see Aggie, say I sorry, how bad I feelin'. She not want see me."

"I heard that, too. I went looking for you."

"Follow me around, eh? Say me be good boy . . . not drink beer. Go back home, be with Rosa."

"It's best. It may not seem like it now, but when you're feeling better . . ."

"NEVER be *feelin'* better!" Stepan shouted furiously. "*Never* with Billy dead, and it my fault . . ."

"It's crazy to think that . . ."

"Like I kill Billy myself . . . I know it, Aggie know it. Why she not talk to me." He pointed an accusing finger. "*You* don't know nothin'! But I say you, me an' Aggie, *we* know the Goddam score!"

Fulton sat in silence, helpless, as Stepan swallowed down the beer on the table, and signalled an order for eight. "Stepan, I've had two. I don't *want* four more."

"Is for you, two . . . for me, *six.*"

"Oh, for Christ's sake!"

"You not drink, I drink all." Stepan shrugged disdainfully. "Make no difference . . ."

The waiter brought the order, telling Stepan, "barman says that's it. No more."

"Goddam sum'n'a'*bitch*!" The waiter backed away, watching Stepan.

"It's the law, Stepan," the barman called. "Nothin' personal . . ."

"Be *fuck* yourself, eh?" Fulton tensed as the room went quiet. But then Stepan slumped back, shrugging. "Hokay . . . is fair . . . I not make trouble . . ." He met each watchful eye, affecting nonchalance. "Anyhow, no fit place drink for Billy when every yahoo be hootin' and hollerin' . . . not give a shit, nohow . . ." He told Fulton curtly, "we get out of here."

"It's better, Stepan."

"Oh, that for Goddam sure . . ." He gulped a beer. "You got my truck?"

"Right outside."

Glass by glass, without stopping, Stepan drained all eight beers. "Maybe too drunk for truck. Best you drive."

"I'd call that a good idea."

"We goin' home," Stepan directed. "I tellin' Rosa about Billy. She understand this time. Not get mad."

"I'm sure she'll be fine."

With everyone watching him, Stepan swayed over the littered table. "Be only drink maybe thirty, Highpockets. Thirty nothin' for a fella be drink fifty easy!"

*

Rosa was still not at home.

"Tamara said she was visiting," Fulton explained.

"All Goddam time visitin', makin' yack-yack . . ." Riding home in the truck, Stepan had become increasingly morose. "Good thing she bendin' some other bugger's ear 'stead of mine."

"What do you feel like doing?"

"*Feel* like?" Stepan gave Fulton a rictus grin. "*Feel* like goin' back in beer parlour."

"STEP-an!"

"What I *do* . . ." He gestured around at the neat, silent kitchen. "Is what any fella do in his own house."

"Just wondered if you need anything from me?"

"You be fly Billy home, Highpockets . . . be help me cuttin' wood. Be gettin' me safe home." Stepan snorted with sudden laughter. "Reckon you do enough for one day . . ."

"Now, look . . ." Fulton suppressed irritation. "I thought of maybe sticking around . . . some company?"

"Thinkin' I need you hold my hand? Maybe I do somethin' stupid . . . shoot myself in head?"

Fulton was shocked less by the statement than by Stepan's seeming perception of his thoughts. "Hell, *no* . . ." He tried to jest. "That's not your style . . ."

"Not wantin' you stick around," Stepan said harshly. "Who *need* you? Not here nor *nowheres*!"

"Well, okay . . ." But Fulton was experiencing that foreboding which would plague the start of an emergency flight. Stepan, very drunk, could be in shock over the death, hag-ridden by ghosts. Angry and hurt, he sought, like a wounded animal, to hurt in turn indiscriminately; others . . . or himself. He said worriedly, "if you want *anything*, you know where I am."

"Yah . . . thanks . . ." The aggressiveness was gone; Stepan sounded merely weary. "Best thing for me is be on my ownsome . . . go sleep it off."

Fulton nodded agreement. "No harm in that."

"Not be fit company for man or beast." Stepan managed a small smile, and waved Fulton away. "Go on home. Rosa come soon, then no more to be worry over . . ."

Fulton looked across from his door, waving to Stepan, standing there at the kitchen window. But Stepan did not wave back . . .

*

The chili was heating, the rye bread sliced for buttered toast. Fulton stood in the doorway watching the first grey tinges of evening above the distant mainland mountains. He sipped a beer, following Rosa with his eyes as she made her slow way up from the village, returning from visiting . . . and when she visits, he reflected, she really *visits*. But there would be much to talk of this day in Blackfish Harbour. He wondered how much Rosa knew.

Would she be aware of Stepan's early return, and why? And of his almost-inevitable reaction to tragedy and loss, seeking solace, without success, in alcohol?

She called up, waving, "how you doin'?"

"Okay, thanks . . ." His smile was hesitant.

She halted, watching him. "*Stupid* woman . . . what kind of question that? Everyone talkin' . . . this terrible, *terrible* thing. Keep thinkin' . . . few days past, Aggie be down to Vancouver and see her sister, and I give Billy his supper. Aggie come back two days gone, and now . . ." Her face twisted. "Never see him no more."

"I didn't know about that." It made it worse.

She said with wonder, "and my Stepan not even scratched . . ."

"You've heard, then?"

"Sure . . . whole thing." Rosa nodded sombrely.

"That Stepan's home, I mean?"

"Yah . . . is so. You bring him, eh?"

"He's inside now. I was just with him."

She asked flatly, "he been drinkin'?"

"Some . . . yes." He went hurriedly on, "Rosa . . . he's taking it hard. He saw it . . . what the cougar did to Billy."

"I hear all this." She nodded again.

"He's got it in his head that he let Billy down."

"Old fool birdbrain . . ." She was smiling sadly. "He pull stunt like that, we be havin' *two* widow women!"

"He thinks it could've made the difference."

"Like all times, he *wrong*. Thinkin' he Goddam Superman . . . 'specially when he full of beer . . ." She eyed Fulton. "He *bad* drunk?"

"Not what you'd call bad . . . and only because of Billy," he insisted quickly. "He went to see Aggie Langewische, but she wouldn't talk to him. That hit him hard, too."

"So he go beer parlour?"

"Take it easy on him, Rosa," Fulton pleaded. "He hasn't forgotten his promise, or fallen off the wagon."

"You say me not?"

He asked, "you know what we say in English about drowning our sorrows?"

"Yah . . . I hear about that."

"That's what Stepan's done . . . to help him get through it. Tomorrow, you'll see, will be different."

"Can understand that okay." She nodded pensively. "Him and Billy be like brothers . . ." Her young-girl smile came on. "I go easy, Jack. Be real nice lady to my Stepan."

*

He felt some optimism: Rosa had understood and accepted. Stepan would be forgiven his lapse . . .

The shouting began as he was clearing away the supper dishes. With sinking heart, he went to the door to listen.

Initial reaction was one of anger: what was the *matter* with Rosa: she had *promised*. Allowance would be made . . . leave it alone, ask no questions . . . The words were muffled, but the yelling, Rosa's shrill and furious, Stepan's answering bellow, could not be mistaken.

He thought of going over there, trying somehow to mediate and appeal to reason, but the savagery of their latest quarrel unnerved him. Even as he hesitated, the outside door burst open, and Stepan appeared, reeling into the yard, stumbling, then sprawling. Still clutching an almost-empty whisky bottle. He was hopelessly staggering drunk, his face bloodied, visibly swelling. As Rosa followed him out, raining kicks and blows on his bowed head . . .

"Bastard man . . . BAS-tard! They say me go easy . . . give you break. And okay, I say . . . OKAY . . . !" Stepan, on hands and knees, mumbled something, and she smacked him hard across the head. "Nobody say me nothin' about Goddam bloody WHISKY!

Bad enough you beer, beer, beer . . . but *that* sheet stuff . . . not NEVER!"

She shoved at him with her foot, and he sprawled full length: she stood over him, stocky legs astride, reaching down to snatch at the whisky bottle, but he roared at her, clinging to it, and they struggled, panting and cursing as most of the remaining whisky spilled into the dirt . . .

Stepan became still, then, staring in furious disbelief at the small, muddy patch. Until he looked up at Rosa, and the face Fulton saw then was not that of the Stepan he knew, nor of anyone he would have wished to know . . .

"GOD-DAMN' YOU FUCKIN' BITCH-WOMAN!"

In those brutal words all the resentment of the years was hurled into Rosa's face: she took an involuntary step back, and they watched each other in frozen silence. Until, as though in disbelief, she demanded, "*what* you say to me?"

But Stepan's bolt was shot; he could only gape at her, as stunned and unbelieving as she.

Rosa's face went stone-hard, and when she spoke again, she did not shout. "No need for you to say . . . I hear *fine*. All time I stick with you and your drinkin' . . . all time hatin' it. Now you say me *that* thing, I gettin' to know where I stand with you. Well, now is no *more*!" She chopped a hand downward with finality. "Is *finish*, eh? Finish me . . . finish you . . ." He watched her from bruised, puzzled eyes. "You talk that way, know what you say me? You don' give good God-*damn* for me. And okay, same here, don't give no more for you than pinch o' dry coon-sheet! With *you* is *finish*!"

"Woman . . . Christ sakes . . . listen to me . . ."

"You get *out* this house . . . *out* this yard! Not come back here no more . . . not *never*, Stepan Kereniuk!" He sat in the dust, all protest stifled as her meaning became clear. "Go be live somewheres else . . . your boat . . . on beach. Be *drop dead*. I not care. You show up here, bother my Tamara, bother me, you go to jail! You thinkin' not, you *try* me, bloody man!" Rosa strode to the door, then paused, looking back, her expression set and unyielding.

"Mean what I say to you! Now you go away!" The door slammed behind her.

With difficulty, Stepan regained his feet to stand staring bemusedly at the door, clutching the whisky bottle. He swayed there for a full minute before lifting the bottle to swallow the last drops of liquor. He frowned at it until, face twisting, he hurled it at the house. It shattered against the wall, and he yelled his defiance. "This MY house, too! Nothin' *you* say goin' keep me out my house!"

With that, he gave up, picking his lurching way to the road, a forlorn and lonely figure. Fulton watched as he went off down the hill . . .

Stepan had been an unbelievable fool to drink whisky, *and* in the house where Rosa must discover him. Yet, certainly, he had suffered enough to make him drink to excess. The feeling would not be denied that Rosa, even with justification, had been needlessly harsh.

She knew of the day's events, had been forewarned: she knew her man and his shortcomings. She would have known what he felt, how he would—must—react.

Stepan had gone out of sight, and it was not difficult to imagine where his destination would be: thirty-odd beers and a half-bottle of whisky under his belt, he would be primed to continue.

*

For the second time that day Fulton fretted over the need to go after Stepan; to see if something could be salvaged from the ruins of a partnership . . .

Common sense prompted inaction: it was Stepan's business, and Rosa's . . . stay *away*! Stepan had said it earlier . . . 'who needs you?' They're well and truly put asunder, he reflected with regret. Now *you* hold your peace . . .

But emotion offered its counter-argument: *how* was he to leave it, feeling the weight of his concern for Stepan. There could be no honour, no decency, in turning aside. To do so could risk incurring an outcome worse than any intrusion might.

In his present state, wounded and grieving, Stepan was unstable, potentially explosive. Filled with grievance, he would be scenting trouble and, as the expression had it, would surely find it . . .

The day faded into blue dimness, and Fulton sat on, undecided. The Blackfish lights came on, ringing the bay, marking the water with golden streamers. Floodlights below illuminated the hospital's emergency exits, and the Nurses' Residence offered an ordered row of warm radiance. Somewhere down there, behind the lights, Tamara would be at work, unaware of this fresh, possibly final family crisis.

He checked his watch, deciding . . . fifteen minutes more. Then, if there were no developments, he would go and look for Stepan. Down to the shoreline road, peek inside the cafés and the beer parlour. If he was not in any of those, then the hell with it . . .

He jumped at the shrilling of the telephone; until then the party-line had been unusually quiet. He listened, and it was his ring, and . . . Alice Royle, he decided. A crack of dawn booking . . .

"Jack, I do apologise for calling you so late," Ichabod said. "But I think we should meet."

"Now . . . ?"

"I'd not trouble you if it wasn't rather urgent."

It was more than a mere guess that this would be to do with Stepan. "Can't we discuss it now?"

"I believe you're on a party-line?"

"Around here, who isn't?"

"You'll be aware, then, of the attendant problems . . ."

The Blackfish Harbour telephone system provided few private lines; most residential numbers shared party-line facilities, each installation with its coded ring. Which, when rung by the operator, was the signal for all others on the line to pick up their receivers.

"This," Ichabod announced in pulpit tones. "Is *not* for shameless busybodies!"

They both heard the sharp intake of someone's indignant breath.

Fulton laughed. "*That's* tellin' 'em!"

They arranged to meet outside the hotel, and Ichabod added mystifyingly, "Mister Pedersen is with me. We're both quite concerned . . ."

He hurried down the hill, perplexed: what else *could* it be but Stepan? Who was probably in a jam somewhere; the beer parlour seemed the likely place. But then, how was Pedersen involved? And what grounds were there for his and Ichabod's 'concern'?

The others waited at the hotel entrance, from where the beer parlour's late-evening uproar was audible. Fulton demanded, "is Stepan in there?"

"You've figured it's him, then," Pedersen said.

"Who else?"

"He's long gone," Pedersen confirmed. "He *was* here, knockin' it back."

"Until he became difficult." Ichabod added, "and was ejected."

"So where's he gone?"

"That's what *we* want to know," Pedersen declared. "And pretty damn soon . . ."

*

Stepan had spent a quarrelsome hour at the beer parlour, and been warned for his behaviour.

"He appears to have been particularly unpleasant," Ichabod offered.

"I hear somebody decked him . . ." Pedersen asked, "or was that Rosa?"

Fulton confirmed this, and enquired, "is that it? Or am I missing something?"

"*We* wondered . . ." Ichabod raised baffled hands. "If you might know something we don't?"

Fulton was exasperated. "You *said* this was important. But *what*?" He saw them exchange looks. "What I *know* is that Rosa and Stepan have had the brawl to end all brawls. She's kicked him out . . . for good, she says. And it sounded as if she meant it."

"I'll be damned . . ." Pedersen was nodding. "Looks like it's addin' up."

"*What* is?"

But Pedersen persisted, "you seen nothin' of him?"

"Christ, Olaf . . . wouldn't I have *said*?"

"Jack," Ichabod said. "We're inclined to think that Stepan may intend doing himself a mischief."

"What . . . ?"

"Like blowin' his stupid Uker-rainian brains out," Pedersen finished.

Ichabod grimaced distaste. "It would *appear* so . . ."

"Appear? When he comes in my store drunk, buys a shotgun and shells, pays cash on the barrel? It'd *appear* so, all right!"

"In the state he was in?" Fulton was aghast. "And you sold him . . ."

"I'd've showed him the Goddam door!" Pedersen looked indignant. "But I wasn't there. My lame-brain assistant done it." He explained, "they was workin' late, stock-takin'. Store was shut, but the lights was on, and Stepan comes hammerin' at the window. They said to beat it, but he went on hammerin'. So, because it's Stepan, they let him inside . . ." Pedersen spread exculpatory hands. "Night *or* day, you don't turn down a sale."

"Not even to a staggering drunk wanting to buy weapons?" Fulton was scathing.

"It was that dumb kid . . ." Pedersen wore an abject look. His worried gaze flicked between them. "But, like he told me, Stepan was upright, under his own steam. He knew what he wanted, and was polite. Cash in hand . . . sixty-eight bucks."

"He made the sale, but was still concerned enough to tell *you* about it?"

"Look . . . am *I* on trial here?" Pedersen demanded with heat.

"Olaf . . . it's all right," Ichabod soothed. "But Jack has a point. Why *did* he tell you?"

"Somethin' Stepan said," Pedersen replied sulkily. "Young fool got to thinkin' about it after Stepan took off, and figured he should check with me. Because, when Stepan was lookin' the gun over, he said it was for finishin' off some job." He added, frowning, "somethin' about seein' to hisself for good."

Fulton said with finality, "that's *it*!" They watched him, frowning. "You should've acted, instead of wasting time phoning me, then us debating it!"

Pedersen'a eyes were cold. "So what's *your* answer?"

"This is in Porkchop's league."

They remained undecided. Ichabod ventured, "it's only our supposition . . ."

"But enough to scare you!" Fulton told them, "think! Stepan drunk, depressed, with a grievance . . . *and* a gun? Talking of finishing some job? Even a dimwit store assistant can hit the panic button over it once the nickel drops."

"Yes of course." Ichabod was subdued.

"It *may* turn out to be nothing, but Porkchop would still want to know about Stepan running around town armed . . ." Impatiently, Fulton turned away from them.

"And where are *you* headin'?" Pedersen demanded.

"Back to the house."

"While we get stuck with talkin' to the Horsemen, eh?"

"It's not that . . ." Fulton shrank from the picture forming in his mind, wondering why these two could not see it . . . a terrible sensing which he feared too much to define, had him running full tilt, leaving the other two to stand gaping after him. Running to warn Rosa . . .

*

All the way, up the hill to the house, he was praying half-aloud . . . *let* me be wrong! Make it just some cock-eyed bee in my bonnet. Grant me that, and I'll live gladly with the laughter and ridicule that come later . . .

Chest burning, he pounded up the steep, punishing slope, following the broken road past fallen trunks and rotting snags of trees, the legacy of land cleared for building lots that were never sold, for gimcrack houses destined not to be built. Running, it was like a hateful *dream* of running, getting nowhere on leaden feet, a malicious treadmill. At every step the wish repeating like a stuck record: 'let me be wrong, or, if not, let me be in *time* . . . !'

Until, exhausted, he came up into the shadow of his rented house, and stood, struggling to breathe, snatching the seconds needed to slow his overtaxed heart . . .

Drawing in lungsful of air, he peered over at the bigger house, at the yard and sagging woodshed, illuminated by the outside light. Seeing the slabs from the afternoon's wood-cutting lying where the Indian youths had dumped them . . .

Seeing with grim despair Stepan there, standing with his back pressed against the woodshed, watching Rosa, who faced him from the open kitchen door. Both were still, even their eyes, and, for a chill moment, Fulton was reminded of two fighting cats. Which would freeze so, motionless, until the spitting scream and flying claws. Rosa, stolid and unyielding, arms folded across her bosom. He, bizarrely, with one foot bared, the boot and sock lying in the dust. Clutching, two-handed, a twelve-gauge, double-barrelled shotgun. Holding it by the barrels, the stock on the ground, the twin muzzles pointing into his face . . .

As from somewhere down the hill, there came the sound of an abused car engine: twisting his head, Fulton saw the glow of brake lights as the vehicle made a hurtling turn into The Row to vanish behind the high school building. And he listened and watched, helpless: there was nothing more, he thought then—and was to think again in years to come—that he could do, or would have dared to do. As Stepan spoke in a child's brittle voice that cracked against the savage words it uttered, "you be thinkin' I make Goddam joke? Then I *showin'* you right now is no *joke*! You never *listen* to me . . . so now you be *watchin'*!"

Rosa, still and silent, and Fulton afraid to move, of interrupting, upsetting disastrously this most frail of balances between them. Feeling the small flicker of hope: what he feared most did not seem to be in Stepan's mind to do. Stepan was geared for violence, but a violence, it did appear, directed at himself. Or . . . hope strengthening at the thought of . . . a ploy? The stage set with care for Rosa's benefit, the bare foot, the weapon aimed as it was, the words of threat or promise. To con Rosa into backing down? *Could* that be the extent of Stepan's purpose, a big act . . . ?

Fulton knew deep anguish then as Rosa refused the bait, jeering, "is big talk . . . like everythin' with you . . . talk, talk, always *talk*!" The ploy, if intended, was not working: Rosa was too shrewd and knowing. "You try this bullsheet trick, think I knuckle under . . . say forgive, forget?" She snorted scornful amusement. "*You* the one be forget. Because it not happenin' . . . not *never* . . . !"

And, somewhere down the hill, the abused car screamed on, drawing nearer.

"You see me? I not *give* a damn!" Rosa flapped a derisive hand. "Sure . . . go shoot yourself . . . be good thing. Knock sense in your head. But make no difference . . . you be alive, be dead, not come back in this house. Nobody want you . . . nobody care. Maybe . . ." She was laughing at him. ". . . best *thing* for you be good and dead!"

And Fulton knew as surely then as if the intent had been expressed in words, what would, *must*, happen now. Because Rosa had pushed and pushed until she went that perilous inch too far, and Stepan, now, could not draw back as the weapon spun in his hands, reversing, the stock coming under one arm, both barrels pointing at Rosa as she turned away . . .

Over the car's racket, now very close, its lights bathing the house as it tore into the yard, he heard the cracked, almost childish voice of Stepan, "GOD DAMN YOU, ROSA . . . NOW YOU BE LOOKIT *HERE*!"

Rosa turning to face him once more—it seemed so slowly—her eyes meeting his with the first widening of beginning recognition as, at short range, he fired, and the full charge of buckshot tore her chest open . . .

In Fulton's eyes, then, everything splintered; it was as though he, too, had sustained some enormous destructive blast, all impressions fragmenting, mere scraps and tatters: the dull, flat report of a single discharged barrel echoing off, losing itself in black depths beyond the nearby treeline . . . Stepan standing, the shotgun loose in his fingers, watching the fallen Rosa with an odd, puzzled smile. Like a child whose violent play had ended in a manner unforeseen. Because the make-believe corpse of the bad guy did not rise to its feet and make friends again, but lay unmoving under the harsh glare of a single high-wattage bulb, with a spreading lake of blood on scrubbed floorboards. Playing the game no longer; tired to eternity of the game. Rosa, felled and broken, half-shrouded in her wrapper, dressed for bed and for sleep . . .

The car, all blazing lights, had halted beside Stepan's parked truck: Fulton saw its doors swing wide, Prokopchuk and an unknown constable vaulting out, coming forward, crouching by the truck, their Service revolvers drawn . . .

It made no sense, lacking reality, in the way that a waxen exhibit would lack while conveying an *impression* of events. Until an intruding voice could revive it, and better, perhaps, that the voice had not? Prokopchuk, his pistol in both hands, aimed, commanding, "Stepan . . . don't do anything! Set the shotgun down . . . now!"

The constable aiming also: Fulton saw how he glanced nervously at his superior, as if for guidance, when Stepan offered no response, but went on staring, hurt and baffled, at Rosa's body.

"I won't say it again, Stepan . . ." The words seeming to penetrate; Stepan's head slowly turning until he faced Prokopchuk, squinting against the headlights' glare. ". . . Put it *down* . . . right away!"

Stepan nodding, spreading his arms, a gesture of seeming submission. Still grasping the weapon.

"That's getting there," Prokopchuk soothed. "All you need do is let it drop."

And Stepan, nodding, not speaking, was bringing the gun back upon himself, aligning the barrels once more with his face . . .

"STEPAN! DON'T *DO* IT!"

But Stepan was doing it, jamming the stock into the ground as his foot lifted, his bare toe feeling for, finding, the trigger guard. The *second* barrel, Fulton remembered, and broke into a stumbling run, at last freeing himself, too late, from the bonds of his inaction. Hearing as he moved, from somewhere, the crack of a pistol shot, the musical sound of shattering glass, Prokopchuk's furious shout, "Jack . . . STAY THE HELL *AWAY* . . . !"

Too *late* as a second pistol shot was echoed by the shotgun's popping boom.

In the light, Stepan lay on his back, unmoving.

THIRTEEN

"There's a good pulse, Sarge." The constable looked up expectantly.

"That's no thanks to us, or him . . ." Prokopchuk seemed vexed. "What a God-awful mess." He asked, "no wound?"

"Nothing . . . he missed completely. Knocked himself silly with the blast, I guess."

"Cuff him. We can have him checked at the hospital." The constable secured the handcuffs. Stepan groaned, but did not stir. Prokopchuk stared accusingly at Fulton. "And where the Sam Hill did *you* spring from?"

"I was here all the time."

"Olaf said you'd headed this way. Damned fool thing to do."

Fulton, numbed, stared back: Prokopchuk's irritable words, his own reply, seemed distant, detached; like watching an implausible movie. "I wanted to warn Rosa."

"Nice try . . ." Prokopchuk glanced once at the body in the doorway.

People were gathering close to the house, pale-blob faces reflecting the lights, and Prokopchuk turned an official scowl on them. "*All* of you . . . stay *back*. Better still, go *home*. There's nothing here for you to see . . ." Most stayed, and, "bloody ghouls," he muttered in disgust, and turned back to Fulton. "When exactly *did* you get here?"

"In time to see everything. They were quarrelling . . ." Olaf Pedersen's Ford pulled in to the yard behind the police car.

"Did you try and intervene?" Prokopchuk demanded.

"No. Just then, Stepan was gearing up to shoot himself . . . was going to do it in front of Rosa, to show her, I suppose . . ." His own voice sounded to him oddly high-pitched; he wondered if he was becoming hysterical. "He'd *planned* it . . . you can see that, the boot and sock off. Stepan *meant* it that way . . . !" He drew several breaths, and felt some control returning. "They were talking, Rosa listening. I couldn't butt in in case I made it go even more haywire . . ." His eyes met Prokopchuk's. "But Rosa wouldn't believe him. She ridiculed and humiliated him, the way she always did." His vision blurred through welling tears.

A hand was gripping his shoulder, Prokopchuk saying, "easy, Jack. Take your time."

"It's okay. But it's not easy, this."

"It never is."

In a little while, miserably, he could resume. "I'm certain . . . I swear it . . . he didn't know what he was doing. It was like a slap in the face . . . shock, you know? And he just turned on her." He insisted, "Stepan wouldn't have done that knowingly. For Christ's sake, he loved her! You wouldn't believe the number of times he's told me that unasked. I *know* it's true!"

Prokopchuk pressed, "and you saw it all?"

"Everything . . ."

"Which means, Jack, you're our best witness. Perhaps our only one."

*

Two more constables arrived to assist the investigation. Both houses had been cordoned-off. Olaf Pedersen drove away, to return minutes later with Doctor Denkman and two stretchers. Denkman and Prokopchuk exchanged curt nods.

Rosa received her official pronouncement of death, and Stepan, semiconscious and moaning, was given a cursory examination. He was pronounced unhurt except for severe powder burns to the face and neck: not one pellet of buckshot had struck him. He could have an observation bed at the hospital, Denkman declared, but it was not vital. He was fit for the lock-up.

"I'm sure you'll give him your best care and attention, Sergeant." Denkman grinned. "Such a rare, important bird."

"He'll be looked after," Prokopchuk assured him frostily. "But if I have any doubts, I'll haul you out of bed personally."

Denkman left with the body in the Ford.

"Wish they were taking Stepan, too," Prokopchuk admitted. "If he'd done the job properly, he'd have escaped the rope."

"For Stepan?" Fulton was shaken. "You can't mean that!"

"It's what's handed down for murder in this country," Prokopchuk reminded him brusquely. "And that's what we'll be charging him with."

"But . . . it was meant to be suicide!"

"Who says so?"

"I told you what I saw . . ."

"You saw the way it *looked.* A man all set up to shoot himself. But was that on the level, or to bamboozle his old lady? Can you prove he had suicide in mind? More to the point, can Stepan?" Prokopchuk's mouth tightened. "For sure, *Rosa* can't."

"But I *do* know it! I think you do, too . . ."

"Could be . . ." Prokopchuk was noncommittal. "It's a point you'll be free to make when you give evidence. But I should warn you, it may not stack up so well against what look like the facts. That Rosa wouldn't buy Stepan's argument, so he killed her."

Fulton could not leave it there. "What about his state of mind?"

"The insanity angle?"

"Wouldn't you call *that* insane?"

"In the heat of the moment, maybe," Prokopchuk allowed. "But I imagine psychiatric tests will show Stepan's got all his marbles."

"Shock, then? Billy Langewische's death . . . ?" Fulton sought desperately for reasons, justification, for *anything.* "He'd been drinking for hours, beer . . . a bottle of whisky."

"Who made him drink?" Prokopchuk answered his own question. "Only Stepan. No one twisted his arm, or forced it down his throat. And, in criminal law, drunkenness is no defence, and never more so than in capital cases. Plus something else to consider."

"*What?*"

"Think about it . . ." Prokopchuk watched him, expressionless. "Stepan wasn't too drunk to return to the beer parlour when Rosa kicked him out. Nor too drunk to find his way to Olaf's store, buy the shotgun and shells, then make a remark before witnesses that implied violence, whether self-destructive or murderous. Considering how it's worked out, it wouldn't take a Clarence Darrow to convince a jury it was the latter."

Fulton muttered, "Jesus!"

"I'm truly sorry . . ." The regret was more than token. "But Stepan's given the prosecution all that's needed to establish malice and intent. And it's those that get people hanged."

One of the slow-prowling constables called out, "can't find anything else, Sarge. Looks like it's the twelve-gauge, the ammo box and the two shells."

"Wrap it up," Prokopchuk directed. "We'll do the fine toothcomb drill in daylight." The constables abandoned their fruitless quest with undisguised relief.

Prokopchuk, fingering his chin, eyed Stepan's truck which now leaned drunkenly over a flattened tyre with a fresh bullet hole in it. "Between ourselves, Jack, I agree with you. I wish to hell Stepan's aim the second time had been better than ours . . ." He glanced at the constable who had accompanied him in the car, who was looking sheepish.

Fulton was mystified. "I don't get it . . . sorry."

"My worthy colleague here let off what was intended as a warning shot. And killed a window stone dead." Prokopchuk pointed out the shattered kitchen pane. "Then, trying the same stunt, I manage to go off—literally—half-cocked, and blow up a tyre . . ." The constable was trying without success not to smile. "Pistol shooting was never my strong suit." He glanced again, sternly, at the constable. "Good to know I'm not alone."

"Care to look here, Sarge?" It was the constable standing guard over Stepan. "He seems to be back with us."

Stepan sat upright against the woodshed, arms locked behind his back, head lolling forward. He mumbled to himself unintelligibly. Prokopchuk leaned down. "Stepan, can you hear me? Do you know what I'm saying?" Stepan muttered something, and Prokopchuk's voice sharpened. "No I *haven't* got a beer for you! Forget that, and listen . . ." He raised Stepan's head. "*Look* at me . . . it's Porkchop." The constables hid their grinning faces.

"Porkchop . . . ? What's up . . . you got beef with me?"

"Now that you mention it, I *have*." Prokopchuk was affable.

"Make you feel good, eh?" Stepan sounded weary, and vaguely belligerent.

"If you want the truth, it makes me feel lousy."

"Yah, I *bet*!" Stepan chuckled thickly. "You get me thirty day in Oakalla for drunk on day my best friend get killed? And you say me you feel *lousy*?"

Prokopchuk glanced once bleakly at Fulton. "Stepan, it's more than that this time."

"That why you got the Goddam cuffs on me?"

Prokopchuk said quietly, "tell me what you know about tonight."

"Like I say . . . be drink for Billy. Get in fight, maybe, with some sum'n'a'bitch? Don't know for sure."

"What about Rosa?"

"My Rosa . . . yah . . ." Stepan grimaced as though in pain. "Remember now."

"*What* do you remember about Rosa?"

"She find me drinkin' rye. Crazy thing . . . don't even *like* rye . . . can't handle that hard-tack stuff. Rosa gettin' mad with me . . ." At first halting, the words gained fluency. "She punch the shit out of me . . . throw me out o' the house. Then I get mad back."

"What happened when you got mad?" Prokopchuk's questioning was gentle and unhurried.

"I call my Rosa bad, dirty name . . ." Stepan's face crumpled. "That too much . . . she say we through for good this time. Say me get out, not come back."

"Did you do that, Stepan? Get out?"

Stepan frowned, struggling to remember. "Sure . . . do that hokay. You don't argue with Rosa."

"So where did you go then?"

"Go back in beer parlour," Stepan admitted at once. "Thinkin' maybe I get hotel room . . . stay there till I gettin' back with Rosa. But just be forget that. Be drink and drink, and feelin' bad . . . think of terrible thing I say to her. Thinkin' then I want to die, eh?" Again Prokopchuk and Fulton exchanged looks; Fulton's expression demanded . . . what did I tell you?

Stepan's head dropped forward once more, and Prokopchuk patted his shoulder. "There's no hurry." Stepan nodded wordlessly. "But what else can you remember about the beer parlour?"

"Somethin' I say, or maybe do, but they get mad as well and throw me out."

"Okay. And where did you go then?"

Without hesitation, Stepan replied, "go Pedersen's store."

"Why go there?" Prokopchuk leaned forward intently.

Stepan lifted his head. "Be doin' shoppin', eh?" He looked puzzled. "What for else?"

Prokopchuk did not answer that. "What were you shopping for?"

But Stepan looked blank. "Seem like . . . gone out of my head. Remember store be closed. Folks inside doin' things . . . say me come back tomorrow." He offered unhappily, "everywhere I goin', get throwed out, go away, come back tomorrow . . . don't *never* come back!"

Prokopchuk prompted, "so you were never in Olaf's store?"

"That what I sayin' . . ." Stepan sounded aggrieved. "You not hear so good, Porkchop?"

The listening constables looked away.

"I need to get this clear in my mind," Prokopchuk explained gently.

"Then be get *this* clear! They *closed* . . . not open up, not for me."

"You didn't buy anything at all?"

Stepan answered with unarguable logic, "when store *closed*, how for Christ sakes you goin' *buy* anythin', eh?"

"Good question . . ." Prokopchuk chuckled. "And you don't remember what you did after you lucked out at Olaf's?"

He waited patiently as Stepan grappled with his elusive memories. "Maybe be pass out somewheres? Or some kind fella bring me home . . . ?" He sagged wearily. "Not feelin' good, an' you keep askin' me things."

Prokopchuk enquired quickly, "are you sick, or hurt?"

"Got Goddam sore head," Stepan complained. "Feel like it burnin' up . . ." He cried out then, "what in hell *happenin*? How come I here, and feelin' so bad?"

*

The patrol car and the constables had left, taking Stepan, handcuffed and bewildered, with them.

About to leave, Stepan seemed to recognise Fulton for the first time. "They gettin' *you* here, Highpockets?" His seared face twisted into an abashed grin. "Maybe *you* say me what this all about?" The constables waited, allowing Stepan his moment. "Can't think what I s'posed to do . . ." He searched Fulton's face. "You know what I do?"

"I know, Stepan . . ." But Prokopchuk, frowning, was shaking his head.

Stepan saw the movement. "Is so bad? Must be . . . you gettin' face like wet week, Highpockets." The grin stretched. "What I do . . . *kill* somebody?"

A constable touched his arm. "Let's go, Stepan."

Prokopchuk issued crisp orders: Stepan was to be segregated from other detainees, and left to sleep. No statement was to be taken that night. One constable was to return with the car, then to remain to safeguard the crime scene. It seemed to Fulton, listening and watching, that the directions held no meaning for Stepan . . .

Now all that remained were the bullet-shattered window, the blown tyre, the shards of Stepan's hurled whisky bottle and, just within the house, the huge blackening stain of Rosa's blood. Some persistent idlers lingered beyond the pool of light.

Prokopchuk, furious, turned on them. "That's *it* . . . all of you! Nothing left to see, so get the hell *out* of here!"

Slowly, muttering, they melted back into the enveloping dark . . .

Hesitant, Fulton asked, "was that real with Stepan . . . or an act?"

"The forgetting?" Prokopchuk gave a nod. "I'd call it real. I've come across it before, *and* heard it confirmed clinically. Shock, and the narcotic effect of heavy drinking. Enough to induce a form of temporary amnesia. It's said to be a kind of reflexive defence mechanism."

"But temporary?"

"Just about always. Stepan'll wake up in the morning, and I pity him when he does. Because it'll all be in has mind, clear as a bell."

*

Prokopchuk required a written statement. He grinned without mirth. "In case you get the amnesia bug as well."

"I wish I could." Fulton nodded. "But, okay."

"I'll run you down when the car returns. Get someone to bring you home when we're through."

Fulton said, "there's something I want to do first."

"Yes . . . ?"

"See Tamara at the hospital. She's on till midnight. I must find out if she needs anything, or if there's something I can do."

"In that case, because there are things I have to check out as well," Prokopchuk said heavily. "Maybe we can both find strength in numbers."

It was past eleven when they reached the hospital. In the reception area, an orderly was unloading forceps from a steriliser unit. Nurse Paulen was at the desk, bent over paperwork. She glanced up, her expression hardening as she saw Prokopchuk. "Yes?"

No less coldly, Prokopchuk replied, "I imagine you know why we're here."

Fulton saw how they bristled at each other, their reciprocal anger and bitterness, and thought . . . hardly the stuff of impending marriage. He stayed back, not speaking, as they sparred.

"Is this about Tamara Brenko?"

"It is."

"Then it's all in hand." She stared at him with disfavour. "We've seen to everything."

"Care to be more specific, Julie?"

"It's a medical matter!" Her eyes flashed. "Of no concern . . ."

Prokopchuk cut her off brutally. "It's a matter of *murder*! Her mother's in the morgue, Stepan's locked up!" She watched him with shocked eyes. High colour touched her cheeks, and she was beautiful then, Fulton reflected. The orderly had stopped working to listen avidly. "Or didn't you know that?"

"Well . . . no." She was nonplussed. "I mean . . . we had no idea . . ."

"And here's me thinking of you . . ." He smiled without mirth. "With your finger forever on the pulse."

Fulton wondered if Prokopchuk had at last got wise to his fiancée and her ways. Or had he known all along, and gone on hoping until hope withered, and the drab realisation came that he wanted no more of her. Or of Doctor Denkman who played jazz piano, and liked to play around, and did not give a hoot what Sergeant Prokopchuk thought or felt . . .

Nurse Paulen had recovered some of her poise. "We know of a death, and whose, but not how or why." She sounded petulant. "No one's gone into details . . . *that* part's no concern of ours . . ." She caught sight of the listening orderly. "If you can only stand around, would you do it somewhere else?" The orderly hurried out with lowered head.

"Feel better now?" Prokopchuk wondered ironically. She glared at him. "Well, now you know it all." He asked, "and you say you've taken care of it?"

"Yes I *do* say!"

"Miss Brenko knows her mother's dead?"

"Of course."

"And her whereabouts . . . ?" Prokopchuk suggested acidly, "if *that's* any of your business?"

"It's certainly none of yours . . ."

"Beg to differ. It's very much police business."

She looked vexed, but revealed, "she's resting in one of the private rooms."

"Any chance of . . ." He gestured at Fulton. ". . . Jack and me talking to her? It shouldn't take long."

"None whatever." More certain of her ground, Nurse Paulen stated, "she's too shocked and distressed . . ."

"Tell me who isn't . . ." Prokopchuk seemed to speak more to himself.

"Doctor Denkman has ordered sedation, and she's sleeping. He says she's to be seen by no one before morning."

"And what Doctor Denkman says goes."

She reddened again. "He *is* the doctor."

"That's one of his talents . . ." Prokopchuk gave a tired shrug. "Okay, I'll be back in the morning. It's important that she hears from an official source what's happened." He insisted coldly, "no gossip or tattle. This, for now, is under wraps." She did not respond, and he softened a little. "She must *not* go up to the house yet, Julie. Maybe not ever."

It was like a moment of truce as they eyed each other, strangers now.

Until she said quietly, "we have spare rooms in the Residence. We'll have one prepared. I'll see to it personally that Matron knows the score."

He said with approval, "good for you." And, turning from her, walked out without another word. Fulton, about to follow, glanced at her once more. She did not appear to see him, gazing, stricken-faced, at the door through which Prokopchuk had vanished . . .

He was waiting beside the car, watching Fulton's approach with exhausted eyes. "I'll give you that ride home."

"What about the statement?"

"Screw that! We've all had enough for tonight. See to it in the morning."

"If you're sure?"

"I am." Prokopchuk pointed to the car. "Get in." And confessed, "I could use the company . . . maybe a little talk?"

"Sure. If it'll help?"

"You never know."

Prokopchuk drove slowly up through The Row, going by Hawaiian Jim's darkened house at night patrol speed. He gave the looming building a passing glance. "There's one mean old prick who'll get a big charge out of this." He told Fulton, "Stepan and that bloody cripple hate each other's guts."

"I'd heard about it, but not why."

"No one seems to knew except them, and they're not saying. Expect we'll have a tough time keeping Jim and his brood away from the magistrate's hearing and the inquest." Prokopchuk's tone was very dry. "He'll be itching to gloat out loud."

The car wound on up the hill, and the two houses came slowly into view. Outside the larger one, the porch light still burned.

"Be all right in your place?" Prokopchuk enquired.

"I'll have to be . . . I live there . . ." Fulton admitted, "as long as I don't look out the window." But that thirty-yard gap could not now provide sufficient distance. The width of the continent could not give him that . . .

He saw Prokopchuk watching him in the dashboard glow. "We could check you into the hotel. Technically, your place is part of a crime scene. And, as you're our prime witness, I can justify the expense with Vancouver."

"It's okay . . . really." Fulton shook his head. "I need to be close to the phone in case Alice wants me . . ." He remembered then . . . that's what I was thinking of when it rang earlier, and it was Ichabod. "She can get pretty fierce if her pilots go AWOL."

Prokopchuk parked again beside Stepan's truck. The bystanders had disappeared. A constable approached the car, and Prokopchuk rolled down the window. "Everything all right?"

"No sweat, Sarge. The company got bored seeing nothing, and pissed-off with me for *saying* nothing."

Prokopchuk smiled a little. "We'll make a cop of you yet." He promised a relief as soon as he returned to the office.

"Appreciate that, Sarge. I'm busting for some coffee."

"Bust some more," Prokopchuk told him. "Everything comes to those who wait."

Fulton reminded him, "you said something about a talk? Or have we had it?"

Prokopchuk nodded. "Five minutes? Can you spare that?"

"More if you like."

"That should do. It's not much of a story, and I reckon you've pretty well got the gist now . . ." After a pause, he said, "you saw how things were back there with Julie and me?" And laughed shortly. "How could you *miss* seeing?"

"I could tell there was a problem . . . yes."

"You're good on understatement, I'll give you that," Prokopchuk said. "With the two of us, it's never been anything *but* a problem."

"Then I'm sorry . . ." Fulton was growing uneasy, but he had sanctioned this discussion.

Prokopchuk said flatly, "you'll have heard things."

"Not all that much . . ."

"Jack, if you haven't, I'd say you're the only one in town!" Prokopchuk gave another harsh laugh. "The way the wise-guys and know-it-alls around here air their views, you couldn't fail to be *somewhere* in the picture. Sad thing is, though, those same wise-guys and know-it-alls, where Julie and I are concerned, have got it dead right." Fulton did not reply, but then, it was Prokopchuk who wanted to talk. "Now I'd say it had just about gone far enough." For emphasis, he banged both hands on the steering wheel. "I got sick and God-damned tired of being two-timed." His voice was level, seeming calm, in contrast with that single agitated hand movement. "Of having my nose rubbed in it by Julie and her part-time romeo . . ." He made a wry face in the dashboard glow. "Except that the bastard's full-time now, I guess. And I wish him the joy of it. There's not been much joy for Julie and me . . ." He glanced across at Fulton. "Let me make a guess at what you're thinking."

"All right."

"You're thinking . . . here's the Mountie hotshot, Mister Big himself, off on a humdinger of a self-pity kick. His pride's hurt . . . his ego's dented . . ." The tone was dry. "All of which is true."

"If it's any comfort," Fulton told him. "I wasn't thinking any of those things."

"No? What then . . . if I may ask?"

"Only what I said before. That I'm deeply sorry."

"Then thanks . . ." Prokopchuk nodded. "All this revelation is, I admit, the lead-up to an explanation of sorts." He drew a breath, let it out. "My reasons . . . although no excuses. There *are* no excuses for being chronically bad-tempered, and, with that, a pompous prick into the bargain . . ." Fulton smiled involuntarily at the thought that, somehow, sometime, he must have winkled that out of my head. "My trouble since way back has been taking myself far too seriously." He admitted, "different in the Air Force. There, when you're a crew, all in the cart together, someone's always ready to pull you off the high horse, make you see the funny side . . . the joke. Even when the joke is *you*. Not the same now, not on the Force." He was shaking his head. "Here, to some degree, prickhood goes with the job, and there are added points for pomposity . . ." He turned to face Fulton. "When it boils down to it, I'd say I rate about average as a cop, although in pistol-shooting . . ." He grinned briefly. "I'm not even up with the non-starters . . ." Fulton listened to these outpourings with growing fascination. "But, when it comes to being the aforementioned prick, right out of the training manual, then I lead the field by a country mile . . ." He guffawed and Fulton smiled back edgily. "If only you knew how many times I've pissed myself off, and wished that I knew how to change."

"Maybe you're being too tough on yourself?"

"Can you believe that? What *I* believe, Jack, is that you've got it wrong."

"Suit yourself." Fulton shrugged. "But it's possible."

"Although I should inform you," Prokopchuk said with ponderous mirth. "That, on this day, your Sergeant has hit the end of the road, and made his move. One long overdue."

"You haven't *quit*?"

"In a manner of speaking."

"The Mounted Police?"

"Nothing so drastic. I need the Force. Police work and flying Halifaxes are all I know. And there are no Halifaxes left to fly."

"No . . ."

"So, if I'm still true-blue, '*Maintiens le Droit*', and let's all have fun on the Musical Ride . . ." Prokopchuk maintained his cover of heavy playfulness. "What other big move have I made? Well?"

"Julie Paulen? You've called it off?"

"*There* now . . . is that so difficult?" But the hollowness of the banter was becoming more evident, and the voice broke slightly. "It's gone on too long, the horsing around, playing hard to get. You know?"

"I think so," Fulton said.

"Life's too damned short!" Prokopchuk said with sudden sharpness, "and, with that in mind, I went and pulled the plug."

"How did she take it?" Fulton was remembering Julie Paulen's dismayed look.

"She's one very put-out lady, and why? Because I got in first. Julie was just waiting for her moment, once she'd got that jackass Denkman all tightly packaged . . ." But the facade of bravado was cracking, the weighty jocularity foundering in a sea of now-unconcealed misery. "I've kicked her in the teeth, and she's gone, and that *has* to be a good thing for me." Prokopchuk drew in another long breath. "But, with all that, I can't deny that she's still there, under my skin. And, along with Rosa and Stepan, it's something that's been on my mind all evening."

*

She felt panic, not knowing where she was: this was not her room but a dim place, alien, yet somehow known. She could hear the sounds of activity, voices, low laughter, footsteps hurrying by, rubber heels squelching on polished surfaces. The sound her own shoes made on the wards when she was on duty . . .

DUTY, she remembered, and her heart slammed in shock.

She had been on duty . . . was beginning to sense something awful happening, but what? Something connected with this room, and her being in it: in her mind, confused half-impressions, eluding her when she tried to grasp them. Like trying to recall dreams that only faded as you reached out . . .

She compelled her mind: what *was* it? She had been on shift, four to midnight. No memory, though, of the shift's ending, of saying goodnight to the graveyard crew, walking up to the ugly, raw-boned house against the treeline where her bedroom window and the porch light always glowed welcome. None of that remained, and its absence baffled and frightened her as her presence in the strange room frightened her.

She turned her head to examine her surroundings, and pain exploded in her skull: trip-hammers beating at her temples; she heard the heavy rush of oxygenated blood pumping through vessels close to her ears. Nausea rose in her throat; she fought the spasm, lying, jaw clamped, appalled by the thought of vomiting all over someone else's room.

But the incautious movement had allowed her a glimpse of the room's fittings—two visitor chairs, a bedside locker, a high window with the blind down. Light seeping through the blind's fabric, and around its edges. Enough to recognise one of the single-bed private wards. She was *in* hospital, then . . . a patient? She had no idea of how, or why, and lay puzzling until, gradually, the uncertain images began to harden and take shape. And the awful echoing words that she longed to deny even as she knew they could never, now, be erased.

Remembering the horror, one of the images became . . . Doctor Denkman. Not smarmy now, the over-confident cocksman with the knowing grin, but sombre-faced, looking drawn, his mouth working as though he struggled to shape the words. Until he found the way to utter them, the worst words in the world that began, "it's about your mother . . ." Remembering his look of relief when *that* part was said, and he could become once more the physician, clinical, detached. Examining her with unrevealing eyes, ordering a room—this room—made ready. "Keeping you here tonight . . . we'll give you something."

Silencing her when she tried to refuse. "You're not going home, Tamara . . . that's official. Believe me, it's for the best."

His evident concern had touched her, and helped to release the first tears. In the depths of numbing shock, she could feel gratitude towards Doctor Denkman, could almost like him then . . .

After some time—it seemed long—Matron came to take her hand, and tell her of another room prepared for her at the Residence. Echoing Denkman's insistence that she must not go home. Sergeant Prokopchuk, it appeared, had ordered it. Which would be what Doctor Denkman meant about 'official'.

When she was ready, Matron was with her for the walk through the corridors, past Reception where everyone she knew stood grave-faced, as though for a royal visit. Noting as she went the averted eyes, a few uncertain smiles, quickly suppressed: this was no moment for smiling. Some murmured things, the words not registering: she half-sensed Erica, looking stricken; Kirsty Watanabe reaching out to touch her arm.

She was outside then, with the morning fresh on her face, cooling the dry-fever heat of her body. Like fever, too, the whirl of disordered thoughts, trite and empty, skittering away, fleeing from cruel, savage truth: how thin Matron's arm is . . . but then she never eats . . . lives on coffee and cigarettes. Remembering how, last night, she had seen the unpleasant coarse hairs sprouting from Doctor Denkman's nose: how could Paulen *stand* that? Wondering . . . will I like the room? Didn't know there were any free . . . hope I haven't pushed someone out? Don't have a toothbrush . . . and I'd like some clean underwear. The sting of sudden irritation . . . I wasn't *expecting* this . . . if I'd only *known* . . .

The thought, black and searing, like the knife going in . . . known *what*? That I'd need a toothbrush, bra, panties . . . comb and soap and towel? Because MY MA IS DEAD . . . ?

*

Fulton telephoned Alice Royle to let her know where he would be. "I was an eye-witness, and they need my written statement."

"Oh, poor *you*! How absolutely awful . . ." She was in one of her 'mother-hen' moods. "And so sad for all concerned."

"It's that, all right," he agreed. "Although, with respect, I don't see how 'poor me' comes into it. I just happened to be there."

"Yes, we've all heard . . ." She sounded breathless, "how you went up there alone to try to avert a tragedy."

And *now* who's been shooting off his face, Fulton wondered? "It might be better to concentrate our thoughts on Rosa and Tamara."

"Oh, *quite* . . . of course. We're all aware . . ."

He cut in deliberately, "and let's not forget Stepan."

"But surely . . . that terrible man . . . ?"

He closed his eyes, *telling* himself that the words stemmed merely from a thoughtless moment. Alice Royle, for all her faults, was not wilfully vindictive.

It's the shock, he thought: the whole town would be in shock . . . Billy Langewische killed, then Rosa; Tamara brutally orphaned. Stepan facing a capital charge. Too much to deal with when, yesterday, none of it had happened. Plus everyone knew Stepan, a local 'character' among so many. Few in Blackfish Harbour had not liked and admired Rosa. After this, what could anyone think, or say . . . ?

He did not wish to debate it with Alice Royle, not now, although there was the need, he felt, to point out, "let's not forget 'innocent until proven guilty'."

"That's true, of course . . ."

"And *two* sides to every story?"

"Oh, I quite agree."

"And how many of us this morning can claim to understand even *one* side?" He ended, dispirited, "I'm sure *I* can't. So let's leave it to those who can."

Alice Royle became brisk, and perceptibly cool. "I shall contact the R.C.M.P. should anything come up for you in the next little while."

"And if I've left, try the hospital," he said. "I have a call to make there. After that, I'll be at home." *Home*, he thought . . .

*

He looked across the yard as he left the house, and shivered, seeing the everyday *ordinariness* of things over there. It appeared unchanged, normal, no hint anywhere of violence and tragedy. The outside light burned still, and the door stood open: a *living* Rosa had opened that door, and he had the impression even then that she might appear, wave to him, call out good morning. But, instead, a uniformed constable slowly paced, looking bored, and, in the road, there was a returned knot of muttering onlookers.

The constable gave him a wave. "How you doin', Jack?"

"I've done better."

The onlookers watched him hungrily, picking him apart with their eyes, a woman in curlers pointing him out to her companion.

"Lousy business," the constable allowed.

"You might well say that."

"Beats me how you could stand to spend the night there."

"It's all I've got." Fulton gave him a grin. "And I had you to protect me."

But, as he trudged down for his appointment with Sergeant Prokopchuk, the constable's remark went with him: it was a good question. How, precisely, had it been possible to return, seemingly so matter-of-fact, waving good night to Prokopchuk as he drove away. Then, like an automaton, to strip and wash and clean his teeth, and climb into bed, and *sleep*! When, mere yards away . . .

Must have been more shock, he reasoned vaguely. Such oddball behaviour could only be put down to shock . . . ?

*

Prokopchuk took the statement in person, then Fulton read it through, surprised and disturbed to find how clear and factual and *emotionless* it was: grief and pain and fear had not confused the mental images, nor—as he might have wished—dulled their pain.

He had recounted the events in careful detail, from the moment of the witnessed brawl with Rosa, through Ichabod's call, the hotel meeting, the things discussed there. Up to the moment when Stepan fired . . .

"And, within seconds, *you* were there . . . I'd heard you coming . . . burning out your motor." He shook his head. "A half-minute sooner and you might've stopped it."

Prokopchuk nodded, expressionless. "And we'd have nabbed Stepan for waving a shotgun around while drunk."

Fulton offered quickly, "that about getting there sooner . . . it's no criticism."

"It should be," Prokopchuk said. "I'm criticising myself."

He sent the hand-written statement out for typing, and they waited, drinking coffee. He asked Fulton, "any flying today?"

"Not so far, but Aunt Alice is riding herd." Fulton grimaced wryly. "She'll holler if she wants me."

Prokopchuk wanted to know, "how much longer before you head back East?"

"Eight weeks or so. I have to report to Centralia in Ontario in October. But I've promised to spend some time with my parents on Bowen Island. So I'll probably leave a week or two early."

"Will you be able to ride it out here until then?"

Fulton frowned. "If you'd asked me that last night, I'd have said no. Got my ticket on the next Q.C.A. flight out. But now, after some sleep . . ." He thought again with wonder that it had been deep, dreamless, quite untroubled. Not a care in the world! "Well . . . it's not long, is it?" He eyed Prokopchuk uncertainly. "I have to. I'm your star witness."

"Oh, we'd come looking," Prokopchuk promised. An attempt then at lightness. "You know us, we always get our man. Even if, in the process, some windows and tyres come unstuck."

Fulton smiled mechanically, but the forced levity clashed with the gravity of the moment . . .

Prokopchuk mused, "funny thing, you going to Centralia."

"Do you know it?"

"Do I *ever*. It was a flying school when I started out in 'forty-one."

"Were you there?"

"Not far away. I flew Cornells at Aylmer, about fifty miles down the road on the Lake Erie shore. I did my Harvard training at Moose Jaw." They discussed changes in the Air Force. "We called the Harvard the 'Yellow Peril'," Prokopchuk recalled. "Because of its paint scheme, and the fact that it could be quite a handful if you didn't stay on the stick. Then, if you survived it, they gave you a pair of wings and shipped you out as half-baked cannon fodder . . ." He was shaking his head. "Nowadays, only eleven years on, and it's all fifty thousand feet and sound barriers . . ." He turned. "Well? What?"

The constable-typist stood in the doorway. "All done, Sarge. Not exactly pretty, but best I could do with two thumbs."

"You're too funny to live," Prokopchuk told him.

"Original and two carbons . . ." The constable laid the smudged sheets on the desk.

Prokopchuk, examining them, observed with deceptive mildness, "reminds me of the one about the monkeys and the typewriters."

"Sarge . . . ?"

"How, if you gave all the monkeys in the world typewriters, unlimited paper and time, between them, they'd write the *Encyclopaedia Americana*."

The constable took his cue. "That's very good, Sarge."

"Beat it," Prokopchuk told him. When Fulton had signed each page, Prokopchuk rose. "That's about it for now, Jack."

"Okay . . ." Fulton hesitated. "How's Stepan this morning?"

"I thought you'd never ask."

"Wasn't sure if I should."

"He's not at his best," Prokopchuk admitted. "Not at all."

"Why . . . what's happened?"

"*Use* your head!" Prokopchuk's glance was bleak. "What do you *think* happened? He woke up with a full memory. He's in there now with that for company."

"Yes . . ."

"No prompting needed. When we looked in, he was sitting up. He remembered it all, he said. He had done it, and wanted to get it off his chest."

"How . . . was he?"

"Calm. Very quiet and polite. He's had some coffee. Now he's sitting there, staring at the wall." Somewhere, a phone rang and rang. Prokopchuk called irritably, "do *I* have to answer that?"

A voice said, "sorry, Sarge . . ." The phone stopped ringing.

"Stepan wants to confess," Prokopchuk said. "Sooner the better, he says."

The voice from the outer office was saying, "About one o'clock, Ma'am? Yes, that's fine . . . we'll tell him."

"Bet a buck that's for you," Prokopchuk said, and then, "we'll get Stepan in when you've gone. Take his statement . . ." His brow creased. "We'll charge him." He looked up as the constable appeared at the door. "You again?"

"Message for Mister Fulton, Sarge."

Prokopchuk smiled. "I win the bet."

"I didn't take it," Fulton reminded him.

"Can't depend on anybody anymore." Prokopchuk told the constable, "let's hear it."

"A trip up to Bella Bella," the constable replied, and looked at Fulton. "Want you there at one o'clock."

Fulton made rapid calculations: a hundred and twenty air miles, clear day, little or no wind. Take off at eleven-thirty, he decided. Which still leaves me time to call at the hospital. "Did Alice say what's up?"

"Indian woman . . . expecting, but no sweat. A suspected *placenta praevia*," the constable added importantly. "They want her in for tests and things."

"What's with the witch doctor claptrap?" Prokopchuk eyed him. "You studying medicine, or just spending too much time sniffing round the nurses?"

"I'll never tell, Sarge." The constable grinned and left.

Fulton began, "don't suppose there's any chance . . . ?"

"None. Not even to say hello, or ask if there's anything he wants, *or* try and cheer him up," Prokopchuk said flatly, "sorry, Jack, but Stepan remains under wraps . . ." A hint of irony crept in. "It's the law, that old standby."

"Sure. Okay . . ."

"Only a lawyer can see him now. And, as our local man doubles also as magistrate and coroner, that kind of narrows the field. Stepan'll have to go to Vancouver where he can hire someone, or have one appointed."

Fulton stared at him disbelief. "He'll be before the bench . . . unrepresented?"

"A preliminary hearing, remember?" Prokopchuk pointed out, "a formality. A reading of the charge and our request for custody. Which, as it's a capital case, we'll get automatically. No evidence will be led."

"Does that mean I won't have to be there?"

"I should think not. You'll be wanted for the inquest, and you're a must for the trial. By which time a defence will have been prepared." Fulton nodded acceptance. "As for the other points," Prokopchuk went on, "we'll say your hellos for you, and see he gets the best care." He watched Fulton. "Trust us. We're small town cops doing a job. Not the Gestapo. And Stepan's playing ball, making it easier for us . . . and himself."

*

There was no one at the reception desk, and he waited.

A voice behind him stated, "you'll be looking for Tammy."

Fulton turned. "Hi, Eric."

"Nice to see you again . . ." The orderly hesitated. "Although hardly *nice*, given the current situation."

"No . . ." Fulton explained, "I wondered if Tamara's up to receiving visitors?" He glanced around. "But the place seems abandoned . . . nobody about."

Eric pouted. "Am *I* nobody?"

"With the exception of you," Fulton amended.

"It's mid-morning chaos time," Eric said. "Bedpans, bottles, back-rubs, lovely urine specs. Not forgetting medications, dressings, backside-wipings, *and* our worthy clutch of M.D.s twittering about, dispensing placebos and platitudes." He snickered. "Chasing their professional arses in ever-tightening circles."

"Why do I get the feeling, Eric, that your heart's not entirely *in* all this?"

"Oh, it's *in* it, all right," Eric assured him. "Just that it's *hardened* somewhat." He gave Fulton an arch look. "But to prove it's all in the right place, still, I'm going to do you a big, fat favour."

"I can hardly wait."

"It's because . . ." Eric smirked at him. "I *like* you."

"Why is it those kind words tend to worry me, Eric!"

"Bitch . . ." The orderly sighed. "But, all the same, for your ears only, visiting rules no longer apply to Tammy. Matron's moved her into the Residence. She's off duty, with strict orders to *stay* off U.F.N."

Fulton was disappointed. "I won't be able to see her. Not in there."

"Strictly speaking, no. The Virgins' Retreat is most *verboten* to lovely, hairy male animules. Except . . ." Eric fluttered his lashes. "In my case. For reasons I can never quite fathom, I'm considered safe."

It compelled laughter, and laughter, that morning, was much-needed. "All that privilege," Fulton said. "And nowhere to go."

"You *do* have a bitter tongue." Eric was reproachful, until a small grin appeared. "But good to see a smile. Perhaps we've managed to buck you up a little?"

"You have . . . and thanks."

"Well, now, there's even *more* . . ." Eric crooked an inviting finger. "Come wiz me to ze casbah. And I might *just* reveal where Tammy's holed-up."

"What about the rules, Eric?"

"Balls to the rules! Rules are only worthwhile when they're getting bent!"

*

Her room was larger than his own combined kitchen and lounge, with a high ceiling, and painted throughout in clean, sterile white. That starkness was softened by dark blue drapes framing French windows which opened on to a long communal verandah.

A feminine room, with easy chairs, a bureau and dressing table, a built-in closet with louvred doors. Fulton noted the framed prints on the walls; a bright Dufy, Van Gogh's 'Sunflowers', a Norman Rockwell design for a Saturday Evening Post cover: a shabby woman with a small boy at a table in a truckers' diner, their heads bowed at grace over their cheap meal. Wall-to-wall carpeting matched the blue drapes . . .

In a low voice, Tamara explained, "before . . . when this was the hospital building, it was a two-bed semi-private ward."

She sat on the bed, her back against the wall, legs tucked under her. Still wearing her rumpled white nurse's dress.

It was all she would have, he realised: she had come to work yesterday in the usual way, and then could not go home . . .

He offered, "it's a nice room." Tamara only shrugged. "Is it all right for me . . ." He faltered. "Do you *mind* me coming? Now, I mean."

"No." She met his worried gaze. "I'm glad. I wanted you to."

He stood before her, unable, it seemed, to find anything suitable to say. He should have taken her into his arms, held her, *embraced* her: that was natural now between them. But tragedy made a stranger of her . . .

Until she asked softly, "don't I get a kiss? Or at least a hug?" She held out her arms. "Maybe just the hug would be best."

"Well, sure . . ."

"Only because I've almost certainly got a terrible breath. All I had for cleaning my teeth was liquid soap and a finger."

He breathed again; he had feared her rejection. "Damn it . . . come *here*!"

She rose to him, and they held each other with all their strength, their mouths pressed together, and he felt the way she trembled against him . . . heard the sharp sob catch in her throat. Her lips were dry and hot, like someone fevered, and tenderness for her, and a terrible pity, moved him. He pressed her face against his chest, murmuring, stroking her hair, seeking words of comfort. "I'm here, baby . . . right here always. We'll find a way through this . . . make it work out." He insisted fiercely, "it *will* work out, Tamara . . ." And stopped himself; it was perilous to offer too much. He switched tack. "Don't worry about . . . well, *things*. I'll get you a toothbrush, and anything else you need, at the Rexall. Whatever you want from the house . . . clothes . . . things like that . . ." But he felt her shudder as he spoke of the house, and caught his breath: it was so unbelievably tricky. Like picking your way through a minefield without a map . . .

"I can see to that . . ." She was shaking her head. "I'll go later, and . . ."

"I think . . . you shouldn't, not yet. Not for a while. Better to stay here until things are quieter."

She agreed dully, "I hadn't thought of that."

"It's for the best. Let me see to the other things."

"Thank you, Jack," Tamara said formally and politely.

They watched each other in silence, and he could see the effects on her of strain and pain, the black ache of sudden, savage bereavement. She seemed somehow *shrunken*, her eyes huge in the pinched face, lids swollen by weeping. In embarrassment, she turned from him. "Don't look at me . . . I'm a wreck."

He began: "You look fine . . ."

"Oh, for God's *sake*!" Her voice rose, shrilling. "Who are you kidding? I've seen myself in the mirror!"

"Baby . . . I'm really sorry . . ." Her outburst had shaken him.

"And so am I . . . there I go again . . ." She bit her lip hard. "There's never the need for that kind of talk with you. But still I do it."

They held each other still, but the first fierce power of the embrace had lessened; she felt limp in his arms. He wondered, "would you prefer it if I went?"

"Only if you want to."

"You know I don't . . ." But there was a catch; there was *always* a catch. "Although I'll have to soon."

"Do you have to fly?"

"Yes . . ." He mentioned the Indian mother-to-be: *she*, at least, provided a safe, neutral alternative to what weighed upon them both.

Tamara listened, seemingly attentive. "More likely to be a breech birth than *placenta praevia*. They're pretty common among the Indian women."

"What's a breech birth?"

"Just that. The foetus gets twisted around in the womb," Tamara explained gravely. "The rear end shows up first instead of the head . . ." She asked, "how long will you be gone?"

"Shouldn't be more than three hours. At the most."

"I'll still be here."

"Please be," he said.

"Where else *is* there now . . . ?" And she went on in a low, hating voice, "after what that evil son of a bitch did to my mother . . . to *us*!" He watched her, unable to speak. "I want them to take him out and *hang* him! KILL him!"

He muttered, "It's very likely that they will."

"*Good*!" She spat the word. "And I'd like to be there and see it happen. I'd *do* it to him myself if they'd let me . . . like a God-dammed *shot* . . ."

"Tamara . . ."

"The thought of seeing him there while they get him ready for it . . ." Her strained voice was rising. "Then watching him suffer . . . like he made *Ma* suffer!" Useless, and improper, for him to suggest that Rosa had not suffered, had not even *known*. "And, afterwards, I'd dance on his . . ."

"Tamara . . . *stop* that!" he said sharply. "Cut it out *now* . . . do you hear me?"

She started like someone struck, and then her eyes cleared. "I beg your pardon, Jack." She was curtly polite. "I let myself get carried away. All the same, I know what I said, and meant it . . ." She faced him squarely. "That was *me* talking."

"That's what worried me."

"Does it put you off? My ugly side?"

He made an attempt at lightness. "I think maybe you read that somewhere."

She did not deny it. "If so, it has its place now."

"I hate to see you torturing yourself."

"You mean bad-mouthing *him*? Jack . . . that's not *torture*. Just thinking of him going through hell, and talking about it, it's what I need to keep me sane!"

He was silent, helpless before her anger and hatred, the first *full* awareness of her monstrous loss . . .

She stabbed her finger at the floor suddenly. "Listen!"

"What . . . ?"

"Don't *talk*," she snapped at him. "Listen for once!"

He did so, chastened, hearing all the usual sounds of a summer morning at Blackfish Harbour: gulls squabbling shrilly around the salmon-packing sheds, the wheezing thud of a one-lung fish boat ploughing across the bay. A truck went rumbling by along the shoreline road, fading with a blast of airhorn. Inside the Residence somewhere a floor polisher whined, rising and falling . . .

Observing him intently, Tamara asked, "do you hear it?"

He sat very still, concentrating his mind, and became aware slowly of the faint, muffled humming that seemed to come from somewhere beneath his feet. Accompanied by a barely-perceptible tremor. He looked at her doubtfully. "Is that what you mean?"

"It's in the basement." Her eyes never left his face. "And we both know what's there, don't we?"

Appalled, he began to protest, "you can't . . ."

"That's the electric motor you hear . . . keeping everything cold." Her voice seemed filled with a kind of wonder. "It only runs when there's someone *in* there . . ." An ugly edge of hysteria began to emerge. "They've taken Billy away to get him ready for burial . . . the only one left is my *mother*!" Her eyes were wide, blankly-staring. "I sit here like some V.I.P. with a suite at the Hotel Vancouver. While, right under me, my mother's stuck away in a God-damned *meat locker*!"

FOURTEEN

There was a delay at Bella Bella, and it was late afternoon before Fulton returned. Circling the bay, he spied the unfamiliar Beaver at the seaplane dock, painted in the blue and gold livery of the Mounted Police.

At the dock, Jackie Seaweed informed him, "come up from the big city to take old Stepan away. Got here an hour since. Some bigshot Staff Sergeant with a briefcase an' a big arse, two more in suits and ties, and the driver." He grinned satirically. "Lot o' weight for one little piss-artist that shot his old lady." He began hauling the fuel hose off its drum-reel.

Fulton asked, "are they taking him today?"

"Couldn't say . . ." The Indian crawled out on to the lift strut, and pushed the nozzle into the filler pipe. "Depends on the beak, I guess. Hear tell Stepan's up in front of him now."

Fulton recalled Prokupchuk's words: the magistrate's court was a formality; the hearing of the charge, the automatic award of custody. I'm not needed, he thought, and was obscurely ashamed of the relief he felt . . .

"Them Goddam Horsemen don't screw around," Jackie Seaweed observed with mocking admiration. "Nothin' but the best for Stepan. Private plane . . . enough cops to make up a poker school. If it wasn't for what comes later, might almost be fun . . ." To be certain that Fulton grasped his meaning, he parodied a hanging man, the lolling head and protruding tongue, one bunched hand lifted, pulling on the rope . . .

Sickened, Fulton turned away to study the shining, immaculate police aircraft. Mustn't get mad, he told himself . . . start bawling Jackie out for his lack of sensitivity. It was only his weird sense of humour. Prokopchuk had said it: who knew what went on in an

Indian's mind? For Jackie, it was the way it was, and could happen to anyone . . .

"Jack, you want a ride, you better get the lead out," Olaf Pedersen called from the pierhead. "I got a lady here to get to hospital."

"Coming . . ."

He asked to be dropped off at the Rexall drug store. "Some things Tamara needs."

"She's at the Residence, eh?" Fulton nodded. "You seen her?"

"This morning."

"How's she takin' it?"

"How would *you* be?"

"Yeah . . . sure." Pedersen glowered at the road before him. "Sweet *Christ*! If we could just turn the clock back a single Goddam *day*!"

At the drug store, Fulton purchased a toothbrush and paste, added a wash cloth, soap, a nail brush and a bottle of Listerine. He spotted an ornate flask of imported toilet water, and asked for that as well, telling the assistant, "a little surprise."

She smiled at him. "Wish someone'd surprise *me* like that."

Up at the house another constable stood guard, but there were no onlookers now. The outside light was off, but the door remained open. Two men in coveralls knelt there, peering at the blackened stain of Rosa's blood.

"Whiz-kids from Town," the constable explained. "Forensics freaks . . . and what *for*?" He sounded put-out. "We got a prisoner, a confession, a *prima facie* case." He added, grinning slyly, "*and* a top-flight witness." It was okay, he said, for Fulton to visit Tamara's room. "That poor kid. You go on up and get what she needs. We're about through here. Soon's the crime-busters call quits, I'm going to lock up." He promised, "but I'll wait for you."

*

She had asked for denims, shirts, her blue pedal-pushers. She needed socks, a sweater, sandals and a pair of saddle oxfords. She had balked, colouring, when he mentioned night attire and underwear. "I'm not keen . . . sorry . . . on anyone rooting around in my things."

He insisted gently, "they're only clothes, baby. And you need them."

"It's just so . . . *embarrassing* . . ."

"I've seen you without, and vice versa. That didn't embarrass you."

She murmured, "*that* was different."

"Come on now . . . tell me what you need and where to find it. And a suitcase to put it in. I'll simply pack, and won't root."

"You swear?"

"Tamara . . ." He gave her a smile. "I don't usually get off on women's clothes." And was vastly relieved when the smile was returned.

"*That's* a mercy."

"Unless, of course, you happen to be in them . . ."

It had been, he recalled now, not unlike flying through a heavy squall line, which was violent and physical and frightening, and could toss an airplane like a leaf. But you found, usually, once you were past the turbulent leading edge, that it weakened and went away, leaving only an exhausted calm.

Following her terrible lament for her mother, Tamara had been swamped by her agonised weeping. Her private storm had gone on for what seemed like a long time, and he had grown anxious. He had a trip to fly, and must leave soon, and knew that he would not while she remained in that state. It would have to be the hell with the trip, simple as that. It was not as though there was any great urgency: the Indian woman was coming in merely for observation and tests. It would not matter that he was a little late, and, if it did, too bad . . .

In time, though, like the squall, it passed, leaving her quiet, and strangely remote. Something akin to *resignation* appeared to supplant the earlier corrosive anger, and he wondered, hoping but uncertain, if those might be the first small, tender shoots of acceptance and healing emerging. In a little while more, they found that they could talk together almost naturally of everyday things like toothpaste and saddle oxfords and underwear. And she could even, for brief moments, smile . . .

*

He had vowed *not* to root, but the fact of being in Tamara's bedroom, alone, with her permission—albeit reluctantly given—was enough to excite curiosity.

He knew Tamara now, and loved her, and could believe that he had her trust. Thus, he reasoned, it should have been possible for him to be at his ease in *her* space, rather than as it was, moving about with the guilty air of a voyeuristic intruder. He was ill-at-ease, feeling himself somehow *observed*; the half-belief in a presence at his shoulder, suspicious and critical of his slightest move. To the point where, as he timidly explored the room, there was the urge in him to explain and justify the small things he did, and apologise for them. Yet, what he did do was harmless enough, and need not have given offence; no more than the wish, by being where he was, to *experience* Tamara more.

So, slowly, it became that he *could* justify his gazing about to study the pennants on her walls, from Seattle and Victoria and Vancouver, the Yakima Valley, and Juneau and Ketchikan in Alaska.

He gazed at her single bed on its pinewood frame, made up neatly with tucked 'hospital corners', the pillows from which the dolls and stuffed animals of her childhood stared back at him with glassy self-importance.

One door of her clothes closet stood open to reveal her coats and dresses on hangers, among them the electric-blue party dress she had worn on the night of the dance.

On the dressing table, he came across the framed enlargement of a snapshot: Rosa and Stepan arm in arm, she with her young girl's beaming smile, her head resting on his shoulder. Stepan proud and puff-chested in a bulky three-piece suit and wide necktie, clutching a fedora. Like a contented *mafioso* and his moll posing against the background of the Grouse Mountain chairlift . . .

He peered with troubled eyes at the grey images, and wondered if he should remove the picture, or conceal it, so that Tamara need not be confronted by *that* reminder when, or if, she should return here. He could do it, and leave a note of warning and explanation for her to find. It was not a *bad* idea, and yet he wondered, would she thank him for it, or view it as an intrusion? He stood, irresolute, the picture in his hand, and then, with a quick, shamed movement, put it back in its place as his nerve failed him . . .

That done—or not done—he devoted himself to the agreed task of gathering her needed clothes, arranging them with clumsy fingers within the feminine powder-blue suitcase found on top of the closet. He grinned stiffly at the case, anticipating the chagrin it could cause him, the ill-concealed mirth of passers-by as he made his way through the village with the wretched thing in his hand. All that could be hoped for, he decided ruefully, was a paucity of passers-by.

It was as he closed the case, and was turning to leave, that he noticed the other snapshot, one of several tucked into Tamara's mirror frame. Hasty, blurred at the edges, taken perhaps on sudden whim, but, unmistakably, the Seabee. Caught 'on the step' at the moment of take-off, blunt-nosed and purposeful, cleaving the calm water into whiteness. A three-quarter front view that, with sharper definition, would have looked good on the cover of an operator's manual. Taken, he believed, from the long seaward-facing verandah of the Nurses' Residence with its wide view over the bay. And what trip would that have been? Tamara had never spoken of it . . .

He smiled again, fondly now, thinking of Eric's words that day: '. . . she shoots to the window to watch you take off, with this gooey look on her face . . .' And, on one occasion, she had had her camera with her.

*

Walking back to the Residence with the bright suitcase in his hand seeming to shout its presence aloud, Fulton came down The Row as the preparations were being made to move Stepan out to

Vancouver. And found Olaf Pedersen standing before his house, watching the R.C.M.P. barracks fifty yards away.

He turned, smiling, and looked at the suitcase. "Off on vacation?" He saw Fulton's pained expression. "Only kiddin'. It's Tamara's bag, and you're takin' her some things."

"How did you work that out, Sherlock?"

"Elementary. I sold her the bag. Knew it straight off." Pedersen's shoulders lifted. "The rest, you and *it*, just falls in place . . ." He sobered. "You made it in time, Jack." He nodded at the barracks, the small, restless crowd gathered outside.

Fulton studied the tableau edgily: the waiting police car with its motor running: Sergeant Prokopchuk on the front lawn by the flagpole, in conversation with the Beaver pilot, another sergeant in a tailored Eisenhower jacket. The bystanders silent, but with an almost palpable air of expectancy about them, watched over by two constables.

"They're gettin' him out quick," Pedersen confided quietly. "There's been lots o' feelin's stirred up, both for and against."

Fulton demanded, "What's been said?"

"Two camps, seems like. Bunch of pricks talkin' about lynchin' Stepan on the spot, given half the chance . . . another bunch talkin' about him gettin' a raw deal, and how Rosa pushed her luck too far . . ." He snorted derision. "Split about fifty-fifty, and the whole damn' kit an' keboodle's full o' piss and wind."

Fulton took in the information, and resolved to reveal none of it to Tamara, although he did not delude himself; there was no chance of her being shielded completely. In due course, if not all, then she must hear *some* of it, and no prizes, he reflected, for guessing which of the two camps she would favour. But, he resolved, she won't hear it from *me*. I'll plead ignorance . . . don't know, don't *want* to know: see, hear, speak, *think* no evil!

Later, maybe, once the healing process had taken hold, and Tamara was better-equipped to deal with it, *then* something might be said. With the hope that, when the time arrived, she would understand, and be able to forgive his deceptive reticence . . .

"Here they come," Pedersen was saying.

Two men were emerging from the barracks, one the small, bent figure, instantly recognisable, of Stepan; drably-clad, head bowed, submissive. Seeming detached from, unaware of, where he was, or what was taking place. He was bare-headed, and Fulton saw the way his thinning hair caught the wind. You expected change, he thought, but Stepan looked no different: he seemed, indeed, almost comfortingly familiar. Until you noticed the handcuffs linking him to the big, red-coated staff-sergeant.

Which ruined that spurious appearance of normality, tarnishing the reviving mind-pictures of Stepan at the supper table, in the rackety beer parlour, on a quiet shore at sunrise, cutting wood.

The manacled pair went first to the car, followed by Prokopchuk and the pilot.

Stepan did not look up when the shouting began; appeared not to hear the cries, whether of support or vilification. And perhaps, Fulton mused, the police had advised that? To react by non-reaction?

Over fifty yards the voices came clearly, a confusion of opinions, the high shouts of women rising over all . . .

"Hope to Christ they throw the *book* at you!"

"*Wife-murderin'* son of a *bitch*!" from a shrill, furious woman.

"Don't you pay 'em no never-mind, Stepan . . ."

"Lousy, rotten BASTARD . . . !"

"Keep your pecker up, ol' fella . . . we'll see you back here soon!"

The turn of another woman to tell him, "you go straight to *hell*, Stepan Kereniuk!"

Conflicting with the intended comfort of, "screw 'em all, Stepan . . . you never done nothin' wrong! She had it comin' . . ." Stepan's head came up at that, an angry movement, and the Staff-Sergeant spoke to him quickly, as though in reminder, or warning.

"They're goin' to *hang* you . . ."

"When you get home, we'll buy you a beer, Stepan!"

The constables, watchful and wary, held position, dominating the crowd, noting the faces and threats. Yet the watchers, for all their vociferousness, remained orderly.

And Stepan, seeming once more oblivious, waited docilely beside the grey official car as Prokopchuk and the staff-sergeant exchanged final words.

Until the tableau shivered into shocked silence, all heads turning as one, as the great bass voice boomed down over them. Like the voice of an angry, hate-filled god . . .

"KERENIUK, YOU COCKSUCKER! YOU BEEN *BEGGIN'* FOR IT . . . NOW HERE IT *IS*!"

Fulton gazed up numbly at the ugly brown house where the cripple sat in his wheelchair, surveying the activity below with bitter pleasure.

"Hawaiian Jim . . . !" Pedersen too, was looking up with hot eyes. "That diseased old son of a WHORE!"

The cripple's face was intent, filled with vindictive triumph: a mahogany moon-face, the head hairless but for a fringing of white above the ears. Above a body once-powerful, made gross by the years of confined inactivity.

Two younger men, carbon copies of the elder, with the same dark Polynesian features, stood behind and to each side of the wheelchair, a brace of loyal acolytes who nodded and grinned as the voice echoed once more . . .

"FIGURED TO WAVE YOU G'BYE, KERENIUK! YOU HAVE A REAL NICE TRIP, EH?"

Hawaiian Jim, Stepan's detested adversary—for reasons which Fulton had never known, and realised now, almost certainly, never would—was laughing massive delight as his sons whistled support.

"GOIN' TO LIVE IN THE BIG CITY, I HEAR . . . FOR JUST A *LITTLE* WHILES!" The laughter was breaking up the word-flow. "BEST WATCH OUT FOR THAT CITY LIVIN', KERENIUK! THEY SAY IT CAN BE THE *DEATH* OF A FELLA!"

Stepan's head was up, his gaze fixed on his old enemy, and even at that distance, Fulton felt the shared loathing like raw current. They faced each other for what seemed a long time, and there was silence from the watchers, even from the police, and no movement. Like the stillness at a cenotaph, the uniformed men at attention, the throng immobile and respectful . . .

Until the staff-sergeant bent his head, murmuring to the prisoner. Who nodded without expression, and stooped to enter the car, the big policeman clambering in behind him, his wide-brimmed hat knocked askew by the door's rim . . .

Hawaiian Jim, though, was not finished. "REMEMBER AND SEND US A POSTCARD! LET US KNOW HOW YOU'RE *HANGIN'* OUT, AND . . ."

"*JIM*! YOU BLACK-ARSED, HEATHEN SON OF A *BITCH*!"

Fulton started, flinching, as Olaf Pedersen bellowed in a voice as huge and threatening as the one from the brown house. The store owner was glaring up, and Hawaiian Jim stared back, frowning and silenced, across the gap. "Best you SHUT UP now, Jim, or, by JESUS, I'll be up there and SHUT YOU UP!" Pedersen stabbed a finger at the cripple and his sons. "AND YOU TWO PUNK BASTARDS AS WELL!" The words were wilfully, brutally provocative, sufficient to induce an explosive response, but all three remained still, staring back down, not speaking. "And you KNOW God-damn' well I CAN and WILL!" Pedersen was scowling. "I whipped your arses before, and I'll be happy to *again*!"

The brief spell was broken; there was movement once more before the police barracks. Voices chattered excitedly, and there was laughter . . .

"One more WORD, Jim . . . that's all it takes!" Pedersen promised. "And I'll wheel your fat carcase straight down, and tip it in the SALT-CHUCK!"

Someone gave a long whistle, and a man's voice cried out, "give 'em SHIT, Olaf!"

Pedersen, watching the cripple, ignored them all. "All right, Jim . . . you get back in your HOLE . . . WHERE YOU BELONG!"

A woman who sounded like one of those who had harangued Stepan, yelled, "good for YOU Mister Pedersen!"

"She prob'ly owes me money," Pedersen muttered at Fulton. "Or else lookin' for discounts."

"Way to GO, Olaf!" A man this time.

"Screw YOU, Jim, and your drunken bastard kids!" another woman bawled. "Nobody likes any of YOU round these parts!"

Mingling with the cries came the sound of an engine: Fulton looked over to see the police car speeding away, the bystanders following it with baffled eyes, some voices crying out protest or last-minute curses. Until, as the car took the curve beyond the B.C. Packers' warehouse, and was lost to view, they seemed to lose purpose and cohesion, and began to drift away. The two constables rejoined Prokopchuk by the flagpole.

Pedersen observed heavily, "guess that takes care of that." He watched the brown house still, where the cripple and his sons were no longer to be seen; the unkempt, littered yard was empty.

Fulton gave him a strained smile. "You were taking on a handful there, weren't you?"

"*Those* pricks . . . ?" Pedersen made a disdainful gesture that would have been apparent to any watcher up there. "They're full of shit . . . all mouth and no brains."

"And what if it had been the entire clan?"

"Same difference . . ." Pedersen turned his back deliberately on the house. "It'd just have took me a little longer to teach 'em some manners. That's if they'd stuck around for the lesson."

They stood and watched together until the police Beaver was airborne, the snarl of its engine echoing back, ghostly, from the mountains. The sound died slowly away as the machine dwindled against the bright southern sky.

"If I was you, Jack . . ." Pedersen was eyeing Tamara's pale blue suitcase thoughtfully. "I'd get the hell out of sight with that thing before folks start gettin' ideas about you!"

*

At a superficial level, at least, life at Blackfish Harbour appeared to return to normal in the days following, although an undercurrent of tense excitement persisted. All talk everywhere was of the murder, and of Stepan held on remand at the Oakalla Prison Farm in Burnaby. There was talk, also, of Rosa's funeral, soon to be held.

Other diversions caught the public's notice fleetingly: the burial of Billy Langewische, the news that Clara's baby would be okay, but that the young Indian woman would carry some heavy scars for the rest of her life.

In the beer parlour, toasts were drunk to Langewische's memory, and all were in agreement with the assessment of one drinker, "all's I can say is that must've been one mean old mount'n lion to get one over on Billy."

Still more glasses were raised to the post-script declaration, "not no more he's not . . ."

The assembled heads continued to nod when someone else offered sombrely, "lucky thing Billy never knew what he started with that cat . . . Stepan and his old lady, and all."

Much speculation centred upon Tamara's continuing presence within the community. She had resumed her ward duties, and was staying on at the Nurses' Residence, acknowledging the impractibility of returning to her home. Much of the talk was favourable and sympathetic, although some was to prove painfully and embarrassingly gushing.

There were those, also, who reacted more cynically. With beliefs and comments centring upon Tamara's supposed inheritance. Rosa was gone, and Stepan was a cinch to get the rope, it was stated. And Tamara must be, almost certainly, the sole heir. There were the two houses, and the land upon which they stood. Those alone, with Stepan's boat—old, but in excellent repair—tossed in, would add up to a tidy bundle. For sure, it was claimed, there was plenty in the bank: both Rosa and Stepan had been cagey with money: what Stepan squandered on liquor was peanuts beside what he salted away. And all that sitting there, up for grabs. A good-looking kid like that, and rich, too? Something there, all right, for some sharp young stud to latch on to.

Not a few people expressed baffled admiration for Tamara's decision to stay on. "Takes *some* God-damned guts! I'd've high-tailed it on the first boat out. Wouldn't find *me* stickin' around after *that*!"

Fire season had begun, the hazard increasing relentlessly with the passing of each baking, rainless day. The woods were explosively dry; a lightning strike, a single careless match or cigarette butt, could set them off; even the lens effect of raw sunlight through a shard of broken glass.

Soon, the Forest Service ordered the cessation of all logging and sawmill operations between Kelsey Bay and Cape Scott.

Fulton would not have denied his relief at the decision. He had had his fill of axe and power-saw injuries, the constant stream of broken choker-setters, the battered victims of bunkhouse feuds.

Calls for the Seabee's services went on, but were now mostly for injured fishermen, or those hurt in domestic accidents. He flew back to their homes a number of Indian patients discharged from hospital who were entitled to transportation at public expense.

The slow-down left him with more leisure time, but few means now whereby to enjoy it. Before her mother's death, he would have spent every possible free moment with Tamara, exploring and exploiting the region's restricted amenities, while allowing their relationship to develop and mature. That, now, could not be, and while he told himself that he understood and accepted, it was a situation that could chafe.

He found comfort in the knowledge that she had not turned away from him, but merely pulled back into some kind of protective shell, eschewing all but the most necessary—and brief—of human contacts. By means direct or oblique, she was hearing those things that were being said of her. Inevitably, also, in the public spaces of the hospital, there would be repeated, frequently painful encounters with over-reactive sympathisers and well-wishers; those genuine, those merely curious or self-seeking.

Offers came to her bewilderingly: of shelter, food, clothing, money, company; hands to be held, ears into which she could pour out her grief, shoulders upon which to cry. All she had to do was *say* . . .

Until, demoralised, Tamara fled to the sanctuary of her borrowed room, declaring her readiness to see only Fulton, Annie Markham, her closest friends and—surprisingly—Ichabod. For the preacher, tactful and perceptive, placed no strain upon her, but assumed instead, quietly, the role of supporter and friend, and then only in need, when *she* should need.

Tamara and Fulton went out seldom, when they could be reasonably certain of avoiding unsought encounters. Mostly, they passed their time together in her room—the rule forbidding male visitors had, by unspoken agreement, been relaxed temporarily—or else in the Residence lounge where they were left, after smiles and brief greetings, to their own devices. Sometimes, merely for the sake of change, they would wander along to the recreation room for a few listless games of table tennis.

Their talk, too, had become perfunctory and similarly listless: they could not plan or aspire now, nor address those personal matters which remained close to their hearts. Instead, after a kiss and a hug, he would ask how she was feeling—always, in these early days of terrible loss, a tricky question—and if there was anything he could do for her, or that she might need. She, in turn, would profess a dutiful interest in the activities of his days, and offer at least the appearance of attentiveness. After which, always too soon, there would remain only the one topic for discussion. The strained silences which ensued then were always to be preferred.

They went no more to the coffee shop, or to Hong's Café, places where they would at once be recognised and discussed in whispers; she as 'poor Rosa Brenko's kid', he as 'the one that seen it happen'.

Tamara gave up her badminton evenings, and avoided the Legion dances which had resumed after a brief hiatus in respect for her mother, unable to endure the sudden silences which greeted her appearance, the sidelong glances and murmurings, the abashed avoidance of eye contact.

On a few occasions, usually late, they would venture cautiously out to walk together to the end of the nearby Forest Service pier to stand looking down at the moored ranger's launch. They would clasp hands, or he would draw her to him in silence as they listened to the night's sounds, and the soft wash and suck of black tides around the pilings. It was during these short, stolen times that he was most conscious of her *withdrawal*: she had raised her own defensive barriers against a world from which she felt herself estranged, and viewed, rightly or wrongly, as hostile. For as long as it took, then, even for him, there could be no *entrée* . . .

Longing for her in every way, he would try to convince himself that he *did* understand: that her immediate need of him lay in the support and comfort he was able to provide simply by being there. Beyond those clearly-marked limits, for now, it could not be expected to go, nor did he let himself imagine that it might. The rewards—if those were to be for him—for patience and forbearance would come later, when something akin to that yearned-after normality really did re-enter her life, and perspective was regained. Until that time, he could, and *would*, accept, learning how to live with the situation, the awkward, sometimes precarious *status quo*.

For himself, as the summer progressed, there was the awareness of a deepening inner tension, a tightening of the nerves inducing a sick dread that defied logic, reason, or full comprehension. He could recognise that it was to do with the impending inquest and criminal trial, and the part that he must play in those. It *was* illogical, *and* unreasonable, because there was nothing in these events for him to fear. He endeavoured, without much success, to make himself see the realities, but was hounded by something near to a terror of the judicial process which comes so often to those who have never run afoul of it. In his life, he had not received so much as a parking ticket, and could reflect with irony that he was a fair-to-middling working example of what it took to be a solid citizen, God-fearing, law-abiding, dull . . . and scared silly. Facing his now-imminent encounters and duties, even though in the guise of the so-called 'good guy', he found himself experiencing the irrational guilt by association—and its accompanying panic reaction—of the naive and the innocent. He would be compelled, as he saw it, nervous and jittery, to stand like one condemned, facing the close, critical scrutiny of a coroner and jury, later a judge and another jury. Made to suffer—what was the expression?—'the slings and arrows' of cross-examining lawyers, one of whom was being paid to shred his testimony and show him hostility. Facing throughout, as he saw it, scepticism, disbelief and ridicule. He feared that, and the prospect of it, and nothing more than the fact, in due course, of having to go through this ordeal in the presence of Stepan, and as Stepan's legal *adversary*. With the awful knowledge that every word uttered under oath would serve to strengthen the case against Stepan.

There it was, he could recognise then, the hard core of his concern, and recognition only deepened the dread, filling him with the leaden sense of his own guilt.

There was, also, the cruel paradox that those things he would say at the trial must please Tamara, whom he loved and desired to serve well. There was nothing more in life, Fulton believed, that was of greater importance to him than these feelings for her, or that desire. Yet that was an aim to be achieved by his hastening Stepan's way to the gallows or, if not that, to a lifetime of imprisonment.

For the first time, he could begin to grasp the true meaning of the term 'horns of dilemma'. There was his love for Tamara, his belief in her return of that love. He was, though, deeply fond of Stepan: his natural instinct was to *help*, to try with everything in him to save him. Something which, he could believe, Rosa would have wanted. But Tamara wished for Stepan's death, and would not yield in that, nor compromise. What I say in court, Fulton knew, could give her what she wants, and earn me her gratitude, even as I sell Stepan down the river. The true and painful horns of bitter dilemma.

FIFTEEN

It appeared that almost everyone in Blackfish Harbour had turned out for Rosa Brenko's funeral. A sombre procession followed Olaf Pedersen's Ford, pressed into service that morning in its official role of hearse, as it bore her to the hillside cemetery above the Indian village.

Fulton was at Tamara's side, silent as her mother was lowered into the earth. Noticing, as he looked about, how people watched them, enduringly curious, avid for sensation. He was glad that, at least, they kept their distance, as though sensitive to Tamara's desperate need for privacy. It was only as the service concluded that she began to lose some of her stiff composure, weeping then with quiet bitterness.

But it *was* over, and they could leave, cold and aloof, an island of bereavement in the surging, living human current.

Until Olaf Pedersen, waiting at the cemetery gate, found them. "I was figurin' maybe you kids could use a ride down?"

As he chivvied the dispersing mourners with light touches of the horn, he offered, "unless you got other plans, we could stop by my house . . ." Explaining, "the Missus put together some eats and coffee."

Tamara hesitated, glancing back at Fulton for guidance. He gave a quick nod . . . *accept.*

"That's really kind of you, Mister Pedersen." The response was dutiful, and wooden. "And very nice of Madeleine to take the trouble."

"No trouble . . . forget about that." Pedersen's glance met Fulton's in the driving mirror. "Okay with you, Jack?"

And Fulton, wondering if Pedersen had noticed the silent exchange with Tamara, nodded. "I'll just have to let Alice know."

"Use our phone." Pedersen glanced at Tamara. "Look, don't worry about Maddie. I know she can be a motor-mouth sometimes . . ." She smiled faintly, and Fulton remembered the evening when she had told him . . . 'it'll be all over town when Madeleine gets hold of it.' "But she don't mean no harm, and anyway, we talked it over last night when she come up with the idea of the coffee klatsch." He smiled encouragement. "Just a few close friends . . . nice and easy."

There were ten guests, all residents of The Row. Tamara, who seemed almost glad now of the diversion, introduced Fulton to the high school principal and his wife. He shook hands with the manager of the B.C. Electric power station whom he had seen last playing in the band at the Nurses' Dance. Madeleine Pedersen was revealed as a dumpy, cheery woman, not formidable, who gave him a single close, searching look, then, after a hug and a few soft words for Tamara, appeared content to withdraw and devote herself to the needs of her guests . . .

Pedersen led Fulton aside. "I'd asked Ben Gilliam to stop by, but he reckoned it wasn't such a hot idea, and he'd better stay away."

"Because of Stepan?" Gilliam was the village attorney who served the community as magistrate and coroner.

Pedersen nodded. "After shippin' Stepan to th' pokey, he felt it was best he stayed out of sight. Wanted to offer his condolences, though, and I wondered if you'd pass 'em on to Tamara?"

"Of course I will . . ." Fulton glanced across the room to where Tamara was in conversation with the wife of the high school principal. The two young women were smiling at each other, and their smiles could ease some of his anxiety about her. "Although I'd say there was no need for him to steer clear. It's likely she would've wanted to give him a hug and a kiss." He confessed, "she hates Stepan for this . . . wants him to hang."

"And would she feel any better when it's done . . ." Pedersen demanded bluntly, "Jack, you seen it all. Reckon he should swing?"

"No I don't. Not ever . . ." Fulton glanced across again at Tamara as if fearful that she might overhear. Softly, he appealed, "what's to be gained by it, Olaf? It can't help Rosa, and I'll never believe she would've wanted such a thing, an act of revenge."

"It's still murder, though. And never mind how she just *might've* tipped Stepan over the edge with that temper of hers, and her mule-headedness, and all. Still remains there's no justification, and no makin' out any which way that she ever deserved what she got." Pedersen's tone was severe; he watched Fulton stonily.

"But still . . ."

"Hold it right there, Jack. Let me guess. You're thinkin' on what you seen first. Stepan with the shotgun pointed at his own head. All fired-up to do it with his big toe, like them crazy Jap soldiers done in the war sooner'n surrender."

"It's a point in Stepan's favour . . ." But Fulton felt an uneasy stirring of doubt.

"And a pretty damn' good one, I'd say. When the time comes, Jack, make sure you get a hearin' on that." Pedersen's brow creased. "Same time, we can't change the fact that even a half-smart prosecutor's goin' to rip it all up to ratshit."

"Porkchop suggested much the same," Fulton admitted, and it was painfully clear then: a flimsy line of defence based upon unsound reasoning, with no substantiation. Held up to ridicule by the prosecution as a self-serving ploy to counter Rosa's determination to bar Stepan from the house.

Which, it could then be claimed, when it backfired, had been sufficient to induce a vindictive mood leading to murder. It would not be difficult, after that, to bring the jury to the belief that murder had been uppermost in Stepan's mind from the moment of leaving the beer parlour and setting out to purchase the weapon and ammunition.

"It's not like he said anythin' about actually shootin' himself before other witnesses that can bear out what you say," Pedersen pointed out. "All he said to my jackass assistant was somethin' about *finishin' a job*. Which could mean anythin' . . . shoot yourself or your old lady, shoot a moose for dinner, or shoot your sick dog. What'll stick in folks' heads at that trial is that Stepan bought the gun, said what he said, then did what he did. Don't need no Christly lawyer to tell you that . . . could do it myself."

"And yet," Fulton persisted stubbornly. "I *did* hear him say it."

"Sure you did . . . no doubt about that. But who *else* did? Stepan never said it to you, only to Rosa. And you comin' out with that, the prosecutor fella's goin' to thank you very kindly, and tell the jury what you heard was some bullshit Stepan cooked up to get Rosa to take him back. All you seen and heard, he'll say, was Stepan play-actin'."

And Fulton reflected glumly that, if these were the beliefs being echoed among Stepan's supporters, then Stepan stood very little chance at all. He managed a wan smile. "Olaf, you're doing such a jim-dandy job for the prosecution, maybe you could turn your arguments around, and take on Stepan's defence, instead. You'd probably get him off."

Pedersen did not return the smile. "I don't think he'd thank me if I did. Not from what I've been hearin'."

"What *are* you hearing?" Fulton studied his face. "And from whom?"

"Porkchop again," the store owner replied. "Although strictly off the record, all right?"

"Of course . . . fine."

"It sure as hell looks like Tamara's gettin' one of her wishes already. Because Stepan's really *sufferin'*."

Stepan Kereniuk had been wracked by an agony of guilt and remorse without respite from the moment of wakening after the shooting.

"He's takin' the longest nosedive in the world," Pedersen said. "With no bottom anywheres in sight."

"Except maybe at the end of a rope," Fulton interjected harshly.

"And that, itself, is somethin' that don't seem to worry him a hell of a lot," he learned then. "That's from Porkchop, too, and you never heard it from me, eh?" Fulton nodded wordlessly. "Seems Stepan won't quit talkin' about how he knew exactly what he done to Rosa, and so he wasn't lookin' for no breaks. Tellin' Porkchop, and anyone else that'd listen, how he *wants* to die . . . so's he can find Rosa somewheres, and tell her how sorry he is to her face. He told Porkchop, Porkchop *says*, if they decide to spring the trap under him, that'll suit him jus' fine!"

*

The inquest hearing was not prolonged. It was, as Prokopchuk had forecast, little more than a concession to the rules of procedure, the offering of facts for the official record.

Ben Gilliam, now fulfilling his office of coroner, gave a sympathetic ear to those summoned to testify. There were only four to be heard: Sergeant Prokopchuk as senior investigating officer, supported by his accompanying constable; Doctor Denkman, who had certified the death and carried out the autopsy, and Fulton.

Awaiting his turn to be called, Fulton had not missed the deliberate manner in which Prokopchuk and Denkman avoided eye contact: the engagement was ended, and the interloper had got the girl. Antipathy and awkwardness, however, persisted . . .

Photographic evidence was produced, together with the shotgun and the two spent shells. That gun, Fulton mused absently, must have had one of the shortest careers on record: purchased, fired twice within minutes, then seized . . .

His name was called.

He recounted the events witnessed, avoiding the temptations of embellishment and hindsight.

He had been surprised, and encouraged somehow, by the presence of Ichabod on the jury panel. As the hearing progressed, though, he felt less certain about one of Ichabod's fellow-jurors, Oscar Towerstone, the village barber, a small, bustling figure with a prim toothbrush moustache and wire-rimmed spectacles. Puffed with the brief importance of his position, Towerstone had seized with eagerness upon the coroner's invitation to the jury to question each witness.

Fulton, weighing his own minor role against the criminal and forensic evidence of the policemen and the doctor—professional witnesses—had hoped that he might be spared a grilling. A hope dashed as Towerstone informed the bench, "I got a few questions for this-here witness, Your Honour."

"Yes . . ." The coroner eyed him musingly. "I reckoned you might have, Oscar." He fluttered his fingers at the barber. "You may proceed."

"Thank you kindly, Your Honour." Towerstone turned, smiling, to Fulton. "Is the witness quite at ease?"

Fulton eyed him with caution, then allowed, "the witness *is* . . . as much as anyone can be under these circumstances."

"Oh, right . . . sure thing." The barber inclined his head in agreement. "Mean to say, it's all so *tragic*, and everything. Just wanted to make sure you was *psychologically adjusted*, you know, to facin' up to my enquiry?"

Fulton stared back at him with undisguised astonishment. "How's that again?"

There was restive movement in the room, some smothered laughter.

"*Mister* Towerstone . . ." With asperity the coroner pointed out, "we have all noted the manner in which the witness, freely, has made himself available to us. Nothing he has said so far, nor his demeanour, lead me to believe that we should question his state of mind."

"Okay, Your Honour." The barber, unruffled, nodded affably. "Thank you again very . . ."

"Oh, just get *on* with it, Oscar . . . *do*!"

"Sure thing, Your Honour." The barber turned once more to Fulton. "All I need to know, sir, on the night in question, did you see anything more'n what you said you seen?"

Fulton raised baffled hands. "I'm sorry, but I don't have a clue as to what you're talking about!"

The barber hooked his thumbs into his lapels. "I put it to you, sir, you are an *airplane pilot*."

Fulton, nettled, snapped back, "you don't have to *put it* to me at all! I *am*!"

The room rocked with mirth, and the coroner, lacking a gavel, was compelled to still it by bawling irately. Fulton, laughing himself, could see Ichabod shaking his head slowly, his habitually grave features split into a wide grin. Until the coroner's will prevailed, and order was restored.

"Now, look *here*, Mister Towerstone!" The coroner did not try to conceal annoyance. "This is not a theatre, or some arena where grandstanding is encouraged. We have no requirement for the antics of a Perry Mason!" The barber was looking crushed. "Now I must ask you just where it is this line of questioning's taking us?" He shook an admonishing finger. "Precisely what bearing does the witness's profession have upon matters in hand?"

"Your Honour, it's like this-here . . ." The barber, his aplomb restored, drew himself up to face his inquisitor. "It's on account of pilots they got to have pretty damn' good eyesight . . . better'n most, so's they can do their job. And him bein' a pilot with good eyesight, maybe he seen other things goin' on than what he says he seen?"

The room was quite still, as though in anticipation of the impending explosion from the bench. Seconds ticked by . . . then the coroner nodded. His tone was mild as he enquired, "what do you say to that, Mister Fulton? Anything overlooked?"

"Your Honour, the gentleman is quite right," Fulton replied. "I do have excellent eyesight . . . it's essential in the trade." He looked pointedly at the barber, and the barber's thick-lensed wire spectacles. "But, despite this, I can say truthfully that I saw *only* what I saw, and reported in my statement to the police."

Faintly smiling, the coroner glanced at the barber. "There'll be nothing else, Oscar." It was a statement rather than a question.

"Matter of fact, Your Honour . . ."

"*Thank* you, Oscar . . ." The coroner nodded genially at Fulton. "I see no reason to detain you longer, sir."

"But, Your *Honour* . . ." The barber lifted imploring hands. "I got a whole raft of things I still need to ask this-here witness . . ."

"I'm sure you have, Oscar . . . I'm sure you have." The coroner was patient. "You've done a remarkable job today, but I have to tell you enough's enough. You'll need to hold on to your questions till some other time." He suggested gently, "maybe you two fellows could get together over a cup of coffee, and give it a good airing."

The jury's deliberation was brief: the foreman delivered the unanimous verdict according to the letter of the law: that the deceased, Rosa Natalya Brenko, had suffered death by unnatural and unlawful means which required further investigation. Fulton saw Ichabod watching him across the room, and grimaced response. Thinking of one more nail driven into Stepan's coffin.

*

Ichabod spooned sugar into his tea, and added milk until the liquid assumed an ashen-grey colour. He removed the tea bag with fastidious fingers, then stirred vigorously, and Fulton could hear the spoon grating in the bottom of the mug. The small sound reminded him of the night at supper when, rattled by Rosa's wrath, inattentive, Stepan had over-sweetened his coffee . . .

"Apropos nothing in particular, I feel that you came through your ordeal with credit and dignity," Ichabod observed.

"It wasn't as much of an ordeal as I'd expected," Fulton confessed. And thought with a fresh pang of the coming trial which would be another story. No first names there, no mild indulgences or moments of farce. He smiled for Ichabod. "Except when Sweeney Todd got his hooks into me."

"Be grateful that you didn't finish up in a meat pie."

"From the way he was looking at me when Ben Gilliam shut him up, I'd say I had a lucky escape." Fulton drank some coffee. "How did you make him agree to a unanimous verdict? Threaten to break his legs?"

"Poor Oscar. I do believe all the fight was knocked out of him by Mister Gilliam's short shrift. He was convinced of the sinister, of villainy and deviltry and conspiracy. But we brought him round by reducing everything to a level that he could grasp. That Stepan *had* shot Rosa, and confessed to it. That both action and confession are corroborated by a credible witness . . . *with* splendid eyesight." Fulton grinned. "And, furthermore, that we were not a trial jury . . ." Ichabod began to chuckle. "And if one did not cease immediately to be a prat, we would be compelled to shove one's long list of questions up one's arse!"

"My, my . . . and from a gentleman of the cloth?"

"One did but lend one's support," Ichabod murmured. "And there does come a time when one feels, as it were, *driven*?" His face grew solemn then. "It does help, doesn't it . . . a little laughter? I fear, though, that until this dreadful business can be put behind us, there is to be no real place for that."

SIXTEEN

The date for Stepan's trial had been set, and the notification commanding his attendance—a subpoena, really, Fulton supposed—came like a low blow. He read the date in August, thinking . . . only three weeks, and the knowledge brought the anticipatory dread sharply back.

"You'll be going to Vancouver." Tamara's tone was flat and unrevealing.

He eyed her uneasily. "That's where it's being held."

From the Residence verandah, where they sat in dimness, they could watch the floodlit activity on the decks of the *Chilcotin* which had docked earlier on its regular northbound run to Ocean Falls. The ship was sleek and powerful, one of the new craft coming in to service to replace the old-stagers which had served the up-Island communities for decades. Tamara would go on duty at midnight: at ten, restless and fretful, she suggested that they should walk together to the Government dock, and view the vessel more closely.

He hesitated. "There could be people about."

Tamara was still on edge, keeping herself distant from the watchful eyes and gushing tongues; the community's insatiable thrill-seeking curiosity. And yet, at that moment, she seemed not to care: he sensed a difference about her, a hint of excitement that she suppressed with difficulty. He saw her nod, and make a wry face. "Bound to be. But, this late, maybe not so many we know?" She pointed out reasonably, "those returning will have gone home, and the ones leaving should be on board, or too busy to bother with us. It'll be okay."

She was right. Only two of Lucky's Transfer trucks were on the dock, loading newly-arrived freight. A few Indians, remnants of the crowd which gathered always to greet the passenger ships, remained.

As they watched the preparations for departure, he filled Tamara in on the details, as he knew them, of his summons to the forthcoming trial, expecting . . . he realised then that he was not sure what to expect by way of response from her, and was relieved by the cool, detached manner with which she greeted his news . . .

Until she said abruptly, "about your going to Vancouver. I'm going away, too."

He assumed at once, troubled, that she was thinking of attending the trial. There was no need for that: she had no function to serve; would be present as a mere spectator: in that role he feared the effect the proceedings could have upon her. He did not want to believe that thoughts of vengeance, a desire to gloat over Stepan's downfall, would prompt her attendance.

He probed cautiously, "Vancouver, you mean?" And felt better when she shook her head.

"No. Just away."

"That's good . . ." He smiled encouragement. "You *should* get out of here . . . give yourself a break."

"I mean . . ." She wore a troubled look. "To go *right* away."

He was nonplussed. "For good?"

"I think so . . ." She reminded him quickly, "I would've been going, anyway."

"Your nursing training . . . yes." When she made no response, he asked, "will you tell me where?"

She met his anxious gaze frankly. "I'd always want *you* to know. I'll go to Victoria for a while . . . stay with friends. They've already invited me."

"Well . . . that's great." He wondered, "you say . . . for a while?"

"Afterwards . . . guess I'm not sure yet." There was something studiedly offhand, about her shrug. She said with deceptive lightness, "maybe back East, you know? Toronto, or Montreal? I've always wanted to go there . . ." She told him, "the farthest east I've been is Banff and Calgary on the Greyhound." Her glance at him was quick, furtive-seeming. "But I *will* keep in touch, if you want me to?"

"You know I do, Tamara. What kind of cock-eyed question is *that*?" She smiled, and took his hand, clasping it tightly. "But, baby, I have to ask . . ."

"About my training?" He nodded, and she admitted, "I'm thinking of dropping out." She looked down at their joined hands. "I'll maybe give it some more thought after Victoria."

Trying to conceal dismay, he urged, "think good and hard. I hope you'll reconsider."

"Do you believe I should?" Her eyes came up to search his face.

But, he shied away from that, not wanting to risk intrusion into her affairs. "It's for you to decide, of course. I know what I'd prefer, but I shouldn't interfere." He imagined that he saw disappointment in her eyes. "Although it's a very good qualification . . . a career."

Tamara asked in dry tones, "a future?"

More certain of his ground, he insisted, "there's going to *be* one . . . that's how it goes, no changing it."

"Oh, sure . . ." Her voice was low and bitter. "Some brilliant future it's going to be!" She watched, seemingly intent, the crewmen readying the ship for departure. "As for profession, or career, who needs them now?" She turned once more to face him. "I'm going to be pretty well off, Jack. Did you know that?"

He nodded. "There's been talk."

"I'll *bet* there has!" The pain showed anew as she said, "I probably would've been, anyway, at some time, when . . . only, like *this*, it was never expected." She drew a shaky breath, then resumed more calmly, "the busybodies got that part right. Ma worked hard all her life, and knew how to look after money . . . the Old Country ways. The *kulak* mentality never left her." Her voice was cold and still. "And *he* always . . . made good provision. From the money angle, it was a sound partnership. I can't deny that . . ." Her eyes brimmed and her voice choked, and she made herself go on. "They invested cagily . . . provincial and federal bonds . . . gilt-edge . . . things I don't know about. Although I'll have to begin learning now, won't I? Because of . . . what he's done, while I won't be rich, as long as I don't do anything stupid, I can expect to be comfortable for the rest of my life."

All he could offer was, "Tamara . . . I'm so terribly sorry."

She went tonelessly on, seeming not to hear, "and, if they hang him, I probably get that as well . . ."

On the walk back to the Residence, she said, "I'll need to go to the house and get some more of my things . . . I've been ducking it too long. My clothes . . . stuff I'll want to take with me. Then there's everything else that needs boxing up for storage."

He asked, "must it be you?"

"There's no one else now, is there?"

"But I'd do that for you gladly," he protested.

Her hand squeezed his. "Jack, that's sweet . . . and I'm grateful for the offer . . ."

"Well?"

"But you wouldn't have a clue where to start looking . . ." She hesitated before adding, "although there's something you *could* do for me."

"Just say the word."

Tamara asked quietly, "would you mind going with me . . . to the house?" She pulled a self-mocking face. "I know I'm being a weed, but I don't think I'm ready yet to face that on my own."

*

Fulton gave silent thanks for the unknown hands which had erased the huge bloodstain at the entrance. The shot-out window had been repaired, and he wondered if Sergeant Prokopchuk had drawn upon public funds for the repair, or chosen to meet the costs from his own pocket, saving on the paperwork and possibly humiliating explanations . . .

He followed Tamara along the passage to her bedroom, sensing the air of creeping neglect that already pervaded the house, hearing the echoing hollowness of their footfalls in the emptiness.

Tamara's face was set: she looked straight before her, paying no attention to her surroundings.

The smell of incipient decay was everywhere; the warm, trapped air musty with the blending of dust and damp and stale living. The windows were grimy, which the fiercely house-proud Rosa would never have permitted, the sills littered with dead flies and moths. In every corner spiders had set their snares, and a philodendron was bowed and yellowing on its stand at the end of the passage.

They had brought grocery cartons, and he helped Tamara pack her belongings into them; they worked together in tense silence, conscious of the almost-palpable oppressiveness of the silent house. Fulton noticed that the snapshot enlargement of Rosa and Stepan was no longer to be seen, but could not imagine who might have removed it. Perhaps the same kindly hands that had scrubbed away the bloodstain . . . ?

When three cartons were filled, Tamara spoke for the first time. "We're going to need a cab to move all this."

"I'll phone for one." He waited as she gazed abstractedly about the room, then wondered, "what about your other things?"

"I'm still not sure." She gestured uncertainly. "A lot of it's junk I'd have thrown away . . ." She grew pevish. "I'll just have to figure something out . . ." She's on edge, he thought, and on *the* edge. Just being *here* was enough for that. He watched as she plucked the picture of the Seabee from the mirror frame, and her tone was more gentle as she assured him, "*this* isn't junk . . . and *won't* be thrown away."

He smiled. "Happy to hear it."

"Did you see it when you came last time?"

"Yes."

"Hope you don't mind . . . ?" She glanced at him sidelong. "My taking it?"

"I'm tickled pink . . ." He rolled his eyes at her. "Just glad I wasn't doing anything stupid at the time."

It earned him a returned smile. "I thought you were managing pretty well."

"Makes a nice change . . ." He told her lightly, "probably better to have a picture of the airplane. I'm far from photogenic, and I hate posing for a camera . . . even yours."

"That was something I meant to ask you," Tamara said. "But I guess I've got my answer now."

"If you really wanted, I'd fight the phobia," he offered. "On condition that I get to take the next one on the roll. Of you."

Her smile lingered, warming perceptibly. "I think we can do better than that . . . let's see." She opened a drawer, took out a leather portrait wallet. "This was taken last fall when . . ." She faltered momentarily. "When I was in Vancouver with Ma. She insisted on having it done, and . . . well . . ." She handed the wallet to him. "If you'd like? See what you think."

He studied the formal pose by a competent studio photographer: the Robson Street address gold-stamped into the leather. Sepia tones emphasised her dark beauty, the fine bone structure, as did the vaguely Spanish or Mexican clothing; a low-cut blouse with a gathered bodice that flattered her shoulders and breasts and firm upper arms, the full skirt falling from the slender waist to below the knee. Her neck was unadorned, the head held proudly. She faced the lens with a suggestion of boldness, and the small, questioning smile did not quite reach the cool Tartar eyes. She had brushed her hair out below her shoulders in the way that he liked . . .

She said softly, reflectively, "better days, Jack."

"It's lovely, Tamara." He was deeply moved. "*You're* lovely."

"Aw, *shucks* . . ." For a magical moment they recaptured the old playfulness. "You say the *sweetest* things."

He matched her mood-shift. "Don't I just . . ."

"May I take it that you approve?"

They held each other, laughing, and even then he felt the tremor rising from within her, sensed the mingling of tears with laughter. He murmured into her hair, "I'm knocked out, baby. Can't come up with a single original superlative."

"Don't worry about that . . . it's yours, anyway."

"But, something so terrific . . . how can I just take it?"

"I've *said* it's okay. It's only a photograph . . ." She uttered a strained laugh. "Not an icon of the Orthodox Church. Just your girl's picture in a fancy folder."

She humbled him. "I *like* that . . . my girl's picture."

"That's how it is . . . if you choose?"

"And *how* I choose!" He was beaming at her, and his nose was prickling. "I want it."

"Say no more . . . and quit worrying," she told him. "It's not the only one. There's a framed enlargement downstairs. That was Ma's . . . the whole purpose of the exercise. She wanted one of me . . ." For the first time then since the killing, she spoke of her mother easily and naturally. She lightly touched the wallet in his hands. "Maybe I was just holding on to this until Mister Right showed up."

Their eyes met, and held. "And . . . has he?"

"Kind of seems that way." She studied his face. "You must be *someone* pretty special. Who else could steer my mind away . . ." Her lips compressed for a moment. "From those other things?" Her arms were around him tightly as she asked, "Jack . . . would you kiss me now, please, and really mean it? And when you've done that, take me away from here?"

*

Alice Royle announced, "you'll be going to Vancouver on Thursday, Jack."

For some time now he had been on first name terms, the mark of her particular favour. But . . . it's Monday, Fulton thought, perplexed. Since when did we ever get three days' notice of an impending emergency flight? "What's so special about Thursday?"

"If you fly your machine after then," she informed him, "you'll be in violation of Air Regulations, and *we* shall be liable for penalties."

He remembered, "the old bird's time's up for her C. of A."

"It's all been seen to . . ." Alice Royle's eyes glinted as she added, "I should like us to be quite clear as to who or what we refer to as 'the old bird'."

The Seabee's annual Certificate of Airworthiness was due for renewal, and the aircraft must be flown to the Sea Island base for an exhaustive inspection, and the necessary repair and replacement work.

"The actual date is Saturday," Alice Royle said. "If you fly down late on Thursday, that'll allow us a full day of legal leeway, and we can still extract some revenue time from the aircraft and yourself."

He looked at her with respect. "You think of everything, and all the time."

"It is what one is paid for," she declared virtuously.

Fulton's mind was racing ahead . . . thinking of *Tamara*. Who had tendered her resignation at the hospital, since when he had been living with the painful certainty of her now-imminent departure. Puzzled, too, and hurt, by her failure to reveal her plans to him. He had no idea of her leaving day, or of how she planned to travel.

He saw now a way of learning these things, and of a possible role for himself in those plans. It would not, in the end, diminish the pain of parting, but could, at least, postpone the moment. If he managed to swing this, he thought with growing excitement, then it would be possible to enjoy her exclusive company for that extra time. A time in which to discuss further still-uncertain hopes for a shared future. Something better than an uncertain promise to 'keep in touch'.

*

"Don't see why not, Jack." Mike Denholm's brows lifted quizzically. "Must do what we can to encourage puppy love."

Fulton gave a rueful laugh. "Hope Head Office agrees."

"They'll get used to it. Anyway, I'll tell them I okayed it. In the finest traditions of Harry S. Truman, the buck stops here."

"Thanks, Mike. I'm very grateful."

"Forget it . . . I'd do it for a dog." Denholm chuckled. "Shame, though, about her going to Victoria."

"I agree. But what makes you say that?"

"Well, with you going late Thursday, that means a Vancouver night-stop. For which, by the way, the company picks up your tab for room and board. Then, come Friday morning, they'll have a temporary replacement aircraft for you . . . one of Campbell River's less-than-salubrious 'Bees." Denholm added, "Sierra-Quebec. Which I happen to know is a clunker. But, all that aside, seems a pity you and your girl couldn't hang out in Vancouver for a while, and . . . well, I'm sure you can work out the rest for yourself."

SEVENTEEN

Tamara asked with wonder, "you mean . . . you'll fly me there?"

"That's the general idea. If Thursday afternoon's okay with you?"

"Thursday afternoon's *terrific*!" Her beaming smile gladdened his heart. "Or any other day you like."

He said, relieved, "that's great . . ." Everything was simply . . . falling into place!

"I think that's what I should be saying . . . *again*." She shook her head as if in disbelief. "All the way to Victoria? Really?"

"Really . . ." He fixed his smile in place, and tried not to think of the solitary night that would follow in some nondescript Vancouver motel. "I can take you to Pat Bay airport, or, if you prefer, we'll do it in style, and land bang-smack in the middle of Victoria Harbour."

"I don't know where you came from . . ." She reached out to touch his face. "Or what I did to deserve you. But, I'll be there and ready . . ." She confessed, "I guess, maybe, I'd been waiting, hoping for something like this. Mooching about, all set to go, yet not quite able to do it. In spite of all the talk to the contrary, actually hating to go . . . because that meant leaving you."

He felt the tautness in his throat. "You only had to say."

"How? I couldn't afford to charter you . . ." She pulled a face. "Even if I *am* said to be well-off. Besides, you don't do charters."

"Not the kind I'd ever want to fly you on. But now, I've got to go, and it's a non-revenue trip with a seat going begging . . ." He said gravely, "even though you'll be leaving me once we get there. Everything after Victoria, for me, is going to be a very much down hill."

They were together in the Nurses' lounge. Tamara's final shift had ended, and she had been—as she put it—'dabbling at packing'.

"Olaf has offered to store everything until I'm settled, and can make up my mind what to do with it all. When I say the word, he'll simply clear the house for me . . ." She looked down, frowning. "Although, so far, I haven't thought a lot about that."

"Well, there's no big hurry, is there?"

"I guess I probably will sell up, and cut my ties here . . ." Tamara's eyes were distant. "As for *his* stuff, they can burn it . . . dump it in the salt-chuck . . . do what they damned well like!"

It was late, and they were the only ones left in the big, overstuffed room. She turned to him to say impulsively, "Jack . . . I'm not leaving *you*. I couldn't . . . not now. Any distance between us will be only miles." He sought for some grain of comfort in that. "We're going our separate ways, but then that was always in the cards . . ." She watched him with troubled eyes. "So where's the real problem? We *will* get back together when the time's right."

"I like to think of that." He nodded. "But, right now, it's all so vague and uncertain. Like a gamble."

"Jack, shape up, will you?" She clutched his arms fiercely. "Try and get it into your little pointed head that you're the one tie I'll *never* cut!"

*

He was delighted to find that the Seabee's front passenger seat had been re-installed. Jackie Seaweed explained with ponderous irony, "it was Bob Peters done it. He's been seein' too many mushy movies. Worked it out you'd have a hard time grabbin' a feel with the lady sittin' behind you."

"That," Fulton informed him, "doesn't sound like any mushy movie *I've* ever watched."

"Anyhow . . ." The Indian was grinning. "She can park her butt beside you, and you two can get on doin' what comes natural."

"You're an incurable romantic, Jackie."

"That's me." The Indian nodded agreeably.

They looked up as Olaf Pedersen's Ford rolled along the pier, rattling the loose planking.

Jackie Seaweed murmured, "don't forget and let us know how it went when you get back, eh?"

"The trip, you mean?"

"Sure . . . yeah. That part as well!"

Tamara came down to them in her white blouse and blue pedal-pushers that would remind Fulton always of going with her to the Private Place. It was a place, he knew, that he would not be visiting again.

She was wearing flat shoes for travelling, and her dark hair was tied back in a long pony-tail: his breath caught as he thought again of how beautiful she was. And, like a knife twisting, the bitter knowledge of her *going* . . .

Olaf Pedersen followed heavily behind, burdened with the powder-blue suitcase, a matching vanity case, a canvas grip. That case, Fulton decided, smiling, looks no better on him than on me . . .

Tamara said breathlessly, "hi!"

"Hello, there . . ." He watched her, feeling his delight in her tarnished by the emptiness of desolation. He tried to re-assure himself: she's not gone . . . not yet. And made the ache worse as he asked, not thinking, "all set to go . . . ?"

"I've brought a terrible lot of junk. Sorry."

"You could've brought the whole house. I'd still have taken it."

"Please . . ." She looked strained. "Don't speak of the house!"

"Christ . . . !" Something else said without *thinking*. He could have bitten off his tongue.

"It's just me," she offered in a low, contrite voice. "I'm still too prickly."

She hugged Olaf Pedersen, who told her, "you come back soon. No matter what, this is your home . . . people care about you here." Her voice was breaking as she thanked him. He gave Fulton a fierce glare. "Look after her, or I'll have the hide off you."

Fulton nodded, not speaking, making himself swallow the needless resentment engendered by the rough words. Telling himself . . . everyone's hurting today.

He waited as Jackie Seaweed gave Tamara one of his rare smiles, and told her, "you take her easy . . ." Before turning aside to stow her bags in the aircraft.

She was peering into the cabin. "Hey . . . you've put back the seat!"

"Just for you, as you're not a stretcher case . . ." Fulton avoided studiously Jackie Seaweed's sardonic eye.

*

They climbed straight out from Blackfish Harbour, not looking back, setting course down the long arm of Johnstone Strait.

He ventured, "surprised no one came from the hospital to see you off."

"I asked them not to," she explained. "Anyhow, they gave me a party last night."

It had been a muted affair: coffee and sandwiches and a cake; the suggestion by someone of champagne flown up from Vancouver on Q.C.A. Had been vetoed as inappropriate to the moment.

Everyone off duty had been there. Tamara told him, "it was really very nice." He noticed her set face.

The Matron had presided. The hospital administrator made a speech that steered an uncertain course between jocularity and a more seeming gravity. There had been a farewell presentation.

"They must've emptied the Rexall of its complete stock of perfume . . . not that there was ever much there . . ." She seemed amused. "I've got Chanel and Revlon and Elizabeth Arden . . . you name it. Enough to keep me fragrant till I'm eighty . . ." She hesitated before adding, "they gave me silver thunderbird earrings and a matching pendant . . . beautiful Indian workmanship. Trouble is . . ." She was looking down at her folded hands. "Thunderbirds will remind me always of Blackfish . . ."

He attempted to joke. "I'm busting to see you . . . *and* smell you, in all that good stuff."

She nodded, smiling reflectively. "Have to save them for you."

They flew over Kelsey Bay in the high golden light, and he

made the turn through the pass to Campbell River. Already, in the crystal air, they could see the distant blue expanse of the Strait of Georgia widening before them. The dark, tumbling folds of the Vancouver Island mountains flowed away, softening, to the southeast, becoming hazy-grey where they appeared to blend with the barrier of the Washington shore, the seaward thrust of the Olympic peninsula.

Down there, he thought unhappily, almost within view now, lay Victoria and its sheltering inlet. For the first time, he found himself regretting the *speed* of flight. Even at a Seabee's snail's pace, you still got there too soon . . .

"They made me an offer," Tamara said then. "That there'd be a job waiting after I graduate. Anytime I wanted. I almost puddled-up all over them," she admitted, and the sad smile was there once more. "As you can guess from that, I'd said nothing about quitting."

He asked, "is it still only a possibility?"

She gave a slow nod. "Guess I've still got some more heavy thinking to do."

He seized the opportunity. "Then . . . if it's okay to put in my two-bits' worth?"

"No need to ask, Jack. Although I've got a shrewd idea of what's coming."

"I'll say it anyway. I wish you wouldn't quit, Tamara. I hope you won't. That's all."

"A very modest two-bits' worth . . ." She wanted to know, "would it matter if I did? Whether I get my R.N. or not makes no difference to *us*, surely?"

He answered, moved and pleased, "nothing will change *us*."

"So?"

"But you haven't actually gone off nursing?"

"No . . ." She answered with considerable irony, "but I think you'd allow that I've been through a rough patch lately? And that, just now, my head's kind of topsy-turvy?"

"That's what's on my mind more than anything when I ask you not to quit, and go wandering off around the country, thinking and remembering."

She asked, "brooding?"

"If you like."

"And, instead, study and hard work, lots of iron discipline, will help quieten my addled brain? The therapeutic effect?"

Fulton shrugged and said, "it makes sense, baby." There was a need, though, to clarify and justify his argument. "They'll certainly run you through the mill, and there'll be no time for anything but the books and the job."

"You still don't seem to get the picture, do you?" There was a hint of chill in her voice. "I'll never, *never* be able to stop thinking of my mother."

Her words made him defensive, and inexplicably irritable. "*Okay* . . . that's accepted, and no one in his right mind would suggest that you should. And maybe you're right, and I'm wrong, and, yes, you ought to drop out . . ." He heard the harshness, and stopped himself: she was nowhere near ready for rough handling. The wounds were still too raw. "Please . . . forget I said that."

"Jack, I know what you're getting at, and I *am* grateful . . ." She touched his arm.

"But I still have to think this through, and get myself squared-away. Now I know for sure how you feel, I promise to take that into account. You'll be a definite influence on what I decide."

"My turn now to be grateful." He nodded and smiled. "I couldn't ask for more."

The Seabee was passing over the Air Force station at Comox, and Tamara reminded him, "soon, that'll be you. You'll be the one going away." Her smile was wistful.

"Fine, yes . . . but at least with a purpose." He said insistently, "and that's what I feel *you* need. To find yours, you need look no farther than Vancouver, and things that are worthwhile and positive, and can actually *help* you adjust. You can be busy there, and useful, instead of aimless. And I'd say *busy's* what's needed."

Comox fell behind, and they flew on in silence until, at last, Tamara asked the question he had been dreading. "What will you do after you let me off?"

"I'm trying very hard not to think about that . . ." It could not, though, be avoided, and he told of going on to Vancouver, of the temporary exchange aircraft to be flown back in the morning . . .

"Oh, *wow* . . . !" She gave a little, breathless laugh. "An honest-to-God night on the town!"

"Shacked up in some crummy motel on Lulu Island," he pointed out ruefully. "While there's you in Victoria."

"Must you go there? To the motel?"

"I could go to my parents, but it's a long shlep out to Bowen Island when you're stuck with no car. By time I got there, it'd be almost time to start back."

Tamara suggested lightly, "it does seem a wicked waste."

"And a crying shame!"

"Although it needn't be . . ." She left a deliberate pause.

He said, puzzled, "I think you lost me."

"Would that Lulu Island motel be quite so crummy," Tamara wondered. "If you took me there with you?"

He gaped at her. "You're *serious*?"

"I wouldn't joke about something like that, Jack."

"No, of course not . . ." But he was confused. "What about your people waiting in Victoria?"

"What *about* them? They're expecting me when they see me. There's no mad rush."

He felt excitement: this was exactly what Mike Denholm and Jackie Seaweed—in their preferred ways—had hinted at. What had been beyond his hopes and dreams: the hated moment of farewell deferred once more; the night alone with her . . . and a night could seem like *forever*!

"It's quite simple . . ." Tamara sounded matter-of-fact. "In the morning, I take a bus downtown, or the Inter-Urban, and catch the Victoria ferry." Her smile was that of a conspirator. "I've always wanted to make that cruise through the Gulf Islands. Then I'll get a cab out to Saanich. Easy . . ." A question lay in her eyes. "If *you* want?"

"My God! What do you *think*?"

"Just making sure . . ." She said impulsively, "Jack . . . let's *do* it!"

*

The motel lay on the far side of the river, between Marpole and Richmond, close enough to the airport for them to hear the aircraft movements clearly. A dozen worn units behind an electric sign that vied ineffectually with the bright early evening. Their assigned room was basic and clean, and everything worked. No one had commented upon the arrival of an Island Airways pilot with a companion: the carefully-rehearsed quip about 'co-pilots' was not needed.

Walking to their unit, Tamara murmured. "Perhaps this is the norm? Aviators arriving in mismatched pairs?"

"*Un*-matched, maybe," he corrected her lightly. "But I'd never call *us* mismatched."

But the edgy bawdiness went flat as the door clicked behind them. The moment, they were finding, and the place, lacked the sweet spontaneity of that long afternoon at the sea's edge, seeming, instead, charged with intent and purpose.

Other than during strained moments in the Nurses' Residence, and at the empty house, they had never been alone together in a bedroom. In this anonymous place of many hasty trysts, they sensed the contrivance, even the faint whiff of something shoddy. Constraint fell over them, and they faced each other with the big bed between them, plagued by unwelcome misgivings which neither could utter.

They would begin to speak, then break off, smiling in shared embarrassment. He grew protective and solicitous, quizzing her, offering unsought assurances, until, exasperated with him, she exclaimed, "I'm *fine*! Just quit *nagging*!"

He begged her pardon, and she his, and they unpacked side by side in silence. Tamara said that she would shower; she felt grubby after the flight. He sprawled out on the bed, watching her with baffled eyes as she gathered her toilet articles. She came across to kiss him lightly. "Sorry I got owly with you."

"It was justified. I must've sounded like a stuck record."

"Maybe a little . . ." She stroked his forehead. "Guess we have to expect it to be tricky at first. We'll be fine soon."

He smiled up. "You promise?"

"I can almost guarantee it."

He followed her with his eyes as she crossed to the bathroom; he heard the shower's soft drumming, soothing in its steadiness . . .

Until it seemed that the sound grew louder, more harsh, seeming to take on a hard, metallic edge: there was the disturbing half-belief that the water was moving closer, coming on to soak him where he lay. One more of Tamara's little jokes? Like the one with her bathing cap and the ice-cold sea water?

Although . . . he puzzled over it drowsily . . . not so much a water sound, as a heavy, rumbling drone, *machine*-like. Since learning to fly, his mind had attuned to the sound, unmistakeable, of compression, pistons rising and falling within hot, polished, beautifully-wrought cylinders, building up to the explosions of gases that provided the driving force . . . induction, compression, ignition, exhaust, millions of times between each take-off and landing. He felt the tremor of that immense power; the synchronised hooves of thousands of horses shaking the earth, and the building surrounding him . . .

As the climbing aircraft on departure from Vancouver International thundered overhead, and his airman's ear registered four Pratt & Whitney R-2000s, each driving thirteen hundred horses in hand. A Douglas DC-4 that galloped south across endless plains of sky.

Waking, he listened with closed eyes to the fading rumble, pondering the southbound heading . . . United Airlines, or Northwest Orient. Early evening run to Seattle, Portland and San Francisco-Oakland . . .

The engines had faded to a distant muttering; the motel room was back on its foundations, and he noted that the shower sounds had ceased. He lay at ease, waiting. Until a small, piqued voice informed him, "if you don't *mind* . . . I'm starting to freeze here!"

He caught his breath as he saw Tamara at the bedside, slender, golden-tanned, her body still wet in places where the towel had not passed. Naked—and he amended then, *almost* naked—nudity enhanced by tiny, delicate silver thunderbirds, one at each ear, the third suspended from its chain to rest above the smooth breasts.

She stood for him, her wet hair pulled back from her forehead to fall heavily down her back. His eyes roamed freely, feasting on her, on the sweet curves of hip and thigh, the nipples aroused and hardened, the dark triangle of pubic hair . . .

She accused, "all you could think about was that damned *airplane*!"

"Not any more . . ." She stood only inches from him, and he reached out with an arm to encircle her waist. "Now that my eyes are open to reality."

The bonds of restraint parted, and he could draw her down to him, relishing the silk-over-steel firmness of her body under his fingers. She came without resistance, and her closer proximity brought him the dark richness of expensive perfume.

"It's 'Blue Grass'," she whispered. "Like it?"

"Love it to bits." He breathed the fragrance deep. "That's one hell of a going-away present."

She kissed him lightly. "See? I kept my promise. Saved them for you . . ." She kissed him once more, less lightly. "And . . . one thing."

"Yes?"

"Who said anything about *going away*?"

*

The motel did not provide food, but there was a 'half-ways decent' café ten minutes' walk away along the road to Brighouse.

It was a glorified diner, but its plain fare met their needs, and the coffee was good.

Smiling face to face across the scuffed formica table, they agreed that there was no need for the customary preamble, artfully staged, of candlelight and wine. They were already well beyond that, and ham and eggs and coffee would do. Within an hour of leaving it, they were back at their motel room . . .

They made love wildly, with a hunger that, it did seem, could never be satisfied. They would lie back, gasping, exhausted, believing themselves spent, and, within minutes, no word uttered, would reach for each other once more, their bodies dictating terms to minds which relinquished joyously all curbs and controls, becoming compliant for the long duration of their stolen speck of time.

Before, they had known each other only a little, and then hesitatingly. Now, with eyes and hands and limbs, with mouths that drank their fill of each other and thirsted still, they explored and discovered to the farthest regions of themselves, tasting and savouring; pausing awhile before plunging yet again, tireless, into the vast pool of shared sensations.

Until, near dawn, they were sated, and could collapse upon their ruined bed, delighted with each other, with no secrets, it did seem, then, left uncovered.

In the cool dark, when even the great airport across the river lay silent, they could whisper their words of love and hope for a while longer, and still imagine that there might be no ending, no moment of parting.

EIGHTEEN

Fulton waited outside the courtroom with the dread gnawing like sickness, breathing the stale, motionless air that compounded odours of stone and wax polish, the tang of disinfectant from some unseen washroom.

He studied furtively those others around him awaiting *their* summons on comfortless benches, those who chose to stand, or pace back and forth.

People singly, with nervous cigarettes, ignoring the No Smoking signs, probably unaware of them: people in groups, chatting grave-faced in this place without laughter. Some stood before the windows to gaze with undisguised wistfulness out at a world of normality from which, for whatever periods of time, they now found themselves excluded.

Some who waited were known to him: the tight, aloof knot of Mounted Police in their scarlet tunics and snowy lanyards; Sergeant Prokopchuk stern in the midst of his constable servitors, the two plain-clothes forensics men.

Beyond bare greetings, the obligatory 'good mornings', there had been no contact, and Fulton was quick to sense that an attempt to link himself to their group would be rebuffed.

He wondered, observing the police, with so many here for court, who would be left back at Blackfish Harbour to mind the store? Was that handled by temporary replacements, or by some long-practiced sleight-of-hand to conceal the manpower shortage? Could it be, simply, that the community's unruly elements were left to kick up their heels unchecked until full strength was restored, and the crack-down could begin . . . ?

Fulton found himself thinking of . . . *theatre*. That each of them present was no more than an actor waiting in the wings for a cue.

All in costume, ready, the resplendent police and the soberly-respectable plain-clothes men. He, himself, in a blue summer suit; the first time for months that he had dressed so. Going over his lines, considering his role in the grim drama that had begun already beyond closed doors a few paces away.

Perhaps, he mused, it was this theatrical aspect of the judicial process that made film and television courtroom dramas so enduringly popular . . .

He looked up, startled, as the door opened, and a clerkly official figure emerged to call an unknown name, and one of the forensics men, grimacing, detached himself from the group.

And . . . the preliminaries are over, Fulton realised, and felt his nerves tighten. It was stepping up a gear, moving on, one by one, towards the moment when it would be his name they called. Thinking of theatre, he recalled an operatic work in his father's L.P. Collection: Poulenc's 'Dialogue of the Carmelites'. In which the nuns, waiting at the foot of the guillotine, sang together, and, at intervals, there would be one less voice. Until there was *only* one . . .

He remembered, like a welcome balm, Tamara's letter, and drew it out to read for . . . he had lost count of the number of times.

'Dearest Jack,' she wrote. 'We both know what day is close, and where you will be, and so I want to get this off to you quickly, hoping that it will be there before you leave Blackfish.

'There is little time if I'm going to make today's mail, so I'll have to keep it short. Yet there is so much I want to say to you, and have committed to paper for good. All of that, though, must wait for another letter, or, better still, for the next time when we are together. For now, please make do with knowing that I love you, and only you. I'll be knocking on wood, and crossing my fingers (and my legs!) until I hear again that you feel the same for me? I keep thinking that, just as so many pretty horrible things have happened, and are happening, that you have come into my life, and that, just maybe, there really *is* a God?

'It's still too soon for me to know if I'm pregnant, but after those unbelievable things we did together it would not surprise me if I was. Would you mind terribly? You must never start thinking I'd use it to try and pin you down, like some blackmail thing. That's not my way. All the same, married or single, in sin or out of it, I would want to have and hold your—OUR—baby.

'Making due allowance for developments of the situation above, it may please you to know that I've been thinking hard about my R.N., and have decided I WILL NOT DROP OUT. I guess I've always known I didn't *want* to quit. So, if I'm not yet a mother-to-be, then I *shall*, after all, be a nurse-in-training. But whichever way it works out, I WILL be nursing!

'All my thoughts are with you in these grim days ahead.

'All my love always, TAMARA.

'P.S. I do know that Ma would have been thrilled to bits about us, and would have loved a baby.'

With the letter, he had brought her photograph also, and looked at it now, linking her calm, lightly-smiling face with the warmth of her words to him.

"It helps, Tamara," he told her picture softly. "You, and your thoughts shared with me. With you, and those, I can ride this out."

*

Seeing Stepan's face alight with undisguised pleasure as he walked into the courtroom, was, he felt, the worst moment, one that he would never be able to forget.

Stepan, he realised, *had* been watching for him, alerted by the call for 'John Stuart Fulton'.

He faced Stepan as he took the oath; he could not have looked away, shaken by that smile, the conspiratorial wink . . . as though they were pulling a fast one together on Porkchop. The way the mouth shaped the soundless words of, "hel-lo, High-pockets!"

With that stamped upon his mind, still he must deliver his damning truths about Stepan's actions, hating to do it, *hating* himself. Doing it because it was his inescapable burden of duty under the law.

Because it was, quintessentially, an open and shut case that must, nonetheless, be heard through, the trial, like the earlier inquest, amounted to little more than a formal, solemn recounting of known facts.

The prosecution led Fulton through the events witnessed, keeping it low-key, avoiding theatrics and hyperbole, and he could not fail to notice as he provided answers, how these tactics were impressing the jury.

Stepan sat quietly throughout, almost unmoving, paying close attention. Stepan in a grey gabardine suit of old-fashioned cut, a hideous hand-painted necktie, and Fulton wondered if that was the suit worn in the snapshot with Rosa . . .

Counsel for the defence, left with little but a rearguard action to fight for his client, did his best, basing his arguments upon extenuation due to extreme and unnatural provocation by the deceased. A level of provocation, it was claimed, which had caused reason and self-control to be lost. A situation exacerbated by personal tragedy suffered earlier on the day that the offence had been committed.

True, it was acknowledged, the accused had consumed a quantity of alcohol sufficient to intoxicate him to the point where he could no longer exercise judgement . . .

Fulton, remembering Prokopchuk's warning of the inadmission of drunkenness as a defence, waited for what must be the prosecution's certain challenge . . . and was puzzled and relieved when none came. The impression gathered was that both bench and prosecution were allowing the defence more than the usual latitude in a hopeless and thankless task.

He drew from Fulton—who declared it willingly—Stepan's declaration of intent to Rosa to take his own life. "It was what we expected him to do from the start."

Defence counsel pressed, "could you be more specific? What was expected, and when was the start?" Adding, "you refer also to 'we'. Who's 'we', Mister Fulton?"

Stepan leaned forward intently as Fulton ran through the stages beginning with Ichabod's telephone call, culminating with the conversation outside the hotel. "We all believed that was what Stepan had in mind. He had lost his best friend, actually witnessing the events which cost him his life . . ."

The court was still, only faint sounds of the city outside intruding: the rise and fall of an emergency siren, the nearby hiss of airbrakes. Another world, remote, alien-seeming.

"Yes, he drank a lot, and was very drunk . . ." Fulton began to experience the return of self-confidence: if the prosecution was going easy on the drinking side, then let's milk it for all it's worth. "The drinking was, I believe, the attempt to drown very real and deep sorrow, and to lessen the depression felt over his latest quarrel with Rosa."

"Were such quarrels commonplace?"

"Yes sir, they were."

"Can you throw any light on why this should have been?"

Fulton spoke of Stepan's habitual drinking, weighing that against Rosa's fear and abhorrence of alcohol.

"What did you feel on that evening about Rosa Brenko's behaviour towards my client?"

Fulton drew in a breath. "I felt that she over-reacted."

"What led you to feel that?"

Fulton considered his reply with care, then made it in a clear voice while pointedly not looking at Stepan. "Rosa knew of the death of Stepan's friend, Billy Langewische. She knew that Stepan had been in the beer parlour, drinking."

"Did she learn of the drinking from you, Mister Fulton?"

"Yes, she did. I met her as she was returning home, and explained the situation. I asked her to go easy on Stepan."

"How did she respond to that?"

"Favourably. Saying she understood, and would give him a break."

"Did you have any reason to doubt her good intentions?"

"None whatever. Rosa was a decent, kindly and honest woman. She had a fierce temper, but could handle it most of the time. And her word was always her bond . . . like Stepan himself."

There was a stir and a muttering. The judge looked up questioningly. Fulton glanced in Stepan's direction and was surprised to see him shaking his head, his expression one of agitation . . .

"Mister Fulton . . . could you provide an explanation as to why Rosa Brenko broke her word?"

"I should think it was very much because of what I knew myself at the time, and told her."

"And what did you know and tell her, please?"

"That Stepan was drunk on beer . . . which she was used to. What she discovered subsequently, and what I didn't know, was that he had also consumed the best part of a bottle of rye whisky. I had believed Stepan when he told me he would go straight to bed and sleep off the beer, and had told Rosa so. Whereas, he was still drinking hard, and whisky, I guess, was too much, and she hit the roof."

"Now, Mister Fulton, could we discuss further what you refer to as Rosa Brenko's *over-reaction*? Would you describe that more fully?"

"As I stated, it must have been the whisky," Fulton insisted. "Rosa hated drinking, period. Beer was bad, but hard liquor would have been the final straw. I believe she just couldn't forgive that."

"Sufficient, then, to cause her to physically assault my client?"

"That is correct."

"An assault which you witnessed?"

"Only what took place *outside* the house," Fulton stressed.

Defence counsel nodded. "And, following that assault, is it true that Rosa Brenko ordered my client to leave the premises, and not to return?"

"Yes, it is."

"Did you overhear any threats made to my client by Rosa Brenko?"

"She told him she would summon the police and have him arrested if he came back."

"How did he respond to that?"

"Rosa went inside, and Stepan shouted after her . . ." Fulton decided to make no mention of the shattered whisky bottle. No one had brought that up . . .

"Yes, Mister Fulton?"

"He said he'd return, and that no one could stop him."

"Was that all?"

"There was nothing else."

"No threats of violence? No talk of getting even?"

"There was nothing else," Fulton said again.

"Thank you, sir."

Question and answer, back and forth, going over the drab, tragic events: Stepan duly leaving the house, re-visiting the beer parlour. His ejection from there, then the trudge to Olaf Pedersen's hardware store. The purchase of the shotgun and shells . . .

Defence counsel played one of his meagre cards. "Mister Fulton, what fears did you express concerning my client?"

"That he was shocked and distressed, his state of mind made worse by alcohol, and that he was possibly, even probably, planning to kill himself."

"*Self*-destruction, then? Not murder?" The defence counsel glanced meaningfully at the jurors.

"No, sir. We never believed that. About murder." Fulton's cheeks were hot with the realisation of *perjury*. You went tearing back to the house for that very purpose; to warn Rosa of possible violence to herself . . . you were thinking of murder *then*! But, again, no one had asked him about that. He prayed guiltily that no one would. "Stepan loved Rosa . . . we talked together, he and I, of that, and he told me of his feelings for her. And Rosa, no doubt whatever, *knew* that Stepan loved her . . ." The defence counsel nodded encouragingly. "I believed then, absolutely, what he told me, and I believe it still . . ." He looked across at Stepan, as if to challenge contradiction. "Whatever has happened, and I don't seek to minimize the gravity of it, Stepan Kereniuk is a good, caring man who would never have thought deliberately of harming Rosa. But his feelings, and his volatile nature, *could* have made him decide to take his own life in front of her in an exhibitionist way, and grief and depression could have firmed-up that decision . . ."

"Your Honour . . ." The prosecuting counsel was on his feet. "Your Honour, I must raise serious objection to the witness's statement." He sounded regretful, a more-in-sorrow-than-in-anger tone. "But this is less testimony than *testimonial*, and, furthermore, based entirely upon personal belief and opinion."

"These points are noted . . ." The judge gazed without visible rancour at Fulton. "Mister Fulton, you have made clear to us your friendship and compassion for the accused, and this does you both credit. It is not my intention, then, to have your words stricken from the record. I must, however, point out that the points you make are, indeed, grounded upon opinion, with only some basis in fact, and so must be ruled as irrelevant."

Fulton answered humbly, "I apologise, Your Honour . . ." Within, though, he was elated: the rebuke had been an easy price to pay for that heaven-sent opportunity to speak out for Stepan. True, Stepan *had* killed Rosa, yet it should not be possible to condemn the man, only the *act* . . .

He was smiling inwardly, thinking of the prosecutor's fair complaint about 'testimonial'. It had been that, all right, and shameless; under oath, he could not have denied that he had waited, and begged, for just such an opening. Now, there was the comforting knowledge that what he had said *would* remain upon the court record, and in the mind of each jury member, a valid word of extenuation. And could that be the gesture of a sympathetic judge already pre-disposed toward mercy . . . ?

*

Stepan Kereniuk felt the burn of anger and hurt and bitter disappointment. The questions went back and forth maddeningly between his lawyer—some unsought stranger hired-on at the insistence of other hired strangers—and Highpockets who, for all these months past, he had believed a friend, trustworthy . . .

He sat mute, compelling muteness with difficulty as, before his eyes, they betrayed Rosa. The anger seared him, rising like a tide to the point where he must speak . . . or *bust*. Here and God-dammed now . . . !

In a cracked voice that overrode the near-conversational tones of lawyer and witness, he commanded, "*listen* to me! All of you . . . be listen!"

The court shivered into stillness, waves of shock moving out from the hub of him: he saw the lawyer gaping up, the way Highpockets gave a little questioning shake of the head.

"Needin' tell you people something . . . got to say it!" He was on his feet facing the bench, feeling defiance and a fearful expectation: he was not meant to talk out of turn, his lawyer had said; that could be bad . . .

Yet, as the Court waited, the judge only looked at him mildly, speaking words that Stepan could not grasp fully. "Mister Kereniuk, I should make clear that you are represented by Counsel empowered and . . . one would expect . . . equipped to pronounce on your behalf. Later, should you wish, you will have your opportunity to speak. Until then I advise you to remain silent . . . let your Counsel pursue his task."

But Stepan shook his head. "Sir . . . Your Honour . . . this be something only I know to say. No one else . . . not this good man helpin' me out. He doin' his best, but I got to tell you how he and Mister Fulton be got it all wrong . . ."

The judge wondered, "and is this germane to matters in hand?"

Stepan eyed him, lifting bewildered hands. "Sir, I . . ."

"If it please the Court . . ." Defence counsel had risen. "May we seek a short adjournment while I consult with my client?"

"Might be a good idea . . ." The room rustled as the judge consulted his watch. "Fifteen minutes?"

"That should be ample, Your Honour."

Fulton remained in the witness box as the judge left the bench, watching the inaudible exchange between Stepan and his lawyer. In less than ten minutes they were finished, Stepan sitting back, looking triumphant. The lawyer, with troubled face, waited, toying with a pencil.

The judge returned. "Do we have agreement?"

Defence counsel, subdued, confessed, "I have attempted without avail to dissuade my client, Your Honour. The request to speak stands."

The room stirred with interest as the judge declared, "this being Mister Kereniuk's day in court, I am inclined to respond sympathetically. He may have his say."

Fulton, forgotten in the witness box, waited for the prosecution's objection, but none came, and, as defence counsel bowed his head as though in weary defeat, he felt a return of despair.

The judge addressed Stepan. "I ask you to be brief . . . to waste as little as possible of the Court's time."

Stepan bobbed his head. "Yes, sir . . . Your Honour. Little whiles back . . ." He gestured apologetically. "That word you say . . . I not get the hang of it."

"'Germane', Your Honour," defence counsel put in.

"*That* the one," Stepan agreed. "My friend here . . ." He smiled at the lawyer. "He say me what it mean. An', Your Honour, it *that*, hokay."

"Then let's hear it." The judge grinned fleetingly.

Stepan hesitated, glancing about him as if uncertain how to begin. Until he said, "Your Honour . . . seem all I be hearin' is folks gettin' the wrong end o' the stick." He turned to Fulton. "Highpockets, I listen to you talkin', all your questionin' and answerin' what you do is make out like this all my Rosa's fault." His mouth tightened. "Makin' it sound like she *deserve* what I do to her . . . like she beggin' for it. Well, you thinkin' that, you got it wrong, an' I don't let you get away with it. No, *sir*!" The words were firm, earlier anger replaced by a note of regret for the seeming lack of understanding of something so clear-cut and apparent. "I got to say you, no matter what it mean to me, that not the way of it."

Every eye was on him, the warm heavy air silent, charged with tension. His counsel sat, looking resigned, and Stepan went on.

"Like I say to Mister Fulton sometime . . . like he say you now . . . yah, I love my Rosa. Right from word go . . . never no changin'. She gone now, no bringin' her back, and it *my* fault. But I still lovin' her." Another glance at Fulton, the question in the eyes . . . don't you remember? Didn't you *believe*?

"I know what people try an' do here . . . get me out o' big Goddam jam I get myself in, an' I say thank you." He turned his face to the judge. "But if you sayin' bad things about my Rosa so's to help out, don't *want* that. Too high the price havin' to pay. Rosa, she never, *never* deserve things I do to her all them years wi' the drinkin', then . . ." Stepan faltered, made himself go on in a choking voice. "She not bring one itty-bitty thing on herself. All she do is try straighten me out until she see it no good, an' send me on my way. Doin' that, like everything else, she done the right thing, an' that for *sure*." He nodded to indicate that he was finished, and offered apology. "I take too long time say these things. Just find out now how sayin' things take a lot longer than do for *thinkin*'!"

Fulton, looking around, observed both counsels smiling. Some of the jurors exchanged amused looks.

Only he, it seemed, could find nothing to smile at. Not with the realisation of the deep impression Stepan had made upon his listeners, nor the certainty within him that, unlike the first, Stepan's second suicide attempt might now succeed . . .

NINETEEN

Fulton announced bad-temperedly, "you were right about *one* thing."

"There's something for the record book . . ." Mike Denholm eyed him. "What?"

"This bloody airplane *is* a piece of junk!"

He had landed from what should have been a twenty-minute round trip to Port Hardy.

"What seems to be wrong with it, Jack?"

"*Nothing* seems . . . it's what *is*. I could save us all time by listing what's right!"

Denholm wondered mildly, "you wouldn't be going prima donna on me, would you?"

"After three horrible hours flown in this thing, I'm sure as hell going *something*!"

His troubles with the replacement aircraft began within forty minutes of taking delivery: an oil seal shredding at two thousand feet over Georgia Strait, with the irony of an emergency landing at Campbell River, the Seabee's usual home base. Where he had found a measure of satisfaction in pointing out the evidence, the tail assembly blackened by thrown engine oil.

Airborne once more with apologies and a fresh seal installed, the manifold pressure gauge had ceased to function. While inconvenient and irritating, this was not life threatening. Fulton knew enough now about Seabees and their ways to judge his power settings by ear. It did seem, though, to provide fair warning for his ongoing involvement with the aircraft . . .

Mike Denholm offered scant sympathy. "What did they tell you when you hired-on about Seabees and oil seals? They're endemic . . ." Fulton nodded grudging agreement. "Busted seals and blackened tails are the classic signs of the hard-grafting 'Bee . . ." Fulton expressed doubt and derision with a snort. "Wonder to me you haven't hit the problem sooner."

"That's because we look after our airplanes." Jackie Seaweed looked up from pumping water seepage from the Beaver's floats. "Unlike them Campbell River pricks."

Fulton wondered, "and the boost gauge?"

"Gauges get old and wear out."

"Almost as quick as pilots," Jackie Seaweed declared, smirking.

"Shut up, Jackie," Denholm told him, and promised, "we'll replace that with one of ours. Then, when they bring our aircraft back, we'll shove the duff one back in theirs. Nothing to it . . ."

Now, though, Fulton thought, there had been the Port Hardy trip.

Denholm invited, "tell me about it."

"Bloody landing gear . . ." Fulton stared accusingly at the retracted wheels. "First it wouldn't go down, then it wouldn't come up."

"Looks pretty up to me."

"Only because I was mulish."

There had been a requirement for a rare runway landing at the Port Hardy airport. Circling the field, Fulton's repeated attempts to lower the wheels had proved unavailing.

"Pumping away for nigh on ten minutes . . . thought my arm would drop off."

"So, what *did* happen?" Denholm considered him thoughtfully. "Seeing as you've still got your arm."

"That's what I love about you people . . . your warmth and compassion," Fulton said, peeved. Denholm and the Indian were laughing. "I was about to head back here when, suddenly, down she went, and I landed."

"Good for you. And then?"

"I took off again, and, this time, it wouldn't come up. I was almost back here before I got any action. Otherwise, I'd have had to sit on my arse at Hardy."

"I'll get Bob to have a see," Denholm promised. "Could be

just dirt in the hydraulics. Anyway, we'll be rid of this beast by the weekend. Till then, try and avoid wheel landings."

"It's quite incredible," Fulton informed him acidly. "How you can always come up with an answer for *everything*."

Two days had passed since his return from Vancouver and the trial. Advised that he would not be recalled, he fled the court, vastly relieved that, for him at least, it was over. He could not have stayed; there was nothing more to say on Stepan's behalf, and nothing more, Stepan had made clear what he wished to have said.

There was no Q.C.A. Flight to Blackfish Harbour until the following day. He contemplated twenty-four hours alone in the city, Tamara in Victoria, time heavy on his hands, and thought of his parents, of the comfortable, welcoming house on Bowen Island. Too bad, he allowed ruefully, that his parents and his childhood home should occur to him merely as a last resort.

*

He found, perversely, that he was almost glad of the daily anxieties posed by the troublesome temporary Seabee. He approached it each morning with caution, in combative mood, forever on his guard against it. It occupied his mind fully for the duration of each flight, freeing him for that length of time from worrying speculation over the continuing trial and the outcome of that . . .

He came up to his front door and, from habit, glanced towards the big house.

It still looked so damned *normal* with gold August light glowing on unpainted clapboard walls, on the dusty yard and crumbling woodshed. At some time, someone had been in and lowered the venetian blinds: the covered windows made him think of blank, dead eyes. As if the house, forsaken, had simply let life drift away. He shivered, and pushed open his door as the phone began to clatter his ring code.

Without preamble, Alice Royle wanted to know, "Jack? Have you heard?"

"Heard what? I've just got in, and . . ." He broke off, then said, "Stepan?"

She stopped him. "Not on the telephone, dear. We know how *that* is."

The wheel had come full circle: Ichabod had called on that night with the same warning . . .

She asked, "would you mind popping down?" Promising: "I'll make some tea."

*

"It was on CBU," Alice Royle explained. "The one o'clock news bulletin." She enquired formally, "will you take milk with your tea?"

He nodded, asking tersely, "was it the verdict?" And what else *would* it be . . . ?

"Yes. It's guilty, I'm afraid." Her eyes were troubled. "Although that was more or less expected."

"Did they say what? Murder? Manslaughter?" He held his breath.

"Murder," Alice Royle replied.

So . . . why the shock, he wondered? As though someone just hit me with a two-by-four! She had said it; it was *expected*. "Anything about the sentence?" Telling himself, it needn't be the worst . . . it could still be jail . . .

"Next week," he learned then. "They have to consider the probation, medical and psychiatric reports . . ." She hesitated. "Those can effect the outcome, of course."

"Yes . . ."

She went on, too quickly it seemed to him, "actually, they said very little . . . sounding almost blasé about it, as though they couldn't be bothered . . ." She watched Fulton anxiously. "I've heard that these news people have access to information the rest of us seldom hear, that they sometimes know things in advance. It could be that they've got word of what's going to happen, and that it's nothing particularly awful."

He made the appropriate agreeable sounds for her, but his forced words lacked conviction. "Just have to wait and see. You never know."

That was the problem . . . not knowing.

TWENTY

Three days after the verdict, the forest fire exploded on Minstrel Island, raging out of control, one of the worst on record.

From Blackfish Harbour, thirty five miles away, the great pillar of smoke was clearly visible, topped tens of thousands of feet up by a cap of cumulus cloud where the rising moisture cooled and condensed.

Rain was needed desperately, but the British Columbia coast, celebrated for its prodigious rainfall, remained stubbornly dry. The hot days passed in succession, the late summer sunlight unimpeded by cloud. High pressure ruled the roost, the weathermen were saying, a vast, hovering Pacific system that showed no inclination to move on.

*

The fire brought its attendant upsurge in emergency flights; the victims of burns, those suffering the effects of smoke inhalation. There were others injured by falling trees, the ones mangled in accidents with tools and heavy equipment.

Fulton flew out the corpse of a man discovered in an area where the fire had been beaten back. A mystery figure, unknown to anyone: there were no reports of missing persons. The body was unidentifiable, a grinning cinder shrivelled by the appalling heat to child-size, the features seared away, the eyes melted. The gaping aperture of the mouth contained the few worn, stained teeth of an elderly man. He baffled everyone, and there was no time for bafflement: he was marked as a John Doe, dismissed as some old Indian sleeping off an illicit bender, caught, passed-out, by the flames. You never could tell with Indians . . .

He bore the grisly relic to Blackfish Harbour: an autopsy was required, although it was expected that little would be learned. The sack containing the body lay on the back seat; there was no requirement for a stretcher, or an accompanying first-aid man. The sack took up less space than a suitcase . . .

Jackie Seaweed tossed it into the back of the Ford. "For sure it's not no white guy. You bastards stink different when you cook up."

Fulton exclaimed, "*Je*-sus, Jackie!"

"Things is startin' to get back to normal, looks like." The Indian gave their returned, restored Seabee an affectionate pat. "It was gettin' so's I couldn't stummick that new paint smell!"

*

Fulton was aware, as usual, of the way that conversation faltered as he pushed through the coffee shop door. One or two people nodded, or asked, "how's she goin'?"

He was well-used to it. The murder, trial and verdict remained hot topics, and his role in it all made him the object of ongoing curiosity, enough to bring on those sudden silences.

There was a vacant stool at the counter, and he sat, thinking that while the response to his appearance had been par for the course of late, there did seem this time the sense of something more pointed and intense, that the eyes assessed him more keenly.

The waitress brought his coffee. "Heard you out flyin', Jack." There was a suppressed excitement in her voice.

"Down to Minstrel . . . someone to bring out." He did not elaborate upon who or what.

"You won't've seen today's *Sun*, then . . ." She produced a copy of the Vancouver daily. "Just in on Q.C.A. Special edition, too."

He read the banner headline, thinking dully that . . . Stepan made the front page. Four words in boldest type: 'DEATH SENTENCE FOR KERENIUK'.

"Pretty grim, eh?" The waitress, and everyone else, it seemed, watched for his reaction.

He eyed her bleakly. "The worst."

No one else spoke or moved: it was like a prepared dialogue between the waitress and himself, with the others serving as their rapt audience.

"That's really terrible," she was saying. "Whatever he done, he was a real nice fella. Him an' Billy, we all really liked 'em." There was compassion in her gaze. "And he was a good friend of yours."

"He was, and he still is," Fulton replied in a cold, clear voice. "He's not dead yet." And saw how the watching eyes flickered and dropped.

He forced himself to read the story, registering with growing bitterness each salient point: the sentence based upon the unanimous verdict and the findings of the medical experts. Which were—similarly unanimous—that the accused had been of sound mind, cognisant of his actions and of their consequences.

Although recognised as contributing factors, shock and grief were not felt to have affected adversely the mind's balance, and could not, in the light of that finding, mitigate the act. With intent and malice established to the satisfaction of the jury, no sentence less than the maximum prescribed under law could be imposed. An appeal would be automatic . . .

It's like I just *said*, Fulton thought wildly. He *isn't* dead, and it's *not* over! There would be the appeal, which left a chance, some lingering hope. The appeal could change everything . . . !

He thought with anger of the judge: that soft-spoken, kindly-seeming, two-faced old *hypocrite*! You could have given him a break, he railed silently. A spell in the B.C. Pen would have been more than enough! In *French* Canada, it would have been judged with common sense and reason; a crime of passion, an ungovernable explosion of the mind. And acted upon with mercy. But *you* had to go the whole self-righteous, Protestant, English hog! The fact notwithstanding that killing Stepan could not bring Rosa back, and, dead or alive, *Rosa* would not have sought that awful penalty, or *any* penalty! Unlike you, with your gentle, *deceitful* words, your inflexible, dry-as-dust legal mind!

Until in a while, the slow, sad awareness returned to remind him that Stepan, himself, would, almost certainly, find no fault with the judgement, or the price now demanded of him. He sat cold-faced: the waitress and other customers, rebuffed by his words, keeping away, eyeing him covertly.

He could not kid himself by blaming others; judge, jury, a defence lawyer rendered impotent by his own client. Stepan alone, and with malice *this* time, had laid himself open to this. Fulton thought furiously, Christ! He had all-but dictated his own sentence! The judge needed only to pick up the ball and run with it.

Fulton recalled the wet night, the rice grain patter of rain on the shingled roof; Stepan huddled in his borrowed blanket. It seemed long ago, and *what* had Stepan said then? That, before he hurt Rosa, he would die himself? Now, with no choice left, there remained that one price to pay, and mere token atonement. Paid, though, willingly, by whatever means. Corny as it must sound, it remained that Stepan Kereniuk was ready and prepared to die for love . . .

TWENTY ONE

"Something official-looking came with this morning's mail." His father sounded blurred and distant on the poor line. "From the Department of National Defence."

"My Master's voice," Fulton said.

"Addressed to F-oblique-O J.S. Fulton. Care to explain to me what is an F-oblique-O?"

Fulton smiled wryly: far off at the hub of the universe other people had been wasting no time. "It means 'Flying Officer', Dad. Your former naval person son has become the property of the R.C.A.F." He heard his father's chuckle. "What's funny?"

"I was pondering your turning up there in uniform, and being arrested for impersonating a naval officer."

"Good point," Fulton conceded. "Must be what it is . . . the word from Olympus about when I'm to show my face."

"Should I send it on, or read it out?"

"Read it, Dad, please." Fulton laughed. "By time the pony express got it here, I could find myself AWOL as well as incorrectly attired."

It was the expected order confirmed to report at Number 1 Flying Training School, R.C.A.F. Station Centralia, Ontario.

"They've included travel vouchers, and not ba-a-ad . . ." His father sounded impressed. "A roomette to yourself on the train from Vancouver to Toronto, plus all meals." He grumbled down the line, "in *my* days of servitude, we bloody-well marched. *And* foraged!"

"May I remind ex-Corporal Fulton that this is trans-Canada and not the country road to Passchendaele . . . and that rank has its privileges?"

"And may ex-Corporal Fulton remind F-oblique-O Fulton that he's not too big, too old, or too high-up to have his behind warmed for him!"

"Read me some more." Fulton urged, "what was that about *meals*?"

"At Toronto," he learned, "you connect with the Dayliner to London . . . London, *Ontario* that is."

"Of course, Father."

"There's a number for you to call from London. Whereupon a car will appear to convey your idle carcase to your new abode." His father's despair came through clearly. "*More* burden on the poor bloody tax-payer!"

*

Mike Denholm wondered, "how much more time can you give us, Jack?"

"I know it should be thirty days' notice . . ." Fulton was apologetic.

"In your case, no." Denholm grinned. "We've more or less had you on notice since you showed up here."

"Could I say . . . another ten days?" He mentioned the promise to spend time with his parents.

Denholm nodded. "Not forgetting, of course, a young lady in Victoria?"

"You read me like a book."

"Ten days ought to do," Denholm agreed. "That'll give us enough time to dig up some other dimwit to take your place."

Fulton murmured, "you make it all seem so worthwhile."

"All the same . . ." Denholm punched his arm lightly. "We're going to miss that happy, smiling face."

Making his way home, Fulton dwelt upon Denholm's comment, and was heartened. Nice to be missed . . .

Alone in the house as dusk came down, he found himself thinking, with unexpected nostalgia of this bizarre summer spent at Blackfish Harbour.

He had eaten supper, was pleasantly, reflectively drunk on most of a bottle of Alice Royle's home-made rhubarb and parsnip wine. The wine had been an unexpected gift, one which he had accepted politely, although with reservation. He had encountered such products in the past, not always satisfactorily.

On sudden whim, he chose—as he saw it at first—to bite the bullet, and take a glass to accompany his meal: it would have been churlish not to give the stuff a try. And had been agreeably surprised by the wine's blend of the tart and the smooth, the fruit evident, the parsnip less so, with a pleasing hint of sweetness. That subtleness, though, was deceptive: it was only after the third glass that he began to feel its power, and thought, amused . . . it's hit me like a bomb!

With that realisation came the memory of Alice Royle's untypical diffidence as she presented the bottle, "just a little something of mine . . . I *do* hope you'll enjoy it . . ."

He chuckled, thinking with bleary fondness of 'sly old Aunt Alice . . . a real dark horse'. Staunch pillar of the community, and a first-rate moonshiner with it!

It was the wine, though, that awakened the nostalgia, sharpening its edge as he thought of leaving soon. He was, he knew, going to miss this crazy place, its crazy people. He poured his fourth glass of parsnip and rhubarb, and felt regret at finding the bottle almost empty. He could have handled some more . . . quite a bit more . . . he decided, of that good vintage . . .

He sat at the window with his wine, watching the village lights far down the hill, and their reflections on darkening water. Thinking of . . . *tragedy*. Which, he discovered, bolstered by wine, could not wholly dim the mood of the moment. Even with the pain and anguish of recent weeks, the trial's outcome, the frequent horror and ugliness of his work, the lasting memories would be affectionate ones.

Now, he found, it was possible to reflect upon it with something like peace: this shabby outpost as durable-seeming as the proverbial house of cards, with its volatile mix of inhabitants. It's *grabbed* me, he concluded in boozy contentment. And made me a whole hell of a lot different . . .

He was smiling as he thought of . . . *Llareggub*.

Recently, in New York, the strange and beautiful play-poem had received its hasty, première, performed by out-of-work actors, directed, front and centre, by the poet himself. And someone had thought to leave a tape recorder on the stage. That recording of 'Under Milk Wood' made in the auditorium of the Young Men's Hebrew Association, with Dylan Thomas reading his own key roles, had become already a cult collectors' piece.

In his cups, Fulton envisaged a credible response to that mythical Welsh village right here on the British Columbia coast. God knows, the setting's perfect, he decided. There were oddballs galore, past and present, to match Blind Captain Cat and the Reverend Eli Jenkins. You'd find vigorous counterparts to Butcher Beynon and Bessie Bighead . . . to Polly Garter, Dai Bread and No-Good Boyo . . . Rosie Probert, Sinbad Sailors and widowed Mrs. Ogmore-Pritchard . . . asleep in Bay View with her ghostly husbands, one on each side. Wacky as they were, Fulton mused dreamily, Blackfish Harbour could match them, one on one. The faces and names paraded before him, as though in audition: Ichabod and Alice Royle, Jackie Seaweed and Olaf Pedersen, the Brothers Hong, Hawaiian Jim, Oscar Towerstone, Annie Markham bent lovingly over her eclipsing double bass. Sergeant Porkchop and Nurse Paulen R.N. Fulton drank some wine, and considered . . . Charlie Abalone, who would award half-shares in salmon seiners to white men who'd marry his daughters. Aarvo Taarkanen, woodchopping his own foot: Mister Nemlander striding to the hospital with his fingers in a paper bag . . .

A darkening of the memories then as he recalled . . . Billy Langewische . . . Rosa Brenko . . . Stepan Kereniuk . . . Tamara Brenko.

What to call this literary gem of mine, he wondered. We've got the setting, the people, all we need now's a *title*. He sipped some wine. My kingdom for a title . . .

Remembering Stepan on a still morning that was touched with feather strokes of apricot and saffron light. Stepan raucous outside the bedroom window, "HIGHPOCKETS! We be go *cuttin' wood*!"

Fulton poured the last of the rhubarb and parsnip, and pondered this idea for a little. 'Cutting Wood'? It seemed to fit . . .

*

"Jack? Got a minute?" Olaf Pedersen stood at the entrance to his store. "That's if I'm not disturbin' you?" The irony could not be missed.

I walked right by him, Fulton realised . . . didn't even see him there. Engrossed in my throbbing hangover, and thank *you*, Alice Royle! Praying that, for a few hours more, no one would want him to fly . . .

He turned back. "Sorry, Olaf . . . miles away."

"So I noticed . . ." Pedersen beckoned. "C'mon in. Somethin' you ought to see. *And* get your John Henry on."

Fulton raised protesting hands. "I'm signing *nothing*."

"Wait and see . . . this may change your mind." Pedersen led the way to the counter at the back of the store. "Take a look at that."

It was a petition: foolscap sheets with ruled columns for name, address, occupation, signature; a number of names and signatures already in place. There was a bold heading: 'PUBLIC PETITION SEEKING CLEMENCY IN THE CASE REGINA V. KERENIUK'. On a clipboard that bore the bison emblem of the Royal Canadian Mounted Police.

Pedersen wondered mildly, "still worried about signing?"

"Lend me a pen, Olaf . . ." Fulton's eyes were stinging.

"My pleasure . . ." Fulton scribbled in his particulars. "It choked *me* up, too, when he brought it in."

"When who . . . ?"

"Look at the lead signature." Pedersen tapped the bison emblem.

Wondering, Fulton read, 'Eugene Peter Prokopchuk. Box 9, Blackfish Hbr., B.C. Sergeant-in-charge R.C.M.P. Detachment'. The signature a bold, indecipherable scrawl.

"What d'you reckon . . . stickin' his neck out like that?" Pedersen said levelly, "could be he won't be a Sergeant-in-charge much longer, eh? Maybe not even Sergeant."

Fulton frowned. "Why do you say that?"

"Would've thought it obvious. It's somethin' no Horseman in his right mind'd ever do."

"I don't understand . . ."

"Because he's a *cop*, Jack . . . and cops don't take sides, the rule-book says. They do their job, and leave what's left to the lawyers and judges. S'posed to be impartial. This, with his name on top, makes it so's Porkchop's not like that no more. He's took sides and, far as the Force is concerned, the wrong one, you'll see." Pedersen asked then, "notice somethin' else?"

Fulton studied the sheet. Annie Markham was there, and 'Denkman—Medical Practitioner'. So was 'Julia Paulen—Registered Nurse'. Andrew George Skilly—Ichabod—stood high on the list with 'Ben R. Gilliam—Attorney-at-Law'. Olaf Pedersen had signed as 'Merchant', beaten into third place by 'Alexander Seekings—Salesman'.

"Who's he?"

"The birdbrain kid that sold Stepan the shotgun."

"I thought you'd canned him?"

"Changed my mind . . ." Pedersen shrugged. "Couldn't really blame him. He never asked to be born stupid, any more'n his boss did. And talkin' of stupid . . ." He arched his brows at Fulton. "Still don't get it, do you?"

"Okay . . . what have I missed?"

"Porkchop's the only one. Not another cop's signed. Wouldn't surprise me if he told 'em not to . . . made it an order. Good career move on their parts, lousy one on his."

"You were *serious*? About his job?"

"It's one hell of a thing he's done there. But I'd call it badly thought through." Pedersen was looking pensive. "I just happen to know Porkchop's well thought-of on the Force . . . the war hero thing, and havin' friends in high places. But there'll be no keepin' this out of sight. It'll get sent off, and scrutinized. Provincial Gov'ment for sure, maybe Ottawa, too, and the Governor-General. They'll see who set it up, then watch the shit fly."

"*Would* they bust him?"

"Maybe not . . . but who knows? I can see 'em, though, shiftin' his arse out lickety-split, sayin' he can't be even-handed around here no more. He could wind up on traffic in Dawson Creek." Pedersen pulled a face. "With a big red line ruled under his future."

*

"Haven't seen *you* in quite a while." Sergeant Prokopchuk eyed him questioningly. "Come to confess something?"

"In a sort of a kind of way." Fulton smiled.

"So much for a quiet day . . ." Prokopchuk pointed to a chair. "In a sort of a kind of way . . . shoot."

"I wanted to offer congratulations. For the petition."

"Thanks, but . . ." Prokopchuk's mouth drooped at the corners. "I'd call those a mite misplaced."

"It was an incredible thing to do."

"Or quixotic, or stupid . . . or plain crazy." Prokopchuk asked, "did you sign?"

"Of course."

"Then welcome to the booby-hatch."

"Olaf showed it to me . . . *and* lent me a pen."

"He's great for twisting arms, is Olaf."

Fulton offered, "he's concerned about you."

"Well, he can forget it, because this had to be." Prokopchuk was curt. "I'm not meant to have any thoughts on the matter, but I'll never believe Stepan deserves this."

"No . . ."

Prokopchuk gave him a dry look. "But all the same, I've been a silly fellow, eh?"

"I shouldn't think anyone here would fault you for it."

"We'll have to see." Prokopchuk was silent for a moment. "Where I *have* been foolish is in imagining that a petition, even if signed and sealed by the Queen and Prince Philip, would make one bit of difference."

Fulton's heart lurched. "Why do you think that?"

"Stepan's timing was lousy. Just now, a reprieve would not be a vote-getter. Too many bloody pressure groups climbing on the bandwagon in cases where men kill women. To the point where they can't, or won't, see extenuating circumstances. For them, it's cut and dried. A woman's dead, a man killed her with what's seen as intent, and only the one penalty fits the bill. These are vocal people, Jack. Conservative, staunch and true, the nation's backbone, salt of the earth . . . whatever you care to call them . . . and, with all that, merciless. They represent a lot of votes."

Fulton demanded, "what about the Governor-General? A Crown appointment? He doesn't have voters to worry about."

"But he *does* have a fat coterie of advisers who do," Prokopchuk pointed out. "Who'll be advising like crazy, and guess *what* they'll be advising? It would take *some* G-G to buck *that* floodtide. And our current incumbent isn't that kind of G-G."

"If you know all this," Fulton wondered. "Why get up a petition? Why, as Olaf says, stick your neck out?"

"Because there's a *need*." Prokopchuk's glance was flinty. "Someone has to. Yet for all the hoo-hah I keep hearing around here about justice and standing up for rights, no one else among the citizenry seems quite prepared to make the first move. So, as Olaf so rightly says, it's my neck. And why? Because although that poor little bastard sitting in Oakalla hasn't got a fucking prayer, and, from what he's told me, doesn't want one . . ." Fulton nodded dumbly. ". . . it remains that he has the right to have people care about him . . ." Prokopchuk let out his breath, and grinned ironically. "That's my story, and I'm sticking to it."

"You shame me," Fulton said.

"How do I do that?"

"Because I doubted you, and questioned your motives. Sorry."

"Forget about it. You're probably not half as sorry as I'm *going* to be. But, what the hell?" Prokopchuk laughed shortly. "You know who's to blame, really? Or . . . who should be thanked?"

"I give up. Who?"

"Julie Paulen."

"You've talked *this* over with her?"

"Julie and I haven't spoken since the night of the murder. But, if she had still been in my life, I wouldn't've dreamed of pulling a stunt like this . . . would never have *dared* . . . the risks to our shared security would've been too great. But now, with it over, all those ties and responsibilities shelved, I can take chances I wouldn't have considered as a prospective married man. With Julie, I'd've played safe, and been unhappy about it. Without her, I can do what conscience dictates because it's my neck *only*. It may not do any good, but, at least, I can live with myself."

Fulton allowed a few thoughtful seconds to pass. "About Stepan . . ."

"Every-damn'-thing's about Stepan." Prokopchuk cocked a sardonic eye. "What?"

Fulton told of his now-imminent departure, that he would be spending time in Vancouver. "I'd like to be able to see him while I'm there. Was wondering if you knew how, or if, I could?"

"All inmates, including those condemned, have visiting rights," Prokopchuk declared. "Usually confined to family, close relatives and lawyers. You hardly qualify, Jack."

"He has no known family left, and the nearest relative is Tamara . . ."

"Who, for damned sure, won't go near him."

"So, would that improve *my* chances?"

"Could do, perhaps . . ." Prokopchuk nodded thoughtfully. "I'd need to find out."

"Would you? Please . . . ?"

"That's all it would be, eh? A visit?"

"I swear it." Fulton smiled edgily. "No files or hacksaw blades. And I wouldn't sell my story to the papers."

"Glad to hear *that*."

"I'd take out an affidavit if you . . . ?" But Prokopchuk shook his head. "My feelings are not unlike your own."

"Oh?" Prokopchuk invited dryly, "tell me all about your feelings."

"That by going there, seeing him, talking to him, I could, like you, show him that people *do* care."

"Okay . . . so one more question. Knowing how Tamara feels, what's she going to say when she knows you've been paying sympathy visits?"

"I'm hoping she won't," Fulton confessed. "Not until enough

time has passed for her to be able to deal with it. And, when she can, I'd be the one to tell her."

"It's your decision," Prokopchuk said.

"Yes."

"Leave it with me. I'll find out what the score is, and let you know."

*

Tamara looked up from the letter, feeling the tight knot of desolation form within her. It was like living again that moment of first realisation of her mother's death: she wanted to cry out in protest: *why* must I endure *that* again? Brought back by lines of words on paper, the final, damning evidence of betrayal.

She looked again at the signature, seen before so often appended to surgical reports and patients' notes. A bold scrawl, big and blowsy, she thought then, like the one who penned it. It seemed to gloat from the page, smug, without conscience.

She read again, taking in each nuance, all the squeezed-out drops of tattle, comparing it with the other letter received earlier. Which she had not wanted to believe. This, though, supported that other; there was a mutuality to them, like a set, a matched pair, each corroborating the other's malicious truths. There could be no arguing against them; they would withstand any moral assault or appeal.

Tamara stared through the window of her room, not seeing now the bright day out there, the movement of people and cars in the hospital grounds and parking lots.

The plain, functional room lapped her around, offering its small comforts that she could not then acknowledge; her books, papers and study folders on the desk. In the closet, her street clothes and white uniforms neatly hanging: the single chair draped with an old high school letter sweater. The bed made up with a military precision.

She stood with the ache of fresh bereavement, her immediate companion: it *was* a death of sorts, of hopes and dreams. As real as pain, as crushing as an intolerable burden. Until time had passed, bringing a return of reason; her mind clicking in, beginning once more, slowly, to move forward. Towards *action* that was, for her, the worst possible . . . and the only action to take.

She cleared the desk and laid the two letters side by side where she could refer to them. She sat down, took pen, pad and envelopes, and began to compose her response.

*

Only a few casualties remained to be flown during the last days. He brought in an old Indian from Knight Inlet who had drunk himself to the brink of eternity on the alcohol strained from melted boot polish. There were late pregnancies from Sointula and Sullivan Bay, and one from Winter Harbour that unnerved him as he pondered the possibility of flying with one hand, cutting the umbilical cord with the other. In the event, the child saw the world for the first time from the passenger seat of Olaf Pedersen's ever-dependable Ford.

He spent his now ample free time largely at home, reading, doing chores, waiting for the telephone to ring.

Two days after meeting with Prokopchuk, he saw the patrol car pull in to the yard. He met the constable at the door. "Sarge asked me to give you this . . ." The constable handed over a buff envelope. "Some information you'll find useful, he says."

Fulton read the short note: a name, a New Westminster telephone number. 'Tell him your story as you told it to me. He may be able to help. Good luck.'

And goodbye, Fulton thought. There was a finality to the words that made it clear no further contact was needed, or desired. Porkchop had done what he could, and now had his own problems to deal with. Not even necessary to call and say thanks. Finish, over . . . *quit.*

But, once in Vancouver, he would call the number, and speak to the name. And see what came of that.

*

Since leaving Blackfish Harbour, Tamara had maintained regular contact, writing to confirm her starting date at the Vancouver General Hospital, following which he received a succession of cards from Seattle, Spokane and Coeur d'Alene in Idaho, reporting on a holiday, a long swing by car with her Victoria friends through the States of the Pacific Northwest. It was fun, she wrote, but she missed him, wished he was with her, and longed to see him again: could they get together, if only for a few hours, when he passed through on his way to Ontario?

So that, two days before he was to leave, he was happy and unsuspecting when her latest letter arrived.

Alice Royle handed it to him when he looked in at the office. "You're in luck today."

He took his letter to the coffee shop.

The first page was headed simply 'V.G.H.', with a date two days earlier. He read 'Dear Jack', and felt a premonitory chill. Her other letters and cards had offered more affectionate greeting: this, coldly-formal, alarmed him. He skipped nervously to her closing signature, finding, dismayed: 'With deep regret. Yours sincerely, TAMARA'.

He read on with the dryness in his mouth, aware of his heart's heavy beat. 'I have been putting off writing, yet knew that I must because it would be unfair to say nothing, leaving you to find out only when you tried to call me. This isn't easy, but here goes. I hope that you get it in time.

'I keep wondering if you remember things we discussed on our first flight together? What I said, all high and mighty, about loyalty, and expecting loyalty to be returned?'

I remember, he thought, and felt sick: there was no real need now to read on, he knew what was coming. He had tried to walk the tightrope between Tamara and Stepan; had taken that gamble . . . and lost.

He read her hasty words, anyway. Because the words, although they damned him, were *hers*.

'In the past we've laughed at the way Blackfish people are nosy and gossipy, everyone else knowing your business before you know it yourself. Well, it's been happening again, only, this time, it's no laughing matter.

'I've heard what was said in the court, Jack. How, knowing what he had done to my mother, you still defended him. I know what was said about testimony and testimonial. And your remarks about my mother that made it appear that you think she brought THAT on herself.'

It wasn't meant to be unkind, he protested silently. I told the truth when asked. I was under oath. Except, he remembered again, with a fresh rush of guilt, when it came to those things you chose to conceal. Remembering how pleased he had been by the prosecutor's acid comment. Not stopping to consider how it might rebound. As it *had* . . .

'In time, if it had ended there, I might have got over that disappointment, started thinking straight, finding ways to forgive, maybe, even to forget.

'But, this morning, more from the horrible Blackfish grapevine. Now I know about Sergeant Prokopchuk's petition, everyone rushing to sign up and SAVE that lousy bastard. And among them, I find, is you. And that's too much. From where I stand, I can't forgive, and won't forget.

'I do still love you, and it's going to be horribly hard trying to change that. I don't believe, though, that I could ever fully trust you again. I'd always have doubts, questions, and that's no way for relationships, or loving, or marriage, to be.

'I won't see you again, Jack, not for a long time, and that time could turn out to be for ever. Please accept that it's over. I ask you not to contact me. I won't open your letters, or take your calls if you do call, so please don't embarrass us both by trying to get in touch. I HOPE that, some day, I can forgive, but, right now, I don't see much chance of that.

'Almost certainly you won't know the people who wrote to me about the trial. Suffice it that there was a group there from Blackfish, and they couldn't wait to spill the beans. They were cruel letters, and I despise them all, but can't argue with the truth. As for the petition news, that was Julie Paulen. I know it was spite, and she's an even worse bitch than I imagined. Probably her cock-eyed way of getting back at Porkchop for dumping her, by making everyone else's life a misery. But she did tell me, and that, too, has the ring of truth.

'In closing, I should add that there's no baby. Goodbye, Jack.'

*

There was to be a get-together at Alice Royle's house on the eve of his departure. She had summoned the entire Island Airways contingent to plan it like a military operation. "We'll have total privacy at my place, and Mister Seaweed and his good lady will be able to enjoy a little drink with us in peace . . ."

The law that forbade the consumption of alcohol by Indians was backed up by stiff penalties for drinkers and providers alike.

"That's real kind, Missus R . . ." For once, Jackie Seaweed looked nonplussed. "But you could get yourself a whole raft of grief if we get busted."

"In my home, with the curtains drawn," she stated calmly. "Who's to know?" She looked around. "I shall invite only close associates and friends. Upon whom we can depend for discretion . . ." Fulton saw her watching him. "We're going to have a jolly time."

Mike Denholm was laughing. "Alice . . . you make that sound like an order."

"My *dear* Chief Pilot," she informed him. "That's precicely what it *is*."

Given the choice, Fulton would have opted not to attend. Yet, with no way short of sudden death or terminal illness that would not give offence, he made the effort.

It was a good party and, despite his unhappy pre-occupations, he began to enjoy himself.

Alice Royle, in her dated ball-gown, was a gracious hostess. She provided a cold buffet, and plentiful wine, beer and liquor: far from impromptu and last-minute, Fulton realised, the gathering was evidently long-envisaged.

Jackie Seaweed, spruced-up and stiff in a boxy suit, was there with his young wife, who smiled, hardly spoke, and sipped Seven-Up. Jackie spun out a single rye and ginger ale before forsaking the rye.

Present were Madeleine and Olaf Pedersen, with Annie Markham, Mike Denholm, Bob Peters and their wives. Fulton spied Ichabod in a corner, beaming myopically at everyone, nursing a bottle of beer.

There were toasts, speeches, and the presentation of an engraved tankard to 'CAPTAIN JACK FULTON—ISLAND AIRWAYS, BRITISH COLUMBIA—Fly With Us & You'll Never Walk Again!'

After supper, a space was cleared for dancing to records of Glenn Miller and George Melachrino.

Ichabod, tipsy and mellow, danced decorously with Pauline Seaweed, informing her and all others within earshot gravely, "I remember Melachrino well . . . in England, during the war, you know. He was *Sergeant-Major* Melachrino then . . ."

The dancing awakened painful memories of holding Tamara at the Nurses' Dance. Only a few short weeks ago, when Rosa had been alive, Stepan free, and life was looking good. Now Fulton could think only of never dancing with her again, never seeing her . . .

"Give that to me at once, Jack," Alice Royle commanded. She took his drink and set it on a nearby table. "Sometimes one must take the initiative. You are, therefore, Mahomet, I the mountain. It's not the done thing, but I don't know how else to make you dance with me." She gave him a mock-arch look. "If you can bear to dance with a crone?"

"You're no crone," he told her with vinous gallantry. "You're *love*-ly."

"If you'd said that to me in, say, nineteen-twenty, I might have concocted a maidenly swoon. Now, though, I'm worldly-wise, and a tough old boot to boot."

She danced expertly, adapting herself to his frequently clumsy footwork.

"You've done this before," he accused.

"Danced?" Her eyes sparkled. "Or picked up comely young men?" He laughed, and she looked approving. "*That's* better."

"I meant your dancing," he assured her. "You're terrific."

"Thank you, Jack. I've had my moments, albeit in pre-history." She explained lightly, "like riding a bike . . . one never forgets."

"Somehow, that comparison . . ." He laughed again. "Seems less than apt."

"'Laughter the Best Medicine'," she murmured. "As the *Reader's Digest* likes to inform us."

"It does help things along," he acknowledged.

"I saw you sinking into the glumps, and said to myself, something needs *doing*, I said."

"Thank you *for* doing it."

"Feeling better?"

"Actually, a whole lot."

"Then we have not lived in vain . . ." She watched him with concern. "Jack, I have an idea of what's happened. I've become accustomed to Tamara's handwriting, and it requires little perception to grasp that, since her last letter, things are . . . ?"

"Awry," he said.

"And you've been bottling it up." His mouth quirked in response, and she offered, "if you'd like to talk, then I listen well. And not one word repeated elsewhere."

"I know that . . ." He ventured for the first time, "Alice."

She nodded. "You decide, of course. But talking can help sometimes. If it's no, then we'll say no more about it."

Simply knowing that he *could* talk about it; that there was someone who was caring and discreet, with an intuitive understanding, willing to listen, was, he found, as much a comfort as the actual talking would have been. Yet he knew that he would not talk to Alice Royle, preferring, perhaps perversely, not to share, but rather, to hug his secret and its pain to himself.

*

Once in Vancouver, near her, it needed all of Fulton's willpower not to pick up the phone and call her.

He weakened only once, borrowing his father's car to drive out to the great, pale sprawl of the General Hospital. She would be in there somewhere, attending a lecture, or on ward duties. He could spy on the criss-crossing paths, studying furtively the young women in nursing uniforms and street clothes, filled with wistful hope. But she was not among them: that would have been stretching the odds of chance and coincidence too far . . .

He called the New Westminster number provided by Prokopchuk.

A woman, sounding guarded, regretted that her husband was not at home. "You're not some salesman, are you?"

"No, I'm not." He smiled into the mouthpiece.

"We get 'em all the time, insurance salesmen, encyclopaedia kooks. Me an' Dave, we get sick and tired . . ." She seemed to be settling down for an airing of grievance.

Fulton got in quickly, "I was given your number by Sergeant Prokopchuk of the R.C.M.P. in Blackfish Harbour."

"*Gene*? Oh, sure . . ." She sounded relieved. "Gene's an old friend."

"It's something I need from your husband . . . a kind of favour. What he can do, or advise."

"Well, if Gene Prokopchuk'll vouch for you, I guess you must be okay." She gave a little embarrassed laugh. "Say, why not tell me what it's about, eh? I'll pass it on, and have Dave call you." She took his name, and Stepan's name. "Dave'll want to meet you . . . he was in the Air Force in the war, that's how come he knows Gene," she explained. "They was in the same bomber crew . . . Dave was the radioman." She promised, "he'll be tickled pink."

But two days went by, and no one had called. Fulton, with little time remaining, was becoming anxious. He wondered about phoning again, and decided it might be better, when seeking favours, not to push.

*

He came in from a walk across the island, and found his mother preparing dinner. "There was a call for you, dear . . ." She added, glancing at him with frank curiousity, "from Oakalla, the prison."

"Yes . . ." With intent, he had neglected to mention any of this to his parents. "I've been expecting to hear."

"From someone called Dave?"

"That's right."

"Dare I enquire who *Dave* is?"

"You can ask that, or anything else that takes your fancy." But he sighed inwardly. "No secrets from you." Her answering smile seemed strained. "Dave is a senior Oakalla prison official."

"I was not aware, dear, that you listed *jailers* among your friends?"

"Oh, come *on* . . ."

"Come on what?" Her eyes turned chilly.

He answered deliberately, "you're being a snob, Mother. Lumping him in with panhandlers and Skid Row bums . . ." He saw her stiffen. "He's not a friend, not even an acquaintance. Just a contact given to me by a thoroughly respectable sergeant of the Mounted Police . . ." They were becoming snappish with each other, and he paused to draw a calming breath. "Was there any message?"

"He asked that you call him . . . I've written down the number." She made a small concession. "He was very polite . . . charming, in fact." And that, Fulton knew, is as close to an apology as you'll get. She asked, "this will be to do with that murderer?"

"Yes."

"You're never going to *visit* him?" She gazed at him, wide-eyed. "A man sentenced to death?"

"But still a man," he reminded her tersely. "And a *friend* . . ." His tone hardened further. "You know the score, all the things I've told you. The kind of man Stepan was, and is. You know, too, that I was there, and saw it all. Knowing that, that he's not the woman-slaying monster everyone makes him out to be . . . I like, respect and admire him still. And if Dave tells me it's fine to visit, then I'm sorry if you don't like it, but visit I *will*."

TWENTY TWO

Fulton turned his father's car down the hill road leading to the prison entrance, and coasted to a stop, still a hundred yards distant.

There was little about the appearance of the place to intimidate, unlike the grey-walled, gun-towered penitentiary by the river, a few miles away.

A wide expanse of tilled fields and plots that sprawled over a steep slope, clumps of shade conifers, drably-clothed men working with hand tools along the rows, a distant tractor rolling dusty circles behind a high wire fence that cut it off from the surrounding low-cost housing and pinched gardens. The prison farm clung to its hillside, offering views out to Burrard Inlet and the North Shore mountains. The buildings lay at the end of a drive guarded by a chain-link gate.

It looked peaceful and industrious. But then Oakalla, with one exception, was a low-security, low-risk establishment where convicted men served short sentences. Unless destined to end their lives there . . .

Fulton asked for Dave Le Roux at the gate, and was shown to a cheerless waiting room. Le Roux, when he appeared, was big and smiling, with receding red hair and a crushing handshake. They talked for a while of general things: Fulton spoke of Prokopchuk, and learned that 'Porkchop' went back to the days with the bomber squadron in England. "With that name, how could it be anything else?"

Le Roux said he envied Fulton at the threshold of an Air Force career. "I still miss it. In their odd-ball way, they were good days."

"Trundling around in Halifaxes, getting shot at?"

"That *was* the down side," Le Roux admitted. "But, give it

enough time, and it recedes, and it's the good things that stick in your mind." Prokopchuk, he said, had been a skilled and brave airman. "He deserved those gongs. We all reckoned he should've got the V.C. He sure as hell saved our bacon more'n once."

They finished their coffee; Le Roux stubbed out his cigarette, and the breezy former radio operator became the cool, detached official.

"Strictly speaking, we shouldn't allow this . . . you're not a relative. But Stepan *is* alone except for his lawyer and the chaplain." He added, "we know the story of the daughter . . . Gene mentioned it on the phone." Fulton nodded, blank-faced. "Ever been in a prison before?"

"No."

"Does you credit . . . but I'd better prepare you. With capital inmates, it's not like the time-servers. With them, we can be a little more free and easy . . ."

Visiting time would be thirty minutes. There would be no direct contact: he would talk to Stepan by a telephone link through a glass screen. The meeting would be supervised. "If you've brought anything for Stepan, leave it with me," Le Roux directed. "It'll be examined, but once that's done, I'll see he gets it without delay."

Fulton handed over the two cartons of cigarettes, and Le Roux wrote out a receipt. "Fine. If you've got no questions, we'll get going."

Fulton had no questions.

*

Something surreal, nightmarish, about talking on the telephone to someone seated, clearly visible, three feet away.

Stepan in prison garb, looking small and old and pale: weeks of incarceration had erased the weathering of the open-air life. His hands, folded together before him, were cleaner than Fulton remembered, the grime gone from under the coarse nails.

He pointed then, smiling, at the handset. "Cock-eyed way to do business, Highpockets."

"What I was thinking. Weird."

"They say me gettin' visitor. I say sure . . . who?" Stepan was beaming now. "They sayin' Mister Jack Fulton from Blackfish, big important name, and do I wan' to see him? And be tell 'em Goddam right . . . that my friend Highpockets. Wheel him right in."

"I *was* wondering if you'd want to."

Stepan appeared puzzled. "Why I not want?"

"Last time . . . in the courtroom, I don't think I was very popular with you."

"Oh, then . . . yah, maybe. You be make me pretty mad that time, hokay. But I stop and think . . . all you do is try and help out. Can't stay mad with you for that, eh? Even when you get him all wrong."

Fulton smiled. "That's something we're never likely to agree on."

"Dumb-fool kid . . . goin' to save the world? Can *get* mad, sure, but, like I say, not be *stay* mad."

"I'm glad . . ." Fulton wondered, "how are you keeping?"

"You know . . . fair-to-middlin'."

"Are they treating you well?"

Stepan looked amused. "Well, see, this not no fancy hotel. It's the pokey, Highpockets, and I know all about that now. Even so, they pretty good, talk to me nice . . . call me Stepan. Grub's not so bad." He began to laugh. "Whole lot better'n the ratshit Hong's Café send in when Porkchop got me locked up. Even Porkchop say me sorry for *that*."

"Good to hear it's . . . going well."

"Well, with fellas like me, and what they got to do, they try and take her easy. You nice with them, they nice with you . . ." His laughter crackled in the earpiece. "Exceptin' maybe the last liddle while . . . not so nice then. Hard to be nice when . . ." The laughter ceased. "They say me it not take long. Finish real quick."

Fulton said with difficulty, "Stepan . . . none of that's certain."

"That judge fella say so. *He* ought to know."

"Don't forget the appeal. That could make all the difference."

"Nothin' no one say goin' to change *nothin*!" Stepan stared hard at Fulton. "In court, *you* try and change things, and what happen? Don't do single thing . . . still wind up here."

With urgency, Fulton told him, "many people are trying to help. There's a petition circulating in Blackfish and around. When I left, they'd already collected a thousand signatures. Everyone's saying how *wrong* this is!"

"Thousand, eh?" Stepan looked impressed. "Never knew they *got* so many folks." He chuckled over Prokopchuk's initiative. "Well I be go to hell! He done that for me? Porkchop gone sick in the head?"

"It's not that at all!" Fulton replied testily. "He did it because he believes you're getting a raw deal. Believes it enough to lay his career on the line!"

"Hey . . . simmer down, Highpockets . . . I only jokin'." Stepan watched him through the finger-smeared glass, a hostile barrier between two irreconcilable states. "Don't get your water hot."

"Sure . . ." Fulton grinned, abashed and rueful. "Sorry."

"Got to be *nice* to me . . ." Stepan was reproachful. "Everyone else nice, so how come you bawl me out?"

"Stepan . . ." But Fulton could not continue.

And heard the thin metallic voice soothing him, "take her easy . . . got nothin' to worry about." Fulton thought wretchedly, that's supposed to be *my* line! "Next time you seein' Porkchop, be say him that Goddam fine thing he done. Say him thanks, but not want him get in shit over me. Not for somethin' be doin' no good." He stated flatly then, "see . . . I *want* for this thing to happen like the judge say. From start I say this to Porkchop . . . don't *want* no appeal, no bastard gettin' me off. Want to get it over, and go find Rosa . . . make things good with her again."

Fulton whispered, "sure, Stepan."

"You say these things to Porkchop?"

"I won't be seeing him again." Fulton explained dully, "I'm taking tomorrow night's train to Toronto."

"Yah . . . be forget." Stepan brightened. "I been in Toronto one time. When I come from Ol' Country . . ." An eager note entered his voice. "Nice town. Got big lake like Goddam ocean. Boats on him bigger'n the one I come on from Ol' Country."

Fulton listened to the flow of Stepan's reminiscence. Memories, and their reviving, had to be good: Stepan recalling the events of his long-ago could lift us both. Up and away . . . out of this place . . .

"No-good bloody country, though," Stepan was complaining. "No mountains nowheres, and no trees. Not what a fella can call a *real* tree . . ." And then, coldly, wilfully, he broke the spell. "Me, too, not seein' Porkchop no more. Real shame . . . I get no chance say thanks, get maybe shake his hand."

Fulton suggested quickly, "write to him, Stepan. He'd be pleased."

"Thing is . . . not write so good, Highpockets." Stepan looked embarrassed. "Not gettin' around to it . . . always busy doin' other things." He confessed, "best I do be write name on company cheques before I give 'em to Rosa." His mouth drew into a thin line of pain. "Not enough for letter-writin'. Leave all that to Rosa and Tamara. They the ones with brains."

"Maybe I could do it for you?"

"Hey . . . is good idea!" Stepan looked pleased. "But big trouble for you, eh?"

"No trouble. I'll do it tonight. Mail it first thing. It'll be in Blackfish in a couple of days."

"Highpockets . . . be like this fine! Not like other things . . . this somethin' I wantin' doin'."

Fulton said wryly, "my attempt to make up a little for past mistakes."

Silence fell between them. High on one wall, a clock ate away relentlessly at their small ration of time.

"You do good back East," Stepan said then. "Make me happy I used to know you."

"Never *used to*, Stepan . . ." Fulton's voice caught. "We'll always know each other."

Stepan grinned at him. "Still good friends, me and you?"

"Absolutely. Count on it."

"Friends like some times when I haul you out of bed, we go cuttin' wood? You say me 'fuck off, Kereniuk, or be kick you in arse'." They were both laughing. Laughing through tears, Fulton thought. "How's about we headin' down in my old Dodge . . . and you wettin' your pants for way I'm drivin'?"

"You scared me out of a year's growth, you crazy old bastard!"

Their mirth echoed hollowly in the airless space, and, from his chair by the door, the jailer watched them. Stepan raised a thumb to him. "Is hokay . . . no problem?"

And the jailer smiled back. "No problem, Stepan."

Quietly then, Stepan spoke into his mouthpiece, "be thinkin', you know? Wonderin' . . . about Tamara?"

Fulton told him what he could, trying to avoid anything that could inflict more pain. There had been enough pain: Stepan must never know the extent of Tamara's bitter loathing. He spoke of her leaving Blackfish Harbour, of staying with friends, the long car trip through the north-western States . . .

"Now she's at the General, studying and working hard." He saw how the news pleased Stepan.

"And how you and her makin' out, Highpockets?"

He had anticipated the question, knowing it must be faced. He would have preferred to lie, to brush it aside with the claim that everything was fine, no problems. It was unlikely that Stepan would hear to the contrary. Yet he knew instinctively that that would not work; he would never be able to act the part convincingly. He said, "sorry, but we're not making out at all."

He offered a hastily-edited version, the good, and the bad which had begun for him with the arrival of Tamara's last letter, carefully minimising the events of the trial, and the effect that those had had upon her.

Stepan, as he had known would be the case, was not misled. "Looks like all *this* my fault, too, eh?"

"There's only one person to blame, and you're looking at him."

"You know that, how come you do this crazy thing?"

Fulton made the attempt, at least, to explain those conflicting feelings and emotions tugging him in different directions, of seeking—vainly—a balance between love and loyalty on the one side, friendship and concern on the other . . .

Stepan demanded irascibly, "who *say* you do these things? Who *say* throw it away for nothin'? Was it *me* askin' this? No, *sir*! I not ask you, not Porkchop, not no other bugger!" He brought the flat of his hand down hard on the ledge before him.

The jailer warned mildly: Fulton could hear him through the receiver, "cool down now, Stepan. Take her easy."

"Hokay . . . is hokay."

And Fulton told him with bitterness, "thanks a *lot*."

"Now you feelin' pretty bad, eh? 'Cause I not sayin' what smart, wonderful fella you are? Not stick Goddam medal on your chest?" Stepan scowled at him. "No good you get sore with me . . . better gettin' sore with your stupid *self*!"

"For Christ's sake, I *am*! About everything . . . the whole screwed-up way I've handled this!"

"Now maybe you get smart? What you goin' to do?"

"How would *I* know? It's over, she's said. She doesn't trust me, or believe she can forgive me . . ." Stepan made a derisive noise, and Fulton stared at him in accusation. "You think that doesn't matter?"

"Goddam Highpockets . . . I give up on you. You been to college, you officer, s'posed to be on the ball? Rosa thinkin' this, Tamara, too . . . talk all time about what a sharp cookie you are. Horseshit!" Slowly, pityingly, he shook his head. "All I see now is you act like dumb bunny!"

"Tell me something I *don't* know!"

"Hokay . . . I tell. You thinkin' because she mad with you now, she goin' stay mad all the time? Any more'n *I* stay mad?"

"She's made that pretty damned clear . . ."

"What you got . . . rocks in your head? I *say* you already, no one stay mad *forever*. You think, after all that time, me and Rosa, I not knowin' this?" Stepan closed his eyes for a moment. "Different for sure with me . . . Tamara hate my guts for what I do to her Momma. That another thing."

Fulton ventured, "Stepan, it's not that bad . . ." A gesture silenced him.

"Don't be bullshit me. Even in this place, get to hear things. I *know.*" Fulton said nothing. "With me, she got reason stay mad for good. With you, no. Not goin' to happen."

"Wish I could see it that way."

"You lookin' for big brass band . . . folks wavin' flags? Before you get it in your fool head? Hot *damn*! She *say* you in letter, birdbrain . . . still be *lovin'* you, eh? Sayin' not trust, not forgive . . . that how she sayin' you on her shit-list for now. But not for *ever*. Some time, she be cool down, see things different, see 'em *straight*. She be sorry then, sure as hell, wantin' changin' things. I see this, sittin' in the pokey. How come you, sittin' out there, you don't see it?"

But Fulton, tormented by guilt and uncertainty, could not bring himself yet to accept: the offence was too grave. Tamara warned me from the start, fair warning. I knew the score, and still went ahead and got it wrong, tilting at windmills . . . my one-man crusade. *Unasked* . . . !

Stepan commented dryly, "I see you still sittin' there, but reckon you not *here*."

"Going through it in my head. I've read Tamara's letter over and over. While I'd like you to be right, I can't see that you are."

"So, that's it, eh?" The contempt came through the phone. "Goin' to quit, then . . . run away."

"That *stinks* Stepan!"

"Same as quittin' . . . and runnin' away!"

With suddenness, he saw the funny side of it; like someone switching on an unexpected light. "There's no getting around you, is there?"

"I do some pretty Goddam stupid things sometimes . . . bein' stupid's what be get me in here. Same time, not born yesterday. Can still see what's under my nose."

"And I can't?"

"Sure looks like it . . ." Stepan leaned forward until his face almost touched the glass, saying in a low, fierce voice, "you be *listen* now. You got itty-bitty sense, you don't quit on Tamara. Hokay . . . sit tight liddle time, sure. Let her simmer down . . .

she will. Then write her nice letter, call on the phone. Go visit. And . . . you know what?"

"I don't. But I think I'm about to."

"Bet you case o' beer she *don'* kick you in the teeth. Do it right, goin' to be *all* right." His gaze held Fulton's. "I don' got to live in world much more. No problem for me. But you and her goin' be stuck here awhiles. You good for Tamara, she good for you. Rosa say that, and she *right.* Don't you be crazy and quit, not without one more kick at the cat. That what I sayin' you, Highpockets, and it *so*." Stepan was grinning triumphantly. "Sum'n'a'bitch . . . *yah*! You know me . . . I always get it right in the end!"

TWENTY THREE

The train was warm and softly-lit. His roomette was ready, the bunk turned down invitingly.

He left Vancouver on time to the minute, looking out at the glowing city sliding past the window, the waterfront with floodlit ships lying alongside, or at anchor in the First Narrows. The pace was unhurried, and would remain so for the next eighteen hours of the long climb to the Continental Divide and Alberta. He listened to the muffled wheel rhythm, adapting himself to the train's quiet sway, peering now into suburban darkness, the warning lights, the bells, halted cars at the crossings. Waiting, tensed, in expectation of the final distant sighting . . . and never mind that it was *morbid,* and certain to make him feel bad; there was the need in him still to *see* . . .

He spotted it as the train ground through Port Moody, far up on its hill, the square of lights picking out the perimeter fence, brashly-intrusive amidst the softer illuminations from street lights and house windows.

The buildings were visible, palely-washed by floodlights . . . and Stepan would be somewhere behind the walls now, his supper eaten, listening perhaps to the cell radio: he enjoyed, he had mentioned, the New Westminster station CKNW, and KOMO from Seattle. Or he might be playing cribbage: it seemed that there was a keen card school, a slightly macabre permanent feature of the condemned's wing, despite the turn-over of players. Stepan had chuckled, speaking of that, and Fulton shuddered in his comfortable isolation, picturing men who played cards in the evenings as they awaited an end decreed for them by people they did not know . . .

The train had drawn to a halt, side-tracked for something. Outside his door, Fulton could hear life and movement; indistinct voices, a woman's high laughter. The attendant looked in to advise that the bar was open in the club car, and there were free seats in the observation dome . . . although not much to be seen at that time of night.

Fulton smiled thanks at the man, and turned back to the window: he could see all he needed to from where he was . . .

Over there, car lights were dropping down the hill, their beams swinging as they made the turn towards the main gate.

And Fulton reflected on that bizarre human resilience. Upon Stepan Kereniuk facing his shoddy ritualistic death unless, by some capricious twist, the appeals process should extend him a belated mercy. He sat up there, nursing his death-wish, perhaps playing cribbage, or enjoying the easy-listening dinner music on KOMO. Burdened forever, deep within, by insupportable guilt and sorrow. Passing the time leading up to the swift, brutal moment that would lift the burden from him. Yet, with all that, he could find time and energy and interest for the consideration of *my* small problems. And come up with answers, and poke fun, and crow happily over his own cleverness . . .

Fulton sent silent thanks into the circle of distant lights . . . and thought of one thing that he could still do for Stepan. A thing which Stepan would not spurn.

A rolling blast of air-horn, the grind and screech of steel, and the long freight train for which they had been halted went by the window, running the last trans-continental miles to Vancouver.

The half-mile long string of freight cars blocked the view, leaving him to consider his deepening conviction that Stepan *was* right . . . and right to crow about it. It would be unforgivable not to follow that route he pointed out. And, in the following, when the time had passed and the moment came, to tell the girl of the remorse and courage of the man she hated, and of the one way that he had found to make amends of sorts.

The freight had gone by, and the luxurious express moved out, swaying over the switch and back on to the main line.

The way ahead was open, clearly-marked, through to the Rockies and Calgary and Medicine Hat. On to Moose Jaw, Regina and Winnipeg and by Lake of the Woods to the cold north shore of Superior, and around the long curve down through Sudbury and North Bay, driving deep into Ontario. Three days of easy motion during which to apply the mind and explore the ways that there were, must *be*, to put it back on track . . .

The train gathered speed smoothly, running up into the Fraser Valley towards Langley and Chilliwack, and the ring of lights dimmed and went slowly out of view.

EPILOGUE

SOMERSET

The two elderly men, long retired policeman and pilot—sat before the summerhouse together, in late sunlight, the tea table between them with its litter of cups, saucers, milk jug and sugar bowl, the ravaged plate of cookies.

They were silent now, the lengthy recounting—which the policeman had encouraged—ended; time out in which to reflect upon what had been said, the pros and cons. There in the garden, under a sky of rare blue clarity.

A garden shaped into the steep north slope of the Mendip Hills, its green spread lapping the tall old house of sun-baked stone, where birds flocked from choice, the walled orchard filled with the conversations of chiff-chaff, blackbird and chaffinch, a robin's thin trill from somewhere secret within the recesses of an aged yew.

The pilot was content just then to savour the garden, letting his gaze roam down the line of hills guarding the lower ground from incoming sea winds: hills softened by beech woods plunging from the uppermost levels of bare, brown Somerset moorland. While, beneath hills and garden the long blue lake lay quiet, touched by capfuls of breeze as grave swans moved, unhurried, along the farther shore.

Beyond the lake, the land rose once more, dividing into a patchwork of hedged English fields wherein long-established trees cast their shadows, then went away, blueing and softening towards Bath and Swindon, to where towers and battlements of saffron cumulus clawed for altitude.

The pilot studied the clouds, their burnished faces and deep chasms, gauging their inner violence, the hurtling up—and down-draughts, thinking of how, in there, altimeter and vertical speed indicator would reflect the chaotic forces of an uncontrollable rollercoaster ride.

Approaching them, in those days before commercial jets would carry you far above the weather systems, you'd search the cloud faces for the easiest way through, then plunge, fingers crossed, into wild regions of alternating darkness and dazzling light where the rain's roar muffled the engines' sound, and the windshield had not yet been invented that would keep the teeming waters out. There, you fought to hold the wings steady, to maintain the approximation of an assigned en route flight level, wincing and cringing at the sear of violet lightning surrounding you, the bolts discharging with their simultaneous shockwaves. Not up there, deep within the birthplace of storms, the breathless pause between flash and thunderclap, the crack and long, fading reverberation, but a great bell sound . . . a celestial hammer striking down on an anvil vast enough to fill the sky. The way that, once, frequently, it had been . . .

He surrendered memories as the policeman broke the silence. "What we question, then, is the establishment of intent. Malice aforethought made clear to the court."

"Which was *never* established," Fulton insisted once more. "Remember, I saw it. There was no malice, not for an instant, in Stepan's actions . . . other than against himself," he allowed. "But the jury was anti him from the start, and no argument could prevail against that mind-set."

"It's not unknown . . ." The policeman was deliberately noncommittal.

"Sergeant Prokopchuk spelled it out when his petition was making the rounds. Initiating that, still he saw its futility. Because of the way people thought then. Wife-killers merited no consideration or mercy. And justice," Fulton said in a cold voice. "Ends up looking to be as much about mood as with the weighing and balancing of right and wrong. Which demeans justice totally when it's that calling the shots."

Two collared doves alighted nearby on the grass, watching the table sidelong for scraps. "From my point of view as P.C. Plod," the policeman offered. "Whether then or now, I would have done as your Sergeant did. Charged with murder, then shunted it off to the courts . . ." He saw Fulton's expression tighten, and urged, "let me finish, Jack."

"Sure." Fulton bent his head.

"I spoke of then and now."

"Yes."

"Times changing . . . the fickleness of public opinion." He toyed with his teacup, twisting it in the saucer, this way and that. "Just remembering the Rosenberg case in New York. Nineteen fifty three as I recall . . . about the same time as Stepan's misfortune."

Fulton eyed him, wondering. "The atom spies?"

"Ethel and Julius," the policeman confirmed. "Sent to the electric chair with the forceful backing of a furious President Eisenhower. For passing American nuclear material to the Soviets. Stuff which . . . as was divulged later . . . was not all that sensitive. He glanced at Fulton. "A time for Ethel and Julius, and a time for Stepan."

"And now," Fulton said flatly. "Times are different."

"And values, and opinions. Those matters which inflame us half a century on. Trends and fashions much altered." Deepening shadows were spreading over the garden. A breeze, touched with evening's coolness, stirred in the yew. The clouds, dusty and reddening, faded off towards London. "Nowadays, outrage is triggered more by paedophile activities and serial killers," the policeman went on. "By football hooliganism, neo-Nazis, or . . ." He gave a chuckle. "Those caught cheating on high-paying television quiz programmes. Compared with whom inept and foolish atom spies, or accidental wife-killers, are rather small fry."

Fulton seized upon that. "That's how you see it, then? An accident . . . a terrible mistake?"

Although retired, the policeman remained professionally cautious. "Let's suggest, in these times, were we to lay bets among ourselves on a likely outcome, us knowledgeable coppers might well opt for murder discounted, the accused getting five years for manslaughter." But then, Fulton remembered sadly, Stepan would never have settled for that.

Down on the lake the anglers had begun to withdraw their fly-rods. A Boeing sighed down to its landing at Bristol-Lulsgate as the policeman continued, "so, today, might it have been for the Rosenbergs, and quite a number of people believe that. A few years inside, then let it go. But then? Capital charges and prevailing public feeling. As opposed to now, and the feelings of now. There's our difference, Jack." He sat back then, watching Fulton and thinking . . . he's still very bitter. And what I've offered has not helped. And . . . enough of it, he decided.

He allowed some time to pass, though, before venturing, "and Tamara?"

"As you'll have gathered." Fulton looked rueful. "No classic happy ending."

"Did you ever see her again?"

"Oh, yes . . . later." Fulton nodded. "I wrote after hearing of Stepan's death, and she answered very quickly. Then, when I finished up at Gimli . . . the base in Manitoba where I got my jet training and wings," he elaborated. "I was due some leave, and flew out to the Coast." His mouth tightened in momentary spasm. "And there she was."

"I shouldn't think that was very easy."

"Couldn't have been nicer, or more civilised." Fulton smiled with scant mirth. "Old friends meeting after a long break. If you sought no more than that, it was near-perfect." He tossed a broken piece of cookie to the waiting doves, but the sudden movement startled them, and they flew off to perch reproachfully atop the summerhouse. "We had dinner together in Vancouver, and talked a blue streak . . ."

But talked, he was remembering once more, of anything but those things which had mattered to us. Of her nursing training and by-then imminent graduation, and of how it was flying jets . . . a real thrill, I'll bet! . . . and becoming a fully-fledged Air Force pilot. How she was sure I'd never get away with flying for the R.C.A.F. as, once, I had flown a Seabee for Island Airways, ha-ha! Falling silent then because that, or any allusion to *those* days, got us too close to the bone of ugly memory.

Only briefly, and on mental tiptoe, had Stepan been mentioned. Enough to know that, where he was concerned, disparate beliefs and opinions could never be reconciled. Although it *was* possible to gather from what was not quite stated that treachery was forgiven. As Stepan had pointed out, no one stayed mad for ever.

After a quick kiss, the brief pressure of hands, turning from each other at the corner of Granville and Georgia Streets. Friends once more, and that would have to do.

Only a desultory exchange of birthday and Christmas cards following . . . and ending when Tamara married—fittingly and predictably—a surgeon. By then, time had done its healing work; the news brought no pain, and regret—if, by that time, it was that—could be contained within a self-mocking grimace, a just-discernible tightening around the heart . . .

"The rest you know," Fulton said.

"In some depth, I'd say." There was dryness in the response.

"No complaints, if you please," Fulton retorted, grinning. "You invited it."

And, that's better, the policeman was thinking. That smile . . . much better.

"Don't suppose there's any tea left?" a light voice enquired.

The two elderly men turned as the policeman's wife came soft-footed across the grass towards them, and the doves, freshly-alarmed flapped away into the orchard.

"My own fault if there's not . . . I should've come out earlier." She informed them, "but I was watching you from the window with your heads together, and decided better not interrupt. Although . . ." Her eyes held, and withheld, a deeper question than the one she posed. "I did wonder what could possibly make you both look so solemn on such a glorious afternoon?"

BVG